THE RULE OF RANGING

BOOK 1

# ECLIPSE OF THE MIDNIGHT SUN

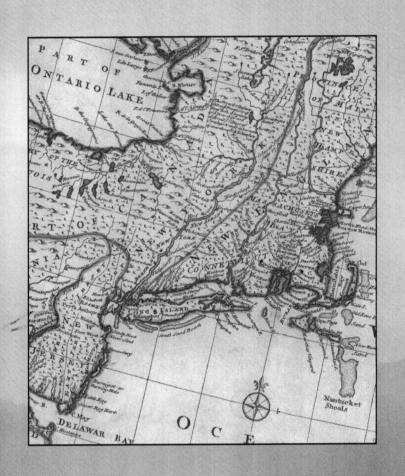

# THE RULE OF RANGING

## BOOK 1

# ECLIPSE OF THE MIDNIGHT SUN

*By*

Timothy M. Kestrel

TIMOTHY KESTREL ARTS & MEDIA, INC.

ISBN-13: 978-0615730080
ISBN-10: 0615730086
Library of Congress Control Number: 2012921753

Book cover design by Glen M. Edelstein
Book interior design by Glen M. Edelstein

Timothy Kestrel Arts & Media, Inc.
1140 Avenue of the Americas, 9th Floor
New York, NY 10036, USA
http://timothykestrel.com

Dedicated to U.S. Army Rangers

*"I am not a man that I am because I was a Ranger.*
*I am a Ranger because a man that I am."*

# THE RULE OF RANGING

## BOOK 1

# ECLIPSE OF THE MIDNIGHT SUN

# PROLOGUE

*Catskill Mountains, New York, 1854*

THE STAGECOACH SCALED UP a precipitous road that wound through the forested mountainside, the four horses pulling and straining against the harness. The narrow, rocky road cut into the side of a cliff forming a shelf, leaving a margin of mere inches for the stagecoach wheels to navigate the deep rut in the road. The lone passenger, a young man in thick glasses and a stylish brown linen suit, leaned out to talk to the driver. He gasped at the panoramic views and the sheer drop down the mountainside next to him. A strong wind blew, forcing the young gentleman to hold on to his black bowler hat. He looked down and saw the road dropping through the trees, and a river gorge full of boulders far below.

The young man gulped and addressed the driver anxiously. "How much longer do we have to go? We must have traveled five hours by now!"

The driver, an older man with a scrubby beard and a nasty scar on his right cheek, held the reins in one hand and urged the horses onward. He smiled back at his young passenger from under an ornate hat with a black plume and gold tassels. He waved his other arm in a sweeping motion over the valley below.

"The scene comes at a cost, sir! We have less than one hour to go, sir," he said.

When the stagecoach finally pulled up to Catskill Mountain House on the leveled plateau, the young man let out a sigh of relief. He grabbed his silver-handled walking cane and proceeded slowly to the edge of a cliff, where the Hudson River Valley stretched below him, as far as he could see. He inhaled deeply of fresh air and imagined, for a moment, how the wilderness must have looked prior to being settled. Turning to get a better view of the hotel, a splendid Early American style mansion with grand entryway framed by large columns, he looked at the large front porch where guests were enjoying afternoon tea.

The man reminded himself that he was not there to admire the scenery, but that he had business to transact. He turned on his heels and walked briskly up the front steps. As he walked through the lobby to the reception desk, a bellboy ran past him to the coach to collect his bags and a young porter standing in front of the baggage room gave him a warm smile. The man reciprocated with a friendly smile of his own.

He stated his business to the concierge behind the front desk. "Good day, sir. My name is Henry Raymond. I am a journalist, and I have an appointment with Mr. Morton."

The concierge greeted Mr. Raymond and bade the porter show him the way. "Seneth, take Mr. Raymond to the suite."

Seneth nodded and led the young man up the wide

staircase to the second floor and down a long hallway. Raymond waited after Seneth knocked on a door until the faint "Come in" was audible from within. Seneth opened the door politely, gesturing for Henry Raymond to enter. Handing his cane and hat to Seneth in the entrance foyer, Raymond observed the spectacular view of the Hudson River Valley through the large windows whose shades were drawn wide. In the rear of the living room, an old man sat in his wheelchair, several paintings depicting landscapes on the walls behind him, to his left and right. The old man was dressed in a morning coat over a dark calico shirt, patterned spring-bottom winter trousers, silk socks and slippers.

"Mr. Morton, someone is here to see you," Seneth announced.

The dark-oak paneled room provided Henry Raymond a whiff of a fine cigar. The suite's furniture arrangement was well-balanced, with two elegant sofas of aged leather and chenille fabric with decorative pillows, a colorful quilt in front of a grand fireplace, and several armchairs and small bow front side table. Shelves full of books lined the wall behind a particularly noteworthy desk. There were mahogany cupboards with porcelain vases full of fresh flowers on top of them. Plush hand-woven wool rugs on the floor muffled his steps.

"Yes, who is it?" The old man inquired in a firm voice without taking his eyes off the paintings, but the porter had already left, quietly closing the door behind him. The visitor found it difficult to form an opinion as to how the old man spent his time in that place: whether the old man would more frequently look at the paintings on the wall or rather admire the breathtaking scenery visible through the windows. Seeing the man's silver gray hair and the wrinkled skin on his hands and face, Raymond realized the degree of the man's advanced age, so he stepped closer and raised his voice.

"Sir, my name is Henry Raymond, sir! I am a reporter for *the New York Daily Times!* Well, as a matter of fact, I am one of the founders!"

The old man turned to face him and seemed to be more than a little annoyed. His gaze was sharp and clear, and his hands firmly held a delicate porcelain cup and saucer. The fire in his eyes and the composed languor of his expression impressed Henry Raymond, who felt compelled to bow.

"I might be old, but do I look deaf or stupid to you, Mr. Raymond?"

Henry Raymond was taken aback with astonishment for a moment. He regained his composure, and bowing politely again replied, "I beg your pardon, sir, no, you do not."

The old man chuckled quietly and then resumed his solemn face. He pointed his finger at Henry Raymond. "I don't give a damn. Did they not advise you at the front desk, Mr. Raymond, that it is my policy to shoot every other reporter asking for stories? I am obliged to inform you, sir, that the first one just left. So what do you have to say for yourself?"

As his host was delivering this news, Henry Raymond spied two .44 revolvers lying on the coffee table, agleam in polished chrome with golden cylinders and beautiful engravings. The pistols were easily within the old man's reach. Raymond's eyes widened, and getting ready to respond, he caught a glimpse of a Colt revolving infantry rifle and a French carbine leaning against the bookcase. He inhaled sharply.

The old man simpered at him and continued, "A reporter, you say. So, you earn your income by writing tall tales, trumped-up stories, and outright lies? I don't think it's a decent way to make a living, by any means. Would you say different? And what brings you to my neck of woods?"

"Sir, with all due respect, and regardless of what you might think of my profession," Henry Raymond replied, looking somewhat discomfited, "I would like to interview you, if at all possible. It is soon the anniversary of the war that began just one century ago exactly, and back in the city, someone told me—who by chance had discovered some old classified military manuals—that you might know something that would be interesting to the readers of my newspaper. You see, I am collecting oral historical recollections for my paper in order to keep them for posterity. My source told me about some rules on how to wage war that date from the last century, and that would be worth an article, and he suggested I speak with you about them."

"Rules, huh..." the old man replied, bowing his head slightly, lost in thought. He looked sad for a moment.

"Yes, long-lost rules regarding a particular new form of warfare that was invented during those days, I was told," Henry Raymond said.

"Not too long ago there was another man, just like you, by the name of Washington Irving, who also collected stories. Interesting man, perhaps, but I threw him out. Now tell me why I shouldn't do the same to you, Mr. Raymond!"

"I am aware of Mr. Irving's work. However, please note that he is a writer of fiction, sir. I, on the other hand, report the news and events and I do not imagine them. The public has the right to know, as I am sure you will agree, Mr. Morton? On occasion we print pieces of historical interest as well, which brings me here, sir."

The old man shook his head as if wanting to dislodge some of his too many memories. "Tell me, Mr. Raymond, if you are an appreciator of art, by any chance? Are you familiar with the Hudson River School?" He gestured towards the paintings on the wall.

"I must admit I only know of their reputations. I am not familiar with their artwork," Raymond replied. He looked at the paintings more out of politeness than interest. His eyes wandered to the scenery outside.

"You should look more closely," the old man encouraged him, "and perhaps you might be rewarded with a glimpse of what I have seen."

Henry Raymond cautiously stepped closer for a better view of the paintings and studied the signatures of the artists. "Thomas Cole, John Kensett, Thomas Doughty ... Wonderful pieces of art," he said, and when he leaned closer, he saw that some of the landscapes had people in them, a line of armed men dressed in green marching through narrow mountain paths.

"These are somehow different from the others. All right, now I see the hunters," Raymond commented.

The old man smiled and nodded in approval. "You have a keen eye for detail. I could add that they are hunters of the most elusive prey: men," he said mysteriously.

"What exactly do you mean?" Henry Raymond asked his curiosity intensified.

"Mr. Raymond, you said you wanted a story, but I see you are empty-handed. Why don't you make yourself useful and fetch me a whiskey, please? I might tell you tales of fame gained, fortunes lost in brutal combat, glory muddled and love everlasting! I am in possession of an epic story in the all-American fashion that has been left untold, until now," the old man replied.

Raymond bowed and hurried back to the lobby lounge and approached the bartender, a young black man. Taking his wallet from inside jacket pocket he ordered the best whiskey in the house.

"Tell me something about the old man who lives in the executive suite. Is he always so grouchy?" Henry Raymond asked once he had placed his order.

The bartender looked at him and smiled. He leaned over to get a bottle of Glenavon single malt from under the bar, and two heavy-bottomed crystal tumblers.

"He is neither grumpy nor mean-spirited, sir. He is just yanking at your chain. He is darned adept at rattling people's cages. Take this, his favorite vice, pour him a stiff drink, and he will be much easier to manage, sir." The bartender winked at Henry Raymond and placed the bottle, tumblers, and a small ice bucket on a tray in front of him.

Raymond nodded, tossed a few coins on the bar, picked up the tray, and eagerly made his way back to the suite. The old man did not seem to notice as he entered, but continued to sit with his eyes closed, as if listening to something-or perhaps someone, Henry Raymond thought. When the old man heard the door opening and closing, only his eyebrows moved slightly.

"Did Gus Junior at the bar say I'm just screwing with you?" he asked.

"Do you mean the bartender? Yes, he did mention something like that," Raymond answered. He placed the scotch and glasses on a table.

"He's a decent fellow. I had the honor to know his grandfather a long time ago. Junior too talks too much, though; he won't let old men have any fun."

Raymond poured two fingers of whiskey into the glasses and handed one of the tumblers to the old man. "Would you like ice?" he asked.

"I prefer mine neat. You don't water down your stories as well, Mr. Raymond, do you?" The old man raised the glass to admire the golden liquid, and then breathed in its vapors. He took a small sip and smiled.

"OK, much better! Now sit down, lad, and shut up. I know it's difficult for a reporter, but take your ears, your pen, and paper and listen. I will tell you about the Rule."

"The rule, I thought there was more than one—" The journalist faltered, because the old man had turned quite serious and stared at him, penetratingly. Raymond took a nervous sip of his drink and almost choked. The strong, smoky peat taste of the whiskey made his head spin. He sat down on the sofa.

"What was it I just said?" The old man leaned forward, whispering, "Are you deaf or dumb or both, Mr. Raymond? Now listen and I will tell you how the forests were painted in red." The old man took a more comfortable position in his chair and began to talk. Henry Raymond listened intently, and soon he felt a bizarre sensation, as if he were being drawn into the old man's blue eyes. The old man's voice started to fade and as Raymond listed, he began to see the story unraveling in front him.

# Chapter I

IT WAS WELL PAST MIDNIGHT, and the sun hung low over the horizon like a battered and stained gold coin. Forests of ancient spruce trees standing guard in the northern frontiers were dotted with dark lakes and turbulent rivers. A thunderstorm had passed through, and gray clouds gave way to rays of pale light. Vast and untamed, the savage wilderness was cloaked in a dozing brume.

The sun cast hazy spikes of light through the dusky trees, and deep in the forests the creatures of the white night were troubled and anxious. Nature's law of the survival of the fittest was like a parasite in the brain that rendered an ever-present, gnawing fear that something— or someone—was always watching them.

Swarms of mosquitoes hovered above putrid bogs, and dragonflies vibrated, skimming over the water's surface. A bee crawled through a dandelion, and over large backwoods of birch trees, the hollow, plaintive call of a cuckoo pierced the silence - *coo-coo coo coo-coo-coo*. In the distance, a column of white smoke appeared to rise straight up to the sky, as if a desperate signal for help in the forsaken rugged border country.

In a clearing in the woods there was a camp, consisting of a lean-to built with poles and spruce branches, and a tapered tent made of long poles tied together at the top and covered with animal hides bound by pegs and ropes. In front of the structures, a fire burned. Two long logs piled one on top of the other were supported by four pegs in each corner. Behind the flickering heat arising from the fire and smoke, the fuzzy figure of an old shaman, his face weathered and wrinkled, sat by the fire, slowly beating his drum. He was chanting quietly.

In the distance across the woods, a hunting party traversed the wilderness, tracking their prey. A small stream of clear, cold water ran over some rocks and stones, creating tiny rapids. One of the hunters stopped to examine animal droppings at a watering hole by the stream. Picking up some dung, he brought it close to his face to sniff it. The moist fetid shit in his hand steamed. Standing, he threw it to the ground, and in one swift motion he jumped across the stream. His shadow frightened a sizeable fish that made a whopping splash in a nearby pool in the stream.

The six hunters disappeared into the woods, and a small fawn appeared. With bulging, darting eyes, ready to bolt at any moment, the fawn emerged from the bushes and stopped cautiously to drink from the stream. The early morning fog was rising to reveal a bog where a herd of moose grazed indolently. The air was still after the storm, except for a slight breeze. Resembling a flickering lamp, a corpse candle appeared to hover over the bog.

The hunters were dressed in buckskins that steamed

from the summer heat and the men's exertions. Armed with bows and spears, the two leading hunters ran silently like ghosts through the woods, communicating only with hand signals. The third man, running right behind them, carried a crossbow, and another had a musket at the ready.

The hunters crossed the stream, and from the corner of his eye, one of the men caught a glimpse of something – it was a moose. The hunters stopped running, closing in on their prey and moving silently through the bushes, pausing only to detect the crisp air for their quarry's slightest scent. The leader made hand signals, and they spread out in a line and approached an opening in the woods.

In the camp, smoke from the fire became more intense. The shaman, wearing a four-wind hat with pointed tips and four colored ribbons in the back, started to beat his drum louder to appease the spirit of their prey and to thank the animal spirits for their food. The wise man rose and began to dance around the fire, falling into a trance with the aid of drum-beating and chanting. Two women dressed in colorful garments of blue, red, green, and yellow came out of the tent and joined him in chanting. The women raised their heads at the sound of a lone curlew, carried on the wind across a lake in the distance.

The sounds of the hunting ritual resonated in the wilderness and reached the hunting party when suddenly, the chanting and drumming ceased. The forest became eerily silent and the trees stopped swaying. Rodents, rabbits and squirrels scattered in terror and a million pairs of terrified eyes peered out from caves and crevices, under rocks and other hiding places.

On the bog, a bull moose with a giant ten-point rack

stopped feeding and raised his head, ears alert, to look around. A rabbit darted across a small opening, zigzagging for its life, being chased by a lynx. Rustling and rushing through the forest, the small animals disappeared into the bushes and the moose, relaxed, returned to feeding.

Faces smeared with soot and coal, the hunters stalked the grazing moose, watching it as they lay hidden behind thick bushes. A dirty hand with sere skin sneaked through blades of green grass and red and yellow cloudberries, parting the tall grass cautiously to reveal a better view.

The leader of the hunt motioned to the men on his right to crawl out, to block the moose from its escape route. The leader turned to the men on his left and gave them hand signals. Slowly, cautiously, each man rose to one knee behind the bushes, ready to give chase. The leader anticipated the closing of the trap, and waited only for his men to advance to the blocking position.

The hunters did not realize it, being fixated on their prey, but there were other hungry bellies in the woods, pursuing the same game. From the early morning mist, a pack of wolves appeared like apparitions, their noses sniffing out the quarry from more than a mile away. The shaggy beasts had their sharp eyes targeted on the moose; they had not detected the hunters.

The hunters froze in place when they saw the wolf pack, but it was too late. The alpha male's eyes had caught the slight movement in the brush. When the gigantic black male saw the hunters, the pack leader snarled a warning to the pack. Baring giant dagger-like fangs, he lowered his massive head and snarled at the hunters, ready to fight for the prey.

The moose in the bog bolted in panic and started its flight from the wolves. The enormous animal thundered through the bog's ponds, splashing and crushing small trees beneath its long legs and hooves. The hunt leader raised his musket above his head with its muzzle pointing towards the moose and shouted commands to his men. The hunters sprang into action. The wolf pack, too, gave chase to the moose.

The wolves and hunters ran in parallel, both keenly aware and wary of the other. Both packs tried to keep an eye on the prey and the enemy at the same time. The men prepared their weapons for a running fight with the wolf pack. There was not enough room on top of the food chain for all of them.

Using a javelin, one of the men hit a wolf that came too close to him, but only managed to wound it. The wolf withdrew, snarling and growling, but continued to chase the moose. The hunter swore and ran to recover his weapon.

"*Perkele!*" He was not summoning the devil as much as recognizing his presence. His agitated cursing echoed in the woods.

Another hunter raised his crossbow and took aim at one of the wolves. He fired, and hit the running wolf in midstride, the broad arrow nailing the whining animal onto a tree trunk, kicking and thrashing as it died.

A third hunter threw his javelin at a wolf, wounding its hind leg. The wolf whimpered and limped away as swiftly as it could go.

The man with the crossbow shot two arrows in rapid succession at the alpha male, both arrows hitting it cleanly in its shoulders. With the impact of the second arrow, the wolf toppled over and fell dead.

The leader of the hunt stopped and raised his musket. He drew a deep breath, took aim, raised the firearm's muzzle, aligned the front sight post with the moose's shoulder blade, and fired. The bullet hit the animal, ripping flesh, muscle, and bone, and a cloud of blood sprayed from the other side as the bullet pierced the animal straight through. The moose bellowed in pain as it fell to its front knees and plowed into a thicket, its hind legs still kicking as if it could run.

Snarling and growling, the remaining wolves stopped and turned to face the hunters. The musketeer swiftly reloaded, his unwavering gaze not leaving the wolves for as much as the blink of an eye. Slowly the wolf pack withdrew, backing into the bushes before vanishing—their bushy tails waving in retreat, leaving only the morning mist whirling behind them.

The exhausted hunters breathed heavily in the brisk morning air. One stopped to remove his hood, locks of long blond hair tumbling down as he looked over his shoulder. He was a young man in his teens, grinning from his banged-up dirty face and blue eyes. Taking off his brown buckskin jacket revealed him to be tall and muscular for his age. He wore a shirt and pants made of flax, but his pants were much too short; he had outgrown them some time ago. The boy tilted his head and smiled victoriously, hearing a wolf howled in the distance. The creature's wailing signaled its great deprivation, which echoed over the vast, sweeping wilderness.

§     §     §

The weather became warmer as the morning went on. The last of the clouds evaporated as the sun came out, and by midmorning the skies were blue. The forest, bathed in sunlight, displayed its rich shades of green. The air was crisp and a slight breeze carried the smell of burning juniper plants from the shaman's gathering.

The hunters loaded the moose meat on a lath stretcher drawn by a team of oxen. The animals were guided by a raggedly dressed old, toothless woman from the village, hired to help the hunters at the camp. The hunters headed back to their village following a rough road through the forest. The teenager in the party tied his stuff to a long pole and carried it over his shoulder, following the others and staying close behind. He whistled a tune to himself and enjoyed the warm sun. The older men teased the old woman, laughing and pulling at her skirt.

"Maybe old Fanny here will have some fun after a hard day's work?" She slapped their hands away and glared at them.

In the afternoon as they neared the village, the hunters came to an open space where a group of men had cleared some trees in preparation to make fields. A group of ten women of assorted ages stood nearby leaning on long poles. Tired looking and stained with soot, they were ready to start working on the slash-and-burn fields.

The hunt leader, the skin on his face made tough and thick through long exposure to elements, shouted to his men. "Okay, fellas, let's take a break!" The hunters removed their large and loaded back bags and sat down on some large boulders by the road. Stealing glances at the younger women, they watched what the other men were doing.

One of the men in the clearing walked around the smoldering piles of boughs and bushes, and turning towards the burning land raised his arms and started to chant quietly. The leader, a stout bald man with a thick blond handlebar mustache and sideburns that hung to his collar, whispered to the young boy.

"Finn, it is time for you to start learning how to prepare the fields for sowing. Look, they are preparing to burn the trees and brushes so that the fire will prepare the ground for cultivation. The man chanting is the overseer. Pay attention to how he is showing appreciation to Ukko, the Supreme Deity, before they start the flames to burn."

The men in the clearing took an old clapped-out axe and some flints, and dug a small hole in the ground in which to bury them. Two other men started two fires using friction wood and flints. The hunt master leaned closer to the boy and whispered again.

"Fire must be started two different ways. That way the two fires compete and the earth will burn readily," he explained.

"Uncle Otvar, when will you let me use a rifle? You know I can shoot," the boy asked.

"Yes, I'll let you have one soon, but not quite yet. Rifles are expensive, and we can't afford to lose one, you know that," Otvar replied, inspecting the lock on the musket.

Once the fire started to spread, the weary women picked up long poles and began turning burning trunks to move them along the field, burning the grass as they went. The smoke blowing from the field smelled like strong black tar. The men tried to rein in the fires, hitting at them with sticks and dense spruce branches to prevent the flames from spreading too fast. Some of the women used large bundles of branches to clean the ashes from rocks and distribute it evenly on the ground. The foreman, Gereon, a stalwart man with a double braided grey beard and wearing a tattered woolen cloak, barked orders at his exhausted laborers.

"Leave a birch tree or two standing for the birds to sing on so that the forest will recover quickly, and we can return here in a couple of years!" Gereon shouted to the men, and turning toward the women continued, "Hey, you old hags! Just finish the job. I might even let you go to the sauna tonight!"

"After the slashing and burning, they will spit turnip seeds into the ash," one of the hunters told the boy, who started laughing.

"What? Seed spitting isn't a real job, is it?" the boy exclaimed, amused. "It takes a real man to hunt, not to burn twigs and branches and boss a bunch of lazy women around! I am going to be the hunt leader – when my uncle allows me to shoot a musket!"

The foreman heard him. Gereon turned and walked up to the boy. "Laugh as you wish, young and foolish lad that you are," he said, "but this land we have now burned is your forefather's first field. It is age-old, like the early poems and stories. These fields feed us, just as the forests that gave you the moose. This field is no different from the stream that gives you trout and salmon to eat. We sow this land by hand, and it provides us logs for our buildings and fodder for our cows."

Another working man nodded solemnly. "This field provides us turnips and barley, and enough seed rye to sell across the sea," he said.

The foreman pointed his fat finger at the boy and continued, "Remember this, boy: in the proper hands, fire is used to cure and mend nature, not destroy it." He turned and pointed to the nearby ridgelines. "This is a well-planned operation that you see. We use only deciduous trees. We also need to consider plane of the land itself, because if it is too uneven, or the roots are too heavy and dense, it becomes just too burdensome to work."

The boy who thrived on action and danger quickly lost interest. He looked around, bored, and saw a smoldering mound and some laborers carrying piles of peat and moss for filling gaps between logs and earth in the big mound. Willing himself to concentrate and learn what he could, the boy became more and more involved and walked up to the laborers.

"And what are you doing? Digging holes in the ground and building mounds to burn wood, too?" he asked the men.

The kiln master was Heribertus, a robust carpenter with a chubby unshaven face and fiery eyes. Heribertus glanced back and answered, "This is a tar kiln, boy, where we get the currency of the world! We sell thousands of barrels every year. Aye, the mighty British Navy itself is our best customer, for they use our tar as a seal for roofing shingles and to seal the hulls and for the treatment of sails on ships and boats!"

One of the workers, a scrawny, muscular fellow, laughed and quipped, "Don't you forget that the tar is also a powerful treatment with strong healing powers for our own bodies! If sauna, vodka, and tar won't help, the disease is fatal!"

Another worker, this one with massive arms and a round face bear many scars, closely inspected the pitch dripping from the wooden spout sticking out from the kiln. He said to the boy, "We use the pitch to make resin to fasten handles to knives, and the ladies like the combs we make from it too." He gave the boy a salacious wink.

Up to that day, the older men had allowed the boy to run carefree in the woods with the wind blowing his hair into tangles and not give a shit about any responsibilities. They had made a promise to his father years earlier and they intended to keep it. The kiln master Heribertus nodded to foreman Gereon in agreement that it was time for the boy to start learning some useful skills. "Look, lad," he said, grabbing the boy firmly by the neck. He pointed to the kiln with a stick. "The heating of wood causes tar and pitch to run away from the wood and leave behind charcoal. I use the birch tree because it is ideal for making extremely clear tar, which we call Russian oil, and that's suitable for leather protection. The by-products of tar are turpentine and charcoal, and by using these deciduous trees, I get also hard liquor. The tar is money, remember that!"

The boy nodded and observed the man closely. "I can see why the tar is like money if the mighty navy buys it," he said, "It even smells like money! Musky and strong, it smells like a man!" He placed some tar on his fingertip to try it, and immediately spat it out. "And it tastes like shit!" he shouted, making an ugly face.

Seeing the boy's face, the kiln master Heribertus

laughed. "Serves you right!" he said, and walked around the kiln to inspect it. "I used limestone on this kiln. It was harder to do instead of just building a more primitive one which wouldn't be more than a hole in the ground, but the work was worth it, boy. An outlet hole in the bottom lets the tar run out. I cut the trees to the size of a finger and stack them densely, and then I cover them with tightly packed dirt and moss. The production would be ruined if air could enter the kiln, because the wood might catch on fire. Then, on top of this, a fire is stacked and lit. After a few hours, the tar starts to run out, and that, my young friend, is money pouring into our pockets!"

Back at the slash-and-burn field, the foreman Gereon was worried about the weather. Standing in the middle of the burning, smoky field, he commanded the women to work harder.

"I've had enough of this lazing around!" he barked at the women. "You'll never get done if you don't put your backs into it, you old hags!" The workers hastily returned to their hard labor, working with more intensity this time.

The hunters picked up their heavy leather backpacks, slapped the oxen to get them moving, and headed down the cattle trail. After a while, they came to the outskirts of their village. In front of a large storage building, they saw the royal tax collector, a stout, burly man wearing a long, black coat and brown shining leather boots. Standing with a large shaggy dog, the cruel tax collector was beating a man with a stick.

"Pay your dues or I will have you flogged and thrown in prison!" the tax collector shouted at the man, who, in his rags, looked absolutely starving and miserable.

"Mercy, Herr Affleck, please!" the man pleaded, cowering fearfully, trying to avoid the tax collector's wrath.

"You miserable scum, my mercy quota is filled for today! Try a different time tomorrow," he said, pretending to think about it. "Wait! There's no time left tomorrow either! You must choose: pay, or pain! Now which one is it?" Affleck demanded his face twisted in anger. He raised his knotted stick for another hard blow.

The boy watched the beating, bewildered. He made a motion to intervene, but Otvar grabbed his arm to stop him. He explained.

"That is Simon Affleck. Do not bother him. He collects for the King what belongs to him. He doesn't give a damn about anything else. Be wary of him and stay away from him as much as you possibly can. The King is the law and we are his subjects. It is our duty to pay what he demands," he said, and pushed the boy to carry on.

The village, consisting of several log buildings forming a large square, was located close to a lake. At its center was a large farmhouse painted in red ocher, with white window frames and trim all around, and a black tarred roof. There was a tall wooden fence with sharpened ends forming a palisade between the buildings. It was a small fortress in the wilderness.

As the hunting party approached home, the villagers met them with cheers. In addition to the moose, the hunters brought squirrels, otters, and fox furs. Young women surrounded the boy, flirting, smiling and poking him teasingly while the other young men in the village stare at him enviously. The crowd was in a happy mood and waited anxiously for the midsummer's day festivities to begin, and everybody was excited, preparing a massive party for the evening. At the farm house, a charwoman placed two young birch trees to decorate both sides of the front door as symbols of fertility and to welcome visitors. Two hired hands carried long tables outside for the festive dinner planned for later in the evening.

A group of young men and women merrily erected a maypole in the village square. Other young men built a large bonfire atop a large rock jutting out of the water. A short distance off, old Petroff the greybeard sat at the sauna door by the lake, thick white smoke billowing from the portal behind him. Petroff tied some young birch branches together with thin branches softened with saliva, peeked inside and threw some water on a pile of steaming rocks in the back corner of the sauna. Even though he should have been used to it, the hot steam that hit him in the face made him grimace and then smile in satisfaction. "The sauna is ready! Women go first!" he shouted.

The young women screamed happily and ran to the sauna, giggling and laughing. They shoved the old man out of their way into the lake and shouted, "Move aside, old man! And feast on this glorious vision!" The women started throwing off their clothes. As they sprinted naked past Petroff, the old man paddled waist deep in the water, ogling their bodies with his eyes wide and his toothless mouth agape.

On the village square, the citizens greeted the hunters with jokes and fun. The young boy found himself surrounded by his jolly friends, Canut, Evert and Machel, all led by a lanky fellow named Brobus. "One day the good Lord came down to earth to bring brains to the people, but unfortunately, Finn wasn't home that day!" Brobus said teasingly.

The young men laughed, and Canut quipped, "Finn might be handsome to look at, and he is mighty good with his hoe on the marshes, but he sure isn't smart."

Finn looked upset. "Stop it! Why are you always teasing me?" he demanded.

Finn was handsome, strong, and brave for his age, but innocent and somewhat gullible. He was known to be strong-headed and snappish, but he meant well. His friends joked about Finn's poor manners, but they did think of him as a little jerk at times, for all of his boyish innocence was mixed with a certain amount of selfishness.

Finn had never known or seen anything outside his village. He knew no one other than his immediate family and the few other villagers. Lacking a formal education, he was highly practical about his farm duties, and he lived freely from one season to the next.

Finn was unusually comfortable in the forests. He had learned to hunt at a remarkably young age, and he knew the ways and habits of the wild animals. He was quite at ease in the wilderness and felt happy in the woods—the forest was his domain.

Finn's mother had tried her best to teach him some manners, but the wild young man simply was not obedient to her in that arena. He felt no need for guidance from anybody, having mastered the wilderness and hunting so well almost on his own. His mastery of the backwoods had encouraged his arrogance.

Finn had learned some measure of humility and man-liness from the stories people told about his father, whom he had never seen, and from his father's posthumous reputation, which made him proud. Finn had not received the usual emotional support because of his absent father during his formative years; his father had been drafted into the army and sent off to war when Finn was only a few months old. Eventually Finn developed a growing indifference to that dereliction. His mother did her best and reminded him constantly to be grateful to his grandfather Padric and uncle Otvar and other village men, who taught him some manners and how to control his quick temper.

Now, being teased by his friends and feeling insecure about himself, he turned to face them. Exultantly he said, "I'm from the house that belonged to my father, and his father before him and his father, who were family men for many moons, seasons, and generations. Whose house are you from?" he asked.

"You are boring me to death, again! Never mind! You always take everything so literally!" Machel said, and turning to the others, he continued, "Let's hope the wedding today is better than the old Rambo's funeral last year. That party didn't even produce one staunch fight or a single new corpse!"

Evert, a youngster with sympathetic, kindly eyes and a friendly smile, ruffled Finn's hair, and wrapped his arm around Finn's shoulders. "Come on, Finn, you spend too much time by yourself in the woods and not enough time with your friends. You should know that we are only kidding!" Evert exclaimed, obviously fond of his younger friend. "Would you like to put some turnips and new potatoes on the hot coals in the bonfire? And then eat them with melted butter and salted herring? You would like that

– I know you would! Be careful! Do you remember what happened last time? You were so hungry and in such a hurry that you burned your mouth!"

Machel agreed with him. "That's right, Finn, and we taunt you because we love you! You know that! It's time to celebrate! Join us! We will sacrifice some grain and meat to Great Otso and drink and have fun, and women like rolling in the fields naked, and we will sneak over there to watch them!" Everybody laughed and Finn smiled, feeling better.

Inside the farm house, the servants were busy preparing salmon and pork. The maids poured mead from large barrels into pitchers and took tankards outside to the tables. The matron of the house, a tall and beautiful woman dressed in a loose linen blouse, wool vest and skirt with colorful stripes, gave instructions to the skivvies scurrying around her on their chores. She said, "Today we will serve the fresh butter and lard. We'll make real tobacco available to our guests too, instead of regular pitch. And make sure there are at least two bottles of spirits for each man!"

The matron wore a red scarf around her shoulders. Usually she wore her long blonde hair pinned up, but when no one was watching she let it free. She had a kind smile and blue eyes, but there was certain sadness. Seeing her son Finn through the open window returning with the hunters brought a smile to her face.

She had remained unmarried after becoming a widow, and she spent her time running the large household and raising her boy. She was quite businesslike with her neighbors and kept private most of the time, so the villagers did not get to know her well. To them, she was simply Missis Marianne, mother of Finn.

§      §      §

Missis Marianne watched her son through the window while she was working with a skivvy named Offilia, and recalled when Finn was a fledgling boy wandering alone amidst the trees around his small village. Early in the mornings he would wash in a cold creek and listen to the birds. He learned to live with nature.

"You have not told him of his father, Missis Marianne," Offilia said, "And why do you make him wear flax? Flax is for the poor people. It is inappropriate for a boy from this house."

Stern Missis Marianne looked back at the maidservant. "When his father was killed at war, Gereon and Heribertus and others promised to look after him," she replied, "and I have vowed to keep my son out of harm's way. That is why I have kept his father's occupation as a soldier, and the way he died, a secret. I do it to protect my boy!"

"But sooner or later he will grow up and learn," Offilia said.

"You must swear you will never tell him of his father!" Missis Marianne said. Raising her finger in warning she continued, "He was a soldier for hire, and he was killed in a war far away that was not his. To my simpleton son there is no soldier father! Hence, he has no desire to follow his father's example, do you see? And he wears flax because no army will demand a simple youth into its ranks or take a jester's services. My beloved son will be protected by his innocence!"

Missis Marianne had noticed Finn's moodiness in his youth. She remembered a day when he was gazing up at the trees listening to the birds. For some reason, she thought that the birds were the reason behind his sometimes melancholic mood, and on a whim ordered the farm hands to hunt down all birds around the house.

Finn loved his mother dearly. Not only was she his mother, but also in his eyes akin to the Virgin Mary — signifying all things bright and beautiful. When Finn heard of her instructions, he ran to her shouting, "Mother, what wrong have the birds done? Leave them be!" He was furious, and he stood in front of her with his hands on his hips. Seeing his glaring anger, she realized her mistake, so she grabbed him up in her arms and kissed him on his forehead.

"You are right, my love," she said. "Who am I to question anything or anybody? What was I thinking? Why should birds stop singing just because of my silly notions?"

"Mother, what is providence?" he asked.

"You should not ask what he is, but rather who he is," she replied, gently rubbing his chin. "Providence is colorful and brighter than a day, and a man was made in his image. This I tell you, my son, so you can go to him when you are in need. He blessed you, and you have to thank him for it. Pray for his advice and ask for his grace and you will prosper. But watch out of the King of Hell, who is black and evil - do not even think of him!"

Not fully comprehending her explanation, he wiggled free from her arms and said, "But I know that thunder is made by Thor's chariot when he rides across the sky!" Finn grabbed his favorite hunting spear and ran away.

The midsummer's night festivities started, and the village people danced around the maypole, which was

adorned with flowers and birch leaf garlands, three
crossbars, and wheels with flowers. The beautiful young
women, healthy and glowing from the sauna, wore colorful
dresses with long striped skirts in dark blue, red, and yellow,
and white aprons. The men wore black trousers and coats,
as well as black felt brim hats. They had colorful striped
vests under their jackets and belts made of brass links and
ornaments, and they wore their knives in brass sheaths.
Grandfather Padric, red in the face from excitement and
jolly after several tankards of ale, praised the young groom.

"Let it be told that in his first attempt to find a bride,
our handsome groom forged himself a wife out of gold
and silver. But he found her to be cold and discarded her."
Taking a deep drink, he belched and wiped his mouth on
his sleeve, and continued, "He then robbed the sister of
the maiden of the north, but she insulted him, so he got rid
of her, too."

The village people passed around tankards of mead
and beer. They teased and pushed each other, and the
village square was filled with laughter.

"The maiden of the north told him that there were tasks
he must complete successfully," Padric said. Making exag-
gerated scary faces he continued his story, "That he must
ski for the demon's elk, and restrain the demon's horse! He
must kill the swan of the River Styx! He must cultivate the
Viper-field, and defeat the wolves of the Forest of Hades!
And if that wasn't enough, he must catch pike swimming
in the Underworld Lake! Only then would he manifest
himself to be worthy of a good wife!"

Missis Marianne put on her scarf before stepping out
to join the party, and right behind her Offilia and other

skivvies brought short barrels of mead. The younger women ran up to her and crowned her with a wreath of dandelions. They announced her playfully. "Here comes Missis Marianne, our magical mistress who knows how to make mead!" The villagers enjoyed the mead she fermented, not knowing that her secret was to filter the mead through juniper twigs in a trough.

Missis Marianne appreciated their favor but was not used to being the center of attention. She smiled a little self-consciously and said, "Mead cannot be made by a man who is too busy, because making it takes both presence of mind and intellect! In other words, it takes a woman to make real hard mead! The fermenting barley wort, malt kiln-dried and soaked in water, cannot be left alone, because it must be gently stirred continuously, and we women know all about watching after everything! An extremely anxious brewer, being hasty, has a tendency to forget that. The high quality of good mead is the symbol of a true artist!" She made a quick bow after her speech.

The village people raised their tankards in a toast. "Hear, hear! Here's to the mistress of the mead!" People shouted merrily.

Youths gathered to dance around the village swing; it was a long seat board suspended by stiff wooden beams between four vertical poles. It was large enough to fit ten people standing up. The young men, trying to impress the women, pushed for speed and stood daringly on the side of the swing, hanging on with one hand only. Every time the swing passed like a giant pendulum it made a swooshing sound and the women screamed in delight.

A group of men sneaked behind a log building.

Glancing over their shoulders, they passed around a bottle of moonshine. A violin player took a swig and grimaced at the fierce taste of the burning liquor. He wiped his mouth with his sleeve, and began to play, marching towards the wooden bridge leading to the surrounding fields. People followed and started dancing on the bridge.

The village people were Christians, but many of the old beliefs and rituals remained strong. Throughout the village, there were wooden statues of bear and moose, their sacred animals. Finn rubbed the belly of one of the bears a few times as he passed it while he was searching for his girlfriend.

"Where's Eva? Have you seen her?" Finn asked Offilia. All of a sudden Padric, in a drunken stupor, nearly knocked him down.

"Did you know, lad," Padric mumbled drunkenly, "that a budding maiden got impregnated from a cowberry she ate and begot a son, but because he was born out of wedlock the execution of the boy was ordered when - lo and behold! - believe it or not, the baby boy started to talk and scolded the people for their poor judgment!"

Suddenly Eva Merthen surprised Finn from behind, running around him and poking at his ribs teasingly. His sweetheart had blue eyes and braided blonde hair, and Finn darted a glance at her in her colorful folk ensemble, breasts bulging underneath under a white blouse with its top few buttons undone. Finn ran after her and grabbing hold of her by the waist, took her to the village swing for a ride. Her merry laughter made Finn feel little dizzy. Taking her by the hands, he led her to the lawn, and facing each other toe to toe they spun around, laughing passionately. Unexpectedly, Finn lost his grip and Eva went screaming and flying backwards through an open door into a storehouse. Finn himself stumbled backwards into a plump bird cherry bush. He quickly crawled out of the bush with his shirt torn open and ran to Eva.

When he stumbled into the warehouse, she was already waiting for him, standing quietly, yet she clearly was excited. He stopped in mid-stride stymied, his eyes darting around the dusty room. Beams of light shone through the cracks in the wall behind her, and the dusty air in shades of grey formed playful patterns around her. Eva breathed deeply, impatiently, her chest heaving. He was mesmerized by her beauty, and noticed her hard nipples pushing against the fabric of her blouse. A small silver bead of sweat ran down her temple.

"Kiss me," Eva said, her voice hoarse.

Finn stepped closer and leaned in to kiss her, but Eva laughed teasingly and spun around to run away. She tripped and fell on some flour sacks. Trying to catch her, Finn tripped too and fell on top of her. They stared into each other's eyes, surprised, breathing heavily.

"Take me," Eva whispered, caressing the soft bareness of his chest.

Finn stared at her and gulped. "Take you where?"

"You're such a sweet fool. Touch me," Eva took his hand and guided it under her blouse to her breasts. He held his breath as his fingertips touched her hot, sweaty skin. He gasped and felt tightness in his throat when he felt her firm breast, and how the nipple responded to his touch.

"See, I like it when you touch me like that," she

whispered. She reached over and cupped her hand over his crotch, squeezing it gently. "Oh my, I knew you liked me too! Ooh, you're a grown boy. Hmm, you are my mighty bull," she purred into his ear, and opening his pants swiftly, slipped her hand in.

His hands trembled as he tore off her blouse and buried his face between her breasts, lustfully kissing and squeezing them. He pulled her skirt up with his other hand and grabbed hold of her firm butt.

In the midst of their passionate encounter, they heard voices outside approaching the warehouse. "Someone is coming!" she whispered, and they got up quickly, pulling on their clothes. They raced out through a hatch in the back of the building and disappeared into the crowd outside.

Around the bonfire by the lake, the young men drank beer and talked about girls, war and hunting. Finn and Eva joined them, straws of hay in their messy hair and rumpled clothes. Before he had a chance to sit down, Finn's uncle Otvar and the old man Petroff called to him.

Otvar said, "Finn, be a good lad and fetch me some food and beer, or seven thousand little devils will come and afflict you!"

"Bring me drink too, you judges, crooks, and thieves!" Petroff shouted drunkenly, waving an empty tankard. Finn left for the farm house and after a while returned with a rack of lamb and a large jug of ale.

Otvar said, "The world is a senectus, which means it is age old, you dumb asses. Wise scientists who have studied the Bible have proven that the world is just five thousand six hundred years old! There are four hundred more years till the end of the world, or even less than that!"

"Who cares?" Petroff roared, ruddy from the mead. "My mind thinks only of a fair young maiden who would become my wife! I say a dutiful wife should be stout, strong-boned, work hard and come from a respectable family stock. Beauty is not necessary and fair skin only makes any woman lazy!"

"The best woman is big-boned, and she is fat and has reddish skin!" Machel said, and laughed hard.

"A good maiden is like an apple, she has red cheeks and seeds inside!" the kiln master Heribertus shouted across the yard.

"Wait! Wait! Wait! A woman should move swiftly and be able in her chores, but she must also be strong and well built," Evert said.

"You know nothing about women! A truly beautiful woman has a round face and a round figure, and large blue eyes. She has a small and straight nose, a small mouth, and thin lips. Her feet must be small, and her ankles should be graceful. She must also have big tits and broad hips!" Otvar declared.

"I'd say slim and slender women are ugly!" Canut declared, and unintentionally emptied his tankard when he fell on his back in the grass.

Otvar sat quietly, smiling and looking smug, listening to the young men around him. He emptied his pipe by tapping it against the heel of his boot. Standing up, he cleared his throat loudly to get their attention and said, "A whip will let a good woman know what is within moderation and appropriate," he said solemnly. He pointed his finger up in the air trying to look sober, and continued, "Only morality can lead to everlasting virtue. Many women are praised for their beauty, but she whose heart is not pure will soon find herself ill reputed."

Padric listened to him, and then busted out laughing, slapping his thighs. "Every man should have an obedient wife, and I'd get one myself too, but then again, I'm already married!"

Eva wrapped her arms around Finn's neck and nibbled on his ear. Making sure that the others were not paying attention to them, she rubbed his crotch, and flirtingly whispered in his ear, "I don't know about other girls, but I just want to have some fun with you, Finn."

§     §     §

Dark clouds were gathering across the fearsome eastern border a dozen leagues distance from Finn's village. As in every generation as far back as people could remember, the Russian Army was being formed into camps, and the troops prepared for war. Rumors of war stimulated the market for officers' commissions, but the purchase system had its flaws - it only allowed the rich to become army officers. Many financially less fortunate young aristocrats sold their services to the highest bidder in any country. In an age when an officer required a private income to live in the expected style, loyalties and oaths were mere commodities. Irish Count Peter De Lacy had the family funds alright, and the flexibility of morals to rise all the way to become the Russian army commander. As he entered his command post, his expression revealed that he was an arrogant and self-centered man, accustomed to getting his wish. The rumors among the troops were that he also preferred perfumed lace under his military uniform jacket and that he had a secret boy toy hidden in his lavish mansion.

A group of his subordinate officers, led by Scottish General James Keith, discussed how many days marching an army could distance itself from the nearest supply depot. General Keith was a professional soldier, dressed in a Scottish uniform with Hessian decorations, which stated clearly, to those in the know, that his services were high in demand by three rulers on the continent. His call to duty, and to maintain his family business, was inherited through a long family line of generals and admirals.

The relationship between Count Lacy and General Keith was functional, appropriate, and loyal, but there was no love lost between the two.

A Norman aristocrat by birth, Count Lacy had served four decades in the Imperial Russian Army. He had hired himself out to the Russian tsar Peter the Great, who bought his duty by showering lavish gifts, land and scores of slaves upon him for faithful service. After Peter the Great died his daughter Elizaveta Petrovna ascended to the throne. Without hesitation, Count Lacy swore allegiance to the new Empress Elizabeth. Eventually, however, his behavior degraded seriously and he became quite brutal in his ways.

General Keith, however, was twenty years younger and had retained more sophisticated Western ways and values. He disagreed with many of Count Lacy's methods and decisions, but being a professional soldier, he decided to keep his mouth shut out of sheer respect to his superior officer's position.

Count Lacy marched in to address his officers. "Gentlemen, you must remember the new strategy, and plan the invasion route along the storehouse locations. We shall advance no more than one, two, or perhaps three days marching distance from the closest supply depot. When we make contact with the enemy, we shall maneuver across the forest and outflank them. In addition, send out bil- leting and road repair parties a day in advance – before the first units move out!" As he made these pronouncements, Count Lacy paraded around the table.

"Sire, our new weaponry puts increased demands on setting up the supply lines," General Keith answered. "In the gay old days, our lancers needed only bread and water, but now the newest musketeers require ammunition, gun- powder, and food. Therefore, we will proceed along the roads between the enemy storehouses, and seize them one by one to sustain our operation. Our strategy calls for a war of attrition that, unfortunately, does not leave us much oper- ational flexibility. At least we will be able to take the initiative on the campaign and force the enemy on the defensive."

Major Lowen, a Hessian officer, pointed to the map on the table and said, "Sire, our spies have reported that the local Finnish peasants are difficult for strangers to deal with due to their wild and violent nature. The officials, clergy, and villagers alike are guilty of violent drunkenness, insolence and robbery on a regular basis, and they simply cross the border at will to evade any punishment. They are said to be trustworthy and helpful to those who have gained their trust, but vengeful and inhuman toward those for whom they feel ill feelings."

"Even the Vikings shied away from venturing too far inland, for fear of encountering the Finnish savages!" General Keith commented.

Lieutenant Johan Kopf emerged from the shadows. He was with the Hessians, who were German soldiers mainly from the Hesse region, hired guns through their rulers by the Russians and British, or who ever could afford them. Kopf was a handsome junior officer, dressed in a Hussar uniform with crest and assorted decorations. He had a little dimple in the middle of his strong chin (which the ladies found quite attractive), and he wore a woolen cap with a skull and crossbones emblazoned on its front.

Prior to becoming one of the Hessian Jaegers, who were employed and organized under the supervision of local gamekeepers and foresters for intermittent military service, Johan Kopf had been a seminary student in Marburg, and because he never knew his father, he sometimes referred to himself as "nobody, from Marburg."

His early plans did not include a military career. On his way to Paris to study theology, Hessian recruiting officers seized him on an obscure pretext. After discovering that he was an orphan without a protector, the recruiters forced the hapless Johan Kopf into the ranks. While he was in their service, senior officers who had served with his father told Kopf that his father had been an ardent soldier. That changed Johan's mind about his future, and he decided to honor his father's memory and serve Frederick the Great.

Johan Kopf received his first assignment with the Hesse Cassel Jaeger Corps. In order to maintain his high standards of living at the palace, the King of Prussia was in dire need of more funds. To raise the necessary capital, he committed the Jaegers to the British Army as hired guns for their military campaigns during the Silesian Wars, a series of wars between Prussia and Austria, and their shifting allies, for control of Silesia.

Johan Kopf's home unit was the Hussar-Regiment No. 5, commanded by Colonel Von Ruesch. During a particularly vicious campaign in Silesia, Johan adopted the death's head symbol emblazoned on the head of his woolen field cap, thus earning himself the nickname "Totenkopf."

Johan Kopf was well-known among his colleagues as an uncommonly handsome and insightful soldier. His superiors recognized him to be an outstanding leader, and the King himself awarded Kopf the Prussian Cross of Gallantry. With the shining new badge glimmering on his chest, Johan Kopf realized that his career of choice was a lucky one.

The Jaegers, dressed in green uniforms and each armed with a rifle and a double-edged sword with grip made from polished black horn, were renowned for their marksmanship skills. In an era when only a few people possessed mechanical skills, the Jaegers' additional worth was based on their ability to operate and maintain rifles, precision tools as the weapons were.

The Jaegers were trained to operate independently of each other, or perhaps in small groups. In addition to their combat role, they were often deployed as forward scouts, bodyguards, dispatch riders, and military police.

By virtue of his natural talent, skills, bravery, initiative, and sheer determination, Johan Kopf soon became an expert in screening, or seeking and destroying enemy's reconnaissance patrols, and as well as scouting and ambush missions. His knowledge of how to read the terrain, combined with his navigation and hunting skills, made him well-suited for the services required of him in his military position.

Never one to be bashful, Johan Kopf was well aware of his skills and abilities. Self-confident and enthusiastic, as he stood in front of the high ranking officers in the command post he saw an opportunity for a promotion and decided to take it. He stepped forward without hesitation to address his commanding officer.

*"Mein Herr und Gebieter,"* Johan Kopf began. "With all due respect, the Vikings were a bunch of pussies! But we must bring own rations with us! The Finnish pea soup is laced with heavy, stinking bear lard. Their half-rotten fish stew tastes like shit, and they enjoy eating meat charred so badly I'd rather eat the soles of my leather boots. No man of class or distinction, sir, who is used to proper nourishment, can eat their local food without disgust and loathing!"

High ranking officers clearly didn't approve of this raw, young officer who had addressed Count Lacy directly without permission, bypassing the chain of command. They glanced at each other to convey their mutual contempt of him, but they remained silent because Count Lacy apparently regarded Kopf with respect.

General Keith glared angrily at Johan Kopf. "Lieutenant, your comment has been noted!" He turned towards the officers. "Gentlemen, the terrain ahead of us is demanding, because we have only a few roads at our disposal, and those few that exist are dreadful for smooth passage. We are going to have to advance several leagues through dense forests and march across unreliable marshes, and we will have to endure wetlands infested with mosquitos. This appalling weather is against us as well, so that we will often be soaking wet. Therefore, in order to fight off cold at night, adequate supplies of spirits must be carried with us, and they will also prevent dysentery and other disease."

The officers were interrupted by a scout rushing into the tent. He wore a uniform soiled by a long journey, and carried a cavalry messenger bag made of canvas. The man bowed quickly and handed a letter to Count Lacy. The officers noticed that the letter had three feathers affixed to it by a royal seal, which served to demonstrate a need for outmost urgency. Breaking the royal device, Count Lacy unfolded the letter, read it in silence, and then turned to his officers. "Sweden has declared war on Russia and has thirty thousand men ready for combat," he announced, waving the letter in his hand. "I have orders to launch the attack across the border! We shall seek and destroy the crown magazines in the vicinity of the town of Lappeenranta. Gentlemen, launch the attack!"

"My spies report only eleven thousand enemy troops," General Keith commented, somewhat surprised, "and we still don't know the exact enemy location."

"Nevertheless, we shall launch a quick search-and-destroy invasion across the border. General, give orders to the quartermaster to issue rations for five days. The camp shall remain in place here and await our return. Enemy supply magazines must be destroyed immediately and efficiently, before their reinforcements arrive."

The officers, leaning over the table, studied the maps more closely. Count Lacy pulled General Keith to the side and explained the strategy behind the mission on which they were going to embark. Aristocrats on both Russian and Swedish sides had their own agenda and worked together in secret. The French did what the French do best and supported both sides, for a price of course.

"General Keith, this is highly confidential information, and divulging it would mean a slow and painful death if you utter a word of this to anybody, do you understand?" Lacy whispered. Without waiting for a reply, he continued. "There is more to our master plan than meets the eye. Sweden will declare war, and in retaliation I will move the Russian army on this expedition. The real purpose is to get the army away from St. Petersburg in order to allow Elizaveta claim the throne. In other words, declaration of war by Sweden is only a ploy, the main purpose of which is to cause a civil war in Russia and raise Elizabeth to power.

"Marquis Chétardie in St. Petersburg has informed me that the king of France will fund the war, at a hefty interest of course, and we will receive the funds in two installments. The king will pay the first installment of one million *livres* in silver upon the declaration of war. Marquis Chétardie has agreed with Ambassador Saint-Séverin in Stockholm that we will get the next installment, two million *livres* in gold, when we launch this operation. Just in case, two more millions have been collected in taxes and loans, should the war drag on longer than expected. After all, several senior officers are in dire need of promotion."

General Keith nodded. "The system makes perfect sense, sir. Elizabeth's sister Anna was betrothed to the Duke of Holstein-Gottorp in northern Germany, nephew of King Charles XII of Sweden, and with Elizabeth in power in Russia, together the two sisters will constitute a powerful alliance." Even the aristocrats occasionally had a hard time following the complicated, congenial and pretty much incestuous relationships among the European royal families.

"Elizabeth is popular with the regimental soldiers. She often visits officers and on my advice even acts as guardian to their children-" Count Lacy's voice faltered when he heard drums and saw troops marching on the nearby road. Abruptly he turned his back on General Keith and mounted his horse, rushing off towards a river crossing nearby. The Russian soldiers passed in review on the bridge, and each of the officers saluted Count Lacy, who sat high on his horse, wiping his brow with a silk handkerchief. The marching Russian troops included infantry regiments, light cavalry units, and Cossacks on horseback wearing long fur hats and long colored waistcoats and open-fronted coats with decorative shell loops. They carried imposing lances that were nine feet long with solid steel tips.

General Keith turned to Johan Kopf. "That pompous ass is more interested in parades than warfare," he whispered. "You, on the other hand, have yet proven yourself, Lieutenant. Follow my orders fastidiously, Totenkopf, so that I can be certain that this operation will provide much fame, power, and prestige for me!"

"Yes sir!" Lieutenant Kopf said, and stiffened up.

General Keith stepped close to him, lowered his voice and said, "Lieutenant, if you fuck it up, I will destroy you. I will break you lower than the lowest private. Do you understand? On the other hand, a job well done will get you a promotion."

Johan Kopf stood at attention. Deep inside, he wanted

more than anything else to earn the Order of the Black Eagle, the highest honor earned in combat. It would prove him worthy of a title and perhaps make it possible for him to become a count. He absolutely believed that it would make him one of the aristocrats he admired, a better person. Resolutely, he said, "I will blitz the enemy and accomplish this mission, sir! Obedience to you is an honor, sir! Your wish is my command!" The corner of his mouth twisted in gross determination to do whatever it would take to obtain a promotion.

§     §     §

In the village, as the sun hovered over the lake at midnight and flames and sparks from the bonfire rose high up to the sky, the party turned into a wild and blurry carouse. The bibulous dancers stomped and pranced on the tables, bawling and laughing. In the village square, two men fought with a steelyard and a knife, although nobody knew exactly why. Machel, Evert, Canut and Brobus watched them struggle, and their hollering and shouting reverberated throughout the green. Padric leaned against a birch tree vomiting profusely, and Otvar chased a giggling naked woman from the sauna to a storehouse. Inside a barn, Finn and Eva lay atop a haystack in an intimate embrace, sleeping under sheep skins.

Early in the morning, Finn awoke when a beam of bright sunlight hit him in the eyes through a crack in the wall. It was midsummer's night. The sun had not set at all and the almost endless days would linger more than a month. Finn took a bit of straw and tickled Eva under her nose. Fast asleep, she wiped at her face with a sleepy hand. He got up quietly, careful not to wake her. She turned on her other side, and the covers slipped lower on her body, exposing her beauty. Stopping mid-stride, Finn admired her naked, taut and tight butt peeking out from the covers. He was mightily tempted to wake her up, but controlling himself, pulled the covers up to cover her and stepped out.

Outside, Finn saw people passed out everywhere – on tables, on benches, on the ground. Padric sat alone at a table, drunk, with a tankard in his hand. "This younger generation can't even handle a little partying anymore," he said, slurring his words. "It was different when I was young. We partied three days straight without any sleep! Mmmm, those were the days."

Finn leaned against a tree and unbuttoned his pants to relieve himself. Breathing a long sigh and tilting his head back, he let out a massive fart. He saw his spear against the stall wall where he had left it during the night. Buttoning his pants he grabbed the spear and headed out over the bridge and across the fields towards the forest beyond. At the edge of the woods he stopped, and kneeling down on one knee he drew in the air and listened to the forest sounds. He remained still for a long time until he became accustomed to sounds and smells of the forest.

Finn deeply inhaled another breath of fresh air, and began to scout the woods for game trails. He ran past the trees swiftly and silently, occasionally stopping and listening to the birds. He jumped over a giant anthill and tripped. He fell down but quickly sprang back up and playfully lunged with his spear at the ants. "Ha! Gotcha!" he said, leaning down close the ant hill and smiling.

He ran off again but a barbed thicket slowed him down. He was just about to bend a small tree branch when he heard horses approaching. Not knowing what to expect, he became both curious and excited. Finn whispered to himself. "Who would that be at this early hour? Maybe it is the Black King of Hell my mother warned me about. I wonder if she thinks I am not brave enough to face him."

He tightened his grip on the spear, the heft of its polished wooden shaft adding to his confidence. Through the foliage, Finn saw a group of horsemen approaching, and he was struck by their colorful uniforms and shining weapons. He stood in awe as the horses neighed, their hooves bounding the ground. He heard the leather harnesses and saddles squeaking, and the clanking of the metal gear. As the lancers approached, Finn gawked at the long steel-tipped spears with swallow-tailed bright pennants just below the spearhead. Finn did not know what to think - he had never seen anything like this bunch. It occurred to him that the riders were so awe-inspiring that they must be the King himself. He threw the javelin into a tree and jumped on the road, kneeling down in front of the riders.

"Help me, dear King, because you are all-powerful!" he yelled.

The front lancers scowled angrily and lowered their spears at him. The first rider behind them was General Keith, who pulled back on his reigns harshly, clearly angered by the boy's sudden appearance. "Who is this stupid boy holding us up?" he asked.

"Help me, merciful King!" Finn yelled again.

General Keith was surrounded by bilingual Karelian partisan scouts, known for their ruthlessness, who acted as his interpreters. He rode closer, and looking down at him replied, "I am not King although I do follow his commands. If you look closer, you will see that we are soldiers in His Majesty's service."

Finn looked back at him, dumbfounded. "You talk about soldiers, but I know so little about them. Could I become a formidable soldier like you, sir?" He asked.

"Join the King's army, and he will grant your wish and make you his soldier!" General Keith replied, slightly amused.

Finn smelled the soldier's sweaty horses, and he admired their swords and their pistols. He looked at General Keith's gleaming armor breastplate with embossed twin-headed eagle.

"That shining coat you wear looks very fine on you sir, but tell me, why do you need it?" Finn asked. He shaded his eyes with the palm of his hand. "Could I make a kettle out it for my mother, could I? If deer wore plates like that, my spear would not hurt them!"

General Keith became agitated and taking off his gloves, cut Finn off. "Enough! Join the King's men and become a soldier, before we press you into the service ourselves! Now step aside, you are hampering our procession!"

Finn spun around and ran into the woods without looking back. Excited, he headed straight for home. General Keith turned to Lieutenant Johan Kopf and pointed to Finn.

"Totenkopf, follow that little jerk! He must know his way around these forsaken forests. Dismount so he doesn't realize that you are trailing him! He just might lead us directly to the storehouse," General Keith ordered, motivated. Without hesitation, Kopf dismounted his horse and handed reins to his sergeant. He signaled the Karelian scouts to follow him and took off running after Finn.

§     §     §

Back at the Catskill Mountain House, the old man took a sip of his whiskey and glanced at Henry Raymond.

"I will teach you a little history lesson, Mr. Raymond, or may I call you Henry?" he said, eager to continue the story. "And you may call me Finn, if you wish. Anyways, for centuries, the kings of Sweden had disputes with the emperors of Russia over one petty thing or another, but always along the eastern frontier in Finland, which, at the time, was the eastern province in the piece of shit Swedish empire, or what was left of it. That awful day, there was a twist to the usual story. The King of France wanted the Russian tsar to force the King of Sweden to join in the French embargo against the King of Britain. So to make a long and complicated story short, an attack was ordered to destroy the warehouse that happened to be in my home village in Finland, not far from the Russian border. Kings, oh, how I hate those nasty old fuckers, didn't give a damn about anything or anybody else! Many people suffered and died according to the whims and want of aristocrats - those arrogant bastards!" The old man spoke furiously, and slammed his fist on the table so hard that Henry Raymond spilled his drink. For a moment, Henry Raymond was concerned; he thought the old man might have a heart attack. He felt relieved when the old man regained his composure.

"Having lost her important grain fields in Estonia in a

war seriously weakened Sweden's self-sufficiency," the old man said, the unpleasant reminiscences making him look ill. He continued, "Raids and robberies across the border were common, and the Finnish people along the frontier were at the mercy of both sides. Border skirmishes, indiscriminate killings, and ethnic purging were the norm in those days, just like what is happening on the Great Plains today!"

For a moment, the old man paused to empty his glass. "Little did I realize it then, but that day of wrath, that dreadful day, my life was changed forever," he said. He gulped down a sob, his eyes fixed on the crackling timbers in the fireplace. "A chance encounter on the road was not that random after all. The kings and queens and other faggots clamored for power and the aristocrats, their loyal henchmen, played their heinous games again! They wanted more pawns and more cannon fodder to play with! Catherine the Great of Russia wanted to be the empress, and she planned a rebellion to seize the throne. The King of Sweden sensed a potential weakness in this plan and saw his opening regain power and glory for his own piece of a shit empire. These two fucking conniving serpents arranged secret deals and soon the body count measured in the thousands! Once again, regular folks got crushed in between the marauding armies..." The old man's voice faltered.

Henry Raymond glanced up from his papers as he scribbled notes on imperial order of battle outlining armies and types of attacks. "Please, please go on, sir," he said.

§   §   §

On his way back to the village, Finn ran through the forest, flushed with the joy from of his recent encounter, and thinking how he would tell his mother about it. He burst out of the woods and ran across the fields, his blond head bobbing up and down in the vast undulating sea of golden wheat.

Behind him, at the edge of the woods, Kopf halted his men. He took out a scope and followed Finn running through the field. He surveyed the village and stopped looking when he saw the warehouse.

"Excellent!" he exclaimed, sucking air through his teeth, motioning to a Karelian scout standing near. "Hey, ugly face, return to General Keith and report that we have found the objective, on the double!" The scout took off running.

Finn rushed over the bridge, ran across the yard, and leaped up the stairs to the farm house. Out of breath and full of excitement, he woke his mother. Shaking her and trying to tell her about the soldiers he had met, his excitement was so great that he could hardly speak. When his mother realized that he had said the word "soldier," she felt her heart sink as she stood up wrapping a shawl around her shoulders.

Finn could not stand still and continued vigorously, "I saw soldiers on the road, and they look more marvelous than anything I could have ever imagined! Mother, I shall become an independent and proud soldier myself, and win glory and fame!"

"Who has told you about soldiers? How did you find out about them?" she asked, and sat back down in shock. She was devastated and felt dizzy hearing her beloved son begging for his own horse so he could leave to become a soldier. Then, looking at his enthusiastic and sincere manner, she realized there was little she could do to stop him. She took a firm hold of her son's shoulders with both hands. She shook him and looked at him sternly. She held up one finger in front of his eyes.

"I worry about you so much! Now listen to me carefully and remember this, my son. I do not want you to leave me and go out and seek danger!"

"No, Mother, but I..."

"Be silent!" she continued. "But if you must go, you must remember this: when you travel in unfamiliar places you must stay away from dark and muddy waters. Cross rivers only where the water is easy and shallow."

"Yes, Mother, but..."

"Be quiet and listen. You must be courteous to all people you meet. When an older man offers his advice you must listen to him, do you understand?"

"But, Mom..."

"Listen! Remember also that you can always get a woman's ring and gain her affection. You should kiss passionately and caress her with love. It will bring you luck and encourage your mind. And you must always remain upright and honest! These pieces of advice will serve you well, I promise..."

"Yes, Mom. Can I go now?" he asked, giving up.

She gently pressed her forefinger to his lips and untied a leather strap from her neck. She showed him an old moose head necklace carved of stone and trimmed with silver, and whispered in his ear. "Here, this belongs to you now, Finn. It was your father's, your grandfather's, and his father's before him. It will protect you and guide you." She kissed the necklace, put it around his neck, and fastened it. He fumbled with the moose head and looked at it curiously.

Suddenly, an alarm bell like a clanging gong rang outside. Finn looked at his mother, startled, and ran out. He saw Brobus rushing in terror to the square from the guardhouse shouting, "It's the Russians! They are here, ready to attack us!"

The village men lying in the yard started to get up, still drunk and clumsy. They assembled in shock and started arming themselves with hunting weapons, pitchforks, and axes. The foreman Gereon pointed to one of the men and commanded, "You, run quickly and alarm the garrison!" The man nodded and staggered off.

The kiln master Heribertus gave orders to his men. "Assemble the women and children, hurry up! We must take them to safety!"

The Cossacks and hussars, commanded by Hessian Major Lowen and Lieutenant Johan Kopf, appeared at the edge of the forest. They were fixated on completing their mission, which was to create havoc along the frontier, and in particular, to pillage the inventory and then destroy parish storehouses that had been full of grain and supplies. Their troops started forming battle lines in the field getting ready to attack. More and more Russian formations came out of the woods and surrounded the Finnish village.

Major Lowen commanded his men, "Form lines!"

Johan Kopf anticipated the coming action with some nervousness. He had never really gotten accustomed to the sounds and smells of battlefields and decided he needed a little encouragement to subdue his uneasiness.

He motioned a soldier to throw him a flask. "I need more schnapps, quickly!" Taking a long swig, he continued, "Men, get ready to attack! Show no mercy! We shall take no prisoners!"

General Keith arrived to inspect the formations. He galloped in front of the troops and looked around. "I don't see His Lordship Lacy anywhere. Surprise, surprise, the man seems always to disappear when the action starts!" The massive formations moved in unison to the beat of the drums.

In front of the warehouse, on the edge of the rolling fields of wheat, the villagers got in position and formed battle lines. They were a motley group, completely unorganized. The men passed a bottle of moonshine around, shouting obscenities and brandishing their weapons over their heads. "Death to all Russian cocksuckers, we'll kill them all!"

The approaching Russian lines vastly outnumbered the villagers. The kiln master Heribertus looked around worried. "Where are our own troops? They should be here soon! We can only hope that they arrive on time!" he shouted.

Then Finnish troops in blue uniforms and tall black hats appeared on the road around the bend, double-timing in formation. Their leader was Colonel Eric Sandels, a tough looking veteran officer of many wars and skirmishes. Foreman Gereon was relieved. "There they are! Get ready to fight!"

The Finnish troops formed defensive battle lines in front of the storehouse, while small cavalry units formed on the right flank. The Finnish troops were raggedy, armed with worn-out old muskets and their scarce defensive lines were hopelessly outnumbered by at least ten to one against the solid lines of Russian formations poised for action in front of them. The village men took positions on Colonel Sandels' left flank. The old man Petroff stepped out in front, a sword in his hand.

"Come on, Russkies! Let's dance!" he yelled at the Russians, making a cutting motion across his throat.

Colonel Sandels estimated the enemy formations and said, "Our age-old Russian nemesis never changes. They come up once again, this time with their British mercenary masters. Captain Lofving, command your troops to get ready!"

Captain Lofving was dressed in green uniform coat. He led a group of Finnish rangers who specialized in guerrilla tactics across the Russian border. He took charge of the troops. "Form the lines!" he barked.

"Hold your positions, no matter what happens we will not ask for the quarter from the enemy, and we will not show mercy to them either! Fight for your father's land and your families!" Colonel Sandels barked encouragement to the men. Captain Lofving assessed the situation and turned to Colonel Sandels.

"Sir, our situation is not good," he said. "We are vastly outnumbered. They have thousands of men, and we have only a few hundred! We don't stand a chance on the open fields! We must withdraw at once and start a guerilla action instead!"

All over the village, men and women were trying to hide their small children and searched for any kind of weapons, anything to use to defend themselves against the invaders. Inside the parish house, Pastor Rombert said a prayer and hid his children in a baking oven, but his wife and six-month-old baby had no place to hide. They had to lie on the floor underneath a single thick blanket.

The battle started around the church and parsonage. Drums beating and trumpets sounding, the Russians launched their savage attack. Bayonets thrust forward gleaming in the sun, they marched forward stamping over the grain fields, ready to crush any opposition without pity.

Colonel Sandels' horse reared, and he knew what was about to happen. "We do not go anywhere except forward! One Finn equals twenty Russians any time! Look, there are not enough hiding places for them to run into!" he barked.

Captain Lofving ordered Finn to reload rifles for him. "Boy, don't think anything, just keep reloading these rifles for my men! No matter what happens, keep reloading until I tell you to stop!"

Colonel Sandels waved his sword. He shouted, "Captain, you support my defensive position here by taking and holding the Cemetery Hill over there. Do not let the Russians have it or the devil will take us!"

Captain Lofving grabbed his rifle and rushed off with his men. Finn followed them, carrying several muskets. Colonel Sandels shouted to the village men. "Villagers, the left wing must hold at any cost! Die in place if you have to, but do not let them outflank us, or we are all doomed!"

The Russians launched an all-out attack to take the high ground, and volley after volley hit the stone wall on the Cemetery Hill. Few Finnish musket volleys cut down Russians, and thick gun smoke spread on the field. Foreman Gereon, in his black Sunday suit and brim hat, stood on the stone wall swinging an old double-edged battle axe, and with precise swings he chopped off the heads of attacking Russian marauders who ventured too close.

Finn dodged behind some headstones, and kept reloading and distributing rifles. A hail of bullets hit a tombstone showering him with debris and pieces of stone. He spat on the ground, and with sand grinding in his teeth, he pulled in his shoulders and continued to reload. He tried to stay calm by muttering to himself, "I'm not afraid, I'm not afraid."

Captain Lofving jumped down beside him and looked at him approvingly. "You are doing a great job, boy! That's the spirit! Keep up the good work!" he said, and grabbing a musket, disappeared over the stone wall.

Overwhelmed by sheer numbers, Finnish positions on the hill were in danger of being overrun. Colonel Sandels ordered his cavalry to help them. A small contingent of Finnish cavalry made a charge, shouting the old battle cry.

*"Hakkaa päälle! Hakkaa päälle!* Cut them down! Slay them all!"

Many terrified Russians in the rear turned to flee, but the front line troops had no time to escape and had to face the raving mad Finns. Desperate Russian musket volleys cut down Finnish horses and men, and surviving riders were quickly skewered by the Russian lancers. Russian infantrymen shouted in agony as they were crushed under the horses falling dead on top of them. The ground turned into a bloody mess, and a kneeling Russian trooper, his stomach split wide open, stared at his own intestines spilling into the mud.

Closing in on Cemetery Hill, Russian sharpshooters

took careful aim at the sole berserk defender, the foreman Gereon who stood prominently on the stone wall, his legs firmly akimbo, single-handedly holding off the attackers with his battle axe. Sharpshooters' bullets hit him in the chest and in the head, and his bullet-riddled body fell on the stone wall. Russians leaped over him and advanced to occupy the hilltop cemetery. Captain Lofving's troops withdrew fighting, under enormous pressure from the Russians, who opened the iron gates and started positioning field guns on the hill. Russian artillerymen threw grave markers and headstones aside and crushed them into pieces under their weapons' heavy wheels. On the field, the Russian infantry was lined six men deep, turning to launch another attack. Young Russian soldiers in the lines, marching shoulder to shoulder towards the dreaded enemy, were frightened and anxious. Rumors circulated among the jumpy Russian troopers that when the Finns went berserk, they would have no chance at all. It was said that the Finnish fighters would slaughter all of them all and tear their hearts right out of their chests.

Across the battlefield from the Russians, the village men took their last swigs of booze and threw the empty flasks away. They were drunk and working themselves into a frenzy, raising their weapons above their heads, raving madly. "Let's go get some fresh Russian meat!" The Finns let out an insane howl like wolves and rushed the Russian lines. Vicious hand-to-hand combat quickly turned into a brutal, merciless slaughter. Men on both sides were shot at point blank range, strangled with bare hands, knifed, maimed, hacked to pieces and drowned as their faces were shoved in the bloody mud. Captain Lofving forcefully drove a maypole through two Russians like a skewer. Colonel Sandels had his horse shot from under him, and quickly wrapping a black bandanna around a gaping head wound, he mounted another horse.

Kiln master Heribertus swung a heavy steelyard in broad sweeps, hitting attacking Russians in the heads. His heavy blows cracked heads like eggs and covered him in bits and pieces of skulls and brains. "Right or wrong, this is for my country! Justice has been served to the Russian scum!" he shouted.

Seeing that his left flank was collapsing and having no reserves to fill the gaps in the line, Colonel Sandels realized the fight was lost. He knew there was only one last thing to do. "Raise the white flag! They will never show us any mercy, but let's lure them in and wait until they send negotiators," he ordered. He gave Captain Lofving a nod.

Pastor Rombert raised the white flag and the battlefield blasts from the roaring artillery, booming muskets, and hammering and clanking swords slowly subdued. Thick grey smoke lingered over the combatants and Finn felt sick from the stench of black powder, sweat, mortal fear, blood, urine and shit.

Captain Lofving shouted to Finn, "Boy, snap out of it and redistribute the ammunition! Take some water to my men!" Finn wiped his running nose on his sleeve, hastily grabbed the remaining pouches of powder and ammunition and some water canteens, and started handing them out.

Russian trumpeters blared out a fanfare and three Russian officers marched towards the Finnish lines intending to negotiate the terms of surrender. They reached the middle of the battlefield when suddenly Captain Lofving's men fired a volley, fatal shots ripping right through the officers' bodies, killing all three of them, making a gory pile.

Colonel Sandels raised his sword and ordered the final assault. He shouted, "It is beautiful to die in front of your own people, fighting for your land, fighting for your own folk!"

The field of golden rippling wheat bathed in a bright light as the sun came from behind cotton clouds in a blue sky. A warm breeze rustled in the surrounding trees and the shadow of a hawk sent a flock of sparrows aloft in flight. Then suddenly, everything turned eerily quiet, and for a moment no one moved. Captain Lofving raised his sword as well, and yelled at the top of his lungs, "Russians, here we come! Let's dance, you motherfucking cock-choking ball-drainers!"

A chill trickled down all the soldiers' spines on the battlefield and made them certain they really felt fear. They felt a sickening hesitation and urgent homesickness, and the stench of the loosening of their bowels made the men nauseated. It was not such a good day to die after all.

"Finlanders, fix bayonets!" Colonel Sandels commanded, his horse rearing and flags flapping in the sultry wind. Hundreds of bayonets made a harsh clicking sound as they were attached to the muzzles. Muskets were cocked and the metallic clinks sealed fates for eternity.

"Boy, this is it! Watch what I do, and follow me!" Captain Lofving shouted to Finn, reloading his musket. Finn glanced at the glaring sun. A drop of sweat ran down his temple, and suddenly he was extremely thirsty and needed to piss at the same time.

Colonel Sandels looked left and right to make sure his troops were ready. He lowered his sword, pointing it at the Russians. "Get ready! Charge!" he shouted, his horse rearing up neighing and spouting spit and froth. A hellish battle cry arose from the throats of the Finnish troops. Soldiers and civilians, men of all ages rushed forward, shouting and howling. The women, armed with sickles, pitchforks and sledgehammers and whatever else they could lay their hands on, followed their husbands and sons. Then, to the Russians' astonishment, even the village children ran after their parents in a desperate attack across the open field.

The young Russian troops could not comprehend this wanton display of sheer defiance. Instead, they watched in horror the approaching bedraggled masses of humanity gone mad.

The Russian troops had been deliberately misinformed and were told something completely different and did not expect this at all. "We were told that the Finnish people were docile!" screamed a junior Russian trooper, pissing in his pants.

"They were supposed to receive us as liberators!" another trooper yelled shaking, and shit his pants.

Major Lowen and Lieutenant Johan Kopf gave firing commands, calmly sitting in the saddle, and all hell broke loose. Volley after volley of bullets ripped into the attacking masses, and ordnance explosions pounded the surf, throwing columns of soil toward the sky. A heavy rain of bullets and shells cut down the Finnish people, the heavy slugs piercing through men, women and children, blasting blood and pink and white matter from their bodies.

Captain Lofving, his face covered in a fine mist of blood like war paint, decided to retreat to fight another day. He led the few surviving men to escape from the killing fields into the woods. Finn started to follow them with old Petroff, but without warning an artillery shell exploded right behind them, and jagged pieces of metal severed Petroff's head from his neck completely. The blast knocked Finn down with a hammer blow of shock and debris, and he rolled unconscious into a ditch.

The shooting lasted for ten minutes until there was nothing more to kill on the field. The horrendous variety and sheer scale of the slaughter left a lingering mass of red gummy mist over the mounds of mutilated bodies. Russian troops gagged on the black powder's thick sulfurous stench. The field smelled like the fires of hell.

When Finn regained consciousness, based on the sun's position, he judged that he had been laying there for an hour. He was disoriented and bleeding from multiple lacerations. He gazed blankly at hundreds of dead bodies around him. As his vision came into focus, the first thing he saw was Johan Kopf and the Totenkopf emblazoned on the head of his cap, sword in his raised hand. Finn heard the "Fire!" commands to the firing squad, and saw Padric and Otvar standing proudly, their heads held high in front of the surviving old men and women. He watched in horror as bullets ripped through Padric and Otvar, and the other women and old men, and bounced off the stone wall behind them.

The Cossacks approached the parish house, and Pastor Rombert rushed to stop them, but the Cossacks knocked him down and then nailed him spread-eagled against a sturdy wooden bear figurine. Inside the parish house, the Russians noticed movement under a blanket on the floor, and stabbed the pile repeatedly with bayonets until the blanket turned red with blood. The Russians heard muffled gasps inside the baking oven, so they locked the latch and started a fire underneath it. Outside, Finn saw the smoke rising from the chimney stack and heard the screaming and crying as the pastor's children began roasting to death.

Finn crawled through the tall grass to the farm house and found his mother dying. Missis Marianne lay on the bench in torn and bloody clothes. She had been raped, bayoneted, and left to die, and she knew her time was limited. "Son, you must find your own way now," she said, coughing blood.

"Mother, don't die!" Finn pleaded, pulling her close.

So powerful was her love for him that she tried to smile at him. "No time left, my dear son," she said, her voice low. "Listen carefully, my beloved, you must go. Save yourself, my dear child, and find Columbia! Run for your life and don't look back! Don't you stop, or you will never hear the birds sing again! Go across the big sea like the Vikings did. You must find Columbia!" Missis Marianne stiffened in pain, coughed more blood, and died in her son's arms. Despairing, crying, Finn shook his mother's lifeless body. "Mother, please, Mother! Please don't forsake me now! I don't care about the birds. Don't leave me, Mother!"

Finn was utterly bereft and confused and understood only that his mother's last wish for him was to find a woman, but he did not know where to go or how to get started.

Outside, Eva and Offilia and three other young women

and a dozen children in the village square were bound together by a rope behind a wagon. General Keith and his officers on horseback appraised the women, when suddenly to their surprise Count Lacy appeared on the yard. Ignoring the astonished General Keith, Count Lacy leered at the two beautiful prisoners, Eva and Offilia.

"You can have the old hags but don't touch the young women! I will select first! All virgins are mine!" Count Lacy ordered.

General Keith shook his head in disgust. Lieutenant Kopf took a sip from his flask and laughed. "May I get seconds, sir?" he asked sarcastically.

Count Lacy continued, "Take the surviving children, young men and women as prisoners. I can sell them as slaves in St. Petersburg for a pretty good amount of money!"

The young women realized that they had to make difficult decisions, quickly. They had to choose between slavery in an unknown place or try to do something about it. Offilia felt an advantage in Lord Lacy's interest, and seeing her opportunity for a better life, she determinedly pushed her conflicting emotions aside. She stepped forward and nodding to a Karelian scout to interpret for her she said, "Sir, I wish to be your bride. Will you take me?" She lifted the hem of her skirt, showing off long curvaceous legs tanned from days of swimming nude in the lake.

Count Lacy leaned down from his horse to have a better look at her. Drooling and leaning even closer, he nodded in agreement and motioned for her to get on the horse. She jumped eagerly behind him in the saddle. Johan Kopf applauded as Count Lacy grinned and displayed a victory sign.

General Keith commanded his horse and approached Eva. She raised her hem even higher to show a glimpse of her pubic hair. Smacking his lips, he told her to get on his horse, and without hesitation Eva jumped behind him.

Finn wandered disoriented on the yard and saw what was happening. He was dumbfounded. "Eva, please, no!" he yelled to her.

Johan Kopf's face gleamed in victory. "Now that is the most fitting grand prize for an old warrior, sir! She will serve all your desires and needs well!"

Count Lacy chuckled and said, "General Keith, yours might not be a virgin, but with a body like that who cares! Besides, if and when you get tired of her, you can always find even prettier and younger harlots!" Keith laughed at his commander's joke and was not paying attention what was happening behind him.

Finn took few steps closer and looked at Eva in quiet desperation. She returned his stare calmly and whispered, "Finn, you were my young stud, but I have a chance to live. I prefer to do it in style, my darling. I will miss how well you fucked me, but a girl must do what a girl must do to get ahead in life." Her voice faltered, and she shrugged.

Johan Kopf heard them talking and he looked at Finn in contempt. "Listen, you idiot! You have just witnessed winners in action. We are the winners, and we take what we want! We want your possessions, your money, and we want your women! Winners take all!" he declared jubilantly and raised his fist above his head.

"I will kill you! I swear I will cut your head off and shit down your neck!" Finn tried to attack him, but he was stopped at bayonet point by the Russian troops who seized him and threw him to the ground.

Johan Kopf laughed contemptuously. "You will kill nobody, you stupid boor!" he said, and pointed to death's head insignia on his cap. "I am the Totenkopf! You are just a pathetic loser, but if you are a lucky sad loser, I might spare your miserable life and sell you to the Russian priests! They know what to do with pretty young boys like you!"

Kopf snickered aloud again as Count Lacy galloped away. Manure and dirt from the horse's hooves flew into Finn's face. Watching Count Lacy go, Keith shook his head in silent disgust, and rode off followed by his squadron. Eva did not even look back, and Finn wiped his face. Betrayed, he was totally despondent, and helpless against the bayonets.

Before leaving, the Russians troops torched the village, which burned furiously with black smoke roiling toward the sky. The mounted Cossacks marched out, and the infantry guarded the straggling prisoners who were tied to the wagons. Finn felt relieved finding his friends Machel, Evert and Canut among them, although they were all wounded and bleeding, in poor shape.

"Finn, you must save yourself," Machel said, and grimaced in pain, "You are the only one not hurt! You must go and make your life worth all of this!"

"Remember us, we are your people," Canut said. "Earn it. Get ready, because we will have only one shot at it."

Evert put his hand on Finn's shoulder and said, "Save yourself and honor us. Don't fail, or we will have died in vain!"

"You must be stout, and keep a noble heart. You're a

true friend, and now you must trust your instincts, and you shall find your way to freedom. Farewell," Canut said and gave Finn a quick hug.

Machel, Canut, and Evert let out glaring battle cries. Jumping on the guards, they started a fight to draw the Russians' attention. In the confusion, Finn rolled underneath the wagon to the other side and into a ditch. He had only one thought, to obey his mother and his friends, and without looking back he ran for dear life towards the forest. The guards responded with brutal vigor. Machel and Canut fought bravely, but they were beaten to the ground and killed. A Cossack ran his spear through Evert from the back, and he fell dead under the wagon wheels.

Hearing the commotion behind him, General Keith placed Eva on a carriage and returned to investigate the situation, and from his horse, he saw Finn running in the tall grain field toward the woods.

"Totenkopf, see that?" He pointed to Finn who was running in the distance. "There is your promotion running away! I'd go after him if I were you! Make sure you bring him back alive, because my plantation needs strong laborers like that fellow! Don't come back empty-handed!"

Kopf spun around just in time to see Finn disappear into the forest, and shouted to his men, "Follow me! After him! Don't let him get away!" Kopf spurred his horse after the fleeing boy.

Finn bent low as he ran through the thickest bushes he could find in order to camouflage himself and elude the Cossacks. He took directions from the sun and headed west. He came to a bubbling brook only a couple of feet wide winding through a ravine. He could have jumped across it, but his mother's advice sounded in the trees, and he hesitated. In the shade underneath the mighty alders, the water looked awfully dark. He heard shouts and a dog barking behind him, and he continued to move along the creek.

Finn thought for a moment that he had managed to evade his Russian pursuers. He found his spear and snapped it from the tree where he threw it and continued to run. Just then, a group of Cossacks appeared and almost caught up to him. Finn dashed through the dense brush in a panic. He fell into a deep ravine, and into the river rapids that ran through it. He nearly drowned fighting the current trying to swim to the other side. The Cossacks started shooting and shots spattered the surface all around with deadly drops of lead. He kept diving deeper, bullets making mad fizzed streaks in the water around him, until he had to come up for air. Luckily, he popped out under a fallen tree that shielded him from sight. Desperately grasping roots and branches, he managed to pull himself out of the water on his belly onto a muddy riverbank. Holding his breath, he crawled through wet and slippery brushwood and quietly slipped away.

§   §   §

When Finn was sure it was safe, he got up and started running. Overcome by his emotions, he sobbed and kept running while trying to fight off his tears. He forced himself forward until the adrenaline rush started to wear off, and his muscles began to ache. His stomach growled, and he realized he had not eaten all day. He only stopped when he could go on no longer and had to rest. Exhausted, he leaned on a tree and allowed himself to feel the full weight of being shattered and abandoned. A devastating grief that left him breathless surged over him like a massive black rolling wave. He could not breathe and as he nearly collapsed, tears ran down his cheeks. He felt sick. His stomach heaved painfully in convulsions, and he kept throwing up until nothing came out. He was ready to give up when he heard his mother's voice urging him on. Looking around surprised to see where she was, slowly and painfully he was able to get up again. He kept looking for her, running wildly around dark pine tree trunks with the ground covered in red moss, like blood.

Finn was soaked, cold, hungry, and badly shaken. He felt sorry for himself, and he had no idea where he was going. As his grief slowly turned to numbness and apathy, his mind tried to stop the terrible memories of his dead family. He emerged from the woods in a state of shock and arrived at an old stone church. He had never seen anything so immense and the towering stone building made him quite nervous. At the gate stood a wooden beggar statue with a hole in its outstretched hand where people placed alms. Finn touched the wooden hand and felt the rough, chipped paint, and it gave him little support.

In the distance Finn's eyes were attracted to a young lady who wore green riding garments of wool cloth, velvet facings with a lace jabot and cuffs. Her horse rested by the stone wall. Finn noticed a sizeable, conspicuous gold ring on her finger. All of a sudden, a young ruffian appeared from around the corner and started bullying the lady, attempting to rob her. The roughneck threw himself against her, forcefully tearing at her jewelry.

"Help me! How dare you?" she screamed. "Young man, this is an insult, let me go! Someone! Please help me!" She tried to fight off the robber who put a knife to her throat, and nicking her skin, he tried to intimidate her in order to remove the ring from her finger. Hearing her scream, Finn remembered his mother's advice how he could get a woman's ring and win her affection, and rushed to help the lady. He grabbed the man's arm pulling him back, and the ring came loose, dropping to the ground. The woman's blouse had been violently torn from her body by the robber's knife slashing, leaving the distressed woman semi-naked and huddling in the grass. Finn hit the man with all his power right in the jaw. The man staggered backwards and dropped the knife, got up, and held his chin. The lady kept screaming for help.

The robber looked at Finn who stood ready with his spear, and then ran away. Finn asked the lady to quiet down, but she kept yelling that he was trying to rob her.

"Be quiet, please! I did not rob you, my lady! I helped you!" Finn said, picking up the ring from the ground. When he handed it to her, she screamed even louder. He grabbed hold of her and tried to calm her down, but she struggled against him. During their scuffle her belt buckle ornamented with precious stones came loose.

The lady tried to protect herself by clutching at the remaining threads of her severed dress and sobbed, "Don't take my clothes off! Let me keep my ring and my buckle. When my husband arrives, you will find his wrath is dreadful indeed. He will punish you for this!"

"Come now, my lady, I did not try to rob you! It was

the scoundrel who ran away when I beat him to protect you, not I!" Finn said, "I am to become an officer and a rich man, surely you would like to follow me and live a life of wealth and fortune!"

She glared at him angrily. "If you treated me as a righteous man would treat a lady, this would have never happened. If the King is willing and doesn't forsake me in helping me across the sea, then you can leave me be, and rest assured that I would rather eat only bread and water in my innocent freedom than love riches on earthly hell with scum like you and your friend!" She cried and spat at him.

Stepping back, Finn held the ring and belt buckle in his hand. He kept her at arm's length as he admired the items. "Well, if that is how you thank me, then I wouldn't care for your husband's tantrums, would I? Winner takes it all! A kiss shall be my only reward!" Finn pulled her forcefully to him trying to kiss her, and fumbled to grab her breasts.

She pushed him away, shouting, "Get away from me!"

"My mother taught me to hold ladies tight and close to me, and they would give me their ring, but you are a wildcat!" Finn said, and stepped back. "But if my presence is not to your liking, I shall continue on my way then, and these will be my reward for helping you!" Finn tucked the ring and the buckle under his shirt and jumped on her horse, bowed to her, and rode off. Finn had trouble at first finding the right position in the saddle because he tried to ride the horse astride, and the lady rode a sidesaddle.

As Finn had disappeared from view, a hateful and cruel-looking Swedish officer in a blue frock coat trimmed with yellow arrived riding a horse followed by a cohort of cavalry. He was the lady's husband, and saw her in torn clothing. "Is this how I deserve to be treated by you, my wife?" He said, viewing her crossly, "My superiors will question my standing as an officer and a gentleman! Indeed, I fear that this display shows that you are keeping a secret lover!"

She tried to raise her torn clothing to cover herself and said, "A clown dressed in fool's clothes arrived, and although he was so handsome to look at, he violently stole my ring and buckle, stole my horse, and fled away!"

"You might as well tell me that he gave you pleasure as well!" the officer claimed furiously, picking up pieces of her clothes and throwing them at her. "I can see it with my very own eyes!"

"The man was just a peasant judging by his foolish clothing and the spear he carried," she replied defiantly.

The officer sneered at her. "I have done nothing to deserve this from you, although you had to give up queen's title for me and settle for being a duchess." He pointed his finger at her and continued. "The trade seems to get expensive for me now. You had better show me the respect I deserve as an officer and a gentleman! But what does it do for me? Nothing at all, now that I have to bear the shame you have brought upon me! Many men beat their women for much less than this. I no longer have an interest in serving you, nor do I want to embrace you or hold you in my arms. Your red lips shall become pale, and your eyes shall turn red with shame!"

She pleaded for understanding. "Sir, I beg of you! Do not abandon your honor because of me, please. You are still a faithful and wise husband. You have a power over me so strong that I am at your mercy. Please listen to me, for the honor of all women, not just mine, and I would rather have someone other than you kill me, so that your honor would remain intact! If you hate me that much, then I want to die!"

He scorned her and said, "My lady, I can see your pride is still intact, but after your shameless demonstration I don't give a damn! I will not sit at the same table with you any longer, nor will I share a bed with you. That's an end to it! No more new clothing for you and your horse shall be an old bag and your saddle old and tattered!"

She leaned against the stone wall sobbing, and pulled her ripped clothes around herself. He looked around and motioned his mounted troops closer.

"Now, the chase is on! I will catch that scum bag that enjoyed your love, and I will challenge him to mortal combat and regain my honor, no matter if fire spouts from his nose like a dragon!" He was furious and sent his soldiers after Finn.

"Go get him! I want his head!" the officer shouted to his men. The Swedish posse galloped after Finn.

§     §     §

Finn saw the tall towers of Hame Castle in the distance across rolling countryside, and riding towards them he encountered many beggars and starving peasants along the road. He stopped to ask for directions from a bald Franciscan friar wearing a brown robe with a chalice, who was collecting alms.

"Hey there, tell me, bald man, where do I find Lady

Columbia?" Finn asked the monk. "I must find her, my mother told me so."

The monk barely glanced at Finn. He shrugged his shoulders and waved his hand toward the castle towers in the south. "Name sounds foreign to me," he replied. "Take this road to Renko. You will find the northernmost point of the pilgrimage route to the shrine of James the Great in Santiago de Compostela. Just follow the old ox road and God will guide you the rest of the way," he said.

"How do you know? Have you been there?" Finn asked.

"No I haven't, but so I have been told. Now bugger off," the friar replied, and walked away.

Finn scratched his head and not knowing where else to go he decided to trust the monk's information, and followed the old ox road. He traveled along the road past beggars and wagons on their way to the market. Soon he arrived at the Hame Castle town customs gate, where a pair of guards motioned for him to stop.

"Dismount and open your bag!" the first guard demanded, while the other circled the horse. Finn dismounted and showed his bag. When he was ready to remount the horse, the guard slapped it with a stick, spooking the horse, and Finn needed all his skills to calm it down.

He shouted to them, "Fools, what the hell is wrong with you!"

The first guard hit him with his steel-tipped staff. "Consider the horse confiscated! We know rascals and wretches like you, you pitiful piece of shit. You must have stolen a horse of this caliber!"

Finn faced him. "Watch it, mister! A ferocious enemy is after me! Let me go!"

The guards glanced at each other, and busted out laughing, slapping their thighs. "A ferocious enemy is after a petty peasant ruffian like you?" the first one said, pointing his finger at Finn. The guards suddenly fell silent when they saw what was happening behind him.

Some distance down the road, Johan Kopf and his Cossacks and the Swedish posse appeared simultaneously, separated only by a hedgerow. Both parties saw Finn and charged at the same time, crashing into each other, taking everybody totally by surprise. Shouting and howling created a cacophony as the men tried to control their horses and fight at the same time.

The two guards were stunned and stood there with their mouths open. The Swedish horses ran over the first guard, the thunderous stomping of their hooves crushed his head wide-open. Johan Kopf's horse was trained for combat. It reared and with his front hoof kicked the other guard in the face turning it into a bloody pulp. Finn's horse reared in fright, and he fell off as the Cossacks and the Swedish soldiers fought with swords and lances, shouting and screaming. The Cossacks' lances were too long for close quarter combat and the Swedes ran through two of the Cossacks with their swords.

The Swedish officer fired his pistol at one of the Cossacks at point-blank range and blew off much of his face. The dead soldier fell from his horse on top of Finn who struggled to get out from under the body. By accident Finn's hand hit some of the bloody mess that had been the dead soldier's face squirting blood all over him.

Another Cossack ran his lance through the Swedish officer who screamed in agony, spitting a long stream of blood, before flopping dead on the ground next to Finn. The dead man's eyes stared at Finn who was trying to stand, but Johan Kopf's horse backed into him, knocking him down yet again. Narrowly escaping the stomping hooves Finn managed to get on his knees and fled into the woods. Kopf, struggling to control his horse, shouted after him, "Halt, surrender!" He and his men fired their muskets at Finn. The bullets made sharp, snapping noises like breaking twigs that narrowly missed him, whizzing through the forest and hitting some trees around his head.

Finn crawled through the dark undergrowth that smelled like rotten eggs. He fell into a hole with a dead animal in it and gagged at the foul stench and muck of the carcass. He felt terribly sick and his stomach began to convulse, raising the bitter taste of vomit in his mouth.

Through the bushes, Finn saw the surviving Swedish soldiers fleeing for their lives, galloping down the road, shooting their remaining rounds at the Cossacks behind them. The Cossacks did not bother chasing them because they saw loot for the taking. They started searching and robbing the bodies, ignoring Kopf, who tried to get them to continue the pursuit in vain.

Finn crawled desperately farther and farther into the lush underbrush to escape the fight. He sighed in relief when he found a suitable hiding place behind a large rock and a giant old oak tree. He dug a shallow hole beneath a clump of flowering lilac bushes, and curled into a fetal position. Wrapping arms around his knees, he tried in vain to fight back tears, but after a while they dried on their own.

After several hours in his secret hiding place alone, even though he was cold and starving, Finn felt safer. His feelings started to dull, but his senses gained strength. He smelled the fresh and fruity aroma of lilac flowers and slowly his body uncoiled until he lay in a prone position. He focused his eyes on the leaves shaped like hearts and remained perfectly still and alert for a long time, and only after he did heard no more noises and was assured that the Cossacks were gone, did he crawl out from the bushes to continue his flight.

§        §        §

The old ox road cut through beautiful forests with ancient oak trees and wound through meadows with gently rolling hills. Finn kept the road within sight but followed the smaller trails close by. He washed in a small creek and felt refreshed, but he was still starving. Seeing a small town in the distance, Finn observed it for a while from his hiding place. There was a medieval gray stone church and a bustling market square with near-empty stalls, where men who looked like former soldiers loitered and drank beer. Finn hesitated, but his stomach rumbled and growled, and he decided to take his chances to get something to eat in the town.

The old soldiers were reservists and paid no attention to Finn. Somewhat relieved, he continued to scout the market square for friendly faces that might be willing to give him some food. He noticed a beautiful young noblewoman with a stern demeanor, surrounded by her chambermaids. Young townsmen were courting the lady, smiling and greeting, but she did not return their glances or smiles as eager suitors passed by. She only nodded solemnly and averted her eyes. Her chambermaids whispered, wondering about her behavior and one of them explained to the rest, "Our Lady made a pledge to a friend of hers that she will not smile at anyone until she meets a faultless man."

Finn happened to walk by them, and upon seeing him, the lady spontaneously laughed aloud, heartily. The maids looked at each other in amazement. Appalled by Finn's rags and earthly odors, they flipped open their folding fans and vigorously waved them in front of their faces. Finn did not understand what was wrong with him, and wondered if the reaction was to his clothes. He sniffed at his armpit, and glancing at his torn flax clothing, he shrugged his shoulders. Suddenly the lady's father appeared, a vicious-looking old nobleman who had forfeited most of his wealth to drink, and he forcefully grabbed the lady by her hair.

"What a sorry sight I see. There goes your reputation," he said with an ugly, angry face. "But I will fix it if I can, and correct it in a way that makes sure your mouth stays closed! There have been many wealthy officers of sub-stance and other prosperous gentlemen passing by here, and they have courted you, but not once have you offered the courtesy of returning their warm greetings. But now, seeing an idiot like that young beggar, you seem happy!"

The man started to slap her. The other women rushed in and attempted to defend her, but he pushed them away roughly. Finn raised and aimed his hunting spear at the man, but other people rushed to intervene and got in between him and the man. Finn pushed through the crowd and forcefully jabbed at the man in the back with his javelin. He said in a harsh voice, "Stop, you coward! That is not the way to treat a lady who happens to like my handsome figure!"

The old soldier froze, his arm raised to strike the lady. He turned slowly, full of hatred, and looked at Finn. "Who in the hell is this clown? You must have a death wish to talk to me like that!"

Finn took a closer look at the man and his equipment and glanced at his own worn-out clothes.

"Listen, you old moron! No one can get away with treating an admirer of mine like that! I will show you who's who! I shall meet you outside town!" Finn looked around and took a glove from someone standing nearby. He slapped the man in the face with it.

The soldier look at him, outraged. "You are an idiot!" he exclaimed. "I will make mincemeat out of you! Follow me to the fields to settle this once and for all!" The soldier got on his horse and rode off. Finn bowed to the lady and followed the man out of the town, leaving her to stare after him, eyes wide.

The soldier waited for Finn in a field some distance away. Finn stopped in front of the man and pointed his finger at him. Finn felt the surging adrenaline rush building up, and let it run and grow until he could not control his anger any longer.

"I am to join the King's men to become a soldier and a winner! Don't try to stop me, either!" He declared, "I am on a mission from my mother, who died in my arms, to fulfill her last wish! Should you regret what you have done, I will tell the King you were drunk, and no harm was done. Give me your horse and your gear and that shall be my reward for defending you. I must be equipped so to become an officer. This is a friendly request, but shall change into a challenge if you do not part with your gear readily. You would do wisely to obey me, old man," Finn told the man.

The soldier scorned him and answered, "Look at who's talking, you shabby excuse of a man. Why don't you swear to take my life, too? Let's see if there is a man in those rags who can take my weapons from me!" He pulled out his rapier.

Finn was adamant. "I shall only be getting what belongs to me, because I will put them to proper use, unlike an old drunkard such as you. So shut up and hand over your gear! I do not have much time!"

The soldier attacked Finn with his sword, but Finn sidestepped his lunge. The soldier drew his pistol and fired it at Finn, but the horse moved, and the bullet nicked Finn's side. Finn shouted in pain and grabbed hold of the bridles, and spooked the horse with his yelling. The startled horse bucked and threw the soldier from his back. The old soldier grimaced with a loud moan when he hit the ground but quickly recovered and stood up ready to fight again.

Finn threw his spear, and skewered the man through his stomach. Finn stepped forward, grabbed the man's sword from his hand, and sliced his throat. A long stream of blood gushed from the severed carotid artery. Gored by the spear, the soldier fell cursing on his back, and died in agony spitting blood and white foam. Finn watched with curiosity as the man died. The javelin made a sucking sound as Finn pulled it out of the dead body.

In a sudden understanding of what just happened,

Finn realized that he had become an outlaw. Not knowing what to do, he walked around the dead man trying to think, fiddling with the moose head necklace. He mumbled to himself, "Oh Mother, look what I have done. I killed a man, and for what? Did I do it because of a lady, or because I wanted his stuff? What should I do? What should I do?"

Making a decision, he looked around to see if anyone was watching him, and not seeing anyone, he started to undress the body. Finn left the torn and bloodied coat to the corpse, but took the dead soldier's trousers, boots, and gear. "Now all I need is a good coat," he said aloud.

A group of rough riders emerged from the woods in full view of the town, across the valley to the north. Johan Kopf really feared that if he failed his mission, General Keith would strip him of his rank and he would end up as a commoner, a petty bourgeois. On the other hand, he enjoyed the thrill of the chase. He figured that his prey would be hungry eventually and would seek food in nearby towns or farms. He led his Cossacks in an ever-widening search circle knowing he would find Finn's tracks sooner or later. They galloped into the town and continued through the streets without stopping. The Cossacks hit the people left and right with their lances and swords. People screamed and scattered in a panic trying to hide. Finn heard the commotion from the town. He slapped the horse, which sent it off galloping, and ran the other way, disappearing into the woods.

The Cossacks arrived at the scene of the murderous fight, and saw the dead soldier's half-naked corpse. Kopf looked around and spied the horse running in the distance. He stood up on stirrups and used his telescope to see that

the horse had no rider. "Shit! We just missed him! Go
after him like a Doberman! He can't have gotten far!"
he shouted, and threw his gloves on the ground, totally
and madly frustrated. Studying a rude map of the area,
he realized that his quarry was trying to get to the harbor
and decided to get there first. He picked up his gloves and
mounted his horse, motioning the troops to follow him.

§       §       §

Finn skirted around the edges of any villages and farms
in order to avoid people, and discovered a decent hiding
place near some large alder trees along the river rapids. He
found a quiet spot by a pool on the river and pulled off his
shirt. Examining the wound on his side, he grimaced. In
a cupped hand he took some water and tried to clean it.
He looked for some large plant leaves and tore his shirt
using his teeth, placing large green leaves on the wound
and dressing it with strips of cloth from his shirt.

Finn knelt down to clear some pollen from the water's
surface so he could drink. He washed his face in the cold
water, and sat down on the riverbank, exhausted. His
stomach growled, and he felt sick. He lay down and closed
his eyes.

He mumbled to himself, "A quarter of an hour. Give
me a quarter of an hour. That is all I need." He looked up
into the trees hovering above him and listened to a bird
singing. His eyelids got heavy, and he dozed off.

Through his slumber, Finn heard the soothing sound
of water running over rocks and stones. The sun glinted
through the leaves and bees buzzed in a field of flowers.

A sizeable fish made a splash in the river. An osprey swooped down and caught the shiny brown trout in its talons. Finn woke up startled from his slumber, and shook his head to clear it and to get hold of his bearings. More alert, he looked around and grabbing his weapons began to search for animal tracks. He needed food badly. He advanced through the woods looking for animal trails when he heard a voice in the distance. He moved forward cautiously along the riverbank until he saw a two-story building by the river. It was an old mill and roadhouse called the King's Inn.

Finn observed the house for a while from his hiding place behind the trees and bushes. He did not see anything out of the ordinary and decided it was safe to approach. There was a fat man in the yard, wearing a suede vest over a white drawstring shirt, and Finn walked up to him slowly. The fat man turned, and seeing Finn, held up his arm demanding him to stop.

"Halt! Don't come any closer!" he commanded.

Desperately tired and hungry, Finn asked him, "Sir, I need something to eat and a place to rest just for a little while. Would you be kind enough to let me stay here, maybe in the barn or stables?"

The innkeeper was angry and armed. He looked at Finn with disdain. "I would not give you a slice of bread if you begged for thirty years! Anybody who asks anything from me for free is wasting his time and mine, because I only look after my children and myself. You have no place in my house!"

Finn said, "But sir, my village was attacked and my family and everybody was either killed or taken away as

prisoners. I have nothing left. I am searching for Lady
Columbia like my dying mother instructed me to do. I will
become a soldier and a master of my own life! As an officer,
I will collect taxes for the King!"

The innkeeper looked long at Finn, scrutinizing him
from head to toe. When he had observed him long enough
to consider him harmless he said, "Well, I could come up
with something, and if you have money or anything of
value, I just might accept it."

Finn showed him the elegant metal buckle he had
taken from the lady. "Don't worry, I can pay you," he said.

When he saw the shining metal, the greedy innkeeper
started to smile. Baring his blackened teeth, he rubbed his
fat hands together. "Well, you are such a handsome boy,
and should you wish to stay with us, you will receive only
the best from all of us in the house. Perhaps you will find
my daughter to your liking?"

"Just give me some food and you may keep the gold if
you feed me tonight, and show me the way to the harbor
town tomorrow," Finn replied.

"That I will do, because I have never seen such a
handsome young man such as you. For a price like that,
I will take you to the knights of the round table if you
want!" The innkeeper smiled and licked his fat fingers. He
led Finn inside and showed him a spot on a wide bench
against the wall. The grumpy old wife brought him some of
the previous day's thick stew in a wooden bowl, and couple
of pieces of hard bread, and threw it on the table in front
of him.

Finn devoured everything and insisted that they leave
early. "We must leave at dawn, and I do not want to waste

any time. We will leave before rooster's call," Finn said, curled on the bench and promptly fell asleep.

Early the next morning, Finn woke up to the smell of a steaming bowl of broth on the table with some chicken, vegetables and cereal grains it. He ate in silence and tried to figure out a plan or where to go, but he could not think of anything. As the sun rose, the innkeeper guided Finn towards Turku, eagerly hurrying in front of him, and climbing atop a small hill they saw the tall towers of the cathedral in the distance.

"It is your lucky day, lad! See, there is the city in front of you, and there you must go," the innkeeper said.

"I want you to show me the way," Finn demanded.

"Young sir, I cannot do that. You see, the townspeople do not like rough country folks like me, but they certainly will appreciate an upstanding young gentleman like you," the innkeeper replied, acting as if he were sorry. He bade Finn farewell with a wave of his arm, and left.

As the innkeeper hurried away, Finn shrugged his shoulders and walked towards the church towers in the distance. From atop a large rock, he had a better view. In the distance, he saw the innkeeper talking with Johan Kopf and eagerly pointing in his direction. Johan Kopf dropped a small purse in the man's hand. Finn hissed between his teeth. "That fat bastard! He's a thief and a liar after all. I should have known!"

Finn turned and entered the city running. He was lost, and could only think of the large body of water his mother told him to cross like a Viking. He smelled the tar and pitch that was used to waterproof the hulls of ships and saw masts gently bob with the swaying water, and searched to find his way to the harbor. Finn was amazed to see so many people in one place. The street smelled of furnace fumes and the tar left an oily taste on his tongue.

The Russian attack had been a swift and successful, the war had been lost and the troubled townspeople expected the Russians to arrive any time to take over the town. Finn passed by a worried storekeeper. "Should I close the store or what I should do? Will the Russians rob us blind and kill us when they arrive?" the man asked his neighbor.

Finn looked for hiding places from the Cossacks in the crowd behind the market stalls. By the cathedral, Finn saw a teenage fellow in the stocks. He was sitting in his own pungent-smelling sludge. Finn stopped to talk to him. "What happened to you? Why are you bound like that? What did you do?" he asked the boy, but the boy did not answer, and just looked at Finn in resignation.

Tax collection took place next to the cathedral, where a group of nervous and restless peasants demanded tax cuts. Mayor of the town Dean Helsingius, in his black robe and black riding boots, was trying to calm the peasants down, urging them to pay their taxes.

The short but bloody war was cruel to civilians but the shaky peace accord left the population at the mercy of soldiers looting and burning, and it was not much better for the survivors. Peasants in raggedly clothes were left to die or care for themselves the best they could. The Swedish regiments retreated in disarray but not before they forcefully commandeered every horse within many leagues. They used the beasts to transport army supplies from the magazines until the horses were totally exhausted and spoiled and were of no use to anybody any longer.

Aristocrats and officers on the run started to hit people who happened to get in their way and had to flee for their wretched lives. People did not receive any payment promised to them for the war effort or receipts for services rendered. Nevertheless, the King of course still demanded taxes to be paid on time, but people could not pay any taxes, simply because they had nothing left to give.

Dean Helsingius waved his hand. "Amidst all this noise, I can see that some people feel they have been ill-treated and cannot fulfill their obligations to the Crown. My tallyman Mechelin here, who is in charge of the collections, can't make any sense out of this because there is too much fuss. One says he might be able to pay and another that he cannot!"

A forlorn peasant woman waved her arms. "What else could we say? We will honor our obligations, but it will cause us extreme hardships and an intolerable burden if we are ordered to pay the grain tax!" she replied.

Tallyman Mechelin got up to leave. "This is useless! These senseless and stubborn peasants don't know a damn thing. I shall return to collect every single penny due!"

Dean Helsingius followed him. "We should allow local clergy and officials to determine who are so poor that they cannot meet their obligations. The wealthier folks shall agree to pay one barrel of rye, one barrel of barley, and two jugs of spirits to the King's coffers." Waging war and feeding an army was expensive, and the King was not going to use his own monies to do it.

Finn made his way past a medieval castle and hoped that he had avoided the posse and Cossacks who had chased him. Across the market square, Finn saw the innkeeper being paid a few coins by Swedish soldiers. The innkeeper waved his arm towards the harbor.

"That double-timing son of a bitch!" he yelled, and ran through a dark alley to another street. Finn hid in the crowd and witnessed a populist trial in progress. He saw one of the spectators take off his fringed leather jacket and put it atop a fence, and made a plan.

Drunken Judge Vijkman, a fat and vindictive man, was approaching his desk, and as he walked he beat people with his walking stick. He sat down behind the desk, holding a small white dog that licked his face. Occasionally, he turned around to drink from his tankard.

"Defendant, I notice your father has already settled this issue with the plaintiff," the judge said, facing the defendant.

The defendant, a tall young man with a mustache, took his hat in his hands and replied, "No, he has not settled it. I have not agreed to anything. If I don't get justice here, I will pay the money owed and seek justice by some other means."

The judge contemplated for a moment. "You shall do no such thing. To whom would you place your deposit money? Your father who has already agreed to pay? Get married, young man, or go and become a hired hand to some good house. This case is closed!" The judge made his ruling and took a long drink.

While the crowd was paying rapt attention to the trial, Finn crept closer to the fringed leather jacket on top of the fence and grabbed it quickly, walking around a wagon filled with straw. All of a sudden, he heard shouts of "Cossacks, Cossacks!" Turning to look, he saw Lieutenant

Johan Kopf and his Cossacks riding into town with a cloud of dust rising behind them. Seeing their swords and lances shone in the sunlight Finn thought, *Who in hell is that son of a bitch? I can't believe he is so relentlessly on my trail. Why doesn't he just give up?*

Finn ran to the harbor and eagerly looked for an opportunity to get away. He had no idea where to go and just followed his instincts. He saw a Dutch merchant ship, the *Vrouw Maria*, and approached a tall, proud looking man standing close to the loading ramp in the uniform of his rank, and armed as well. He was Captain Raymond Lourens.

Finn kept glancing over his shoulders. "Sir, can I get on board?" Finn was frantic. "I am on a mission sent by my mother. I must get on board! Take me to Spain, like a monk suggested to me, please?" Finn asked the captain.

Captain Lourens heard the commotion from the town and saw the two advancing posses approaching rapidly from two different directions, heading towards the harbor. Captain Lourens looked at Finn, who stood there tense with a pistol and a rapier in his belt under his fringed leather jacket, which was slightly too large for him.

"Help us to load these tar barrels, and I will take you on board my ship. This place is going to get too busy for my taste anyway. Be careful not to drop the barrels! This is a valuable export product for European navies," Captain Lourens said.

"I know sir! I know how it is made!" Finn said lifting a tar barrel on his shoulders and carrying it aboard. He quickly hurried back to carry more barrels. Each time he passed Captain Lourens, he bowed to him. "Thank you, sir! Can we go now? Please?"

Captain Lourens counted the barrels on the deck, and when all of them were loaded, he commanded, "Alright, that is enough! Cast off the ship! Raise the anchor!"

Upon seeing Johan Kopf's Cossacks, the Swedish troops became perplexed, and wanted immediately to surrender. Amid the confusion, Johan Kopf cussed and cursed, and tried to go through the disorderly crowd, but he could not get through.

Onboard *Vrouw Maria*, Finn jumped into the cargo holds to hide behind some barrels and flour sacks. "This is it. I do not know where I'm going or what terrible future will be waiting for me. No options left, got to go no matter what," he mumbled, hoping for the best.

Frustrated to the bone, Johan Kopf returned to his camp and angrily threw his gear down in his tent. He prepared a mud bath of ash, peat and hot mineral water in an old wooden feeding trough. He took off his clothes and let out a sigh as he lowered himself into the hot, muddy mixture. He put a steaming towel over his face and quickly relaxed, thinking, If I run with the pack I must play by the pack rules, but I must keep my options open. He dozed off.

Kopf was startled to hear General Keith's voice addressing him. "So you let that foolish beggar get away, huh? I told you to bring him to me!" Johan Kopf jumped up from the trough, his naked body dripping mud.

"But, sir," he started to reply. General Keith stared penetratingly down at him from his horse and cut him off. From his long experience the general knew exactly how to deal with men like Kopf.

"Shut up! I told you, your promotion depended on

apprehending that little joker. Now, let's see, what should I do with you? Ah, yes, some colleagues of mine need fresh cannon fodder in England. At least I'll make some money out of you, and you will get another chance to redeem yourself! Think about it, Lieutenant. Do you want to belong or not? Do you really want to be one of us? Now pack your bags and get out of my sight!"

General Keith turned to his aide. "See to it that he is on the next ship!" he said, and rode off in a cloud of dust.

By that time Vrouw Maria was well offshore, and Finn heard Captain Lourens shouting down to the cargo hold. "You can come out now!"

Finn climbed out warily from the cargo hold and stood at the stern watching the shoreline become smaller and smaller in the distance. The tall masts creaked in the wind, the sails fluttered. Finn walked around barrels of tar stacked amid coils of rope and netting, until he found a place to sit by the outside wall of the captain's quarters, away from the stench of drying fish. He found comfort in the salty seawater tang the air carried, and the refreshing breeze cooling his face. He bowed his head quietly bidding farewell to his homeland, rested for a while, then got up and walked to the bow. On the aft deck, he looked across the vast sea, and saw the sun hovering just above the horizon. Hearing a loud scream above, he looked up and saw a whitetail eagle hovering above looking down at him. The mighty bird screamed again and flew ahead of the ship.

Finn turned to Captain Lourens and said, "My life was not that great before perhaps, but at least I am honest. I wanted to live and grow in peace with my girl, but my desire was answered with unspeakable violence, and my family was ruthlessly taken from me. Now I am all alone, and I am my own master, and answer to no one. I must find my own way now." Finn watched the eagle disappear into the horizon ahead of the ship, and feeling unsettled and frail he twiddled with the moose head necklace he still wore around his neck.

# Chapter 2

FINN ENJOYED THE DAYS AT SEA in the open fresh air, and it made him feel much better. He was eager to learn how to be a sailor, and he did not complain when Captain Lourens ordered him to scrub the deck, among other menial chores. The crew wanted to get to know him better and asked his name. "Finn," he replied morosely. Someone asked about his family name. Finn looked left and right and said, "I don't have one," and turned away. The captain began calling him Orphan Finn.

The work on the ship was hard, and as she visited several ports along the Baltic coast, Finn helped load and unload heavy barrels, sacks, and boxes. Captain Lourens learned to appreciate the quiet young man who stayed by himself, worked very hard, and never complained.

The days turned to weeks, and weeks turned to months. The ship visited many ports in Denmark and Holland. Finn volunteered for guard duty, and stayed on board when the crew went ashore to take advantage of bars and whorehouses. Then one beautiful day, after a full year at sea, the ship sailed on the open sea near the coast of Dover. White cliffs shone in the bright sunlight as the Dutch merchant ship Vrouw Maria approached England. A flock of screaming seagulls hovered over the ship.

Finn's head, shoulders, and torso popped out from the cargo hold hatch. His body had gained muscle mass from the hard work on the ship, and his blond curly hair was now quite long. He wore a white pullover shirt with buttons on the front, a broad black waist sash around his waist. When he pulled himself up to the deck he revealed the rest of his usual ensemble: grey pants with a black drawstring cord, and brown suede boots with two large flaps wrapped around the side of the boot connected with stitched leather laces. He leaned over the railing towards the land, opened his mouth, and tasted the salty seawater on his tongue. He walked towards the stern where Captain Lourens stood at the helm, observing the approaching shore with his telescope.

"Finn, you have served me well," Captain Lourens said. He looked at Finn approvingly. "You are a bright young man and you can carry your own weight. I shall pay you what is due now. Are you sure you want to leave when we arrive in London?"

"Yes, Captain Lourens," Finn replied. "You have treated me well ever since I boarded your ship in haste. You gave me shelter, work, food, and clothes, and even paid me some money. But now I must continue my journey. My dying mother assigned me a mission, and I must obey her last wish."

"Orphan Finn, you are all alone and master of your own fate. Be warned, however, as you must hide from soldiers who force recruits, many of whom are just like you with nothing to lose, into the King's Army, to fight on the continent," Captain Lourens warned him.

"I think I'm ready to look after myself," Finn replied.

"I have no doubts about that," Captain Lourens said, "but you should know that I am scheduled to transport some precious cargo, works of art and such, from Amsterdam to St. Petersburg, and this will take us to Finland again. I thought you might want to return. I'm sure things have calmed down by now. It would be safe for you to return."

For a moment, Finn mulled over the idea of returning to Finland. "Thank you, but I don't think so, Captain," he said. "My people are dead and gone. I did some stupid and terrible things. There is no going back for me."

Captain Lourens understood. "Very well, then. If that is what you want to do, I won't stand on your way. We are going up the River Thames to London. You may disembark there."

The captain steered the ship into the river channel sailing upstream. Finn watched the land and houses onshore in anxious contemplation. When the ship approached the port, Finn turned to another sailor.

"I wonder if this is the place where I can find Lady Columbia," he asked.

The sailor, a toothless and dirty old man, laughed, "Nay, hardly so, lad, whoever she may be! This is London, city of malady, lunacy, and demise! It robs the duped of the sanctity of their bodies, the soundness of their mind, and the honor of their souls! Enjoy it while you are here!"

In the harbor, Finn sniffed the air, and turning up his nose he said, "I don't know about that, but I can sure tell that London is a smelly place! I can smell tar, sea water, rotting fish, fear, and shit!"

Finn helped the sailors cast the ship's ropes and fasten them quayside, and walked up to Captain Lourens to shake his hand. "Thank you, Captain, for everything," Finn said.

Captain Lourens wished him well. "Take care, Finn, and keep your nose clean." Finn put on his leather jacket, tucked his weapons under the waist sash, and jumped up on the pier carrying a small backpack. He waved to Captain Lourens and the ship's crew one more time before melting into the crowd.

Finn walked through London's dirty streets, unaccustomed to all the fuss and hustle. Seeing so many people in one place made him uneasy, and a little jumpy. He heard people on a street corner talking about the King who was away in Europe waging a war again, and he understood that they spoke in fear of an impending invasion.

He cut through small alleys and arrived in a market square. A street peddler with a pale, greenish face rushed to hustle his wares. "Young fellow, you must prepare yourself against carnal diseases with a new innovation: lambskins! I sell the merchandise in packets of eight and tied with silk for the well-endowed dainty fellow such as you! I also have merchandise made of linen soaked in brine, for the less privileged!" Finn was amazed to see the condoms made of animal gut and wrapped in paper, but scratching his head he could not figure out why they were needed. He smiled not believing any of it and waved his hand at the peddler, thinking it must be a hoax.

Near Fleet Prison, Finn saw a shabby crook being arrested for his debt and quickly thrown into prison. He passed iron bars built into the Farrington Street prison wall, so that prisoners could beg for alms from the people passing by. The warden was an obstinate man who loved duty, and money, more than people. He wore a dark triple cape coat with brass buttons and gilt pattern tricorn hat, and was counting a wad of bills at the front gate. Finn became curious and stopped to talk to him.

"Why did you jail that guy you just brought in? How can he pay his obligation if he is in jail?" he asked the warden, who kept counting his money.

"Caging is a productive business here in Britain, my boy," the warden replied. "I charge fees for turning keys to open the doors, or for taking irons off my customers legs, and the Fleet Prison has the highest fees in England!" he boasted.

"What kind of business is it, making money out of throwing poor buggers in prison?" Finn said, thinking aloud, but the warden heard him.

The warden made a sales pitch to him. "For a mere £5, you get your own cell! A few shillings more bring you some food. Or at least a likeness of it! More importantly, you get a regular round of beer or our own prison-distilled gin!"

Finn was appalled by the horrid man and his horrendous treatment of indigent prisoners, and shaking his head, he continued on. As he walked past the Foundling Hospital, a little girl with large blue eyes and a dirty face dressed in ragged clothes started to follow him without saying a word. Finn waved his hands at her to make her stop, but the girl stayed close behind him. After several attempts, Finn turned suddenly and tossed a coin in the air that she quickly snapped in her hand. Finn made angry faces at her, and finally managed to scare her off.

On another town square, Finn witnessed how a group of competing city guides solicited patriotic visitors, some charging sixpence for the premium tour, while others asked only two shillings and sixpence for the same service, to lead them round the patriotic scenes at the Palladian Bridge and the Temple of Friendship.

Finn came to the Goose and Gridiron Ale House by St. Paul's Churchyard. He wanted to get a meal, but the angry looking tavern keeper standing at the door blocked his entrance. The tavern keeper ushered him away, and said, "This is a respectable establishment! Go to the Turk's Head on Greek Street! They allow hoodlums and sailors in!"

On a street corner, Finn almost ran into a loathly lady, a crazy fortune-teller with deep blue eyes and greyish face. She wore loose clothing with black hair under a red scarf with attached coins. She had a deck of fortune cards and an emerald crystal ball in her bag, but she was also turning tricks on the side. She straightened her hem and pushed her sagging breasts back in her dress as she exited an alley, with a man following her buttoning his pants. The man glanced left and right and quickly darted into the crowd. She started following Finn and tried to make his acquaintance, hoping to get him interested in her services.

Finn was not swayed by her sales pitch. "Crazy old woman, why are you following me? I have been around the world before, you know! This strange, troubled place called London town is not the center of the world. What could a filthy crazy place like this give to the betterment of mankind?" He dashed off, hoping to lose her into the crowd.

Wandering through the streets, Finn became interested in a group of gentlemen and naval officers gathered on the steps of the Royal Society in front of a lecturer. The orator wore an expensive suit, a golden heavyweight silk vest and a linen cravat. Lecturing to his audience, he said, "I will now speak to you about the 'wounded dog concept' discovered by Sir Kenelm Digby. The astonishing dust of empathy he has developed can heal at a distance! You see, the dust of empathy is put on a dressing from the injured soul, and even if the dressing drenched with the powder is in London, the person in Dublin will sense it! However, there is one drawback: it causes pains. However, that may be used to your advantage!

"For example, if it is a dog, it will bark in agony. Gentlemen, this is exactly where this remarkable dust is so beneficial for navigation! What you need to define your longitude is a correct time. Now, you simply cut a dog and drench a dressing in the dog's wound, which you keep with you in London. You place the dog itself aboard ship. The ship sets sail taking the dog with it, and at midday, you put the dust of empathy on the dressing. That causes the dog to bark in pain on the ship, and the captain will know it is noontime in London. From this evidence, he can calculate his longitude!" The man concluded, chin proudly high, and a heated debate erupted between gentlemen and officers in the audience.

Finn strolled by the execution dock, where pirates and other water-faring criminals faced execution by drowning in a gibbet made of slats of iron and rivets. The condemned stared terrified at the rotting bodies left in cages from previous executions. They remained in the water, subject to the rising and falling tides, until the bones fell apart. A drunken crowd loitered nearby and sang "Star Anthem."

§   §   §

Wandering through the streets, Finn saw the sign advertising the Bell Inn & Alehouse and entered the pub. At the doorway, he stopped to look around the room where flickering torches lined every wall. A group of men smoked pipes and drank beer from large tankards. Thick tobacco smoke filled the room, and the fragrant scent of the burning leaves, which he found pleasant, filled Finn's nostrils. There was a bar with a few customers and some tables near the dirty, stained windows. Scantily clad barmaids moved between tables scattered in front of the burning fireplace in the corner. They soaked up whatever heat they could while passing out tall mugs of ale. A lively redheaded servant girl in a brightly colored jacket, a black skirt with a white apron and a scarf, came around the corner carrying several large tankards full of ale, almost running into Finn while making her rounds.

She shouted to him, "Out of the way, coming through! Get in, or get out! This is not a place for shy young lads!" She pushed Finn out of the way. He spun around and when he turned back she was gone. The men playing cards at the nearby table laughed. Finn hesitated but stepped in further and found no available seats at the tables. He walked towards the bar looking for a seat, and saw one table where a young man sat by himself.

Finn approached the table and judged by the uniform he wore that the man was an apprentice in the British

Merchant Navy. Very dapper in a short blue jacket and a three-button opening cuff, a mustard colored waistcoat, tanned breeches, and black leather shoes, he had placed a small black tricorn hat and a cudgel-like walking stick on a chair next to him. Finn found his self-confident appearance and friendly demeanor encouraging, but he noticed a stack of books and a sextant on the table, which made him a little uneasy.

As usual, the man had come to the pub straight from the ship to see Elizabeth, one of the barmaids. For some reason, he noticed Finn the moment he entered the pub, which the man found slightly disconcerting, because usually he noticed only Elizabeth. There was something familiar about the stranger; he just could not figure out what. He was curious about the way Finn was dressed and because, obviously, he was lost.

As Finn stepped closer and was ready to talk to him, the loathly lady appeared again from the smoke and grabbed Finn by the arm. Finn wondered whether she had stalked him or was it just a coincidence, but anyhow, he felt uneasy. Her bright smile revealed blackened teeth and Finn could smell cheap rum on her breath. She pushed herself against him. "Kiss me, marry me, and I shall bear you many children!" Again, the men at the table laughed at him. Finn shook her hand loose and hurried towards the young man's table.

"Hey, lad, you better watch out, old Maggie here might take you home tonight!" one of the men shouted, and they all began laughing again. One man spat tobacco in a bucket. Finn looked at the young man sitting alone, and estimated they were close to the same age.

He said, "Sir, my mother, rest her soul in peace, told me to be polite, always be polite. Therefore, sir, it is a pleasure to meet you, and perhaps a respectable gentleman like you would not mind if I joined you for a moment to ask for some advice. I am new in London town," Finn said. The man looked at him briefly and then nodded politely.

"By all means, have a seat," he answered. "Dear Elizabeth, please bring us some more ale," the man asked and lifted his hat and cudgel from the chair and placed them by the stack of books.

He continued, "Wearing a jacket like that you look like a wild man, or maybe some sort of a musician. What are you, sir?"

Finn sat down and introduced himself. "They call me Finn, sir, and I come from the north. This is my first time in London. It is such a vast and noisy place. I am searching for Lady Columbia, as my dying mother advised me, but I have no idea where I should look for her. You wouldn't happen to know where I might find her, would you?" he asked.

The young man greeted him, and they shook hands. "I am James Cook, at your service. I am assigned to the collier *Freelove*, sailing between the Tyne and London. It is my pleasure to meet you," the man said in a pleasant voice. "There are many, many people in London. It is different out there at sea! I assure you that, out there, you are your own master!"

Finn nodded and drank his beer, enjoying the thick, sweet ale warming his throat, and he looked around the noisy pub. He was tired and soon the strong beer made him relax. He heard only a few words of what James Cook was talking about, and tried to concentrate while Cook talked about the duties of a sailor. When Cook delivered his advice to avoid impudent curiosity, Finn pretended that he had heard everything and even understood it, because he did not want to offend this friendly gentleman.

"I hear your advice, and I am on a mission," Finn said. "All I want is some direction. What would you recommend first of all to a man like me?" Now it was James Cook's turn not pay attention. He watched Elizabeth the waitress and smiled at her at every opportunity.

"Having a patron is a must in today's world. You don't get anywhere without one," Cook said absentmindedly, and raised his tankard in greeting to a man passing by. He winked at Elizabeth, who laughed and smiled back at him.

Finn nodded and asked, "I must make a note of that. Anything else I should know, sir? How could I find my way?"

James Cook looked bored, but then his eyes lit up. "Navigation, you must learn navigation! That way you know where you are going. But one problem remains, and that is the issue with the longitude," he said.

Finn had no idea what he was saying. "What is longitude? I heard some men talking about it on the street by the great building," he asked.

James Cook's eyes lit up. "That is an excellent question!" He said, waving his arms in excitement, "Longitude is how far to the east or west you are! Latitude is how far north or south you are! It is no problem for most experienced sailors to understand what their latitude is by calculating how high the sun or a certain star is above the horizon, or simply by the length of day. In order to evade problems with not knowing one's position accurately, skippers, whenever possible, rely on their understanding of latitude. They just navigate to the latitude of their journey's end, turn toward their terminus, and get a course of constant latitude."

Finn leaned closer wondering. "I don't understand what the problem is?"

James Cook cleared the room on the table and leaned over it, arranging empty tankards like pawns on a chess board to illustrate his point. He was almost shouting now.

"Longitude is something completely different, and it is producing big complications these days when everything calls for exchange, travel, and exploration by sea!" Cook said, "Let's assume a ship needs to go west past a cape and then head north for home. But it's cloudy or in the hours of darkness, or there are a lot of islets around so you can't clearly determine if you have passed the horn! At this time, there is no true way to estimate the distance traveled. So you are likely to be wrong about it, think you're past the cape, and go north. Of course, if you haven't passed the cape, you'll head straight on the rocks! And that's exactly what frequently occurs all over the world right now! It is an ongoing tragedy!" James Cook explained, in a loud voice.

An older gentleman in his forties, dressed in a dark green frock coat, walked over to them from the card table. His hair was all ruffled, and he looked a little absentminded.

"Gentlemen, I could not help but hear your very interesting conversation, and notice that you are familiar with the fine art of navigation," he said, pointing at the books and sextant before continuing, "I have an answer to the problem Ensign presented so well. I would like to introduce myself. My name is John Harrison."

Cook pointed to a chair. "Sit down, Mr. Harrison, let's hear your theory," he said turning around and continued, "Elizabeth, more ale for me and these worthy gentlemen, please!"

John Harrison nodded, sat down, and continued, "As you are well aware, in the year 1714, the British Parliament offered a king's ransom in the Longitude Act for any person who could come up with a plan for crafts to determine their longitude with any amount of precision. I am going to claim that prize!"

"Sure. You are quite right," Finn said matter-of-factly, although he had no idea what the man was talking about.

"Many men have tried, and all have failed so far, sir. Tell us about your solution to this pressing problem," James Cook replied eagerly.

Finn looked at both men and nodded with a stern expression, pretending he understood what they were saying. With one hand on his knee, he raised his tankard to drink, but it was empty. He turned it upside down.

"I have invented a watch!" Harrison said, animated. "Not just any watch, but a watch that can be taken on board a vessel and display to the captain the time with utmost precision, allowing him to navigate around the world if need be! I have solved many real-world difficulties, and now I am glad to make my first watch to prove its viability!"

Finn motioned to the pretty barmaid, and as the young girl servant walked by, he smiled and winked at her, asking to bring more beer to them. Flirting with him, the girl showed her tongue.

Cook contemplated what Harrison had told them. "Now how do you propose to do that, sir? We are talking about a leading scientific evolution! It is going to cost you a little treasure!" Elizabeth placed new tankards on the table, but this time Cook did not notice her. She turned away looking a little wounded.

Harrison answered, "Mr. George Graham has already loaned me the money to make my first working prototype, which I named H1, and the Board of Longitude was impressed enough to give me five hundred pounds for a further development, which I shall call H2."

Finn listened to the conversation but his mind was wandering in different directions. He was confused about his feelings. He felt sorry for abandoning his family because he survived and they had not. Distressing thoughts of Eva's deception filled his mind. He tried to harden himself, but in vain.

"I wonder if I can ever trust a woman again," he said quietly. The two men glanced at him but continued talking about sailing.

The men drank and talked well into the night. The servant girl came by again and ran her fingers through Finn's hair. She laughed, and catching him unawares, sat on his lap and wrapped her arms around his neck. He became more interested in her than the two men talking about navigation. She was a pretty, voluptuous young woman with high cheekbones. She blushed easily when she got excited. Feeling her breasts push against his arm Finn became attracted to her, and soon he was convinced that he was deeply in love.

During the evening, Joseph Banks, a boy in his teens and obviously from a well-to-do family, joined them. Clearly young Joseph loved fashion, as he was dressed in tanned breeches and a tight fitting green cotton velvet gown with shot silk lining. He was simply looking for some company and found their conversation stimulating. An outgoing young man, without hesitation or any further ado, he just sat down at the table, introduced himself, and quickly became friends with Finn and the servant girl.

§     §     §

After midnight, Finn and his new friends were the last ones to leave the pub. The servant girl and Joseph held Finn between them, almost falling out of the door together joking and laughing. James Cook and John Harrison, who still talked intensely between themselves, followed close behind.

"Finn, you're a rational man! Remember what I told you and you will find your way!" James Cook shouted, laughing.

"Mr. Cook, I think you should seek work with Captain Lourens who is a close of friend of mine! You could sail with him in the Baltic Sea! With my recommendation, he would probably promote you to a sub-lieutenant on his magnificent ship in no time!" Finn shouted back. James Cook waved his hand to flag a coach and the two men drove off.

Finn was drunk and felt terrific, because he did not feel alone anymore in a big city. Digging into his pockets, he turned them inside out. "Gone, it's all gone! Bloody hell, I must have holes in my pockets, but that's alright, I have new friends!" he said, standing between Joseph and the girl, and slinging his arms around their shoulders. They wandered off aimlessly not knowing where they might find a place to stay.

"Joe, I thought you said your father was a wealthy man! Surely he must have a place we could stay?" Finn asked.

"Yes, he is, a country squire in Lincolnshire and member of the House of Commons. But given the shape you're in, we can't go to his place," Joseph answered.

"So what brings you to London?" Finn asked. "You must be far away from home, you know. Although I don't even know where a place like that might be!"

Joseph kicked a pail, sending it clanging and banging down an alley, and said, "I already told you, I am going to attend Eaton College in Windsor and study nature, history, and botany."

"That's right, you are the flower boy!" Finn said, laughing and groping the servant girl. She pushed his hand away and giggled. They wandered through the streets, and turning a corner, encountered a crowd listening to a priest outside Grosvenor Chapel. The priest preached fiercely to a motley crew of beggars and poor people loitering on the streets. Finn saw the fog rising from the sewers, smelling like rotting flesh and burning hair, and watched how the torches and fires lighting the streets cast flickering shadows on the buildings. He stopped to listen to the priest, swaying on his feet.

The preacher, in black tunic and white tight collar, looked feverish holding his finger high, preaching of the punishment of hell and God's way of destroying offenders. Finn let out a loud burp, and turning against a wall opened his pants to take a piss, and tilted his head back. He started to talk loudly over his shoulder to Joseph and the servant girl, but the priest heard him too.

"Bullshit, I'd say!" Finn declared, with a bout of hiccups. "I'm telling you, that man needs to get laid! I have seen the dead, and they sure aren't pretty! I was the quick one, and they are now gone! The preacher talks about the resurrection of the dead. Fuck that! He's just another bullshit peddler! He can't bring my family back! They are still dead and gone!" Finn leaned his forehead against the wall and moved his feet away from the spraying piss.

The priest saw what Finn was doing and stopped preaching. He looked grim as he worked his way through the crowd towards Finn. The girl was terrified. "Be quiet, Finn. The priest is coming! You are going to get us all into trouble!"

The livid preacher stopped in front of them. "Who are these hoodlums and what is he doing? He is pissing on my church wall! How dare you!"

Finn turned around buttoning his pants, and did not pay any attention to the preacher. He belched, and lifting his leg, let out a loud fart. "Alright, I feel much better now!" He said, laughing drunkenly, "Now all I want is a few minutes in private with you, my beautiful vixen! Come here, pretty girl!" The servant girl took another look at the wrathful priest and ran away, disappearing into the fog. The priest was astounded, and leaning on his walking staff, he held his finger up in the air.

"This is utterly disgusting! This is blasphemy!" he shouted.

Finn swaggered closer to him, "Hey, old man, you scared my girl away! How dare you! And I was going to get laid tonight! Shame is on you, old man!"

The priest raised his staff to strike Finn. "You, you, you... You are a sloshed demon!"

Finn dodged the preacher's blow and grabbed hold of the staff. "Listen, priest, I didn't see your God around when my family was slaughtered! I'm innocent, yet now he makes me feel guilty! Don't come near me with your finger high, I don't think you are much of a match to me! I fought alongside Captain Lofving himself!"

Joseph took Finn by the arm with both hands and pulled him back away from the preacher. "Stop it, Finn!" He pleaded, but in vain. Finn did not listen to him.

The preacher shouted at Finn at the top of his lungs, "A no-good scoundrel like you should get a hold of yourself! Cut your hair! Learn to behave! Get a job!"

Finn pulled in his belt a notch and smirked back at the preacher, "Listen, mister, I am my own master now! Nobody will tell me what to do, like it or not!"

Joseph spied a team of constables who had seen the commotion approaching them, fast. He shook Finn and shouted to him, "Come on, Finn! Coppers are coming to get you! We must run! Run!"

Finn realized finally that he was getting too deep into a sticky situation. Joseph pulled him down the street, and they ran through an alley, finding a place to hide behind a cart and some bales of hay.

All of a sudden, Finn felt tired. "Let me sit here for a little while. Then we can go on... Oh, I already miss her," he said and sat down. The constables went past them, and Joseph sighed in relief. He smirked at Finn and said, "The secularist spirit of your words would have been enough to get you flogged. Worse, if they think you reject God as a doubter, they will most likely hang you. But anyhow, you replied with

astonishing force to the preacher – and he happened
to be a bishop!"

Finn's head dangled almost between his knees by now,
and Joseph hardly heard him. "Bishop, you say? Well, I
showed him, didn't I? Anyway, that last bottle of Bishop's
Finger in the pub was one too many for me. Pleasure is
a devil in disguise, and I think he managed to shove his
finger right up my ass," Finn mumbled with hiccups, then
sighed and passed out.

When Finn and Joseph woke up at sunrise the city was
still covered in thick fog, and they shivered from the cold.
With a hangover, Finn did not feel so brave any more. He
was skittish and jumpy of all the noises of the city waking
up around them. They continued to hide in the alley, mainly
because they did not know where else to go. Joseph did
not want to run home until he knew for sure that the constables were not looking for him. The streets began to fill
with people, and they caught a glimpse of a marching army
corps, and heard a loud crowd in the nearby square. They
became curious and wanted to see what was happening.

"Come on Finn, let's get a move on! We can hide in
the crowd! No one will find us there," Joseph urged him.

When they arrived in the square, a large crowd blocked
Finn from seeing anything. He pushed through the crowds
and climbed on a cast iron fence helping Joseph to climb
over to get on top of a brick wall. Sitting on the wall, they
got a much better view over the crowd's heads. In front of
them, a large town square opened up, filled with people.
Banners flapped in the breeze, and Finn saw that it was a
momentous gathering. There were troops marching in formation with a band playing bagpipes and drums. The regi-

mental color guard presented the colors, and the people cheered.

A stately town crier in a frock coat carrying a roll of paper walked through the crowd flanked by soldiers who cleared a way for him by pushing people out of the way. He stepped up to a platform to address the crowd, and prepared to give a speech. He made a motion with his hand to the band and the drumming stopped. The army troops stood at attention, and Finn pointed out to Joseph a stray dog running amongst the ranks chasing a hissing cat. The man on the podium raised his hand to get people's attention, cleared his throat, and ceremoniously unrolled the paper scroll. The crowd quieted down, looking up at the man on the podium.

The man's words echoed from the surrounding houses as he read from the paper in a loud, commanding voice. "Attention! The treacherous Scots have launched an uprising against the rightful throne once again! The King has chosen Prince William, Duke of Cumberland, to put a decisive stop to the successful career of Charles Edward Stuart, known as the Young Pretender! The King recalled Prince William from Flanders, and today he stands ready to proceed with quelling the rebellion! We shall march north to defeat the rebels and crush them once and for all!"

The crowd cheered and applauded the speaker. Finn stared at the military formations and realized what they had to do. He became excited and turned to Joseph. "This is brilliant! This is my big chance! I will join the King's men and become a soldier!"

"Be careful what you wish for, because you are not in

any condition to make such a significant and momentous decision as that," Joseph replied wryly.

The band started playing the "British Grenadiers March." In front of the troops marched the drummers in the band, young boys in uniforms, to lead them out of town. The people cheered, laughed, and threw rosebuds at the marching soldiers. Women leaned over to kiss the soldiers marching by. Little boys darted in between the soldiers and ran around the marching formations.

A young woman blushing from excitement turned to her companion. "It is the glorious Black Watch regiment! Oh, look at them, the men are so handsome!" she said, admiring the officers.

Finn was intrigued by the soldiers' dark kilts. He saw an officer and approached him. Lieutenant Dugald Campbell, a steely-eyed tough Scotsman wearing an officer's jacket with blue facings, proudly watched his company advance. He had a shoulder sash and regimental badge, a kilt made of dark tartan plaid, with a sword shaped kilt pin and the clan crest. He was young and unshaven, but the way he carried his worn gear, leather sword belt and buckle fitted with a badger head sporran and a claymore sword, which was clean as a whistle and in excellent condition and a nasty looking scar running across his cheek, told Finn that the man was a veteran of many battles.

Finn gazed at the officer's uniform with the mingled feelings of awe and respect. "Sir, you and your troops must be the King's gift to man. You are handsome indeed, like the lady said. May I ask why they call you the Black Watch?"

"We earned our name because our task is to keep

watch for crime and for that we earned the right to wear the dark green tartan!" Dugald Campbell replied without looking at him.

"I want to become a soldier, like you sir! I want to join your company!" Finn said, eagerly.

Dugald Campbell smirked. "Nay, lad, not just anybody can join us," he said, turned to look at Finn more closely. "It takes much effort and training to be professional infantryman! We are the Black Watch after all!" He took a liking to the young man who seemed so eager to become a soldier like himself.

Dugald Campbell nodded to them and followed the formation after the last troops marched by him. Finn and Joseph watched as the troops turned onto the Tottenham Court Road turnpike. Suddenly, they saw constables appear on the other side of the square. They jumped down and Joseph landed on his back, spilling a menagerie of mysterious items, including some coins and beads and a dead frog, out of his pockets. He collected them as fast he could, stuffing everything back in his pockets, and ran after Finn. They hid in a sunken walkway and from behind the iron fence posts they kept an eye on the constables.

"There is only one way! We must follow the troops!" Finn said and jumped up. Crouching low, he kept a line of people between himself and the constables, and followed the troops leaving the city.

"Wait, no! But what if..." Joseph said and hastily collecting his things ran after Finn.

§    §    §

In the Catskill Mountain House, the old man turned slightly towards his guest. He looked at the tumbler in his hand and appraised the dark whiskey. "Henry, did you know that some people call this *uisge beatha*, the water of life? I have always enjoyed smoky tasting whiskey with a hint of peat. Do you want to know why? It's because it tastes like freedom! Drinking the best whiskey feels like running in fields of grain on a hot summer's day!"

Henry Raymond stopped writing. "Mr. Morton... Finn, yes, I guess you are right sir. I can see why you would feel that way," he replied.

The old man looked sideways at him. "During my time I have learned that bullshit comes in many flavors. Getting drunk and stupid in London town did not help me at all that day, quite to the contrary. I was caught by the raging events, but I didn't give a rat's ass at the time. Oh no, I wanted to be a part of it!" He took a sip from his tumbler. "Let me tell you, young man, that we are born in a state of ignorance of nature's law and subject to the whims, attractions, and sensations of the body, and we think there's honor in combat. We should learn to be compassionate toward those who behave badly in the things that they do, for ignorance is the natural state of human beings. Those who live in ignorance are normally self-serving, until they learn their lessons, which usually happen the hard way. But little did I know back then.

"People were struck by invasion panic, because King George II was in Germany waging war with all the regiments, leaving the garrisons empty. The kings and queens and other lowlifes hired Prussian mercenaries to do their dirty deeds, even against their own people, and only the channel separated Britain from the frightening specter of German invasion and hapless Britons being forced to wear leather pants. The rebellious Scots thought it was their excellent opportunity to strike and seek final revenge in order to gain power.

"I did not realize until years later that it was James Cook who gave me a sense of direction in life, and pushed me along the right path. Unfortunately, I wasn't able to follow his directions as I should have and lost my way for a while. I had to endure afterwards many hardships, on so many detours. I tell you, navigating an ocean is easy compared to the turbulent waters and hazards a man faces in life.

"It was then that, for the first time, someone taught me what it actually means to be a soldier. Dugald Campbell. That kilted heathen in his uniform was a sight for ladies' sore eyes. Tall and proud, he was a true soldier's soldier if I ever met one. He was a man of parts, gifted and talented in killing men in more ways than you could ever imagine. He was the kind of man you want standing next to you on the battlefield," the old man said. He stared into his tumbler deep in thought.

Across the table, Henry Raymond put his glasses back on and glanced at the old man appraisingly. He resumed his note-taking without saying a word.

§    §    §

The British troops marched north wearing their distinct red and white uniforms and carrying heavy loads of equipment. Behind the regiments came a succession of horses, ox carts, and camp followers. Finn and Joseph straggled along with a motley crew of families, children, servants, animal handlers and whores. Aristocrats brought their personal effects, silver plates for dinners, opulent wine chests, and even a bathtub, all carried by slaves. One of the regiments had two horses carrying nothing but cigars for the commander's mess tent.

Women and the children were not allowed to ride in wagons, and they had to march alongside or behind them. Some officers started complaining that the multitude of pregnant women near slowed the marching to a halt. On one of the baggage carts a British soldier's wife gave birth to a baby boy in the midst of the heavy rain, and she had nothing to cover her from the weather but a bit of an old oilcloth. The commanding officers ordered the men to get rid of all women and children as were not required, and soon only the whores remained in the camps.

The women who were allowed to stay with the army performed duties such as washing, and sometimes cooking. The provisions for the line troops were running low from the beginning, and on one occasion, Finn and Joseph endured three days without food. Then some farmers brought some foodstuffs to trade in their wagons, and the soldiers quickly plundered everything from the farmers.

In the meanwhile, outside on the moorland in the Highland army encampment, Lady Ogilvy and Lady Murray, dressed in their riding gowns, had followed their husbands on the campaign trail. They listened to the troops singing "Charlie Is My Darling" around a campfire, and watched the soldiers get their weapons and equipment ready for battle. One of the Highlanders jerked a single hair from his head, and wanting to impress the two ladies, sliced the air with his sword, easily cutting the strand of hair in half.

Inside his luxurious command tent, Bonnie Prince Charlie summoned his officers to give his final orders. "Cumberland is advancing with a well-armed, well-trained, and above all, well-fed army twice the size of my own," he said. "I put my own strength at five thousand hungry, ill-equipped Highlanders, and maybe three hundred horses. That's what I have, and with these, I shall make one decisive push for victory to gain supreme power! Where there's a will there's a way! Then in the enemy's court, counsels of prudence could only be counsels of despair. I can see nothing but destruction and misery to us if we should withdraw!"

Lord Lovat, his second-in-command, poured wine into a chalice and replied, "Sire, we are positioned on a moorland outside Inverness. The terrain does not favor our tactics, but it suits the British regulars well. Cumberland crossed the river Spey and pitched his camp twelve miles away from us, outside the town of Nairn."

Bonnie Prince Charlie waved his arm and formed a fist. "So be it, the die has been cast! Lord Lovat, you do not have to like the terrain, but you better hope that a daring surprise might help to redress the balance between the two armies. Proceed with your proposal and commence a night attack on Cumberland's camp at once! Now, get the lead out!"

Lord Lovat emptied his goblet and rushed out of the tent. He summoned his officers and turned to address the troops in formation, and looked self-centered raising his chin. "Officers, assemble the troops! We shall conduct a daring nighttime charge to take Cumberland by surprise while he is still abed! Now go out there and bring me his head! Be prepared to sacrifice yourself so that the impending success will bring immense glory to Bonnie Prince Charlie!" He turned on his heels and returned to his private tent, where he ordered the servant to put a pan full of warmed coals in his bed for the night.

Lady Ogilvy cast anxious glances at Lady Murray who was shaking her head and wringing her hands, both watching soldiers rush out from the camp at nightfall. Their worried expectations proved to be right, because the operation went awry from the start due to the incompetent officers. The Highlanders did not know where they were going, and the conditions worsened on the cold moors during the night, like rubbing salt into an open wound, and soon the whole operation had turned into a disaster. The troops wandered aimlessly around the sinking bogs all night without ever finding the enemy, and their morale declined. Finally, their officers reluctantly acknowledged the futility of the offense, but the long march on the sinking ground wore out the soldiers completely and by the time they made their way back to the camp, they slept where they dropped.

§     §     §

Finn and Joseph followed the Black Watch and arrived exhausted on the other side of the moors. Lieutenant Campbell and his men feverishly loaded their weapons, fixed their equipment, and prepared for the imminent battle. Joseph had to relieve himself and walked over to a bush. Dugald Campbell asked Finn to come closer. "You boys should stay away from the battlefield because I will have no time to look after you two when leading my company in battle! Stay here at the farm, because it is the safest place within miles." He did not wait for an answer and walked back to his troops.

They were close to an abandoned stone farmhouse. Dugald Campbell led the Black Watch marching into battle, leaving Finn to wait for Joseph. When he came back from behind the bush, Finn patted Joseph on the shoulder.

He looked Joseph sternly in the eye. "Joseph, Lieutenant Campbell and I decided it is best for you to stay behind. You are safe here. I have experience in combat, but you are too young. I will come back to get you," Finn said and pointed towards the house. Joseph shrugged and nodded to him and walked into the house. Finn followed the Black Watch, behind the echelons of government forces. In order to see better what was happening on the battlefield, he climbed on top of a large stone marker where he could get a clear view of the battlefield and the ranks forming on the both sides.

Across the moorland, the sound of the British drums beating to arms dragged the Highlanders, still starved and exhausted from the broken night foray, from their sleep. They scrambled to form ranks as Lord Lovat, refreshed after a full night's sleep and hearty breakfast, emerged from his tent to address the troops again.

He took a triumphant position and spoke to the troops. "Men, our glorious revolution is strong, and we are fighting for our rightful place! Since the beginning, we have suffered many a failure, but have never given up our campaign! James Francis Edward Stuart was formally recognized as the Catholic monarch by the French King Louis and Pope Clement. There is no denying this historical fact, nor can anyone deny that our purpose is just! We were unjustly humiliated in 1715, and the laws passed since are nothing more than blatant attempts to suppress us! Follow me, and always be remembered as the righteous ones! Three hoorays to Bonnie Prince Charlie!"

The troops raised their weapons over their heads and shouted, "Hooray! Hooray! Hooray!" They heard the roaring enemy artillery, and moments later felt the ground shake as explosions rumbled around them sending geysers of soil and dirt high up in the air. The Highlanders formed ranks and the officers hastily arranged them in battle formations. Drummers and bagpipes started playing as the ranks closed in on the approaching enemy lines.

Lord Cumberland started his attack with a heavy artillery barrage, to which the Highlanders could make no effective reply. Shells tore gaping holes in the ranks and the explosions threw men high in the air, and legs and arms ripped from their bodies by the barrage rained on the survivors. A young drummer's head was chopped off with grapeshot, but the pressure from the ranks behind kept the headless body standing up, blood squirting from its neck. Artillery shells plowed gaps in the Highlanders' ranks, and they began to grow restive.

"Sadistic fucking animals come and fight us, you pussy-whipped yogurt guzzlers!" a Highlander yelled. Totally exposed in the front line, a bullet hit him in the face and the man fell backward and was dead before he hit the ground.

The Highlanders prepared to attack by removing clothing from their lower body, casting the kilts off to gain speed. Only a true Scot is naked under his kilt. Scottish soldiers wore no briefs beneath the kilt and were routinely inspected by an officer with a mirror to see that each man complied. Kilts were made of heavy woolen cloth so in winter the upper legs were quite warm, and no underwear was actually required, while in summer - being well ventilated - likewise there was no need.

Lord Lovat ordered the Highlanders to attack. "MacDonalds on the left, get ready! In the center, the Camerons, the Chattans, the MacLeans, and the Maclachlans, you are first to the shock! Steady, get ready, charge!" Highlanders rushed forward in clusters of a dozen which formed a larger wedge-shaped formation. The charge gained momentum in the driving rain, and then sleet started to drift into the faces of the exhausted Highlanders.

The well-rested Government troops, supported by five thousand Hessian troops, were ready to take the brunt of the Highlanders' charge. The formed redcoats equipped with muskets and socket bayonets nervously anticipated the direct clash as the ranks of Highlanders closed in on them. One of the senior officers, General Wolfe, told his men to get ready. "Here they come, running upon our front line like a pack of hungry wolves!"

Dugald Campbell ordered his men to hold their fire. "Hold steady! Their attack is fraught beyond compare, and it shall be appropriately received!"

The Highlanders fired a volley and the gun smoke

from the discharge obscured the British aim. After firing, Highlanders dropped their muskets and drew their swords to press forward. They crouched down to avoid the British return volley, and made the final assault full tilt at the British lines, brandishing their weapons, still wearing only their shirts. Roaring Gaelic war cries, the Highlanders broke through the British front line.

The battlefield was full of confusion. The Scots formed ranks on both sides, some with the Hessians in blue uniforms and others with the British in red. The Jacobite cause – or "the rebellion," depending on who was talking – was dedicated to the restoration of the Stuart kings to the thrones of England, and Scotland. In this eternal struggle, brother was pitted against brother, neighbor against neighbor, clan against clan.

Watching the brutal battle from on the top of the rock, Finn could only hope that Dugald Campbell and the Black Watch were ready for the flood of screaming Highlanders. The ghastly sights and horrid sounds of vicious hand-to-hand combat became seared into his memory. No man asked for mercy, and all pity was subsumed in rage and fear. The men grunted, killing, screaming when they were hit, and died with their mouths full of blood. Soon dead bodies, severed limbs and other body parts littered the soaking wet peat on the ground. The Hessians behind the British took up position to cut off any possible retreat for the rebels, and they started the grim task of putting the wailing wounded out of their misery with bayonets and cutlasses. The Highlanders found themselves caught in between two fires, and they died by the hundreds on Hessian bayonets.

In the midst of the slaughter, Dugald Campbell stood on a pile of bodies, the sword in his hand dripping with blood and bits of intestines. Out of the smoke came a roaring Highlander charging at him with a bayonet. Dugald Campbell drew a pistol from his belt and shot the man in the face, blowing the back of his head off in a blast of blood. The dead, faceless man fell at Dugald Campbell's feet, nearly knocking him over.

General Wolfe rode among the troops who were now in turmoil, urging the men forward to attack the enemy.

A wounded Highlander sprawled on the battleground was bleeding profusely. His stomach had been sliced open, and he was trying to push the intestines back in. Lord Cumberland rode by General Wolfe and ordered, "General Wolfe, kill that man! He is a terrorist!"

General Wolfe looked at the wounded man who writhed in agony on the ground. "He is out of the fight, sir! We are not Hessians who take pleasure in such acts! I would rather quit my position than abandon my honor!" Nonchalantly, Lord Cumberland took a pistol from an aide, shot the wounded Highlander in the head, and rode off.

Finn fought the urge to vomit that was brought on by the smell of black powder mixed with the overpowering stench of blood, urine and shit on the battlefield. He was confused by the different types of uniforms amid the smoke and chaos all around him.

Then suddenly, out of the gunsmoke Johan Kopf appeared, slashing and killing wounded men with his sword. Finn was stunned, and rubbed his eyes to make sure. Yes, he clearly recognized the death's head emblem on the cap.

"Totenkopf, you scum of the earth!" Finn shouted, feeling a terrible rage take over him, unleashing all his repressed anger. Switching his pistol to his left hand he lifted a rapier from a dead soldier and faced his enemy.

Kopf, surprised to hear someone shouting his nickname amid the noisy battle, looked around to see who it was. He saw Finn and his eyes widened in recognition. He pointed his sword at Finn. "I shall waltz on your grave!" he shouted over the battlefield clamor.

The men simultaneously rushed forward like two mad dogs, charging across the field with piercing screams. Finn leaped over a pile of bodies in wild despair and swung his rapier. Landing on the other side without missing a beat and ready to attack, a shell exploded close to him. The blast scattered a group of men apart, their bodies shielding Finn from worst of the shrapnel, but the shock wave and falling bodies knocked him down on the ground. He struggled to get back up from under the bodies, ready to fight Kopf, but he had disappeared from sight.

Finn shouted in frustration, "No! Not again! That lucky bastard! I want his head on a platter!"

Finn noticed how the Highlanders started hastily forming up new battle lines. Smoke drifted away and he realized that they prepared to meet the British cavalry charging down on them.

One of the Highlanders rushed past Finn. "Father, father, Lachlan fell, he is dead!" Allan MacLean said.

The old MacLean, riding a bloody horse, looked at his son full of sorrow, and fully knowing the gravity of the situation he said, "Allan, take care of yourself and the family!" His face twisted in anger, he raised his sword getting ready to attack the British, but a bullet hit his rib cage and the next one went right through his neck, throwing him backwards off his horse. He got back up bleeding, his wig and bonnet fallen, and turned to face the charging enemy.

"You white-knuckled bedpost grabbers!" the old MacLean yelled, and cut down the first British cavalry soldier attacking him. He managed to stab another before three Hessian soldiers rode up out of the smoke, killed the old man with lances, and then hacked him to pieces with their cutlasses.

At that moment, Finn's mind was full of the things he had seen that day and the little good judgment he ever had was gone. He did not notice the bullets flying around him anymore and striking the bodies beside him, he did not care about the shots kicking up puffs of dust at his feet or pieces of hot shrapnel zinging by his head did not scare him, because he did not give a damn any longer. He had only one thing left on his mind, one single thought pounding like a hammer in his mind: to find and kill Johan Kopf.

Finn scanned the battlefield, hoping to find the bane of his life. In his rage, he cut down soldiers without looking to see whose side they fought on. Finn shouted on top of his lungs, "Totenkopf! Where are you? Show your ugly face and I shall send you to your maker!"

Finn was oblivious to the grapeshot that was mowing down the Highlanders around him before they could engage the British at close range. One of the Highlanders saw what was about to happen. He cried a warning to his clan, "We are outflanked by the British cavalry!" The heavy cavalry charged on their mighty horses, their hooves thundering, and the horses so heavy the ground literally shook with the charge. The Highlanders realized that they were trapped, and the only option left for them was to make their last stand and just wait for the British. They had no time to pray or say goodbye. The British heavy cavalry hit the Highlanders ranks with tremendous force, and the horses smashed through the lines of men. Then the butchering started in earnest.

Finn sought shelter from the cavalry, and diving behind a rock, he felt as if he was flying in slow motion, as in a nightmare. One of the Highlanders on the rise cupped his hand on his mouth to scream insults at the British, "you maggots," he called them. A bullet hit him in the mouth, and his head exploded. Finn, who was standing behind the man, was showered in the bloody mist, and he caught fragments of skull and brains in his mouth. He choked and doubled over trying to spit out the soldier's gory remains. He started to vomit violently, tears running down his cheeks, and threw up what seemed to be a massive pool of pink projectiles. Discharging his stomach helped him to recover his senses, and afterwards, he felt remarkably better. His wild eyes slowly regaining focus, but his mind remained numb.

The action gradually abated, and after a while, Finn heard only wailing and random shots in the thick smoke drifting across the battlefield. The British and Hessian soldiers rode up and down, wantonly butchering the wounded Highlanders.

On a hillock, Prince Charles watched the routing of his army in tears, as Lady Ogilvy brought a spare horse for him. He mounted the horse and rode off in full gallop without looking back to see if she followed. She was ready to get up on her horse and run after him, but just then Finn appeared from the smoke and took her prisoner.

"Not so fast, Lady! I think there are people who want to talk to you!" Finn commanded her.

"Stop it! Someone help me!" Lady Ogilvy yelled. Finn grabbed her and pinioned her arms behind her. She held her breath and averted her eyes from him. Turning her around, he smiled at her and said, "What a beautiful specimen of a woman you are. Maybe we should have some fun after a glorious day's work? What do you say, Lady?" Finn tried to kiss her.

She fought back, but Finn only laughed, groping her breasts. She was terrified and writhed furiously trying to escape. She pleaded with him. "Let me go, you brute! Stop it!"

She begged, but the more she struggled, the more Finn laughed. He was taken totally by surprise when she slapped him hard with the palm of her hand and then punched painfully into his stomach with her fist. He doubled over but didn't fall. Looking stunned, he let go of her. She fell down pretty hard on her butt, but turning around quickly tried to crawl away. Finn recovered and caught her by the ankle, and harshly pulled her back up by her hands.

He shouted, "Feisty little fox, aren't you, but I know what girls like! Winner takes all! And I think there is a reward for your pretty head, my lady!" He kept fondling her while taking her to Lieutenant Campbell.

She struggled, but Finn held her tight. "I would hold you close to me, just like my dear mother told me! But there is no time now. I must go and get my friend," he said, and turning to Dugald Campbell continued, "Look, sir, what I caught, a wildcat! I guess I have earned a prize for that! Here, take her away!" He gave her a slight push, making her stumble.

Dugald Campbell motioned to one of his sergeants. Finn pushed Lady Ogilvy to the sergeant, who took firm hold of her arms. From the smoke, Lord Cumberland appeared with his dragoons and the entourage approached them. She looked back at him in contempt. Lord Cumberland stopped his horse and said to her, "Lady Ogilvy, I presume. I shall send you to prison, and have you condemned suffering death as a traitor! You shall be sentenced to be beheaded at the Edinburgh tollbooth six weeks after the trial!"

Lord Cumberland nodded to one of the officers who threw a small leather pouch with some coins in it at Finn's feet. Finn picked it up, tossed it from hand to hand, and laughed. He tucked it under his belt and looked around. "Well, I must go and get Joseph. I hope he is alright," he said and headed towards the farmhouse.

§     §     §

After the battle, the British troops hastily collected their own wounded and dead, and began searching for any surviving rebels. Lord Cumberland offered a cash prize of thirty thousand pounds sterling for the capture of Bonnie Prince Charlie, dead or alive. After leaving the battlefield the prince had been unhorsed, and managing to escape his pursuers, went hiding on a farm on an island owned by one Flora MacDonald. She brought him some new clothes and said, "Sire, the money on your head can be no temptation to anyone here, because anyone who earned it would be ashamed to show himself in the Highlands ever again."

"I need a new horse! Somebody get me a fucking horse!" Bonnie Prince Charlie commanded.

She shook her head feeling sorry for him. "I'm afraid you have no kingdom any longer," she said. "Here, sir, put these on. Disguised you will have much better chances in escaping. I will help you," she said, and handed him some clothes. A farmhand helped him to change and soon Bonnie Prince Charlie and his escorts prepared to leave, and Flora MacDonald showed them the way out.

"Charlie's year is over," the farmhand said quietly just as a British patrol rode in to the yard.

Flora MacDonald made sure Bonnie Prince Charlie was safely out of sight and turned to greet the soldiers. "Well, we have tired soldiers pay us a visit. Let me ease your awful day with something lively!" She started to dance to distract the soldiers. She moved swiftly and elegantly, teasing the men.

The troops were excited. "Dance woman, and dance! Dance for your dear life!" The soldiers shouted laughing and applauded her performance. In the background, Bonnie Prince Charlie quietly made his escape disguised as a woman, dressed in a maid's clothes.

The lance corporal appeared and started hitting the men with his lance. "Get moving you dirty sons of bitches! While you are drooling over her ankles, the rebels are getting away! Go after them!" Scurrying away from the lance corporal, the soldiers hurried back into the field. In the melee, Flora MacDonald also managed to slip away.

The Hessian troops kept searching for any survivors and without mercy shot hundreds of wounded Highlanders. Some of the wounded were ruthlessly burned alive, and Finn heard their piercing screams.

Flora MacDonald managed to catch up with Bonnie Prince Charlie, and they continued their flight together. Around the countryside, British detachments hunted down fugitives, looted and burned the houses, drove cattle away, and devastated the country.

A thick fog started to rise and hindered visibility when Finn arrived at the stone farmhouse looking for Joseph. He searched around the yard. "Joseph! Joseph!" he yelled, looking into the barn.

"I'm here," Joseph replied. His voice was barely audible, and he appeared from behind a haystack. Finn slapped him on the back. "There you are! Are you alright?" he asked, stepping outside.

Finn heard a galloping horse and an infernal yell. Turning, he saw Kopf charging out of the fog on a white horse, holding a lance aimed at him. As Finn leaned back, the tip of the lance barely missed him, tearing his shirt, the cold steel scratching across the side of his chest. The lance pierced Joseph through his side, nailing him to the barn wall. Johan Kopf pulled the reins to stop his horse and leaped down, drawing his sword.

"Ha! Nice little trick I learned from the Cossack lancers! Running with scurvy dogs only gets you shot with them!" Kopf shouted to Joseph, and then turned snarling and sneering at Finn. "Do you remember them Cossacks, boy? You cost me a promotion back then, but now I will rectify that little mishap! Surrender yourself, or I will cut off your head and release your little homo buddy from his misery!"

Finn sidestepped Kopf's lunge but tripped and rolled backward. He got up quickly and grabbed a large wooden bucket, hitting Kopf on the side of the head. "I'm going to kill you, mother fucker!" he shouted.

Kopf took a few steps sideways and shook his head, "You miserable cocksucker! Killing you will taste sweet, like a strudel!"

Finn glanced at Joseph who slumped against the wall held in place by the lance. Blood squirted from his wound. Finn yelled at Kopf and charged him.

"You are pathetic, deplorable scum! I will kill you!" Finn launched a fierce attack against Johan Kopf, and forced him to back away from the rain of strong blows. Finn managed to hit him hard in the mouth. Johan Kopf spat out a tooth, his upper lip swollen and bleeding, and slapped the horse so it moved in between them. Finn crouched to the other side underneath the horse.

Finn continued his assault. "I will slice you in pieces!" he shouted. Kopf parried his fierce blows, but then he tripped and fell backwards. His foot became entangled in the reins lying on the ground, and when Finn yelled again loudly the horse bolted, and ran away dragging Kopf behind it. Finn was going to follow him, but he heard Joseph let out a moan.

Finn ran to Joseph, took a firm grip of the lance, and putting his foot against the wall pulled it out of him. Joseph was ashen and started to slide down the wall. Finn caught him in his arms and laid him on the ground gently.

"Joseph! Lay still! I will take you out of here, I

promise!" Finn said, his voice choked with concern. Joseph coughed blood.

A riderless black horse with a bloody saddle wandered into the yard and Finn grabbed the reigns, calming it down. He quickly collected some long poles and rope to make a stretcher, which he attached to the saddle behind the horse, and helped Joseph to lie down. Finn waited for few minutes for sun to go down, and after nightfall, he led the horse on foot. He saw flickering torches in the foggy night and led them deeper into the forest.

In the darkness, Kopf rode back and forth searching for them. "Come out, you little hamster! I know you are here!" he shouted.

Finn stopped the horse behind some thickets. "Oh hell no, you miserable son of a bitch, I must get Joseph to safety first," he mumbled to himself, leading the horse quietly into the night.

"Go ahead, and run like a little schnauzer! But you can't hide!" Kopf's voice echoed in the night. He wondered for the first time why he kept failing to catch Finn, and his right eyelid began to twitch. He smothered a nasty sense of inadequacy.

It was long and painful journey that seemed to take forever. Three days later Finn and Joseph came to a coppice of stately lime trees surrounding a quaint, isolated moorland village. Finn noticed that Joseph was benumbed by the piercing winds on the scrublands circling the limestone dwellings of the upland farm. The village was located at the intersection of four old roads, and they decided to follow a rutted road back towards London.

Finn stopped only to rest when he finally found a well

from which to drink. He doused Joseph's handkerchief and wiped his forehead, but Joseph was too weak to drink, so Finn cupped his hand to get some water in his mouth. Finally, in the early morning hours they arrived at the front gate of a country manor. Finn stopped the horse and looked worriedly at Joseph on the stretcher. He was breathing, but unconscious and coughing blood. Finn picked a dandelion from the side of the road on the spur of the moment and placed it in Joseph's hand, walking a short distance to the door. He rapped with the heavy knocker and soon an old servant appeared, a lantern in his hand casting a hazy light.

"I brought Joseph home. He is hurt," Finn said and heard worried voices inside the house. Troubled people from the house ran outside, and women screamed when they saw Joseph lying on the stretcher and rushed to take care of him. Joseph's father, dressed in a nightgown, was trembling with anger as he looked at Finn.

"What have you done to my boy?" Joseph's father demanded.

"Sir, I... We were in the battle on the moors, and I brought him home, because he is badly wounded," Finn replied quietly.

Joseph's father inhaled sharply and pointed his finger at Finn. "You... took... my boy... to fight rebels... This happened because of you! Get out of my sight before I call the constables!" Joseph's father shouted.

Finn lowered his head, turned and walked briskly out of the gate. He stopped by Joseph once more for a brief moment and gently pressed his shoulder. Finn ran off towards the rising sun until he came to a large alder tree and sought refuge behind it. He was shattered, and sitting down until the adrenaline rush eased, his muscles started to relax. He was overwhelmed by antagonizing memories and horrid scenes of his dying mother; combat; maimed soldiers; and Joseph in agony. Horrifying images that flashed through his head made him shudder, but biting his lip and managing not to cry out loud, he wished for a peaceful place to hide.

§     §     §

Finn was totally drained, tired and hungry when he arrived again in London three days later. He found relief being among throngs of people again, and he welcomed the anonymity of a crowd at a market square filled with rope and candle makers, wheelwrights, blacksmiths, shoemakers and masons. He followed an audience that was gathering for the execution of Lord Lovat on Tower Hill. Finn stole a knee-length hooded cape from an empty market stall, pulling the hood over his head to disguise himself, and grabbed a worn-out leather messenger bag that he slung over his shoulder. Tightly guarded sulking rebel leaders marched towards the execution platform, but their leader Lord Lovat looked defiant as he walked past the spectators. Finn noticed that Flora MacDonald had been caught and followed the prisoners, wearing the scold's bridle.

The British troops dragged Lord Lovat in front of Lord Cumberland, and throwing him down on the ground, started kicking him. "Sirs, have mercy and show leniency!" he begged.

"You old crone, who do you think you are, how dare

you speak to me of humanity," Lord Cumberland said, spitting at him.

The stands around the small hill were full of people. In the center of the square were the scaffolds. The executioner stood by the execution block with his legs apart, resting his arms on his ax. The spectators were excited.

On the stands, young boys sold food and drinks to the people and the noisy crowd enjoyed the festivities. Flags flapped in the breeze, and there was much laughter. Finn walked further into the crowd.

Out from the mob, the loathly lady from the Bell's Alehouse appeared and grabbed Finn by the arm, laughing. She held on to his arm and shouted at Lord Lovat, who stood in chains on a carriage.

"Hey, you ugly old dog, Lovat, don't you think you will have that frightful head cut off?" she said and made a move across her throat.

"You damned ugly old bitch, I believe I shall," Lord Lovat replied.

To Finn's amazement, a group of Hessians appeared across the square, and to his dismay, he saw that the leader of the search party was Johan Kopf, who was inspecting the spectators closely. Men snarled and women hissed at the Hessian mercenaries and spat on the ground in front of Johan Kopf, which made him despise the commoners even more. He was, after all, a superior man to them.

Memories of his family flashed through Finn's mind. He hoped the crowd would attack Kopf, and he imagined how the commoners would chain four horses to Kopf's arms and legs, and they would be made to run in opposite directions, making them pull him apart. Drawn and quartered.

Finn heard Kopf's voice over the crowd. "This town is full of stinking peasants! It awakens the wanderlust in a man of my stature, to want to go explore enemy territory!" Johan Kopf snarled to his men.

Finn pulled the hood over his head and turned away, and the loathly lady noticed him trying to disguise himself.

Lord Lovat walked up to the scaffolds, assisted by the guards. He looked around at the crowd. "God save us, why should there be such a bustle about taking off an old, gray head that cannot go up three steps without three brutes to support it," he said.

Kopf took notice of the old lady and the tall man beside her. Seeing a piece of the fringed leather jacket underneath the cape, Kopf motioned for his men to follow him. Desperate, Finn looked for a way to escape and his hood came off.

Johan Kopf's face turned sour in a rage. "There he is! Don't let him get away! Seize him!" he shouted.

Suddenly, Finn heard the sound of the wood scaffold beginning to crack and then ripping away from itself as one of the stands collapsed. The crowd screamed as many of them were killed crushed under the falling timber. Panicked people forced Kopf to seek cover and Finn dove underneath the execution platform.

On the scaffolds, Lord Lovat looked at the chaos below him and raised his face to the sky. "I suppose the more the enmity, the better the game. It is gratifying and proper to die for one's cause," he said calmly, and submitting his head to the execution block, was beheaded swiftly. His severed head fell into a basket filled with straw, and under the scaffold, Finn was showered with blood. The loathly lady pulled him by the hand and took Finn through the alleys and away from the crowds. She suddenly turned around and pushed him against the wall.

"Now, my boy, you can pay me back!" she said, and groped his muscles. "You surely are strong and pleasing to the eye. Now you can be my stallion and settle your debt to me!" She grabbed his crotch and tried to kiss him. Finn pushed her away, repulsed.

Finn backed away and said, "I thank you for helping me, but ma'am, I will not do what you ask of me! I'm not an animal!" Finn retreated briskly.

Laughing and showing her blackened teeth, she yelled after him, "Come back here, boy! You may not be an animal, but you sure are dumb as a mule! There is no such thing as a free meal! You don't know what you're missing, boy!"

Johan Kopf was very upset, and was trying mightily to maintain his self-control. Pushing people out of his way, he searched out a shadowy tavern in an alley and barged in. *What the fuck I expected*, he thought. *That lucky bastard got away, again! Fucking life is more like a fucking wrestling match in a fucking mud puddle chasing a fucking piglet rather than a fucking picnic in fucking rose garden on a fucking summer's day!* He sat down at a table by the stained-glass window and ordered a drink. He prepared a double dose of absinthe on a sugar cube and washed it down with beer as a barmaid placed a tankard on the table. He took out a piece of paper and pen from his pocket.

"*Liebe meine Mutter,*" he took a deep breath and

started writing, "*It has been long time since I wrote you last time. Rest securely, all is well. We launched a campaign up north and wiped out a terrorist stronghold in Finland. My superiors were extremely pleased with me and I got a medal. Then my expert services were urgently needed against another group of rebel terrorists in England, where I am now. Looks like I am going to get promoted for my bravery.*" He stopped for a moment to think how to continue. "*As you know, Papa was wrong wanting to make a priest of me. In a way he was right, I always wanted to get married and raise a family one day. But now I have started to think that maybe it is better for me to stay alone all my life, and just like my father dedicate myself to serve the King. My soul yearns to be obedient to God, but I am master of my own fate and by profession I am a Jaeger. The hand that can rock the cradle can also be the hand that is dipped in blood! I must harden myself, learn control, discipline and endurance, and I must think nothing impossible. Only women talk about peace, but real men talk about the hunt and war! Even the gods don't live forever and at least, if I die like a Jaeger, I will get a ticket to Valhalla. Your filial son.*" Johan signed the letter and sealed it. Then he overheard someone talking about easy promotions in the colonies and he was immediately curious to find out more.

Several blocks away, Finn dashed frantically onto the street and ran head on into James Cook, who grabbed him by the shoulders surprised to see Finn again.

"James Cook! Man, am I glad to see you!" Finn exclaimed, and sighed in relief. They returned to Bell's Alehouse and Finn was happy to see the servant girl again who rushed to give him a warm hug. She smelled him and turned up her nose when she saw Finn's bloody clothes.

She waved her hand in front of her face, "Oh, stinky boy! Sit down so I can clean you up!"

James Cook and Finn found a free corner table located next to a large fireplace and Finn sat down in a dark corner facing the door, where they sat in silence for a while. "What the hell is going on out there? Why did they crush the Scottish revolt in such a cruel manner? I know there were two competing crowns who wanted to rule, and there can be only one King, but I do not understand the incredible punishment," Finn asked.

James Cook explained. "In Scotland the clans own the land, and their ruler does not. Their system is alien to us, and we must prevent any possibility of a Jacobite revival by crushing the spirit of the Highlanders and destroying the Highland way of life. Our victorious King owns everything, and that is just. The King may do what he pleases with it. Many times large parcels of land are awarded to loyal officers as a reward for their service."

The head waitress Elizabeth came to greet James Cook, bringing food on wooden plates and placing tankards on the table. The servant girl placed a small bucket of water on the floor. Taking a wet rag she wiped dried blood and dirt off Finn's face.

Finn realized how hungry he was and scarfed down bread from the plate. "How does one become an officer? A man must have many merits, and be highly recommended for his skills to command so many men and make life and death decisions, am I right?"

Finn took a long drink. The front door opened, and

some men walked into the pub. Alerted, he covered his face with the tankard, following the men with his eyes. James Cook looked over his shoulder at the men, unconcerned. The newcomers sat down at a table across the room without looking at Finn and Cook.

Cook replied, "No, all you need is money, or a rich daddy. Merit has nothing to do with it. One thousand pounds of sterling will get you a rank of cornet in the cavalry or ensign in the infantry. Higher rank costs more so you must be rich and willing to spend money, or your father's money, and you can climb to the rank of general quite quickly. Should you wish to retire, then you just sell your position to the highest bidder. It is simply an investment, you see."

Finn pulled out a wallet from his waistband, and tossing it in his hands opened it, emptying the copper coins on the table.

James Cook noticed hesitancy in Finn's voice that was not there before. Finn was thinking hard. "I made some money in the battle, but it's not enough if I want to become an officer and command men in battle," he said and paused. His voice became more confident. "I shall be my own master and continue my journey! You see, my mother told me to find a woman, her name is Lady Columbia, but I don't know where to find her." He did not add that more than anything he wished finding a place he could call home.

Cook said, "Listen, you seem to be a nice fellow and I must be honest with you, there is more to it than that. In England, you cannot escape your station. Here, one hardly has a chance of rising from a low class to a higher. Class is like an invisible roof that was placed over you at birth. My advice to you is to find honest service first, and then make plans."

The servant girl sat down next to Finn and placed her hand on his thigh, gently squeezing it. "I heard some customers talking," she told Finn. "There is a wealthy ship owner by the name of John Walker in Bristol who is hiring for new workers. You should go there... And take me with you!" She smiled at him. Finn looked at her and rubbed his chin in contemplation. He looked back at Cook.

"Perhaps you are right, both of you," Finn thought out loud. "I should listen to sound advice when I hear it. I must be smart for once in my life and do what is right. I will work hard, and after having made enough money, I will get myself a commission. I will be just like Captain Lofving and Lieutenant Campbell!"

The servant girl clapped her hands. "Yes! Will you take me with you? Please?" She kissed his neck and nibbled at his ear. Finn kept stealing glances down her open blouse, and his eyes widening, he smiled.

"Yes, I will take you with me," Finn said, "but I must warn you. We must travel by night. This is a secret! No one can see us leave London!"

§   §   §

Finn and the servant girl left London that night. Finn carried a rolled-up blanket over his shoulder and a couple of sacks containing some food. Finn took the girl by her hand and in order to avoid anyone seeing them, they ran from shadow to shadow, hiding in alleys and doorways.

They picked up the pace after getting out of town at

dawn. On their way to Bristol, Finn and the servant girl ran across fields and meadows. When they stopped to rest under a large alder tree, she folded her arms in front of her and looked at him, pouting.

"Wait, we can't go on like this! It is totally unfair!" She complained, "I know your name. You came back for me, but you don't even know my name! Do you even care?"

Finn realized he did not know her name. "Of course I care, silly girl! Now, what was your name again?"

"I am Rosie," she told him and looked away, still pouting.

"Rosie! What a lovely name! You are my dear Rosie!" Finn took her in his arms, and Rosie turned to smile at him coyly. She put her finger on his lips.

"Do you love me, silly boy?"

"Of course I do love you, beautiful Rosie of mine!" Finn looked down at her cleavage again.

She took him by the chin. "My eyes are up here," she said, "I want to be sure. Are you sure?"

"Of course I am sure! Come with me, pretty Rosie!" Finn shouted and gave her a deep, wet, lingering kiss.

Finn wanted to stay away from inhabited areas, and they walked all day in the forest. He enjoyed her company and liked the way she admired the beautiful Oxfordshire countryside they passed through. She smiled a lot and chattered happily how she had never been outside London before. He listened to her soft voice, and it helped him to push the gory battle scenes aside that kept revisiting his mind. They walked hand in hand, and he noticed how the sun shone through her red hair making it look almost carmine, and he sensed her natural, clean sweetness.

In the evening, when it was almost dark, they came to a bridge. Hiding in the bushes Finn made sure they were not seen, and then they rushed across the bridge and into the woods on the other side. Rosie looked for a place to sit down under some towering oak trees.

"I'm getting awful tired. Please find a place for us so we can sleep tonight, my darling," she said.

"We can stop to rest for a moment, but pretty soon I must find a way and then we must keep moving," Finn answered.

"Where do you want to go? What are we going to do in Bristol? Where are you taking me? Do you even know?" Rosie asked.

"I have no idea where I'm going," Finn said quietly.

"You should know. Why don't you know?"

"I don't know because I'm young, dumb and full of cum!" He twisted his face, pretending he had an orgasm.

Rosie laughed, "You are so funny! I know something about boys, and I know you better than you think!"

Finn promised to find a place to stay overnight, if they could just keep on moving a little while longer. He wanted to get as much distance between them and London as possible. Finally, late that night Rosie simply refused to go any farther. Finn led them to a farm where they sneaked into a barn in the dark.

The farmer inside the house woke up because he had heard their noises. It was still dark in the wee hours of the morning. Hearing the horses whinny again, the man got out of bed in his long white night gown and long nightcap. "It must be that damned fox again..." he mumbled, getting up for a lantern. He stepped outside to investigate.

The farmer crossed the yard cautiously. He looked into the hen house but saw only a rooster still dozing, and then he heard the horses again. The farmer walked to the stables and opened the door quietly. He heard more voices inside and heavy breathing from the darkness. He grabbed a pitchfork, and cautiously opened the door ajar, and warily raising the lantern, peeked inside. He saw a young woman bent over against a saddle, standing with her eyes closed and licking her lips. She was flushed and moaning.

"Are you alright, Miss?" the farmer asked and pushed the door wide open. Surprised, Rosie looked at the farmer, her skirt bunched around her waist. Finn was standing behind her, his pants around his ankles, holding her hips. He was grinning from ear to ear. Rosie screamed and pulled her skirt down. She collected her purse quickly and ran out the back. Finn struggled to get his pants up, but he tripped and fell. "You better watch it, mister! How dare you disturb me like that!" he shouted to the farmer.

The farmer took a pitchfork and hissing between his teeth, started lunging at Finn. Finn got up quickly and ran after Rosie, pulling his pants up. Running across the yard, they sent chickens clucking and feathers flying in the air. The farmer shook his fist after them.

Rosie ran fast ahead of him, and Finn had a hard time catching up with her. Finally, she fell into the long grass, laughing. Finn slumped almost on top of her, out of breath.

"Oh my, Rosie was such a bad girl!" she giggled.

Laughing, Finn pulled her up, and they moved on. At sunrise, they found a quiet, shaded place under a clump of aspen trees by a stream. Finn leaned down to drink.

Rosie smiled and pulled him closer. She gave him a long, lingering kiss.

"Did we leave something unfinished back there?" she asked, looking deeply into his eyes. Finn nodded, and she made a murmuring sound as she pushed him down on a pile of soft, pillow-like moss. She jumped after him, and Finn tore off her clothes, throwing them on top of the bushes. She giggled softly in his ear.

Fervently embracing and caressing each other, they rolled on the ground, playfully competing to see who would get to be on top. Finn was amazed at how passionate Rosie was, and feeling the incredible oneness with her, he abandoned himself to her love. Rosie climaxed and slumped down, trembling and breathing hard on top of him, utterly spent. Skimming her fingers through the soft hair on his chest, she asked him to set up camp so they could rest for the day. Finn agreed readily, and they ate what little food they had.

Finn made a spear from a long sallow branch and caught a trout from the stream. He used wooden pegs to secure the fish to a piece of flat wood and cooked it on the side of the fire. Later that evening, in front of the fire, they leaned against a tree in each other's arms. The North Star appeared in the sky, and Finn pointed it out to Rosie.

"How beautiful it is! Funny, but I have never thought about stars before," she said.

"Rosie my dear, there hasn't been too many people in my life," Finn told her. "Some left their mark in me, but now they are all gone. I keep them with me, in my heart. I have seen many awful things, and enough war to last a lifetime. I think I shall be happy to look at only you from now on, my beautiful Rosie."

Rosie looked deep into Finn's eyes. "Anyway you want it, that's the way you should have it," she said, smiling mysteriously.

Finn looked slightly surprised. "Anyways I want I should have it? I like the way you think, woman."

Then words just started to roll out of his mouth. He told her about his life as a boy in Finland, how he had lost his family, and his life at sea, and what had happened to Joseph. She listened quietly while he spoke. Occasionally, she glanced at him, at a loss for words, and worried. She rested her head on his chest and listened, and Finn was surprised at how appreciative he felt.

§     §     §

When they finally arrived in Bristol, Finn and Rosie found a small room at an old inn with adobe walls and a straw roof. They paid the proprietor in advance for the first week, and he did not ask any questions. The room smelled musty and had only a creaky old bed with a straw-filled mattress and one wobbly nightstand, but they were happy to have a roof that did not leak over their heads. Finn felt confident about the future with Rosie. He watched her lovingly opening the window and dancing around the room excited and happy.

She was all smiles. "This is our own first home. This is our love nest!" she said, and started to clean the room pushing him out of the way. Finn kissed her and left to look for work.

Wandering around the town Finn encountered a group

of men standing on a street corner and stopped to ask for directions. Reverend Clarkson, a proud man with grey hair, and his son Thomas were talking about some business contacts they had in a place called Philadelphia. First Finn thought they were talking about philandering and figured the place must be even stranger than London. The gentlemen politely gave Finn some directions, and advised him about where to look for work closer to the harbor.

Finn followed their instructions and entered the regional office of Spears, Bowman & Company and asked for a job. He mentioned Reverend Clarkson's name, and the storekeeper hired him on the spot as a warehouse laborer. He started right away in the warehouse carrying large bales of tobacco coming off the ships. All the workers in the warehouse were children, and Finn realized he was the oldest one of the whole crew. Two boys were told to show him what to do. John, aged twelve, and Michael, aged ten, chatted with him and he followed them around the warehouse and docks.

John told him, "I have been here three years and I work as long hours as men do. Sometimes the work is darned hard and once I was seared in the foot. I have been to Bath once, but I never heard of the testament or who Jesus Christ is. I think cursing and telling defamations is no good."

Young Michael was a serious boy, and he said, "I have been working here I think three months now. They have made me work overtime only once, and that was all night. I worked until the cock crowed and then went to sleep in the back. I had only two hours' sleep, and then I had to work again. I like this work, but the smell of the tobacco made me sick."

In the office, a ten-year-old girl named Mary Beth came to talk to Finn. She said, "You should not fear, this is not such hard labor. See, my work starts at seven o'clock. I get to go home to dinner at two and have an hour free time to do what I want. Then I come back and work until ten at night, but I'm not actually tired at night, and sometimes my master wants me to sleep in his bed, pleasing him. I never went to school. I usually get milk or tea and spuds or biscuits for my meals, and sometimes meat for dinner. I like it here, and I have never been sick since I came here," she told him.

In the evening, Finn returned to the inn, dead tired after a long day of carrying heavy bales. Rosie made them a modest supper of pork, lettuce salad and brown rice, and he soon fell asleep while she was talking to him. She covered him with a blanket and lovingly touched his cheek.

Finn worked hard at the warehouse during the day, and Rosie found a job as a waitress in a nearby tavern. A few weeks later they could afford to rent a little bigger place with an alcove and a small dining table, a two-door wardrobe that delighted Rosie, and more importantly, a better bed with a proper mattress and a bedframe that did not squeak so loudly. The nights were getting colder, and a small coal stove in the corner of the room provided them heat, although they happily spent most of their time under the covers. Rosie took over their finances, and after a while, they had a little nest egg saved up, and could even afford to go out to dinner once a month or so.

They were happy together and did not mind their meager means, and to them, the time flew by so quickly they barely noticed winter at all. Rosie pointed out to Finn how spring was just around the corner, and at nights, they could almost taste the fresh mist in the air as the frost departed the earth. As the sun got higher and heated the previous year's leaves and grass, they enjoyed deeply inhaling the rich smell of the fresh soil that hung in the air with its earthy aroma.

As spring blossomed in earnest, Rosie became radiant. She was able to push the windows wide open. She admired the swollen buds and the few brave bulbs that blossomed early. The sweet smells of green grass were carried inside on the warm breeze. She shouted with joy, "Look how bright the blooming colors are! Were the scents truly this strong, last year?"

Finn was a happy man, and his ordeals started to fade from memory. He felt content and confident about the future with Rosie, and he began to dream about buying a farm or a ranch just like his home village. One morning, slumping beside her after making love, an idea occurred to him: together, they were invincible. They huddled under thick blankets, and she kissed him with the warmth of new love. Finn felt well rested and satisfied, and he was reluctant to get up. "I'd say what a terrific way to start the day! And you, my dear Rosie, are lovelier than ever! But I must get going!" He jumped up and pulled his pants on. He turned to give her one more kiss.

"Today I will be helping Mr. Spears unload a ship at the harbor! He said that I might get a raise!" He grabbed his coat and in the doorway turned to look back at her. She had stayed in bed watching him get ready, and she stretched her naked slender body. He winked at her and rushed out the door.

Finn arrived in the harbor and stopped to listen to William Cowper, a bohemian-looking fellow, who was reciting a poem. "I am shocked at the purchase of slaves, and fear those who buy them and sell them are knaves. I pity them tremendously, but I must be mum, for how could we do without sugar and rum?"

Finn noticed a trading post where threatening-looking slave drivers paraded slaves on a platform, and the air smelled of salt, sweat and distress. Black men, women, and children stood in silence on the platform. They all wore tags around their necks. Young girls stifled sobs of deep despair revealed their misery and suffering. A mother in chains with eyes streaming saw her dear child examined for sale. The woman looked in despair at her husband who could not help them, because his hands were bound and he had heavy chains around his neck and ankles.

A young, beautiful slave woman who caught all the men's attention wore only a sheer garment, which clearly showed outlines of her voluptuous breasts, legs, and pubic hair. Instead of trying to cover her body she shielded her eyes, as she was not ashamed of her body but she was humiliated by her exposed situation. The white men lasciviously appraised her from below while the slave trader ate his lunch with a casual attitude. Finn did not like what he saw and talked to the man who had recited his poem.

"Shouldn't all those people be free? They don't seem to be criminals," he asked.

William Cowper answered to him, somewhat annoyed. "That is a silly notion, young man. If an African imitated a free Briton, it would make a mockery of the very meaning of freedom! Ah, pardon me, I have poor manners. I am

William Cowper, Poet Extraordinaire, at your service," he
said, and made a gesture with his cane, and bowed slightly.

"Sometimes they will escape, then what? They are men
too after all, aren't they?" Finn asked.

"It's simple!" the slave trader replied without inter-
rupting his lunch. "It would be awkward for us to presume
these beings to be menfolk, because to consent to the
notion that they are human, would cause mistrust to follow
- that we are not true Christians!"

Some distance from them, a group of sailors sat on the
pier, and one of them noticed Finn. The sailor pointed to
him and whispered something to his mates.

Finn watched in horror as the slave drivers forced one
of the men down on the ground and nailed every limb to
crooked sticks. Then they took torches and applied the fire
starting with his feet and hands, burning him slowly up to
his head, whereby his pains were unfathomable.

Finn was appalled by the torture taking place, and he
shouted to Cowper. "Some men will go to extraordinary
lengths to gain their freedom. I have witnessed that with
my own eyes!" he said, feeling uneasy about the events.

He witnessed how the slave drivers dragged another
slave and tied him in the stocks to be whipped. Cowper
looked bored as he explained. "Should rebellious slaves
try to escape, they will be broken on the wheel, or they
are gibbeted. Those less directly involved might get away
with a castration, a mutilation of hand or foot or flogging
till they are painful. Sometimes slaves are flogged just to
teach them manners, and like the man there, the drivers
put pepper and salt on their wounds to create a smarting
pain."

Finn was appalled. "They are men after all, aren't they?" He heard a loud whiplash and the slave yelled in pain.

Cowper replied, "You see simply beasts of burden, but nevertheless valuable inventory. They are priced, sold, packaged, freighted, resold, amortized, depreciated, written off, and replaced."

The slave trader finished his lunch and licked his fingers. He spat on the ground and got ready to start his auction. He ordered his drummer to sound a call to raise people's attention. He cleared his throat and made an announcement. "General agents, brokers, commission merchants, my fellow auctioneers, and all other parties concerned!" He declared in a loud voice, "Gather around to make your bids! Fine specimens for sale! Please enter your bids! Only the best available here now!"

Cowper pulled Finn aside. "It appears you are not very familiar with the Triangular Trade."

Finn looked back at the man he found so unpleasant. "You are right, sir, I do not know anything about selling triangles," he said.

Cowper smiled at him. He waved his hand at the auction, "Right, but that's not exactly what this is all about."

Finn looked back at him in slight disgust. "Whatever it is, it makes me uneasy to see men treated like animals."

Cowper drew a triangle in the sand with his cane. He pointed at the drawing, clarifying the trade to Finn.

"Here you see the three points of the triangle. They are England, Africa, and the Caribbean. We sell and ship valuable products from England to Africa. From there, the ship takes slaves to the Caribbean or the colonies in America to work on the plantations growing tobacco and sugar, valuable commodities, which the same ship then transports to England, completing the triangle. It is a profitable business, but the competition is getting more intense every day."

Finn replied, disgusted, "I only see how some people make money on other men's misfortune."

Cowper smiled at him coyly like a politician. "Misfortune, maybe; market demand and profits, most definitely."

On the platform, an older woman screamed as the slave drivers tore her away from her husband and child. The slave trader sold them each to different buyers.

Cowper continued, "Of course, there is also a fine-spun business transporting slaves to the colonies from England too. Some of the best customers on the continent, and in America, buy their laborers from this very marketplace in Bristol. The colonials need manpower on their cotton fields, among other things."

Finn replied, "I would not want to live in a place like those colonies. Where I come from, we are proud of our own labor."

Cowper had nothing to say, having lost all interest in the conversation. He shrugged his shoulders and walked away.

Finn worked the day offloading bales of tobacco, sugar, and barrels of rum from the ship. He was troubled by what he had just learned. He kept an eye on what was happening at the slave auction. He looked at his hands after carrying a load, and tried to wipe them clean.

Afterwards, loading manufactured goods on board the ship, Finn noticed Royal Navy ships of the line in the harbor and admired the naval officer's blue uniforms. A brawny boy named Aiden approached him after they had finished working for the day. He was quite sociable and wanted to drink some whiskey and smoke tobacco, and asked Finn to join him. "C'mon, let's go and have a drink at the pub after a hard day's work. Your girl will wait for you," Aiden said.

Finn hesitated at first, but then agreed to accompany Aiden to the Seven Stars Pub nearby. Aiden waved at the waitress who brought them beer tankards and two shots of whiskey. They stood at the bar watching how the purser proofed a batch of rum for the Royal Navy. The purser demonstrated the best method of treating Jamaican rum before allowing it to be issued to the sailors.

Finn talked to Aiden and raised a toast to his sweetheart. "Here's looking at my lovely Rosie!" he said cheerfully. "And she happens to be waiting for me, so I must be on my way." He was about to leave for home when the sailors from the pier surrounded him in a friendly manner. One put his hand around Finn's shoulders.

The man squeezed his shoulder a bit too hard and said, "Not so fast, my friend. We noticed, out there on the docks, that you were a hard worker. You are not pussy whipped, are you? Surely you have time for one more with us!"

A sailor poured Finn another drink. Aiden took one look at the men and hurried away leaving his cup. The other customers looked suspiciously at the sailors and moved away from them. Finn was annoyed. "Now hold on, you scared my friend off. How do I know who you are?"

The sailor answered, "Don't worry, we are not the Press. We are not going to drop a King's shilling into your drink."

Finn looked back at him, not understanding. "Press, what is that? Shilling, what shilling are you talking about?" he said and searched around on the bar.

Another sailor stepped closer. "The Press is His Majesty's Impress Service, and as by 'finding' the King's shilling in your possession you are deemed to have volunteered for service, as a merchant sailor or for the Royal Navy. It's an old trick a press gang uses," he said and winked at Finn.

A man from another table called to Finn. "Hey boy, that is why some tavern owners have started putting glass bottoms in their tankards," he said, and Finn looked at the bottom of his tankard - it was solid tin.

The sailor patted his shoulder. "Don't listen to him. That is just a nasty rumor! Press officers are subject to fines for using trickery and a volunteer always has a cooling-off period in which to change his mind if he so desires," he said, and the other sailors nodded pretentiously at each other.

"Aye, better one volunteer than three pressed men," one of them said.

Finn straightened his back and said, "Well, I have protection anyway since I am a foreigner and, therefore, cannot be pressed into service!"

"Then you have nothing to worry about!" the sailor said, and poured Finn some rum. Finn relaxed and looked at the sailors and downed the rum. He leaned on the bar and started bragging about his exploits.

"Well, let me tell you this," he started, "I am not just any hoodlum off the streets, I am a seasoned war veteran beyond the ordinary! I took part in mortal combat, in the ranks, with Captain Lofving and Lieutenant Campbell. Both these upstanding gentlemen are excellent soldiers, and they are close friends of mine! I shall become an officer just like them! What's more, I am an able seaman to boot! I sailed with Captain Lourens on *Vrouw Maria* across the Baltic Sea and North Sea!"

The sailors glanced at each other behind Finn's back. The purser showed them thumbs up. "Able seaman, are you? Good for you!" the sailor said and winked to his partners.

An old woman wearing a raggedy cap and smoking a pipe grinned, showing blackened teeth. "Aye, I'll join you for a drink anytime! But young lads like you must be careful! Remember always protect your back, otherwise you'll end up sailing the high seas for the rest your life!"

Finn emptied his glass and faced the sailors. He took a firm stance with his hands balled into fists, and said, "You think I'm a sucker! Let's get this straight! If you try to press me, you got to know how to fight! I am not leaving on any ship in any capacity! My place is here with my dear Rosie, is that clear!" He raised his fists. One of the sailors made a move, but Finn easily blocked him and knocked him down with a blow to the side of his head. The man crashed on his back on the floor and lay still.

"I told you, I'm not such easy prey! You want a piece of me, come and get it!" Finn shouted. The crowd in the bar got up and came to back him up. They did not like press gangs because many of them had lost friends and family members that way. The purser motioned his sailors to back off. They picked up their friend from the floor and headed out the door.

Finn turned his back to the bar pointing with his thumb over his shoulder at the sailors. "Frigging blockheads, can you believe what they tried to do to me?"

Aiden reappeared, and Finn ordered everybody in the tavern a round of drinks. Men told how the press gangs operated and how so many people had ended up in the navy. People had disappeared for years until they were able to come back, or they simply vanished forever.

Finn looked around the warm, cozy pub with its low ceiling, lattice windows, wooden walls and floors and an open fire in the back. The crowd still was in extremely hostile mood towards the press gang. A boozy man with shaggy hair with a drink in his hand slapped Finn on the shoulder. "You did a great job!" he said, just as a constable walked into the pub. The man turned to him and continued, "He'll do your job for you, will he? You're twenty minutes too late, always!"

The constable told the man to get back and pushed his chest. "Touch me again and see what happens," the man said.

Finn stepped in between the two men to calm them down, and ordered drinks. "No, no, let's not fight anymore! They are gone so let's have a pleasant tankard of ale instead, all of us! How about it, will you join me for a pint?"

Aiden stared at his mug, helplessly inebriated. "S-such, such a sottish behavior I have never seen! Finn, you better look out for these boozy broads!"

The crowd relaxed and started drinking happily.

People started telling tall tales, and as more people arrived, the pub was soon one of the most happening places in town. The place was filled with a raucous crowd that got louder as the drinks were cheap, stiff and plentiful.

Finn lost track of time as the evening went on. Some musicians appeared and started playing: a flute, a drum and a violin. A crazy and scary looking gypsy woman with a crystal ball sat in the corner telling people their fortunes. Finn was commended several times for being the hero of the evening. He was more than happy to flex his muscles and show his biceps to admiring women. One of the ladies reached over, and squeezing his thigh, winked at him. Finn slapped her hand away. "Well, I must go now because my fair lady is waiting for me at home, she calls it our lovers nest! Thank you all for your help tonight!" He downed one more drink and walked to the door.

Heading home, hands in his pockets, Finn whistled and hummed a tune merrily and imagined how he would tell a new, thrilling story to Rosie. He walked by a dark alley when suddenly the press gang seized him from behind. Finn struggled and managed to let out a shout for help, but one of the men hit him in the head with a wooden truncheon, knocking him out, and dragged him out of sight. In the dark, the press gang carried the unconscious Finn on board a ship. Behind some barrels and boxes, two vagrants saw in the flickering torchlight its name was "*HMS Hope.*"

# Chapter 3

FINN WOKE AT DAWN to the sound of roaring ocean waves. It took him a while to realize that he was in a hammock in an unfamiliar cargo hold. The swinging nauseated him, and he felt as if his bladder was ready to burst. He got down and sat atop some flour sacks holding his head in his hands and grimaced, feeling the nasty, painful bump on his head covered with dried blood. He had a splitting headache and his mouth was bone dry, with a bad taste of stale rum and vomit.

Finn staggered on a rolling cargo deck towards a light he saw and climbed through an open hatch on the upper deck, hoping to get some water. Still feeling dizzy, he walked to the railing and opened his pants to relieve himself. Seeing the vast undulating waves he realized he was on a full-rigged sailing ship at sea. On top of the surf, noisy seagulls glided against the wind and dolphins breached the creamy waves under the ship's bows. He felt the strong salt wind on his face, and he took a deep breath of fresh ocean air and felt slightly better. As the sun rose higher above the horizon, tall masts and sails were silhouetted against a vast blue sky.

He looked around despairingly, and on the quarterdeck he saw Captain Nathaniel Mumford, an unshaven and harsh looking man in a salt-stained blue coat and shabby white breeches spotted with tar, carrying a whip rolled up in his hand.

Finn buttoned his pants and approached the captain. "Captain, I do not belong on this ship! I urge you deliver me back to Bristol immediately!" he shouted over the roaring waves and screaming seagulls.

Captain Mumford stopped pacing and looked at him. "You volunteered, and now you are a merchant seaman at His Majesty's service! And don't you forget it!" The captain pointed his whip at Finn and continued, "As per regulations, you will receive conduct money and two months wages in advance, from which you are expected to buy clothes and a hammock. The regulations state that volunteers, when they come on board, may be supplied with slop clothes, but the cost thereof must be deducted out of the said two months advance!" He hit the railing with his whip.

Finn's troubled mind was going in different directions, and he looked around searching for clues or landmarks but he saw only the vastness of heaving blue waves. "But I am protected as a foreigner! I cannot be pressed into anybody's service just like that!" he said, losing heart. He began to realize that they would not turn around anyway.

The captain laughed, meanly. "Who gives a shit what you think! Besides, you weren't pressed, you volunteered. A King's shilling was found in your drink, fair and square!"

Finn fumbled with his waistband, frantically looking for his purse. He pointed at a dinghy hanging by ropes on the ship's side. "You can keep the advance, and I have enough money! I will take that dinghy from you, and return to Bristol. We cannot be too far from it yet," he said, feeling a sudden surge of hope.

The captain pretended to contemplate the idea. "Well, let's see. If you pay me one hundred guineas for it, I'll let you have it!"

Finn was stunned. He looked at the captain in disbelief, and then he straightened his back. He glared angrily at the captain. "A hundred guineas, that's outrageous!"

The captain waved his hand and dismissed him. "Take it or leave it! Here on my ship, we have a market economy, do you see? Supply and demand! Seems like you are the only one demanding, and I am the only one supplying, so it is up to me, and me only, to determine the price! So, one hundred guineas it is!" he said.

Beginning to accept his fate, Finn turned away and approached a group of sailors. They were a bunch of unshaven bleary-eyed ragamuffins dawdling, keeping a watchful eye on the captain, expecting his orders or a flogging.

Finn sat down, his head hanging low in depression. "A cruel fortune has thrown me on this ship. I have lost my dear Rosie. She must be wondering what happened to me. She probably thinks I abandoned her."

Sailor Hytholoday, who appeared to be the leader of the group, had sharp-looking features, wore a suit of canvas with doublet and breeches and from the smell of it, he hadn't had a bath in weeks. Contorting his face into an expression of aberrant cunning, he ran his eyes over Finn.

"Don't look so hopeless," he said. "You are in the Navy

now! You won't get rich, you son of a bitch! After all, this is His Majesty's ship, *Hope.* Now where do you think we are going?" The other sailors laughed at the joke.

Finn was depressed and looking around the ship he realized there was no way to get back to Bristol. "I want to go back to my darling Rosie! I am going to marry her, and we are going to get a place where there is quiet and prosperity! Now I guess my luck has turned for the worst, and I am on my way to the end of the world! I've heard there is nothing but untamed wilderness, and vast tracts of barren land," he said

The toothless sailor Skealley took his pipe out of his mouth. He laughed loudly and slapped his thigh. "That is right, America the beautiful, land of the freemen, and mighty savage braves!"

Finn looked very nervous. "Once we get there, maybe I can then make my way back to Bristol and to my Rosie, who must be worried sick about me by now. But what kind of ship is this? I hardly see any cargo," Finn asked, looking around the deck.

Skealley looked mysterious. "Merchandise is in the holds, where else? You might call it black gold, if you will," he said, and winked at Finn, who noticed a whipping post on deck, and a slew of shackles.

"Slaves... I'm on a slave ship..." Finn thought out loud.

Captain Mumford disappeared in his cabin, and the sailors stopped working and gathered around Hytholoday.

"Mates, listen up! We have a new man amongst us! Be careful not to make him work too hard, he is so young and inexperienced! He misses his little darling back home, thinks he can go back and make her happy!" Hytholoday said mockingly, and the sailors howled loudly.

Skealley nodded, and taking the pipe out of his mouth spat over the railing. "He thinks she is still waiting for him, with her nice, plump lips, and a tight, wet twat!" Skealley said, sending sailors rolling on the deck laughing.

Finn looked sternly at the sailors. "I don't give a damn about your silly nonsense! Leave me be! I may be young, but I am already tired of endless war and violence. Perhaps all turns for the better where ever I am going, and I can be all that I can be, my own master, and then return to see my Rosie."

Captain Mumford appeared and seeing the sailors bunched up together, hit the railing with a large stick. "I've had enough of blabbering, and these crazy stories! Back to work! Scrub this deck, you lazy no-good mongrels!" he shouted, sending the sailors scattering. They grabbed the bales as whiplashes dug into their backsides, and the men yelled out in pain.

The sailing was protracted by contrary winds and the captain's inept navigation. On top of that the crew already was disgruntled towards the captain due to his cruel practices. A hated man, the captain could rely for protection only on the two Royal Marine bodyguards who never left his side. It soon became apparent that the ship had taken on more slaves than it could safely carry and conditions on the ship worsened.Seven of the crew and sixty African slaves on the ship were killed by overcrowding, malnutrition and disease. Captain Mumford faced a serious problem because if he delivered the dead slaves to the colonies or if they died onshore, the ship owners in Bristol would have no redress.

*HMS Hope* was a former British Navy warship, and

due to its poor condition, it had been converted to a cargo ship by a consortium of enterprising businessmen under contract to the Royal Navy. There was a slave trade investor on board by the name of John Walker. He was on the way to the American colonies and the West Indies to build valuable business contacts. He flung his sheepskin cloak back to reveal a black frock coat and slightly soiled white britches. Upon entering the cabin to talk to the captain, he took off his fur cap.

"Captain, I do appreciate your actions to protect my investment! The return on my investment is around six percent, but it is significantly higher than national alternatives, which are at present around five percent. Profits from the slave trade are only slightly better than sugar prices from Caribbean plantations and France."

"I would like to point out that my expenses have increased considerably, Mr. Walker. However, my fees are still reasonable," Captain Mumford replied, and John Walker helped himself to more food and wine from the table.

John Walker tasted the wine, smacked his lips, and replied, "Considering risks, maritime and commercial, being expedient for individual voyages, I have mitigated it by buying small shares of many ships at the same time. In that way, I am able to diversify a large part of the risk away. Between this passage and voyage back, I can sell ship shares for little extra margin."

"That makes perfect sense and maybe I can help you to secure some of those profits. I am open for proposals on future journeys on your behalf, provided we agree on the price, of course," Captain Mumford said.

There was a knock on the door and Chief Officer Jack Rackham entered the cabin. He was a tall, strong, well-mannered, and devilishly tidy man who was well liked by the crew. He paid fairly well and let the men have little more of the loot than was usual, and he was seen by them as tough but fair. He liked expensive clothes, mostly black coats and carried two pistols in a sash. He nodded to Captain Mumford, and they turned to look at John Walker.

"I plan to get more cowrie shells, which are used as money in the slave business, in Africa," John Walker continued. "My Italian friend calls them *porcellana,* for their generous clear and shining appearance. In parts of West Africa, the cowrie money is called *cedi.*"

"What does all this mean, sir?" Rackham asked.

Walker smirked. "It means that in order for my insurance to cover the losses, the surplus slaves must be thrown overboard."

Captain Mumford nodded in agreement, but Rackham was appalled. "That is outrageous! They are not things to be simply discarded!" he shouted.

"At ease, Chief Rackham! They are merely slaves, plain and simple! Mr. Walker does as he pleases with his property!" Captain Mumford said.

The captain was an experienced mariner, and he knew that Walker was right, in a horrible way. According to the shipping laws and regulations the slaves were considered consignment, and if they were lost at sea the insurance covered the loss of the human cargo at thirty pounds a head.

Finn listened to the muffled shouting from the after cabin and heard clanking chains and coughs from the cargo hold. He opened the hatch to the slave deck and was repulsed by the smells and sights that awaited him. The stench of urine, shit, and sweat was awful. The slaves were shackled in rows, and men, women, and children were sep-arated into sections. Most of them lay in apathy, and only a few looked up, shielding their eyes from the bright sunlight that beamed through the hatch. Finn was curious to see the slaves and stepping down the ladder onto the lower deck walked cautiously past them trying not to step on legs and feet. Towards the back, he recognized a young woman from the slave market who wore a sheer white gown sitting in the corner. Shivering from the cold she had wrapped her arms around herself.

Finn saw a dark figure emerge from the shadows. Sailor Skealley approached the woman making kissing noises and obscene gestures, slowly opening the buttons in his pants. Finn jumped over and harshly pushed him against the wall.

Finn declared, "She is now under my protection! Anybody who touches her will have to answer to me, is that clear?" Finn pointed his finger to Skealley who spat on the deck and walked away. Finn went over to the storage con-tainer and threw a blanket over her shoulders. He loosened her chains and helped the woman to sit atop some sacks and boxes. He pointed to his chest. "My name is Finn."

She stared at him quietly and wrapped the blanket tightly around her. "I am Prudentina," she replied quietly.

Skealley returned, holding a flask of rum in his hand. He opened the wrist shackles of one the male slaves who staggered to his feet and rubbed his wrists where the handcuffs had left deep marks.

Skealley looked at Finn scornfully and pointed at the

man. "So you like these dark people, you scum, huh? Take a look at this handsome beast. You say you're from the north. Well, maybe you know him because his name is Gustavus Vassa."

Finn glared angrily at Skealley and the slave. "What is this immoral plan? A black man is claiming to be the King who caused so much suffering to my people! You must think it's funny to offend my people like that?" Finn lunged towards him, but the man simply stepped aside. His feet were shackled, but that didn't seem to bother or hinder him much.

"You'd better get some sense! I do not want to hurt you!" Vassa said to Finn.

"Ha! Besides, it's pronounced Wasa, not Vassa!" Finn kept trying to fight the man, but he wouldn't fight back. It infuriated Finn even more. "Fight, I demand you!" he said.

"Stop it, please! My real name is Olaudah Equiano! I was given another name because they could not pronounce it correctly," the slave said.

Finn held back only when he learned his real name. "What a terrible burden somebody has bestowed upon you. First they enslave you and then name you after that horrible King," Finn said.

"You can call me Gus, if you wish," he said.

Sailor Hytholoday came down the stairs looking for his partner Skealley. He saw Prudentina behind Finn, and his face turned into an ugly smile. He made licking motions with his tongue and sneered. "I heard there is some nice and ripe, wet fanny and tight arse for the taking here," he said, and motioned to Skealley to join him, and the two sailors drew closer to Finn. Hytholoday pulled out a knife and Skealley produced a wooden baton. Gustavus who was chained up by his legs couldn't do anything to help.

Skealley tossed the wooden staff from hand to hand, his face twisting in anger. "You're loose cannon on a mighty slippery deck, fucking cunt! Now bugger off before you get hurt, boy!" He snarled between his teeth.

Without a warning Hytholoday lunged at Finn who sidestepped and grabbed a handful of his shirt by the neck and threw him against the bulkhead head first. Skealley stepped forward, baton raised above his head. Finn stepped backwards, and as Skealley rushed forward, Gus managed to trip him. Skealley fell down and Finn kicked him in the head knocking him out. Hytholoday tried to get back up, shaking his head. Finn kicked him in the groin from the back, and when Hytholoday bent down holding his crotch in pain, Finn spun him around and hit him with an uppercut, knocking him out. The two sailors lay in a pile on the deck.

"You saved us," Gus said.

"And you helped me. Anyways, you speak English well," Finn replied.

"You speak it poorly, but I can teach you. I can teach you to read too, if you want," Gus replied.

§     §     §

Recollecting the events on the ship, the old man in the Catskill Mountain House frowned.

"The situation could not have been any worse when I first met Gus. Even wearing his raggedy slave clothing he was a handsome young man, about the same age as me, a vagabond kind of guy with a scruffy beard, if you know what I mean. We started talking, and I learned that he was not only an educated slave but also an excellent soldier, a merchant and an explorer, and he even wrote his memoirs later. Quite an accomplishment, don't you think, from a slave who was standing in front of me that day. But his exploits took their toll, and he was quite confused by them, probably even more than I was, and I was thoroughly screwed up by then! Gus told me later that when we met he didn't have any real goals left in his life. It was because all the abuse he had experienced had made him lose the subtlety of any feelings after being captured.

"Gus had become insensible to everything and had lost hope that he would ever achieve his freedom again. Gus was fearless and didn't care anymore what happened to him. He thought he might even just as well be dead anyway. But he was not a quitter and was going to use his wits to try surviving somehow, that somewhere he would find his way. He didn't care what it would take, but he would prove his worth as a human being to people no matter that mankind has always hated an educated black man all throughout history. Besides, he bragged, grinning as usual, that women were drawn to his wayward-boy attitude. You know what, during the voyage, it was Gus who taught me to read and write, and we became friends. Imagine that, a slave taught a free man the alphabets of freedom."

Henry Raymond was sitting on the edge of the couch. Fumbling with his papers, he urged the old man to continue.

§   §   §

Days turned into weeks, and the ship was still sailing at slow speed. Finn became aware of the crew's mutiny plans but decided to stay out of it. He could not sleep one night lying in his hammock but pretended to sleep when he saw Captain Mumford enter the crew deck quietly. The captain walked by him and started pushing some planks behind coils of ropes opening a secret door in the bulkhead; there was a secret compartment in the ship. The captain disappeared inside for a while and then came back out carrying a small bundle. He looked around making sure no one had seen him.

Out on the gun deck the sailors were getting drunk and singing "Rule Britannia." Captain Mumford, flanked by his Marine bodyguards, whipped some of the men ordering them to disperse and return to their quarters. One of the Marines swung his musket butt, stroking a sailor in the face breaking his nose, which enraged the drunken crewmembers.

Sailors Hytholoday and Skealley led some of the drunken crew breaking into the armory. Drunk and armed to the teeth, the mutinous sailors started bellowing and shouting. Brandishing weapons they launched an attack on Captain Mumford and his loyal crew members. Finn tried to stay away from the melee, but he got caught in the fight. On the quarterdeck, he saw Skealley with a knife in his hand sneaking behind Chief Officer Jack Rackham. Finn grabbed a sword from a dead sailor and took Skealley by the shoulder, and spinning him around drove the sword in his belly to the hilt, saving Jack Rackham's life.

Drunken mad rebels launched another attack from the forward deck. The volley killed the two Marine bodyguards, and Captain Mumford fell, severely wounded. He was still alive begging for mercy when the rebels seized him and heaved him overboard. The waves snatched him as though he was a wisp of grass, and his body rolled over twice with outstretched arms before being pulled under into the depths.

On the stern deck, Jack Rackham rushed to the dead marines and picked up a musket, calmly took aim, and shot Hytholoday in the head, killing him. Seeing their leaders dead, and now being outnumbered, the rest of the mutinous crew stopped fighting, and Jack Rackham took charge of the ship.

The men barely had time to sigh in relief when the cargo doors burst open. The slaves jumped into action taking their only chance, seeing such discord among their captors. Gus helped them to break their shackles, but instead of helping him, the revolting slaves stormed out of the cargo hatches, killing one crew member and wounding several others.

"Gus, you better stay put! Don't go out there! They will kill you if you do!" Finn shouted to Gus, who pulled at his leg irons but couldn't get them loose.

In the dark cargo hold, Finn took Prudentina by the hand and led her to the captain's hideaway built into the ship, and hearing the mutiny on the upper decks, he quickly pushed Prudentina in and following her closed the door behind them. The chamber was hardly big enough for the two of them.

"Captains use hideaways like this for particularly valuable men to hide in if the press gang comes aboard. We must be quiet," Finn whispered in her ear.

Her back was pressed against Finn, and she slowly wiggled her butt against his lap. She felt him get hard and looking at him inquiringly reached down to touch him. He smiled apologetically back at her in the dark.

"You must be happy to see me?" She whispered, "You looked after me and fought for me. Here is my bargain: you protect me, and I will take care of your needs, all needs." She pushed her behind harder against his crotch and looked at him over her shoulder. He tried to fight against his growing lust as her supple fingers swiftly opened the buttons in his pants. First, Finn made a feeble attempt stop her, but quickly overwhelmed by his lust, he could not control himself. Frenzied, he pulled the flimsy garment up over her hips and after more fumbling in the dark, took her forcefully from behind. His powerful moaning and her ecstatic screams were covered over by the shouting and clamor from the upper decks.

Afterwards, Finn leaned against her back, feeling embarrassed and being sorry for having used her. He pulled down her garment and buttoned his pants. Then a thought occurred to him, and he looked at her in the darkness. "I'm sorry if I..." Finn's voice faltered.

Prudentina hushed and cut him off. "We made a deal!" she said. "You must protect me and Equiano all the way, and we are still a long ways from shore. You do that, and I will keep my end of the bargain. Besides, I enjoyed it just as much as you did," she said.

Finn was silent for a moment. "Where do you come from? You must be far away from home. I did not have a choice, and I am searching a new place to settle," he said.

"They came early in the morning and took me and

the other villagers from our homes to Elmina Castle in the Cape Coast," she told him. "Sounds like a place in a fairytale, but I swear it is no fairytale. Like millions of others before me, I was made to walk through the door of no return. Shackled, I was forced to walk the plank over the sharks. I had three choices, to fight and be thrown into a tiny cell with skull and crossbones above it, and then they would starve me to death. Or maybe I could have jumped into shark-infested waters below to be eaten alive. Or I could carry on walking into the ship and get thrown into small compartments with no sunlight, little ventilation, and great filth. The lucky ones of us that survived, we now face a life of slavery in the New World. So don't tell me about choices in life when you have many."

Finn opened the door and led Prudentina back to a quiet corner. On the upper deck, the revolt was suppressed ruthlessly by the crew who had killed seven slaves. The remaining surviving slaves, ten men in all, huddled in a defensive group against the railing. Their leader, a young warrior with a scar-tattooed face and fierce nostrils, muttered something in a strange tongue to his men. The ship's crew circled closer weapons at the ready, certain that the slaves were going to yield. There was a moment of silence as the two groups glared at each other. Then, in a display of defiance at the inhumanity of the slavers, the tattooed warrior hopped on the railing, and without looking back jumped into the waves. The crew watched astonished as the other slaves followed their leader, jumping over the rail one by one into the cold sea.

Hearing the shouts and loud splashes, Finn felt sick when he realized what had happened. "What was the man saying before they jumped?" he asked Gus.

Gus took a deep breath and replied, "He said that suffering requires existence, so death is merely freedom from suffering."

"I am getting sick and tired of all this fighting and killing no matter where I go. At least we are heading to a peaceful place," Finn replied.

First Officer Jack Rackham declared himself the new captain of the ship and made a note to file an insurance claim for three hundred pounds sterling in recompense for the slaves who had jumped into the water. The weather seemed to agree with the new captain because during the following night, a heavy swell was setting in from the east and the ship started pitching heavily. At dawn, the weather was calm, sweet and clear at first, but then the sea turned black and sinister. The swells brought them sailing under unvarying clouds of rain, and the sharp stormy sea sent a shower flying over the quarterdeck.

That morning Finn witnessed a true mariner in action, a sight he would never forget. Jack Rackham, the new captain, ordered the sailors to climb high up on the masts to drop the main topsail and fore course. They came down like the curtain at the end of a dramatic tragedy. The ship responded at once and Finn felt how the ship gained momentum as he gazed up at the royal-mast, firmly parallel with the topgallant and rising high above against the dark blue sky.

*HMS Hope* surged ahead on a hazy, heaving sea, her bow hurling the water aside. Captain Jack Rackham let out an incredible peal of laughter as the ship turned on her heel, her deck leaning sharply and masts groaning. As the winds picked up even more, she steadied on her way heading west running under easy sail in a drift of rain.

Finn stood facing forward at the bow in the lifting rainstorm. The sight of the ship's low checkered hull and her towering masts lifted Finn's heart, and his solemn face broke into a broad smile. "Where are you taking me? What's next, life?" he shouted from the top of his lungs into the pouring rain. Heavy swells coinciding with a heavy roll threw him off balance, and he fell sprawling on the wet deck.

§    §    §

On the new continent, out from the wooded belly of the mountains, below dense forests, rugged gorges and forested ridges, the Hudson River flowed freely but troubled, its dark waters circling in quiet eddies beneath the shadows of projecting rock. Three men had set up a hunting camp below some spectacular rocky outcrops, bluffs with a spar to the fore that resembled a wolverine's head overlooking the river.

John Stark and his older brother William Stark were hunting with their neighbor James Stinson. John and James, who were both in their early twenties, prepared beaver traps close to the river. William, few years older than his brother, was fishing on a rowboat in the middle of the river.

John Stark kept a sharp lookout venturing upstream, past some rocky areas beside the river, and placed his musket against a tree while he was setting a trap some distance from their camp. He heard a rustling in the bushes and went for his musket but it was too late. Suddenly a group of Abenaki warriors rushed him from the scrubs, and he fell into their hands. Their leader was chief named Akiatonharónkwen, but to the Colonials he was Colonel Louis. He was a daunting looking tall man wearing war paint, and a green loincloth around his waist on top of red and blue rawhide leggings and moccasins. The fierce warriors held John Stark tightly by the arms, and Colonel Louis told him to hail the others. "Call your friends, and make them come over here. Do that and we might consider saving you," he said in perfect English.

John Stark recognized the famous chief from his garments, and his long-handled tomahawk and musket with distinctive engravings. "You must be Colonel Louis," he said to the chief, looking at him straight in the eyes. He turned towards the camp. "William, James! I was attacked and taken prisoner! Run for your lives!" he shouted.

The Abenaki fired into the boat, bullets hitting the water and missing William, who quickly rowed towards the opposite shore. In the camp, James Stinson grabbed his musket and rushed forward to help his friends.

"John, run, I will cover you!" Stinson shouted, aiming his musket. John Stark wrested himself away and struck two of the warriors, causing their muskets to shoot in the air. Colonel Louis fired calmly and hit Stinson in the forehead, the bullet snapping his head back. He let out a loud sigh and fell slowly to his knees, and then slumped over on his side.

"James, look out!" John Stark cried, and fearlessly rushed to fight the warriors. His bold attack exasperated the Abenaki so that they started beating John Stark severely and dragged him off to their camp.

"We are hungry, and he can cook for us like a squaw,"

Colonel Louis said. In the camp, John Stark was told to prepare cornmeal for the warriors. He first proceeded to cut up the corn, but then he threw it into the river, and turned to face his captors.

"It is the business of squaws and not warriors to prepare food," he said, ready for a fight he knew would come. To his considerable surprise, instead of being irritated at him, the Abenaki warriors were pleased with his boldness.

"You are a brave young chief, and maybe we can adopt you as a son of our sachem, but first you must pass a test," Colonel Louis replied. The young warriors ranged themselves in two lines, each armed with a heavy stick, ready to hit the prisoner as he passed them. John Stark got ready to run the gauntlet, and worked himself up to frenzy.

"Behold! Blessed be God, my rock," he prayed, "God, who trains my hands for war, and my fingers for battle! God, my loving kindness and my fortress, my stronghold and my deliverer! God is my shield and he in whom I take refuge!"

Surprising everyone, John Stark snatched a club from the closest warrior and made his way through the lines, knocking the warriors down right and left whenever they came within his reach. John Stark escaped with barely a blow, to the great delight of the older chiefs, who sat at a distance and heartily enjoyed the sport at their young men's expense.

Meanwhile, William Stark ran through the woods and came to a clearing. He encountered a massive snarling wolf dog tied to a tree, being beaten by a French officer. William Stark realized the Frenchman was part of the war party that had seized his brother John and killed James Stinson.

Drawing his hunting knife he quietly sneaked closer, and surprising the Frenchman from behind slit his throat, showering the wolf dog with French blood.

William Stark emptied the dead man's pockets and found his commission letter. The beastly wolf dog shook the blood off his thick fur coat and stared at him intensely. Stark walked cautiously around the magnificent animal and cut it loose from the tree. To his surprise the animal did not run away but instead, the wolf dog with its bushy tail at full height pointing straight up in the air approached him, stopped and looked him in the eyes. William Stark knew what the wolf dog was doing, and standing still he looked into the dog's eyes, but then averted his gaze in order not to challenge the beast. The large animal walked up to him and tapped his hand twice with his hulking snout. William Stark petted the giant furry head and rubbed the ears and thought of a good name for him. "I will call you Sergeant Beaubien, after your former master. They got poor Jim, I paid them back finishing by off the Frenchman, and I got the wolf dog. I'd say that's a fair trade. Now let's go get John," he said.

§        §        §

Finn and Gustavus stood on the deck when *HMS Hope* arrived in the Governor's Island harbor of New York. "So, how old are you, Finn?" Gus asked.

"I don't know. My mother told me once, but I didn't get her. All I know is that, I think, I have seen this many summers as having fingers in one hand," Finn replied and showed his hand fingers spread wide, closed his hand and opened it again four times.

"Listen very well. I need to teach you basic calculation as well," Gus said excited, waving his hands.

"You are so educated, Gus. How is that possible?" Finn asked.

"I was lucky enough to have a rich master. He was a Quaker from Scotland, who came to Africa to establish a cotton plantation and a textile factory. As a child, I sneaked into his extensive library at night where I learned to read and write by the candlelight. Then later I wrote letters, kept accounts and managed his household. Unfortunately, he died of malaria and his estate was sold, including all the slaves," Gus replied.

Captain Jack Rackham called for Finn. "The order of the high seas is that the captain has to produce enough men on board to pilot the ship, but we all know that is wide open to interpretation. Here in the colonies, men convicted of petty crimes, adultery, or drunkenness are given the choice go to sea or go to jail, so I will have no trouble finding new crew," he said.

"I don't understand," Finn said, looking puzzled.

"You saved my life, Finn, and I am a reasonable man. If you want to leave the ship, you may do so here. I will give you this one opportunity only," Jack Rackham replied.

"Then I will take my leave and disembark the ship. But I have one more request. I want to take two slaves with me. I'll buy them free if I have to," Finn requested.

Jack Rackham opened the ship's muster records and entered an R on Finn's name signifying honorable release. "I cannot talk about the slaves because, as the captain of this ship, to me they were only cargo. You must talk to the owner or the slave master about them. You will find them in the harbor," he said, and closed the book.

Finn shrugged his shoulders and walked off the ship on the wide plank to the pier and found his way to the market place in the harbor. There was a group of sailors talking and Finn overheard something about the coming war. Finn was stunned when he heard of the pending war against the French.

Finn couldn't believe what he just heard. "Certainly this cannot be so! I am so tired of fighting!" he said to one of the Marines.

"I am dead serious, lad, and worse than that, I am stone sober," the Marine replied to him.

Finn bit his lower lip and nodded his head in determination. "I will not run again, but there is nowhere to go around this miserable place, anyway! I have to find a way back to Bristol!"

Finn found his way to the platform where slaves were being sold. He saw Gus and Prudentina among them. Finn counted how much money he had and glancing at Gus and Prudentina he tried to haggle with the slave trader.

"I'm sorry, lad, there are no bargains today. Too many valuable slaves were lost at sea. The price is what it is. Take it or leave it!" the slaver trader replied adamantly.

Finn was unsure of what to do, and he walked around the harbor contemplating his situation. He was in a strange harbor, in a strange new land, and had nowhere to go. He concluded that he should get a strong partner, and he bought Gus.

"Gustavus, you taught me many lessons during the

voyage. You are now a free man. Please wait here," he said, and went back to the slave trader and paid him. He was given a receipt, and as the remaining slaves walked away in a long line chained together, Prudentina was taken away with them. Finn caught up and walked beside her.

"Prudentina, I don't know what to say," Finn said quietly.

"I know. Go, young man, and thank you for your discreet protection. You did your part well, and you were satisfied of my payment, am I right?" she said and gave him a little sad smile.

Finn turned his back to hide what he is doing from any potential observers. He handed what money he had left to Prudentina. "Here, at least take this," he said. She quickly tucked it under her clothes. They parted company as Prudentina was led away with the other slaves. Finn and Gus walked into the crowd.

Walking away, Finn did not look back, but Gus and Prudentina kept looking at each other until they disappeared from sight. Finn asked, "Why are you looking back as if you will miss her or something?"

"She is my sister," Gus replied. Finn stopped and looked at him surprised, and Gus walked by him. Finn grimaced and caught up with him.

"From now on I will call you Gus, is that alright?" Finn said. Walking through the crowd, they passed by a gentleman riding a horse and wearing a green wool frock coat, who noticed the moose head necklace Finn wore around his neck.

The marine from the harbor was going in the same direction as Finn and Gus. "Where are you from, boy?"

he asked, making conversation. Finn was about to answer when the man heard the question and commented on Finn's necklace.

"Judging by his necklace, the boy's ancestors are Varangian, so he must be from Kvenland," the man said. "They are wanderers and hunters by nature, and call their land Suomi in their own language. I know because my great-grandfather came from there, too."

The marine shrugged his shoulders and walked on. When they parted, Finn and the gentleman in a green coat turned to look back at each other over the crowd's heads. "Wonder who that man on the horse was?" Finn asked Gus.

"I heard somebody call him as Honorable John Morton, member of the Pennsylvania Provincial Assembly. He must be a powerful man. I would not bother him if I were you. Although I must say, there is striking resemblance between you two," Gus said.

"Right, but we must go on," Finn replied, "Maybe we should go and enroll in the army or something. I heard someone saying that the 60th Royal Americans Regiment accepts foreigners. But there might be fighting starting, and I am not so sure about that." Finn suddenly stopped in his tracks. He saw a Hessian army patrol approaching, and it was led by none other than Johan Kopf! He was pulling out a purse with a black cross on a white field, and rosary beads around it to pay his troops.

"Fuck me running!" Finn cursed and pulled Gus over to the side behind a fence out of sight. He could not believe it. He held back his desire to fight Kopf instantly and continued, "No, I got to think straight. Damn it, but I can't afford revenge right now! We need to run the other way. I must get some honest work, get paid and then return to England and find Rosie. Let's get away from the conflict if possible," Finn said.

"We have neither money nor arms so maybe we should ignore the British Army for the time being. Let's go the other way," Gus replied, and they sneaked out of town and got on the Great Conestoga Road towards Pennsylvania.

Back in the harbor, Johan Kopf took a deep breath of ocean air. He was satisfied so far with what he saw on the new continent. He had been awarded a medal for his performance in England and when he heard that promotions were easier to earn in the colonies than in Europe, he saw an opportunity and a short cut to earn his place among the aristocrats. He had decided to get a fresh new start in his career and volunteered for overseas duty. He quickly found himself on a troop transport ship on his way to America. The weather had been good and the relatively quick voyage across the Atlantic was actually fairly enjoyable for him.

Two days later, Finn and Gus arrived in Philadelphia, late in the evening. Townspeople were too busy to pay any attention to Finn and Gus walking wearily walking down the street. They arrived at the Tun Tavern, on which there was another prominent sign lighted by lanterns with bold letters. It read "Peggy Mullen's Red Hot Beef Steak Club."

"Having traveled all night and day sure makes me tired and hungry," Gus said. They entered the building asking for the proprietor and were told that his name was Robert Mullen.

"I have no need for hired hands," Robert Mullen replied to them and pointed towards the back, "but you should talk to those gentlemen over there. They are planning an excursion into the western territories and need laborers and militia."

"Thank you, sir. Why are they recruiting militia?" Finn asked.

"There are plans to launch an expedition to quell the French foray into the area," Robert Mullen replied, and turned back to the kitchen.

On one side, there was a long bar where a recruiter named Benjamin Franklin was working to expand the ranks of the Pennsylvania militia. At a little over forty years of age, he was an athletic man with a high forehead and proud of his hair that was short at the front and sides, and long in the back. Taking his coat off and rolling up his shirt sleeves he ordered a round of drinks for men at the bar.

"S-such an accession of power is to the British e-empire by sea as well as land! S-such growth of trade and navigation! S-such are the numbers of ships and seamen!" he declared, and raised his tankard in a toast.

§      §      §

At the bar in the Tun Tavern, Finn and Gus listened to stories about the many jobs available in the Ohio country, and asked the man next to them how to apply for one of those jobs. "Sir, I was told you represent the Ohio Company of Virginia. I hear you need strong men to take part in your expedition. Here I am, and this is my companion, Gus. We are ready to work hard for you, should you take us," Finn said.

"Not me, talk to those gentlemen over there," the man

replied, taking a drink before continuing, "Talk to Daniel Boone; he needs strong laborers and scouts. Let me offer you a word for the wise, young man. At all costs, avoid going up north to the New France. It is the enemy's country! We are about to go explore east to the Ohio Valley, and maybe we will advance all the way to the Island Of California one day!"

Finn walked around the tavern. He saw a young major dressed in Virginia Regiment uniform coming in with another man. George Washington arrived in the tavern with his older half-brother, Austin. Despite his high rank, he was only twenty-two years old and looked overconfident in his new blue militia uniform walking to the long table. He had obtained his commission and rank through the family connections, and now planned to seek a commission in the regular British Army. He addressed Benjamin Franklin and gave the older man a warm, hard slap on the shoulders.

"You know, old man, not even a distillery full of fine whiskey gives a man such pleasure as does the excitement of the hunt for the most elusive and dangerous game of all, another man, and the ensuing battle of the fittest that can only have one survivor, and one winner who takes it all!" George Washington declared loudly. Finn raised his mug and nodded in agreement.

A high ranking British officer wearing a redcoat uniform walked in, and several colonials turned their backs in silent contempt. General Braddock was an old war horse in his late fifties and looked forward to his last campaign before retirement. He described it as his last action and last chance for glory, to anyone willing to listen.

"Natives should not be regarded as our enemies, but

as our allies. However, we must mount this campaign to quell any potential uprisings!" General Braddock said, and walked to the bar taking off his riding gloves. He threw them on the table and looked at Franklin, and continued, "You say the natives should not be regarded as our enemies. I say that these savages may, indeed, be a formidable enemy to your American militia, but it is unbearable that they should make an impression upon the King's powerful regular and disciplined troops! Your militia, on the other hand, looks like a slothful and languid lot of fellows, hardly fit for military service," General Braddock finished, and looking scornful, took a long drink from his tankard that Robert Mullen placed on the table.

"Th-that, sir is a matter of opinion," Benjamin Franklin replied.

General Braddock raised his foot on a chair, and leaned on it, looking at the men. "Old wise man Cicero said there are two modes of contending, the one by reasoning and the other by force, and he meant war. He said that free men do not speak of the legitimacy of horses or lions!" he declared on a loud voice.

"The c-civil right is derived from the c-civil power, or it should be, sir!" Benjamin Franklin replied, "And so it is the d-dominant power of the state. Now, a nation is f-formed by free men, who join to p-protect their shared values."

"All animals use some form of fighting without any other guide than nature, and all animals see their enemy and the best means of defense, and the strength and scale of their own weapons. Another wise man, Horace, said that the wolf attacks with its teeth and the bull with its horns. Can you tell us where is this ability derived from, if not from inclination? Even a small calf butts with its forehead before its horns appear and strikes with all imaginable fury!" General Braddock said, his eyes sweeping the faces around him.

Washington had been looking for an opportunity to get a commission in the British regulars for some time, and now he saw an opportunity to gain some recognition, so he stepped forward to support General Braddock.

"General Braddock is right," George Washington said. "The man is by nature formed for peace and war. His natural armor is not an integral part of his body, but rather, he has two hands fit for preparing and handling weapons! These two hands serve any righteous man for a pistol, a sword, or any arms whatever, by holding and wielding them!"

Ignoring Washington's comment General Braddock said, "There is only one thing that can be used to repel a force, and it is counterforce! Just as it is only natural to use force to repel a force, the right to resist arms with guns is provided by the divine nature. The laws allow us to take up arms against those that carry them!"

Washington made another attempt. "The lions do not fight with each other, nor do serpents bite serpents. But if any violence ensues to the tamest of them, they are ready to fight quickly and will defend themselves with the greatest alacrity and vigor!"

Benjamin Franklin remained a little skeptical. "Who w-would agree with me, should I argue that the Christian understanding of s-sacrificing our own lives for others is mandated onto us by the law of nature? General, do you honestly b-believe that living according to the raw law of nature is the ch-character of a true believer?" he asked.

General Braddock ordered more drinks and sat down facing Benjamin Franklin. "Religion aside for a moment, Mr. Franklin, the state of affairs you call peace cannot be preserved without a strong army, nor can such an army be maintained without pay, nor pay provided without taxation. For this purpose, we pay tribute to the King, so that his soldiers may be supplied with the necessaries of warfare!"

"Could it be possible for all men on earth to be united in agreement?" Washington said, "Verily, it could happen under certain utopian circumstances, but first they would have to abandon their disastrous and profane rages, and embrace righteous determination and justice toward one another. No matter which means you use, there are times when war is justified, because determined and violent men always exist to disturb the quiet life of lovers of peace."

Franklin leaned across the table. "General, let me m-make clear to you that I don't think there is anything wrong in bearing arms, but to t-take up arms due to rapine motives is a sin indeed, and the c-courage required to defend one's country against the incursions of barbarians, or p-protects one's family and home from the attacks of robbers, is c-complete justice!"

Austin Washington coughed and used his pistol as a gavel to get everyone's attention, and when they quieted down, he opened up some maps on the table and spoke up. "Gentlemen, let me remind you of our original agenda. New tracts of land have been granted to the Ohio Company on the condition that the company shall establish one hundred families near the forks of the Ohio River and construct a fortress to protect them and ascertain the British claim on the land. However, this area is disputed by the French and, therefore, the mission is particularly dangerous! A secondary purpose of this settlement is to establish a regular trade with the local native tribes, deemed necessary in order to maintain friendly relations. We need not only soldiers, but also farmers, hunters, trappers and traders!"

Finn mulled over the conversation. He turned to Gus and said, "Gus, I think we should join in the expedition. Let's talk to Daniel Boone, like the man told us."

They searched the crowd for an older man and the servant had to point him out to them. They finally found Boone sitting in the back. To their surprise, he was a twenty-year-old outdoorsman, trapper, and hunter, surrounded by a bunch of scruffy ruffians older than him. Boone came from a farmer family and was dressed in fringed hunting shirt, leggings, and moccasins. He placed his beaver hat atop a musket barrel that leaned against the chair by the wall behind him. As Finn and Gus approached their table, the men stopped talking. One of them spat out a long, nasty stream of tobacco juice in front of them and smiled, baring his blackened teeth.

"We're here for the expedition," Finn said.

"Can you use a musket?" the man with blackened teeth asked. Finn looked back at him, straight in the eye. "I'm a marksman and so is my friend here," he replied.

Daniel Boone took a closer appraising look at Finn and Gus, emptied his whiskey glass, and without saying a word, nodded to another man to his right.

"You are hired as road builders," Boone said.

§    §    §

The old man at the Catskill Mountain House handed his empty glass to Henry Raymond, who quickly reached over and grabbed the bottle from a side table.

"Long break between the drinks in this place," the old man said, and when Raymond handed his filled glass back he continued, "I learned only later that much to our misery it seemed we had arrived in a hornet's nest instead of a paradise. In America, the British colonies wanted to expand west and began to run afoul of French claims to the Mississippi River Valley. In retaliation, the French began to create a chain of forts along the frontier, and the British efforts to remove them led to open hostilities. The aggressions caused all sorts of anger on both sides, but there were conflicts also within alliances! It was about values that clashed under particular and abnormal conditions. The kind of values that is most difficult to reconcile, because there simply is no clear right or wrong. There is only a series of wicked choices!

"The British often regarded their subjects in America with scorn, and their arrogance towards the natives was well known. They neglected the American colonies but then some aristocrats in Britain realized that the Colonies could pay off the British war debts by taxes! But that was not enough, and the Colonials were also progressively divided among themselves, too! Traditionally they supported the Crown as Loyalists, but then new, rebellious ideas of democracy and such started circulating in secret. The Colonials were used to the raiding parties from various tribes for more than a century; outlying farms were attacked and farmers killed or captured. They often sent their own war parties on reprisal attacks and to obtain new land. Moreover, the Colonials could not accept the fact that women were roughly equivalent to the men in the Iroquois nation. Different nations had been at war for ages with their natural enemies among other tribes. There were also deep divisions within the Iroquois Nation, and brother was pitted against brother when they had to choose between the British and French sides.

"I learned later that the gentleman in the Governor's Island harbor was John Morton. He was in his mid-twenties at that time, a self-educated jurist who was elected to the Pennsylvania Provincial Assembly. He was involved in civic and church affairs and regarded as a caring husband and father, and eventually he had a family of nine children. He was a land surveyor for many years, and was chosen to be the next justice of the peace or a sheriff. His father passed away before he was born, and John Morton was full of pride of his family heritage, especially of his grandfather who had arrived in New Sweden on the *Eagle* in 1654 and was among the New Freemen swearing loyalty to Governor Rising at Tinicum Island. John Morton was a man of grit and resolve, an open-minded and permissive thinker, and a strong supporter of democracy, which was a new way of thinking considered treasonous by many. The people in the secret association were keenly aware of the treasonable nature of their thoughts. However, John Morton was careful not to challenge the Crown publicly because he felt that the time was not right. Even though most Pennsylvanians in his town were Loyalists, John Morton covertly favored independence, he confided in me much later."

Henry Raymond looked at the old man. "Did I understand you correctly, sir? Did you also say you met Mr. Benjamin Franklin?"

The old man grinned and replied, "Surely I did, and I learned a great deal about jolly old Ben. He was born into an unusually large household. His Puritan father Josiah made candles and soap for a living and married twice. He had seven children with his first wife, plus another ten children with his second wife. Ben was one of the younger children, so he grew up in a loud household. His mother Abiah was particularly caring and attentive.

"Despite the fact he never liked school, Ben was a bright and self-taught man who read a lot. He established dialogue and study groups for local intellectuals. He liked fishing and the outdoors. His favorite pastime was getting together with his friends to drink beer and discuss philosophy. We liked him for his writing of *Advice to a Young Man on the Choice of a Mistress.* He stuttered a little, but because of his quick wit, being a muscular man and an excellent swimmer, he was also a favorite of the ladies, and you should not be surprised to learn that he had an illegitimate son, William, from his younger days.

"Because of his humble childhood, Ben was frugal, and at a young age, he decided to become a vegetarian in order to save money. Ben became a wealthy, having sold large numbers of his handbook, and his letterpress business thrived. He was closely associated with the Grand Master of the Freemasons. He voyaged to Europe several times, but despite his requests, his wife Deborah who had a fear of the sea never accompanied him. Ben was a staunch supporter of the British Empire, and after being elected to the Pennsylvania Assembly, he influenced the new militia act, set aside grant funds for defense, and appointed government representatives to carry on a full scale war. He considered Britain a freedom spreading nation, precious and beneficial to its people in England, as well as those in America."

The old man paused to take a sip, "Then there was George, of course. Ben was much older than me, but George and I were about the same age at the time. We were both young and stupid, but in different ways, I suppose.

"A little earlier before we met, George had journeyed to Barbados with Lawrence, who was his half-brother suffering from tuberculosis, with the hope that the weather would be beneficial to Lawrence's well-being. George contracted smallpox during the excursion, which left his expression rather scarred, but protected him against further exposures to the feared malady. Lawrence's health did not improve, and he died soon after they returned to Mount Vernon, but not before he had bought an interest in the Ohio Company, a land acquisition and settlement enterprise whose aim was the settlement of Virginians border areas, including the Ohio Country, meaning the territory north and west of the Ohio River. Its investors also included Virginians Royal Governor, Robert Dinwiddie, who also appointed George a major in the provincial militia. Lawrence's estate, the farm at Mount Vernon and the company shares were passed on to the surviving Washington brothers.

"Governor Dinwiddie wanted to highlight the French threat, and had George's account of the first mission to the Ohio River Valley distributed widely. It was printed on both sides of the Atlantic, giving George an intercontinental reputation, since he claimed that although the British officers fought well, their cowardly soldiers did not, but, on the other hand, his own Virginians behaved like men and died like soldiers."

§    §    §

The following day, as Finn and Gus went to report for duty, they passed a group of men working in a field. Finn said to Gus, "I am sure we are in capable hands here, Gus. Road construction pays alright, although it is hard work. We'll build it, get paid, and get the fuck out of here! Anyways, I must say that the young officer they called Washington in his new, handsome uniform, must be highly efficient because he has attained such a high rank, although he is hardly any older than I am. You know, compared to that old fart General."

When they were gone, one of the men in the field named William Dorie spoke with his twelve-year-old son, Jonathan, and said to him, "You must stand here and be a lookout for us while we work. Keep your ears and eyes open!" Jonathan nodded and sitting on a fence whistled a tune.

Suddenly a band of Abenaki warriors rushed out of the forest, and young Jonathan sounded the alarm with enough time to permit all of the men escape, but young Jonathan was seized and carried off as his father watched helplessly from his place of refuge. Colonial militia was alerted, and a patrol rushed out and passed Finn and Gus who were walking down the road towards the camp. George

Washington was excited, and waving his arms, led his men forward. Finn and Gus thought they were supposed to join the patrol, and decided to follow them. The patrol chased the Abenaki for seven days all the way to the junction of the Allegheny and Monongahela rivers. The frantic search party did everything they could but the kidnapped boy was nowhere to be found.

Washington received new orders by a messenger. "We will set up camp on a meadow near the Youghiogheny River between the Allegheny and Laurel Ridges," he ordered. "I will lead a patrol to reconnoiter the possible routes for building a road north from Wills Creek!"

When the patrol reached the meadow, Mingo warrior scout Tanacharison, who was known to the colonials as Half King, ran to Washington. Half King pointed to the woods in front of them and said, "There is a war party coming to attack us, and they are not far ahead. They are setting up an ambush!"

Washington was sitting under a tree with a piece of long grass in his mouth. "Do you know how many? We might have to withdraw."

"I counted thirty-three French soldiers and warriors," Half King said.

Washington spat out the grass and said, "We outnumber them. We could take them by surprise. This could mean a promotion, or even a commission in the regulars."

"We can gain an easy victory! You will be rewarded!" Half King shouted. Washington picked up his musket.

"We will find their camp and attack before they have a chance to organize!" Washington ordered.

Finn and Gus were standing some distance away, and

seeing the men get their weapons ready Finn realized
something terrible was about to happen. He took Gus by
the sleeve and led him behind a large oak tree. "Gus, I don't
like the way this is going. Let's stay out of this, alright? We
came here to work, not fight. This is not our war," he said,
and Gus nodded.

The militia formed a skirmish line and advanced
silently towards the French across the woods. They found
the French still sleeping in a hollow in the forest. A guard
leaned on his rifle half sleep as Half King attacked him from
behind and cut his throat with his knife. The Colonials
launched their attack with bayonets and killed the sleeping
French. Half King and his Mingo warriors let out a bone
shrilling battle cry.

"Kill them all!" Half King barked.

The first volley killed several French soldiers who were
trying to get up, and the British captured several survivors.
The French captain Jumonville de Villiers was brought
wounded and dazed in front of George Washington.

"You, sir, are now my prisoner of war!" Washington
declared proudly, striking a victorious pose in front of his
captive.

Half King walked up to Jumonville de Villiers from
behind and said, "You are not dead yet!" Without a
warning, he sank his tomahawk in Jumonville's skull
splitting it wide open. The man slumped dead on the
ground and Half King washed his hands with the brains,
and swiftly scalped him.

"Stop, you have done enough damage already!"
George Washington shouted at Half King. "As the commanding officer of this patrol, I shall not be charged with

war crime! You lied to me! They weren't setting up an ambush, they were sleeping!"

"What war crime? He was the enemy!" Half King shouted back.

"He was an officer! Surrendering! He was under my protection! You are nothing but savages, cowards who sneak up on helpless victims trembling in the night," Washington shouted.

"There is nothing dishonorable in stealth! Great is the warrior who is able to catch his enemy unaware and slay him swiftly and silently!" Half King looked at George Washington expressionlessly. He glanced at Jumonville's body on the ground. "I don't understand the white man's ways," he said.

"There will be a counterattack! You understand that, don't you? Men, begin building a log palisade. Quickly! Place the stockade in the middle of that meadow. That way the position will provide a clear field of fire. Do or die! We shall call it Fort Necessity!" Washington declared. The militia started to cut down trees and erected the barricade.

Finn turned to Gus. "Gus, I don't see any way out of here! The forest is full of wild, uncontrolled enemies now that their leader has been killed! What are we going to do?"

Gus ran a little way back and looked for a way, but he realized they were too far from the camp. He pointed to the militia working on the palisade. "That's our only chance, like it or not! We got to join them and take cover behind the walls!" He started running, Finn following close behind. They joined the militiamen erecting poles and logs to form a fort. Then out on the road a line of red-coated soldiers appeared. The men tensed up, but then militiamen realized it was Captain James McKay's company of regular British troops from South Carolina. The militiamen cheered their arrival.

"Reinforcements have arrived! We are saved!" a man shouted when he saw the regulars. Captain McKay started positioning his men immediately. He motioned Finn and Gus to change positions.

"Captain, my name is Major Washington, and I am in command here!" George Washington protested.

"You, sir, may have a superior rank, but my commission in the British Regular Army takes precedence!" Captain McKay replied with authority.

George Washington had to swallow his pride, and paced nervously back and forth. "Fine, while your men remain at Great Meadows, my men shall continue work on the road," he finally agreed.

"Too late for that, I'm afraid," Captain McKay said. "No doubt you are a decent surveyor, but your skills as a soldier need improvement, sir! Don't you realize that your stronghold is sited in a pit and is too close to the tree lines?"

Washington turned around and taking a closer look at the site realized his amateurish mistake. "Well, as soon as we have a chance we will relocate it, I suppose," he said.

The French forces arrived, led by Captain Louis Coulon de Villiers, the dead Jumonville's brother. They quickly surrounded the fort and Jumonville's body was brought to Captain Villiers. He looked at his dead brother and was filled with both sorrow and disbelief. "*Oh, merde!*" he exclaimed, and then turned towards the British fort on the meadow. His troops and warrior allies occupied high ground along the tree line, dominating the area with direct observation and fields of fire.

The French sharpshooters opened fire, their accurate shots killing three British troops. The remaining militia and regulars scrambled for cover, Finn and Gus huddling behind a pile of logs. Outraged by his brother's death, Captain Villiers pressed his attack through the day.

"You're fuckwits and British dogs!" the outraged Captain Villiers shouted to the British, urging his men to keep attacking. "Fucking British cowards are nothing but petty murderers and war criminals!"

The British and militia took cover behind the hastily built palisade, but it offered little protection. Washington rushed from man to man. "Men, remember our earlier attack on the French was justified and honorable! All enemies, particularly the officer, were killed by our first volley in fair combat! You've got to tell that if anyone asks you, have you got that?" he shouted.

Accurate French shots killed four more British and militia. Finn and Gus cowered behind logs and saw only glimpses of the French and warriors in the surrounding woods. The Colonials returned fire, but managed to hit only trees. "It is no use to try defending this position. They are picking us off one by one. What was he thinking about, setting up his defenses this way?" one of the lieutenants asked.

Washington's men were pinned down and soon started to run low on ammunition. At the palisade, a soldier rose up slightly to look behind him. "I need ammo! I am out of ammunition! Bring me more ammunition!" He barked and was hit simultaneously in both sides of the head, which exploded in a bloody mist. His headless body fell on the log palisade.

It started to rain heavily, which made firing difficult, since the soldiers had to cover their muskets from the rain. The British soldiers endured, frustrated, shaking their clenched fists at the sky. Their wet muskets wouldn't fire.

"There is only one way. We must charge them! Fix bayonets!" Captain McKay ordered and stood up on the palisade, sword in his hand. He led the company of two hundred men in a desperate charge, and fifty of them were killed crossing the open field. The attack was repulsed, and the survivors started to retreat back across the open field stumbling, over their fallen comrades, and another forty men were shot in the back and killed.

Finn pointed out to Gus that there were muskets lying on the ground. They picked them up and took positions on the palisades as the British fled across the field back towards the encampment. Enemy warriors pursued the fleeing survivors, right up to the hastily erected log barricades. Gus joined the militia and rushed to fight them, and Finn joined him to defend the fortifications, desperately using their muskets like clubs.

The French lieutenant leading the pursuing warriors was captured, and as the French casualties began to grow the rest of them withdrew back to the woods and the action abated. Captain Villiers reluctantly reassessed the situation and realized that if he pressed his attack on, the troops would suffer terrible casualties.

Inside the fort, Mingo warriors burst into George

Washington's tent, demanding the French prisoner so they could torture and kill him.

"Get out of here! He is under my supervision! Do not touch him!" George Washington stood in front of them with the prisoner behind his back. The warriors hesitated but ultimately left grumbling.

"Hey, you who look like a rusty bullet hole. What did they want?" the French prisoner asked.

"What did they want, you ask? To burn you, for crying out loud, to eat you, and to smoke you in their pipes! But don't worry, monsieur, they will take another prisoner from me over my dead body."

Captain Villiers' messenger arrived carrying a white flag to open surrender negotiations, and looking around the fort he saw many bodies and wounded men. Washington assessed the situation and agreed to meet with Captain Villiers.

Finn and Gus stood on the palisades as George Washington and Captain McKay walked out to meet Captain Villiers in the middle of the open meadow. It was pouring rain and lightning erupted in various parts of the sky. The men stared at each other.

"In exchange for surrendering the fort, pock face, you and your men will be permitted to withdraw back to Wills Creek," Captain Villiers said.

"That is agreeable," Washington replied.

"You look like a man who likes to play with himself." Captain Villiers pointed at George Washington, "That's not all, and the surrender document shall state that Washington is responsible for the assassination of my brother Jumonville!"

Washington's eyes grew wide when he heard him. "I resent that! The death of the officer was not a murder, but unfortunate death of a combatant in a mere border skirmish! Our action was not even an act of war! I have witnesses!" Washington protested, waving his arms.

"You're just a yellow belly whore sloshing a bedpost!" Captain Villiers yelled at him, "I will not let this be forgotten! I shall take this to my superiors! You will pay for what you did to my brother! But for now, in order to avoid any further bloodletting I shall let you withdraw." He spat on George Washington's boots and turned away.

The bereft British began to retreat. Marching out of the fort, Finn and Gus turned to look just as the French threw torches on the palisades and began to burn the fort down to the ground.

§    §    §

Captain Villiers rode full gallop to Fort Quebec to report to Governor Vaudreuil. He rushed in and entering the Governor's office sensed the tension in the room. Governor Marquis de Vaudreuil received Captain Villiers with his field commanders, General Montcalm and General Francois-Marie de Lignery. The Governor had just been having an argument with his new commander who had recently arrived from Europe, but they eased off when the captain entered the office.

General Montcalm was in his usual mood, which was both derisive and arrogant. He did not understand why, having received many medals for his valor and faithful service in Europe, the King had ordered him to New France as the commander of all French forces in North America. He considered his new assignment to the Nouvelle-France as an unfair punishment for something he did not do. He thought that perhaps he had failed in court politics, and as a result, he was sent away.

Being a professional soldier, he did not complain, and to redeem his honor he intended to carry out his duty to the hilt, and would not let anyone stand on his way. Problems started when General Montcalm insisted on the European style of warfare with orderly ranks marching in closed formations to the beating of drums and signal flags, while Canadian-born Governor Vaudreuil favored hit-and-run tactics that had worked so well in the Canadian forests previously. General Montcalm was vainglorious and contemptuous of Canadian authorities, and their preference for guerrilla tactics. He developed open hostility to Governor Vaudreuil and considered the entire administration corrupt.

Captain Villiers reported, "Milord, I have grave news. There was a confrontation with the British bandits on the meadows in the Ohio Valley. It looked like a scene in an abattoir! They murdered my brother in cold blood! I demand my rights to seek revenge, sir!"

The senior officers were shocked and provoked. They stood up simultaneously in anger.

"*Scandaleux!*" General Montcalm shouted.

"The British are monsters en masse!" General Lignery exclaimed.

Governor Vaudreuil remained seated behind his desk. He played with his quill and looked at Captain Villiers calmly. "The British bastards have made their first move, and their first mistake! We have superior materiel! Tell us exactly what happened, Captain Villiers," he said and leaned over his desk.

Captain Villiers stepped forward anxiously. "Cowardly British and their local *poseur* attacked our patrol while they were sleeping," he said, "I engaged the British and inflicted heavy casualties on them *par excellence*! We were getting low on ammunition, and in order to save us from any further losses, I decided to let them leave for the time being. Good news is that, in our *coup de main,* the fort was burned down. There are no marks of any British clique in the area."

"That Washington is a military provocateur! You did the right thing, Captain Villiers. Gentlemen, this means war! Send out reconnaissance immediately!" Governor Vaudreuil declared, and General Montcalm and General Lignery nodded with zest. A clerk in a corner took notes attentively.

"We shall win the war!" General Montcalm shouted, "I will assemble the regulars immediately and shall sabotage all British efforts! I will personally lead the French tour de force!"

Governor Vaudreuil slammed his fist on the table so hard that dishes hopped and goblets fell over spilling wine over maps.

"Not so fast, sir, sit down, I am in charge here!" he exclaimed, and drew a deep breath. "*Touché,* we shall gather our local allies, and we will smash them with all our might!" Governor Vaudreuil made his position clear, leaning over maps on the table. He moved his hand, sweeping over Europe and North America, and made a fist.

His face twisted in anger, and the corner of his mouth was twitching. "We have been attacked without provocation! From this day on, our cause will be just! We will witness an invisible hand at work. This grand competition has been enduring for decades now! It started in Europe, and now it is our turn for glory in America! This war is all about commerce, gentlemen! This is the new hundred year's war, and it is fought for profit!"

General Montcalm had to hold himself in check walking around the table. He was furious at the colonial governor who dared to address him like that in front of other officers. He felt insulted, especially as it happened in front of a low-ranking captain.

Captain Villiers shifted his weight in anticipation and cracked his knuckles, watching the two quarrelling officers.

General Montcalm hissed between his teeth, "We French wish only to trade in peace in America without being constantly harassed by the raving mad British dogs!" He lowered his voice. "It is repugnant to see the insatiable greed of the British nation of bourgeois and witness how they harness the power of their state to their grand ambition of pillaging America! This is the conflict between the two European states that has transformed commercial enterprises into imperial war. Trade is real power! It is indeed the invisible hand, and now it is wielding a French sword!"

"You are right, my Lord! They made a terrible mistake in challenging us!" General Lignery shouted, hoping to steer the conversation to matters at hand. He was worried about the rift between the two commanders, but he didn't know what to do about it.

"We shall use our formidable local allies and launch

guerrilla warfare on them! They know the terrain and enemy locations, and they have been deadly effective before," Governor Vaudreuil said, his face flushed with excitement. He spread out new maps on the table and looked sternly at each officer separately. Then pointing at the maps, he told them his plans.

"Pay attention, gentlemen, and I will gain untold glory! We will initiate a three-pronged war on the British swine. First, I want to extend our defenses at Fort Carillon on Lake Champlain, here. Second, I plan to seize and destroy Fort Oswego on Lake Ontario, here. And third, we will mount an attack against Fort William Henry, here!"

"Excellent! We will begin preparing orders immediately!"

General Lignery motioned a clerk to get going. The clerk bowed and departed hastily. Governor Vaudreuil and General Lignery were overjoyed, but General Montcalm remained silent, and as the goblets were raised in a toast, he remained indignantly aloof. His scheme to gain glory and obtain orders sending him back to the royal court in Paris was not going according to plan.

§    §    §

In the Allegheny Mountains, Finn and Gus arrived back in the remote military camp nestled in the pristine green foothills. Almost immediately the quartermaster handed them picks and shovels, and ordered them to report for road building duty in General Braddock's expedition.

Road construction was a slow and tedious process as surveyors tried to create a navigable route through the forested hills and around the mountains. Loggers felled trees and stumps had to be cleared using oxen. Laborers with pickaxes, shovels, and wheelbarrows carried load after load of silt and sand to fill potholes. Caravans of pack mules, each led by a bell mare with a bell strapped about her neck, loaded with supplies, made their daily trek without stopping. The muleteers were busy because the packs were constantly shifting position due to the lumpy roads and uneven terrain, and often became entirely unbalanced and fell to the ground.

The road work site stretched for nearly a mile and resembled more of a long labor camp than work in progress. The stench around the worksite was terrible because most of the laborers suffered from dysentery and diarrhea, and almost a third of the men were out of action at any given time. What they were able to finish was nothing more than a dirt track that turned to mud in the winter and baked rock hard in the summer. Ultimately it took several months for them to advance a few meager miles.

On his first payday, Gus bought a wide waist belt made of leather, silk, and metal with embroidered lions' tails and legs. He took from his pocket an ivory figurine with an incised face, an accentuated pubic triangle and the legs tapered below the knees. Finn hadn't seen anything like it before. Kissing the figurine, Gus crossed his arms with his hands in a fist while praying at the sky, and then put the doll inside a hidden pouch concealed by a flap in his new belt.

Four weeks later, Finn and Gus were pushing a stuck wagon loaded with supplies on the road construction trail one rainy day. Finn tried to raise the wheel from the mud.

"You sure find my troubles for me!" Gus said, pushing

the wagon and looking at Finn from the corner of his eye.

"You know what, Gus, I have been thinking," Finn replied. "Here in this new country we are set to blaze a path to pursue our own life. Anyways, we should not accept the haughty beliefs of others nor should we find fault with those who lag behind us. What do you think?"

Gus stopped pushing the wagon. "For the sake of truth, my father used to tell me that no matter what happens in life it is my part to keep myself good pure and brilliant like an emerald and whatever the life throws at me, I must remain like that emerald and keep my colors true!"

The British army moved forward, slowly but steadily, inch by inch through the upland forests and meadows. Washington, being sick, traveled on a pallet in one of the wagons. When he needed fresh air he traded the wagon bed for a saddle horse, and rode up to meet General Braddock.

"Sir, any plan to march troops to the fort through a narrow valley is dangerous because of the possibility of an ambush," he warned the general, who hardly paid any attention to him.

"Nonsense, major," General Braddock said and turned to Daniel Boone, "Mr. Boone, send flankers out on each side of the column. To flush out any ambushers, you shall lead scouts roving ahead of our advance guard. Now, move out!" General Braddock ordered.

Despite his young age, on his first expedition Daniel Boone led a group of hunters and trappers. "Yes sir!" he replied and rushed off running, followed by his men.

"This road shall bear my name for posterity!" General Braddock boasted. The column started moving, cavalry and infantry followed carts and wagons drawn by oxen, but General Braddock was not satisfied.

"We are moving too slowly," he said. "The wagons and the sick stragglers at the rear are slowing us down. We need to divide our forces into two battalions. Colonel Dunbar, take one thousand men, including the sick and the wagons and stay behind. I will take twelve hundred of our best men and push forward with the workmen to improve the road for you to follow us," General Braddock ordered.

Colonel Dunbar, Braddock's chief of staff, placed some maps on the wagon. "Yes sir!" he said, and motioned his aide to bring him a horse.

"We must avoid an ambuscade and cross the river at the upper ford. We will then proceed down the far bank, and cross back to the right side again at the lower ford." General Braddock pointed at the river valley ahead. The officers watched as the troops marched by in formation. The drummers and the fifers played "The Grenadiers March."

Washington nodded along with the tune. "That, sir, is the most splendid sight I have ever seen!"

General Braddock, complacent in his saddle, rose up on the stirrups and looked around. "The mission is going according to the plan, finally!"

Daniel Boone arrived to report to General Braddock just as Colonel Cage's horsemen pulled up. "Sir, the French are in sight! You can see that there go their scouts running along the trail ahead, having discovered Cage's advance party!"

"Captain Cage, take your company and engage the enemy! Boone, you will provide flank security," General

Braddock ordered. Daniel Boone ran back to his men, and saw Finn and Gus still pushing the wagon. He pointed at them. "You two, follow me!" Boone said.

Captain Cage commanded his men. "I see the enemy clearly. Troops! Aim! Keep steady, fire!"

On the other side of the long meadow, French Captain Beaujeau wore a red leather decorative collar at his throat. He saw the British in the distance, and to his horror some of the warriors turned to run away. "You damned deserters! Fucking squaws! Get back here and fight!" he barked.

Captain Beaujeau turned back towards the meadow, and at the same moment, the British opened fire. He was hit and killed in his tracks. The men next to him were sprayed with a red, bloody mist and fragments of his skull.

The Abenaki warriors were led by Colonel Louis, who started to mock the Ottawa warriors running away from the fight. "You are afraid of a fight, like squaws! No guts, no glory!" He aimed and fired his musket, killing a British trooper. He took a knife from his belt and threw it at another trooper, skewering his throat.

Captain Dumas took command, ordering his column to split in two. The French disappeared from sight into the dense woods on both sides of the ravine, which the forested road followed. From the hiding places behind stumps and the boles of trees, the French and the warriors poured accurate rifle fire into scarlet-coated British ranks in the open.

The British advanced, with drums and young fifers in the front. A bullet went right through a flute being played by one of the boys, and it exploded in the young fifer's face. The British column was cut to shreds by the raking fire.

"Where is the enemy? We can't see the enemy!" a soldier shouted, his eyes wide in shock.

Captain Cage tried to keep his men under control. "Hold the line! Fire in the direction of muzzle flashes and smoke! There they are, now shoot!"

Daniel Boone waved his hands at General Braddock frantically. "Sir, you must order men into the woods! They are fully exposed out here! Take cover in the woods!"

"Nonsense, we fight like the British soldiers in an orderly fashion, not like cowards hiding behind the trees! Hold the lines!" General Braddock said, still adamant.

Daniel Boone ran back to his colonial scouts. "Well, we're not going to fight and give up our lives like the British! Men, take cover in the wood line!" he yelled to Finn and Gus, who followed the militiamen rushing from the track into the woods. They fired their muskets and killed several French and warriors. In disarray, the British ranks were shooting randomly. In panic, the troops fired at anything that moved, and hit some of the colonials. Militiamen shook their fists at the British.

Captain Cage pointed out targets to his troops. "Identify your targets! Aim your fire!" He barked out orders as small cannon were brought up, but they were useless and did little damage to the enemy scattered in the thick forest behind solid oak trees. The cannonballs hit the trees, dropping to the ground without doing the harm that had been intended.

Washington saw strategic high ground among the trees. He rushed to General Braddock. "Sir, I can take that hillock on the right with my militia! We can outflank them by surprise through the thickets!"

General Braddock spurned him because he was just a militiaman and instead turned to another officer of the regular British army. "Colonel Burton, seize that height with a full frontal assault!"

Colonel Burton took off in front of his men, charging across the open field. His body shuddered as it was torn to shreds with the fusillade of bullets hitting him all at once, and the charge collapsed. The British troops started following the colonials running for the woods.

A group of soldiers retreated in panic. "We would fight if we could only see anybody to fight with!"

General Braddock hit retreating troops with the flat of his sword. "Get back in line, cowards! Back in formation! Stand and fight!"

"Colonel Cage, rally the advance guard! Why is it still in a column? Line the troops up in three ranks just like it reads in the field manual, bringing the maximum number of muskets to bear on the enemy!" General Braddock shouted over the musket and cannon fire.

The bugler sounded a retreat and the advance guard started disorderly retreat. Men were bleeding, and their clothing torn when they came through the lines of the main body. A trooper in a panic shouted, "The French and injuns have infiltrated the baggage train to cut off our retreat!"

Cavalry, infantry, and artillerymen all turned and ran, leaving the cannons. The workmen followed them in terror in the mad dash for the rear. General Braddock was barking orders when a bullet went right through his horse's neck, and the horse collapsed under him, and the general took two bullets, in his arm and his chest. George Washington was riding next to the general and bullets hit his horse in the head, and tore his clothing, but Washington was not even scratched.

Daniel Boone, Finn, and Gus were running in between the two horses changing fighting positions, and dodged the horses falling down neighing in agony, blood spurting from wounds. Washington got up and saw General Braddock wounded and lying on the ground, coughing bloody froth.

Washington realized the general was out of action, and he took command. "I am in charge now! Retreat in an orderly fashion! Soldiers, carry the general to safety! Mohicans, take the front line and hold the enemy! Mr. Boone, get your men and provide supporting fire from the woods!"

Daniel Boone, Finn, and Gus took positions in a clump of trees and fired on the French. They repelled an attack and forced the French back to take cover. Bullets hit trees around them, showering them with splinters.

"Change positions!" Boone shouted to them.

Finn yelled, "Gus, we move and fire in turns! You shoot when I move! I shoot when you move!" They changed positions taking turns and fired again. They repelled another attack but were soon forced to withdraw by the enemy superior in numbers. Withering fire continued unabated from the trees, killing more British. Disorderly retreat continued, and men did not pay attention to George Washington any longer.

The soldiers ran in terror. "Retreat! Fall back!" Shouts echoed in the woods as the terrified troops ran until they finally had to stop, out of breath and too tired to run anymore. Soldiers in tattered uniforms, bleeding and exhausted, staggered into the rear camp where General Braddock lay on a carriage, mortally wounded.

The dying general was bemused. "I'll be damned! Colonials I once despised fared much better than my accursed redcoats. We now know how to deal with the French another time," he said, coughing more blood. Then he died.

Washington declared, "The general is dead. Fool that he was, this was an utter disaster! We were easy targets for the snipers when we could have taken cover in the woods. Almost all the officers were killed, and most of the thirteen hundred men are killed or wounded!"

Colonel Dunbar made an assessment of wagons and troops around them. "We have no other choice but to burn our wagons, destroy the cannon and mortars, ammunition and any food we have left. Speed is of the essence now, and we cannot take them with us. We must try to reach Fort Cumberland!"

"Aw, fuck this for a game of soldiers!" Daniel Boone yelled and threw down his musket. "I have had enough of this piss poor leadership! I am going to unharness the militiamen and return to my father's farm. It's every man for himself, and the devil take the hindmost!" Boone looked around for a way to escape. When the route was clear, he disappeared in the woods.

George Washington was disgusted, looking at General Braddock's body. He motioned to Finn and Gus. "First, you shall bury him in the middle of his own bloody road in an unmarked grave. Then run the wagons back and forth over the grave so nobody will find it!"

Finn and Gus took shovels and hit them in the dirt in the middle of the road. Finn looked around to make sure no one else heard him. "Gus, I think Mr. Boone was right," he said, "When we finish burying the general we will take our leave through the woods and find our way to more peaceful place. Just you and me will go and no one else, alright?"

"Sounds good to me, real good," Gus replied.

After burying General Braddock, they quickly gathered some supplies from the wagons and walked off into the woods. They carried blankets slung over their shoulders, a sash with necessary provisions, and a musket and powder bag.

§    §    §

Finn and Gus walked swiftly on the trail all day long. The path was narrow and soft underfoot, and often wet as it wound in and out of the forest to the edge of a swamp. They were wary of all noises and kept a sharp lookout for anything unusual, because they most especially did not want to run into the French or the British. Gus looked at Finn, who strolled beside him without saying anything. "We did well back there. You know how to fight," he said.

"Yes, we did do well," Finn replied. "I had to learn to fight when I was young. But I did not come here to fight a war that is not mine. We must find work so we can earn enough money to go back to England. Or at least I want to. I don't know about you," Finn said.

"We are like brothers now. I think we should stick together, because that way we have a better chance than just a lonesome dick," Gus replied.

Finn stopped, pushed his cap back and leaned on his musket to think about it for a moment. "You think so?" He said, "Let's see, I'm a poor orphan outsider with nowhere to go and you're a poor, black devil in a white man's puritan world. And you reckon together we have a chance? I'd call you an incurable optimist," he replied, and grasped his musket firmly moving on.

Early in the evening, the sun was setting behind the mountains as they arrived in Bethlehem, a small settlement on the bank of a creek. Farmer John Burnside was loading his cart with supplies, and seeing the two strangers, he offered his help. As Finn and Gus walked by, Burnside said to them, "I can tell you two are lost, or at least tired and hungry. Help me to load these supplies, and maybe I can return the favor?"

Finn was a little surprised, and glanced around to make sure the man had been speaking to them. "We need help, but sir, why would you help us, total strangers?"

"We are Moravian. We do so out of a personal commitment to help the poor and needy," John Burnside said. Finn and Gus agreed with his philosophy, and helped him to load the wagon. John Burnside took the mule by the bridles and headed out of the village, gesturing to Finn and Gus to follow him.

"We certainly appreciate your help. I don't want to sound impudent, but may I ask who Moravians are?" Finn asked.

John Burnside smiled and replied, "To make a long story short, a small group of our brethren we call the Hidden Seed, because they were an illegal, underground group, established a new village called Herrnhut in Germany. The town grew steadily from its inception, and soon founded missions with the Mohegan in the British colony of New York. The colonial government based at Poughkeepsie expelled our people and a small community arrived here in Bethlehem to build a mission in the colony of Pennsylvania."

"Why were you expelled from New York?" Gus asked.

"Main reason behind it was the locals' hostility to the Mohegan," Burnside told them. "You see, our support of the Mohegan led to rumors of us being concealed Jesuits, trying to unite the Mohegan with France. We are missionaries, and the converted Mohegan people have formed the first native Christian fellowship," John Burnside said, and walking on he told them about the hundred-year continuous prayer, and the Daily Watchwords, a selection of Old Testament texts.

Finn listened patiently and shook his head. "Back in the old country I saw too many expulsions. Why can't people just be left alone to live in peace?"

John Burnside glanced at him and replied, "We are not the only ones. The Great Expulsion of Acadians has started up north."

"It is all about loyalty, or perceived lack of it," Gus commented.

Finn thought of something and walked closer to John Burnside, "I've meant to ask you something, sir. Tell me, I saw some Prussian soldiers. What are they doing here?"

"Prussians, or do you mean the Hessians?" John Burnside spat on the ground. "They are bloody mercenaries for the British. Landgrave Frederick II of Hesse-Kassel hired out thousands of conscripted subjects as auxiliaries to Great Britain to support his lavish palace. People hate the Hessians because the men are conscripts, debtors, or the victims of impressment and some are petty criminals."

The road was in terrible condition, full of potholes. The wagon wheel sank in a swallow hole, which was full of mud covered with soil. Finn strained his back pushing the wagon too hard. Then they were moving again as the road went past a small cemetery. Gus looked over the stone wall nervously, and made some frantic hand gestures driving off evil spirits. Inside the cemetery, there were head stones covered with moss. There was a building by the gate. Finn saw how Gus had become a little nervous and asked, "Maybe we should say a prayer. Who lives in that house?" he asked.

"I'm not so sure any prayer would help in this case," Gus said.

John Burnside replied, "We call the graveyard the God's acre and bodies waiting for burial are kept in the building. There is also the Healing Spring, but it's behind the house; you can't see it from here." Finn and Gus glanced at each other, confounded.

"What is God's acre?" Finn asked bewildered.

"Did you say House of the Dead?" Gus wondered aloud and pulled out the figurine from his belt pouch.

"What is Healing Spring?" Finn was amazed, fidgeting with his moose necklace. "I don't know what I am or what I will ever be, but I have to find a way to redeem myself. Would the spring help me?" he asked so quietly that Burnside did not hear him.

Seeing their confusion, Burnside was somewhat amused. "The bodies of our dead are first kept in the house, and then are sown as seed in God's acre, as in a field, so that they can rise again when Jesus Christ returns to the world. The water from the spring holds healing powers," he said.

Gus pressed the palms of his hands together and blew air between his thumbs in a pagan hand gesture and Finn kept glancing over his shoulder as the passed the cemetery. They arrived at Burnside's farm late in the evening. He showed them to the barn, while he led the mule into the stall. He turned to Finn and showed him an empty stall next to it.

"You can stay here. It's not much, but better than staying out in the woods. We will serve breakfast at dawn. You can pay by working tomorrow," he said, and took some blankets from a shelf and handed them to Gus.

"Much obliged," Finn thanked him.

"Tomorrow we celebrate the Love Feast. A sweetened bun and coffee is served to the congregation in the pews by the Dieners, our elders. You are welcome to attend if you wish," Burnside said, and left for the house. Finn and Gus gathered piles of hay to make makeshift beds. Finn pulled his boots off, rubbed his back a bit, and grimaced, lying down for the night.

"Oh yes, much better now," Gus said stretching out.

Finn let out a loud sigh with his arm slung over his forehead. "Love feast, Mr. Burnside said. Now that sounds pretty tasty. I could use a feast of love... with my dear Rosie..." he said, closing his eyes. Soon they were both snoring.

In the middle of the night, Finn bolted up, alert. In the dark, he reached over to shake Gus. "Gus, get up, I heard something," Finn urged whispering, listening to muffled barking of a dog from inside the house. Finn stood up and looked outside through a small crack in the wall. He hushed to Gus to be quiet and motioned him to get his musket seeing some armed figures surrounding the house in the darkness. A war party of five Lenape warriors had attacked the farm. Quietly, Finn reached over to get his musket hanging on the wall, grabbed it and opened the door cautiously. From the house muskets were fired, and muzzle flashes lighted the yard briefly. Two attacking warriors fell down. Finn took careful aim and fired hitting one warrior in the back of the head, killing him.

"There! Can you see them?" Gus yelled and fired.

More shots were fired from the house, and muzzle flashes momentarily lighted the yard again, and a fourth warrior fell dead. The fifth one ran away across the field. John Burnside appeared on the porch with a growling and barking black shaggy dog the size of a pony. He let it loose, and the giant dog leaped and chased after the fleeing warrior. Finn and Gus reloaded and walked out. "That was close. Does this happen often?" Finn asked Burnside.

The men stopped to listen in shock when they heard a dreadful shriek and painful scream from the darkness. The voice was silenced by a brutal growling. Burnside reloaded a second musket and said, "Attacks like this are becoming more common across the whole frontier than last year. Somebody is instigating and provoking the attacks. It means war."

Finn and Gus glanced at each other. "We witnessed how the war got started just a little while ago. So I guess there is no quiet place to be found anywhere?" Gus asked, and looked at Finn.

Finn was exceedingly troubled. "I'm afraid it will be difficult to try to stay out of it. And we have nowhere else to go. Perhaps we could take to the sea again, but where would that lead us? Maybe we should seek advice from some sage man? But where can we find someone like that?" He paced back and forth.

Gus picked up a steelyard and examined it. "We ain't dead yet! We should not depend on others for ideas how to live our lives. They never have any fresh ones when you need them most," he said, and placed the steelyard on the wall.

Finn thought about it for a moment. "Fuck it, man! There's not much we can actually do. Colonies it is then, and besides, this place can't be all that dreadful. I heard there are thirteen of them. Surely we can find one where we can fit in," Finn replied.

John Burnside glanced at them and said, "I appreciate your help, you two. But be aware that the Hessians are camped only few miles from here and will probably be here shortly. They must have heard the shooting and will come to investigate," he warned them.

Finn looked troubled and fumbled with his moose head necklace. He glanced at Gus and turned back to Burnside. "We must take our leave, Mr. Burnside," he said.

"I understand and ask no questions," John Burnside replied. "As far as I'm concerned, you were never here. Just remember this: In essentials, unity; in nonessentials, liberty; and in all things, love."

Finn thought about Burnside's words for a while, and nodding in agreement held out his hand. "Well said, sir, although I must say perhaps somewhat too optimistic, in a funny way."

Gus glanced at him. "Nothing's funny about peace, love and understanding."

Finn and Gus hoisted their packs on their shoulders and picked up their muskets. They departed hastily behind the barn. As soon as the two wanderers disappeared around the corner into the woods, a Hessian mounted patrol rode into the yard, and John Burnside turned to greet them.

On a small hill in the distance, Finn and Gus stopped to look back at the farm. They saw Burnside talk to the horsemen who were led by Johan Kopf. Finn was still, but Gus noticed his stiff upper lip becoming less so, as they disappeared into the bushes.

§     §     §

Finn and Gus followed a trail around a hillside above a ferny stream, dipping in and out of the boundary between the birch trees and pines. They headed upstream, climbing gradually along the hillside and crossing a couple of small gullies before descending towards the stream again. They marched briskly all morning until Finn allowed them to rest in the woods. They set up a small camp, and shared some beef jerky and drank from a water canteen.

"Who is he?" Gus asked.

"Who do you mean?" Finn asked back.

"I am talking about the Hessian officer, who is wearing the cap with skull and crossbones emblem. He is after you, but you thought I wouldn't notice, didn't you?" Gus replied and looked at him out of the corner of his eyes.

"I don't know his name," Finn said and threw down a stick he was playing with, "He killed my family. I met him on the field of battle and fought him with all my might. He seems to be indestructible and I just can't figure out how he keeps tracking me so easily," Finn answered and fiddled with his necklace.

Gus said, "What you leave behind, you may find in front of you. Such is life. Maybe you should confront him once and for all."

"I just don't know! I'd be glad to fight him but, fuck me running sideways, the bastard seems to be almost immortal! It's like God's playing a joke on me or something. Anyways, then I met Rosie and started thinking there's more to life than revenge."

Finn stared back at Gus apprehensively and bit his lower lip. He took some stones and threw them at a tree. The stones bounced off the trunk without leaving a mark.

"I'm not scared of him," he said, "I just don't know how to defeat him, that's all." Finn picked up a branch and tried to snap it. He tried several times, but it would not break. "Encounters with evil should not rattle your composure," Gus replied, "They are merely a part of our earthly existence."

"No shit, duh!" Finn exclaimed. "But what is evil? Something I have seen too many times as it is," he said and finally managed to crack the branch in two against his knee.

They started off again, and after crossing over the creek on a fallen tree trunk, the track soon met the Delaware River, flowing quietly over the easy plateau and on to the head of Delaware Bay. In the afternoon, Finn and Gus arrived in the small town of New Sweden. The townspeople were excited to see troops being mustered. One of the village men shouted in the square. "The war is inevitable now! The young Washington sure did it this time!"

Benjamin Franklin and John Morton were engaged in lively discussion on the town square. Franklin turned back and forth, agitated, waving his hands and said, "Th-this whole dreaded Jumonville Affair is a v-volley fired by this young V-Virginian in the backwoods of America that s-set the whole world on f-fire!"

John Morton solemnly paced back and forth, hands behind him, being reflective. "Yes, I am afraid the whole episode is going to cause much despair for our beloved Columbia," he said.

As Finn and Gus were passing by the men, Finn overheard them and stopped, amazed. He approached the two men and asked, "Excuse me sir, gratifying to meet you again. I heard you gentlemen talk about Columbia. My dear mother, bless her soul, sent me to find her. I have come a long way. Where can I find this Lady Columbia?"

The men stopped talking and turned to greet him. John Morton was pleasantly surprised. "Well, we meet again, young man," he replied, "But maybe you have misunderstood your mother. Let me explain. These are His Majesty's colonies. Some people call them America after Americus Vespucius, but there are many others who would prefer to call them Columbia, the Land of Columbus."

Finn looked back at him first bewildered, and then delighted. He embraced Gus and slapped him so hard on the shoulder that Gus winced. "Now I understand what my mother sent me to find, a new homeland!" Finn exclaimed, pounding his palm of his hand with a fist. "Gus, I'd say Columbia is a lovely name for our beloved new land! I don't care for this Americus! What do you think?" Finn said, making some dancing moves. John Morton laughed and applauded Finn, who felt a tremendous weight was lifted from his heart now that he understood what his mother had meant.

Troops marched by in formation, and young boys ran around the soldiers, playfully chasing each other. Finn remembered the events in London that seemed to be so far away now. He held his head as the memories of Joseph Banks rushed through his mind. He wondered if he was doing alright or if he was alive at all.

A woman walked up to meet John Morton, and he introduced her as his newly wedded wife. "There you are, dear. Gentlemen, may I introduce you to my wife, Ann Justis." She politely smiled at the men who took turns greeting her.

John Morton continued, "I encourage you to seek enlistment with the Royal Americans being formed in New Hampshire for the Hudson Valley campaign. They need people who think of the deep forests as a friend, not something to be afraid of."

"That is where we need to go, right, Gus? But what do they want us for?" Finn asked.

John Morton leaned closer to him and lowering his voice said, "Some may call this imprudent and restless gossip, but I tell you this, young man. First we must secure our liberty, and then we shall build a nation where anyone can rise to become the head of state!"

"Will they accept other than British? Do they accept former slaves?" Gus asked.

Benjamin Franklin glanced around cautiously and

motioned them to come closer. He tapped the side of his nose with his index finger. "Yes, t-they do, all able bodied men are needed now," he said, "I hear that t-there is this one p-particular Captain Rogers, and I think you s-should find him. I hear he is highly unorthodox in many d-different ways with his irregulars. He fights like the M-Mohawks."

# Chapter 4

IT WAS A BEAUTIFUL LATE SUMMER day in the colonial farming community, and the fields were ready for harvesting. There was a chill in the air, the leaves whirled in a gentle breeze and hickory smelling smoke from a fire lingered in vegetation. On the road, Finn sniffed at the air.

"Can you smell that? Is that scent of wood smoke? Look, it's so lovely here, so beautiful! This is almost like the fields of Elysia!" Finn said, in high spirits, although he did not know why. Gusts of wind made whirling blurry patterns in fields of hay, barley, and wheat.

There was a sudden swirl of dust and chaff, and then the country became more focused. There were workers in the fields, reapers who cut grain and hay with scythes and sickles. Young women and boys followed the reapers, raking and stacking the harvest. Older women brought lunch baskets with jugs of water and whiskey to the field at noon, and the workers gathered around the harvest wagon. A woodcutter and a milkmaid joined them. Nearby at the watering place, a young drover herded a few heads of cattle.

A spaniel ran spiritedly around a young woman sitting on a cast iron bench under a corpulent maple tree, and she playfully stroked the gundog. A man in a hunting coat carrying a shotgun courted her. Close by there were sheaves of corn, and the workers saw the young men walking along the dirt road that wound through the fields.

During their journey, Gus taught Finn some more about reading and writing, and even some basic arithmetic, and Finn felt extremely happy about it. The weather was warm and Finn stopped to take off his fringed leather jacket, and threw it over his shoulder.

"Yes, I smell it too," Gus replied, sniffing the air, "There must be a village or town near. There are workers in the fields. Maybe we should take a shortcut through those woods." He pointed to a trail. They hopped over a ditch and followed the path leading into the woods, walking deeper into the forest.

"I'm not sure if we are going in the right direction," Finn said, and stopped to listen, cupping his hand behind his ear, "Wait, I think I hear running water. Let's go this way," he said, pointing with his musket. They turned towards the waterfall and Finn led the way through blackberry thickets along fencerows, when suddenly they popped out to an opening and met three Iroquois women. The oldest looking appeared to be in her twenties and was nearest to Finn and Gus, building a wigwam. She wore a garment made from two skins that hung from the shoulders by means of straps, and a fringed wraparound skirt and Finn noticed her tanned, slender legs, and her moccasins.

Two younger women were grinding corn with paddles and a tree stump made into a tool for grinding. Stripped from the waist up, they were bare-breasted, and both of them wore long necklaces made of wampum with an abalone shell as a choker and white and purple beads of clamshell hanging between their breasts. Finn gulped nervously looking at the women, mesmerized. He felt a little shy all of a sudden, and he whistled and pretended not to stare at their bouncing naked breasts as they worked their paddles up and down. One of the women noticed that he was gaping at them. She smiled and turned to her friend, saying something. She widened her eyes in a dumb look mimicking Finn. They both looked at him and laughed.

The women's split deerskin skirts revealed tanned and lean, slender thighs that left Finn gulping. Their long, flowing hair dressed with bear fat was braided to keep it shining and smooth. Sweat from their labors made their bodies glisten and Finn admired their painted bodies and faces with red, white and blue applied to the forehead and cheeks.

A deerskin mantle hung on a branch, and some gardening hoes and fishing gear leaned against an oak tree. The oldest woman noticed the two men staring at them but did not seem to be alarmed and continued to work on her wigwam. The frame was made of saplings, and she prepared the poles made of sassafras, and the hoops of sweet birch.

"Pardon us for intruding like this," Gus said, taking his hat in his hand approaching her.

"My mother told me to greet all ladies I meet in a friendly manner! My name is Finn, and this is Gustavus," Finn said, and using his elbows, he eagerly rushed in front of Gus. The woman turned her head, and Finn noticed colorful earrings and beaded strands.

"You may call me Spotted Bear," she answered in English.

"Are you from here?" Finn asked.

Spotted Bear rolled her eyes and looked at Gus. "Is your friend always that bright? I am Mohegan, of the Wolf People, if you must know," she replied, and rolling her large, beautiful eyes grinned to the younger women.

"Why are you called Spotted Bear?" Finn asked, pulling his stomach in and holding his breath smiled at her. She rolled her eyes again amused by his act and lashed the last hoops onto the wigwam poles.

Spotted Bear shook her head slightly. "The name was given to me by my tribe mother. Sometimes the sun shines on the grizzly, and there's a blot right behind his neck on upper spine that looks like a snowy smudge." She drove short poles into the ground that supported the sleeping platform frame inside the wigwam.

"May I ask why are you building this hut in the woods?" Finn asked, and leaned his hand against the tree trunk.

"You don't know much about women, do you? I am building it for my moon time," she said. Looking at Gus, Finn shrugged his shoulders. He did not know what she was talking about.

"We would like to talk to your leader. Is there a chief?" Gus asked.

"Which one do you want to talk to?"

"What do you mean?" Finn asked.

"There is a leader who leads the hunt," she said, "There would be a war chief. There are leaders who make sure that the village is protected. We have a lot of different leaders at one time. I am a chief."

"You're a chief? But you are a woman!" Finn exclaimed.

Spotted Bear turned to him and put her hands on her hips. "So what if I am a woman," she looked at him sternly, "People listen to women who are strong. Women are leaders in the sense that they make things happen within the tribe. It's the women who are able to provide the tribe. They are the matriarchs who build the earth lodges, they own the earth lodges, they plant the crops, and till the soil, they care for the crops, and then they own the crops," she said as she continued her work.

Gus said amicably, "It is getting chilly, and if you don't mind, we will build a brush shelter."

Spotted Bear walked over to a pile of bark sheets and cattail mats, and laid some stones aside, which were helping to weigh down the bark sheets. Picking up a finely woven bulrush mat, she measured Finn and Gus with her eyes for a moment.

"Be my guest, but you better stay away from my wigwam and my sisters," she said looking at Finn sternly in the eyes.

Finn and Gus built a lean-to against a big tree some distance from the women. They made a small fire, and Finn kept glancing over to the wigwam.

"Don't even think about it. Remember what the woman said," Gus reminded Finn, poking him in the arm.

Finn was tired. Stretching out on the ground, he soon dozed off. During the night, he had a dream: Spotted Bear came to him to seek his help, let her garment fall on the ground and kneeling before him naked, chastely entered under his covers. She caressed his chest and begged him to spare her from marrying a man, and said she would rather kill herself than being forced into this marriage. She whispered in his ear and promised him sex if he would just challenge the man to a duel.

The next morning Finn and Gus took off early while the Mohegan women were still sleeping. The track passed through endless forest with cedar and towering oak trees. The dense canopy blocked most of the sunlight. At the far end of the track, the old trees soared into the sky high above. Finn was still all worked up about the women.

"I am telling you, Gus! Remember those Mohawk women? They are mighty pretty to look at! We must have arrived in paradise!" Finn said, and playfully punched Gus in the arm.

Gus rolled his eyes. "I am beginning to wonder if you really ever think of anything else," he said.

It was late afternoon when Finn and Gus came to a road and met a gray man accompanied by two wenches. They asked the man for directions, and if he happened to know anyone who could give them some advice. The man told them to seek out a man local people called the hermit in the local Tangier Tavern.

"If it is advice that you look for, seek out Mr. Fronto," he said.

"No worries, you will recognize him right away. It is said that a white dove descends on Good Friday each year, filling the Hermit's cup," one of the wenches said mysteriously.

Tangier Tavern was a roadhouse built with logs and stones, and had a thatched roof with straw. Inside, they met the tavern keeper, Mary Brazier. Her friends and customers included William Plunkett, Thomas Dowden, and

John Jones, rough-looking men transported from Britain. They drank a toast in memory of their friend.

"Here's to Dick Turpin!" They raised their tankards and hit them together, spilling beer.

Finn and Gus saw an older man sitting at one of the tables with two wenches. He had one on his lap and the other sat beside him, his arm wrapped around her shoulders. He was just finishing his story as the young men approached his table.

The man, perhaps in his fifties, wore a baggy, wrinkled shirt with some necklaces made of beads, clam shells and coins around his neck. He had rolled up the sleeves of his worn-out overcoat that had perhaps been brown or some other color, but had turned ashen gray from long hard use. He wore a slightly torn wide brimmed hat and carried a leather bag, a powder horn, and a canteen slung around his shoulder. Finn noticed he was armed with a hunting knife and had a musket leaning against the wall right next to him.

The man was just having fun with the women. "Now that I have completed this story, you lovely ladies will have to speak sweet words to me!" he said, and the women giggled and snuggled closer. Finn and Gus looked around the place and approached his table.

Finn was in a jokey mood and he decided to start with a gag. "Ladies, compared to the wild beauties in the woods I saw just last night, you have noses like a dog's! I admire your braided eyebrows, and your lovely hairy faces!" he said.

The two women gasped in anger and started to unleash a fuming rebuttal at Finn. However, the man intervened and cut them off and looked at Finn. "Obviously, subtlety is not your forte," the man said. "Are you looking for love or mortal combat, young man? Maybe your pride allows you to sit in my humble table and take a little break from your brazen quest?"

"Sir, we seek advice so please, can you help us?" Finn asked him.

"First, mind your language, young man!" The man said loudly, "Always go to the aid of ladies, damsels, gentlewomen, and widows! Mind you that I have these ladies held hostage and brought here for the sheer pleasure!"

Mary Brazier, a burly woman in a loose corset, blushed and beaming smugly brought drinks and placed them on the table. She folded her arms in front of her and looked at the man straight-faced. "Great pleasure you say, my pretty arse!" She quipped to Finn and Gus, "Hermit here was abandoned by his king, and 'Love' was his battle cry. He fought, but eventually was struck with an arrow during a duel with a heathen, pierced through his balls, its iron arrowhead remaining embedded in his flesh!" Mary Brazier drummed her fingers against her arm, expecting the man to return an insult. The two women giggled.

"Woman, there was a time in my swashbuckling youth when I matched wits with the Vagabond King himself! I found love in his court, and when I saved his city in the hour between the dog and the wolf, he made me the constable for a week!"

Without replying, Mary Brazier turned and lifted her skirt a little. She made a teasing, pushing motion at the man with her behind, and walked away.

"What say you, sir, will you help us?" Finn asked.

The older man took a long drink, smacked his lips and wiped off a foamy mustache with his sleeves. He belched, and the other woman patted his stomach. "It would be my pleasure to give you advice, but first you must tell me how you found your way here."

Gus replied, "We met this old gentleman with two ladies who graciously advised us to seek you, and he told us the way."

The man nodded. "He must have been old Gabe, who just left my company. I am Marcus Fronto, at your service. But that's not what I asked," he said, looking at them curiously.

Gus moved his chair to get closer, and leaned on the table. "You seem to be at ease with strangers like us approaching you."

Fronto chuckled. "Ha! Bears and moose might scare me more than people!" he said, laughing. "I know how to deal with a man; wild beasts I am not so sure of. I don't want to brag, but my heart has always been stout before a fight. As a young man, I fought for love maybe too many times, and all I could think of was the female form."

One of the men at the bar, a rough character wearing a shoulder rig over his black coat, walked over to their table and set himself down without invitation. He motioned Brazier to bring drinks to everyone.

"You don't mind if I join you, do you? I am William Plunkett, but you can call me Bill," he said.

"What is it that you do, Mr. Plunkett?" Gus asked as Mary Brazier walked up to the table carrying tankards. William Plunkett pinched her, and she slapped his hand away.

William Plunkett said, "Gentlemen, there were originally four classic professions: Sex, Law, Religion, and War.
Later, man invented Currency, and it became possible to
profess Money. I am, we are, in the business of making
money!"

"And how exactly do you make money?" Gus asked,
cautiously observing at William Plunkett.

"I have the honor of having worked with the gentleman
highwayman, Mr. James McLane himself. He is my master
and my mentor. Do I need to add more?" William Plunkett
replied, and waved to his two friends who walked over to
join them and brought two chairs with them. The men's
clothes were dirty and torn. Both of them had scarred
hands and unshaven weather-beaten rough skin.

"Here are my charming associates, Mr. Dowden and
Mr. Jones," William Plunkett said.

"Did you say McLane? That name rings a bell," Fronto
commented.

"He is well-known for his brave exploits in certain
parts of England!" Jones declared.

William Plunkett leaned closer with squinted eyes
and said, "Aye, one night, Horace Walpole himself was
returning from Holland House by moonlight, about
ten o'clock. I and Mr. McLane decided to stop him in
Hyde Park and ask for directions, when Mr. McLane's
gun went off, by accident of course. The bullet grazed
the skin under Walpole's eye, and leaving nasty marks
in his face it stunned him silly. The bullet went through
the roof of the chariot, and if he had sat one inch nearer
to the left side, it might have gone clean through his
head."

"Walpole, that fat old Squire of Norfolk!" Fronto laughed.

"Now he had the distinctive quality of a man of parts," Dowden agreed, "Who, under different circumstances, would have rewarded a ribbon round his shoulders than a rope around his neck!"

"Curse on the man who owes his greatness to his country's ruin!" Jones said.

During the evening, Mary Brazier kept serving whiskey and the party became louder. The women danced for the men in front of a large fireplace, teasingly opening their corsets and flashing their breasts. Dowden and Jones cheered them on and raising loud toasts, spilled beer on themselves.

Finn bragged about his exploits. Gus listened to him for a while and then told him to shut up. Finn slapped his left shoulder with his right hand. "It ain't bragging because I've done it! I can back it up! Anyways, some people pray, some people brag. What's the difference?" he asked, looking at Gus.

"I pray, but nobody can enslave me! That's the difference!" Gus said.

"Then why do you keep tormenting yourself?" Fronto asked and raised his arm in a toast. "My motto is, six times faithful and six times loyal!" he declared, and Finn noticed a tattoo on his arm depicting a stork and some strange looking letters.

William Plunkett kept bragging. "One particularly profitable year we made a handsome profit in thousands of guineas!"

"What did you do with all the money?" Finn asked.

"We frittered the loot away on fine clothes, gambling, whiskey, and whores, and the rest we spent foolishly!" William Plunkett replied, and all three men busted out laughing.

One of the women moved next to Plunkett's side. Mary Brazier brought new tankards and waited to be paid. None of the men made a motion to pay her, so she shifted her weight on another leg saying, "Hey, who of you fancy gentlemen are going to pay? In King, we trust, and all others pay cash!"

Finn tossed his empty wallet on the table. He stared at it and scratched his head. "Anyways, I don't know how it happened again, but we are out of money, Gus."

William Plunkett slapped him on the shoulder, squeezing it hard. "Where there's a will there's a way! I happen to know that there is a stagecoach expected to arrive in few hours' time carrying certain wealthy individuals with a large purse. Now do we have the will? I am sure we could convince them to give some of their wealth to us!" He nodded at the men, and looked at them probingly.

Drunk out of their minds, Finn, Gus, and Fronto decided to join them. "So be it! Seize the road, trusting as little as possible in the future, which is unknowable, and instead scale back our hopes to a brief moment ahead, and drink the wine while we can!" Fronto declared, standing up staggering on his feet. He shouted to the tavern keeper behind the bar. "Mary, we shall return in three shakes of a lamb's tail!"

"Let's get the fuck out of here!" Gus declared, and tried to get up. The rowdy group left the pub jostling and staggering on their feet.

§   §   §

There was a steep bend in the road where it went around a large rock. Torches threw flickering shadows on the trees encircling the men gathering around William Plunkett behind the rock.

"The coach has to slow down coming around this rock," Plunkett said. He drew out his pistol. "We will be waiting on the other side. When they arrive, Finn, you keep an eye on the driver, while we collect the loot."

"Sounds like a plan," Fronto agreed with a hiccup. The men arranged themselves in a semicircle to wait and soon they heard hooves and harnesses squeaking in the dark coming towards them. The horses neighed, and when the stagecoach arrived around the rock, William Plunkett jumped in the middle of the road. He grabbed the lead horse by the bridles to stop the coach. He waved his musket in his hand.

"Stand and deliver, or the devil may take you!" His shout echoed in the dark woods. The driver, an older man, pulled at the reins.

"What was that, sir? My hearing is not very good." Jones rushed to his side, waving his musket only inches from the driver's face.

"He said *your money or your life*, old man!" Jones shouted. The driver dropped the reins and raised both hands. He stared horrified at the pistol barrel. Two disgruntled male passengers dressed in long frock coats stepped out of the coach, followed by a lady in a silk dress with decorative stitching and linen trimming. She looked horrified and cowered behind the men's backs. Seeing the woman, William Plunkett decided on a gallant act.

"Let me introduce myself!" He bowed. "If you are a man, look to your wallet but if you are a woman, look to your heart. Much havoc I have made of both, for all men I make to stand, and women I make to fall!"

"You are nothing but thieves and murderers, the whole lot of you!" the other passenger shouted.

Fronto stepped forward. "I admit to being a thief and a scoundrel, but I must argue that the chivalric values upheld by you are no different, sir!" He said.

"Sir, we shall take only a part of the loot from a fine gentleman such as you if your wife agrees to dance with me in the wayside," William Plunkett continued.

Dowden waved his pistol, wide-eyed and tense. "Just get the money, and let's go!" he shouted, his voice shaking.

William Plunkett pulled the woman to him roughly by the hand and forced her to dance with him. She sobbed and struggled against him. Finn turned his head to look, and everybody watched the dancing couple. Jones smirked, laughed, and took a couple of steps back for a better view.

Suddenly an ear-shattering shotgun blast made everyone jump. Jones's head was blown off, and the dismayed spectators watched the headless body slowly fall to its knees and slump over into the ditch. The driver held a sawed-off double-barreled shotgun with its smoking barrels in his hands. "Surrender, you maggots!" he yelled, and fumbled for new rounds from his pocket.

Dowden raised and fired his pistol, but being still too drunk he narrowly missed the driver, sending his thrummed cap flying. The driver reloaded quickly and fired on Dowden who dove on the ground, and the shot narrowly missed him. William Plunkett pushed the woman violently against the coach. Hitting her head hard, she let out a sigh, and tumbled unconscious to the ground.

William Plunkett took aim at the driver, but one of the passengers hit his hand with a cane. The pistol went off, the shot hitting the other passenger in the head, who slammed against the couch and the dead man toppled on top of the woman. William Plunkett bounded behind the rock, and Dowden glanced around in panic, saw the driver reloading again, and followed Plunkett.

"Finn, Fronto! We better get out of here!" Gus yelled.

Finn and Fronto ran after Gus who made a mad dash into the dark forest. They followed William Plunkett running through the dense woods, branches whipping their faces until they had to stop to take a breath. Catching up with them, Finn ran face first into an enormous spider web.

"What happened to your mentor, Mr. McLane, anyway?" Finn asked, tearing the spider web off his face.

Breathing heavily, William Plunkett reloaded his musket and spat on the ground. "He stood trial at the Old Bailey, which became a fashionable society affair, and he supposedly received nearly three thousand guests while imprisoned at Newgate. But in the end, he was convicted and hanged at Tyburn."

"Hanged? The man you said taught you everything about highway robbery was hanged! We followed you on this wretched enterprise! Gus and Fronto, get ready for a two hundred mile race!" Finn said, shocked.

Fronto was totally out of breath and gasped for air. "No need for running anywhere, we shall hide in the woods and wait until all is clear," he said and leaned against a tree.

"This is where we part company. We have to break into smaller groups," William Plunkett said, leading Dowden into the woods. They disappeared into the night.

"What are we going to do now? We didn't even get the loot. All that for nothing," Finn said, looking despondent.

Gus was sitting down holding his head in his hands. "That was a sobering experience. Because why? Stupid is as stupid does. I will never drink again!"

Fronto poured some water from his canteen on a hand-kerchief and wiped his face and hands. "Finn, perhaps you should be grateful that the driver was superior to you in vigilance," he said. "You did not have to pay the high price for the loot. In exchange for it, you would have become a thief, and faithless to boot."

"Could be, but we can only hope that the Hessians don't find us now! They will hang us on the spot!" Finn exclaimed.

Gus collected himself and stood up, determined. "I think we better go deeper into the woods and make camp for the time being. That or the gallows, we have no other choice!"

"That is a good idea," Fronto replied. "We must get as much distance as possible between us, and this accursed place. Come to think of it, I think Fort Edward is two score leagues from here as the crow flies. It is a remote army garrison and small frontier town. It's a terrific place to hide. We should aim that way," Fronto said, pointing in the garrison's direction.

Finn felt overwhelmed by the events, and he slumped down to sit on a tree stump. "Fuck this shit, man! I can't even rob a coach properly! I have been nearly killed many times, and I have been accosted, assaulted, and kidnapped! Everything I have loved has been robbed from me, my family, my dear Rosie, everything! What the fuck is the meaning of all this? Life sucks so badly," he said, depressed.

Fronto gazed at Finn, contemplating. "Courage, whippersnapper! Live according to nature, that's the meaning," he said, waiting to see Finn's reaction.

Finn glared back at him, surprised. "What, we should live like some fucking animals in the woods or something? Are you out of your fucking mind, old man?" He stood up.

Fronto let out a sight, pointing eastward with his staff. "Well, seems like I got your attention, but I can tell we have a long way ahead of us," he said.

§     §     §

In Philadelphia, a group of British officers arrived in the governor's mansion. British commanders Jeffrey Amherst, James Wolfe, James Abercrombie, and Edward Boscawen gathered in the library to make new plans for the upcoming campaigns.

One colonial officer stood alone, isolated from the others. George Washington had heard about the meetings and used his connections to receive an invitation as an advisor. He was slightly offended by the pudgy fragrance of the powdered wigs, starched lace, and rich fragrance in the room, but he saw an opportunity seek a commission in the regular British Army. General Amherst, well-dressed in white trousers and a red uniform jacket with lace and blue flaps edged with gold, held a crystal goblet in his hand, while a servant poured him sherry. Washington noticed the blue velvet badge of the British Order of the Garter that the general was wearing on his uniform.

"Gentlemen, we must form an aggressive plan of operations!" General Amherst said. "This could easily be a French attempt to divide the American colonies by an invasion from Quebec! It is my noble duty to stop them!"

Servants brought in an extravagant feast on large platters laden with stuffed quails, roasted piglets, lobsters and smoked Acadian whitefish, and placed them on a large side table along the wall. General Amherst smacked his lips and motioned the others toward the banquet. The senior officers gathered around the table and nodded approvingly, and the servants carrying plates picked courses for them as the officers pointed at what they wanted. Other servants filled crystal goblets with fine wine.

Washington knew there was a serious shortage of food in the colonies, and he was appalled by the self-indulgence as the aristocrats gobbled up more and more food and drink. He coughed into his hand and forced himself not say anything. Junior officers carried rolls of maps and spread them out on a large table.

General Abercrombie, pale-faced and bleary eyed and his hand shaking from drinking large quantities of wine, looked at the maps while eating. "We must start by fortifying Fort Oswego," he said.

Admiral Boscawen, in his blue naval uniform coat, assented. "I agree, and that should be followed by a swift attack on Fort Louisburg and Fort Niagara. I have His Majesty's Ships *Dunkirk*, *Defiance*, and *Torbay* ready for action. If necessary, I can always press jolly old *Hope* back into service too! For now, I have leased her to some old friends of mine for some profitable business enterprises, you know," he said.

General Wolfe disagreed with the naval officer. "No offense, Admiral, but this is land warfare," he said, "I would rather not entrust the land assault to a naval commander. I would suggest capturing Fort St. Frederic and Fort Beausejour."

While the others ate, Washington examined the maps and took notes. "This is a vast territory," he thought aloud, "and that many operations require considerable manpower! But more than that, we need intelligence! What are the French plans and intentions?"

The British officers discussed tactics, and they firmly believed in regular troops and conventional warfare. Being young and lower in rank, Washington stepped aside when the officers moved over to the maps on the table. General Abercrombie was adamant. "We shall convene the regular regiments in the decisive Hudson Valley campaign. The Frogs are no match to the British Army high command!" he said.

"They shall scatter in panic when they see our glorious marching formations!" General Wolfe exclaimed, and looked around extremely satisfied.

General Amherst handed his goblet to a servant, indicating he wanted more wine. He looked at the maps and rubbed his chin. "Perhaps there is an indication of facts on what Major Washington just said, the area of operations is quite extensive, and the enemy formations are largely unknown. We will require intelligence! Perhaps we should send some of these, slow witted they may be, but ever so sturdy militiamen to reconnoiter the French positions?"

General Abercrombie leaned over the map table with his hand hovering over the Hudson River Valley. Over Quebec, he made a clenched fist and said, "We may use local militia in some limited capacity, but the British Regulars are undefeated champions of the battlefield! They shall be our main fighting force! Glory will be ours!"

General Amherst faced Washington and said, "The Hudson River Valley shall be my glorious coliseum! Major Washington, tell your men that it is their duty to perform their roles in it well!"

General Abercrombie was thrilled. "That is right! The men who are destined to die in the arena on this campaign shall die for the established order! We will gain fame and glory! The King will surely reward us!"

Admiral Boscawen pointed out a naval route from England to America. "More troops are on their way, as well. The famous 42nd Royal Highlanders regiment called the Black Watch is among them," he said.

General Wolfe nodded arrogantly to Washington and turned to the other officers. "Yes, I saw some of the Black Watch in action, and they were hugely impressive indeed. But gentlemen, let's be fair to our colonial subjects," he continued. "He may be right after all, and the 60th Royal American regiment is marching north at this moment. Maybe we can use this local talent somewhere, no matter how vague that expertise may be!" The officers laughed and eagerly joined General Amherst raising a toast. "Gentlemen, we shall drink to the King! To the glory of the Kingdom of Great Britain! We shall drink to our fame and fortune!"

§   §   §

Emerging from a sea of deep green, Finn, Gus, and Fronto traveled in single file along a trail in old growth forest. Tree ferns crowded the track as it wound between rotting stumps and fallen trees, and descended to some mossy cascades on a small creek. Suddenly, they heard a commotion ahead and in a flash disappeared from sight in the undergrowth. They huddled together not knowing what lay ahead, but decided to reconnoiter what was happening. Approaching the edge of the woods cautiously they kept hiding in the bushes and saw a road ahead.

Finn moved closer to watch the road and saw a long line of sullen soldiers marching among an army supply convoy, with carts, pack mules, and wagons pulled by oxen. Finn heard whiplashes and the officer's horses neighed. Farmers along the road sold spoiled mutton, salted fish, and bread to the militia troops. Mohawk warriors followed the wagon train.

The retreating soldiers robbed farmers and pushed them into the bushes at gunpoint. One civilian, sitting on the ground crying into his chest, wailed that soldiers had stolen his reins, breeches, and a pocket watch, but none of the other civilians paid him any attention because they were too busy trying to save themselves.

The wagons were filled with rations, hay, ammunition, and wounded men in bloody bandages. A doctor emptied a stinking slop bucket full of half-rotten meat and intestines for the hogs following the wagon. The walking wounded, who suffered from dysentery and diarrhea, had cut the seats of their pants off for easier evacuation. The stench was terrible.

"You know, sometimes it is best to hide in plain sight! It would be a perfect way to hide, if we joined the convoy as laborers," Fronto said. Finn and Gus glanced at each other. Gus frowned, and Finn nodded, delighted.

"That is a bold move, old man. I like it!" Finn said. "Come on, let's go!"

Crouching, they ran to the wagons without being noticed. They stood up, and pulling at their pants buttons, acted as if they had just stopped to relieve themselves, and gotten back in line. Troops on the road did not pay any attention to them. Finn, Gus, and Fronto blended in with the laborers, and Finn gave a thumbs-up as the file kept moving along the winding forest road, which was solidly packed with woods on both sides. They overheard from the marching men that it was Captain John Bradstreet's supply convoy returning from the failed Fort Oswego expedition.

On one side of the road, Captain Bradstreet was discussing his mission with his lieutenants. "I had my explicit orders. My first duties in the spring were to escort a convoy of bateaux to reinforce the garrison at Oswego. Once there, I was to take the necessary men and supplies, and attack Fort Frontenac," he said.

The young lieutenant agreed, "We had mustered fifteen hundred bateaux and three thousand men for the attack on Fort Frontenac, but only a hundred and fifty of them were regulars."

Captain Bradstreet replied, "Since French pressure on Oswego is now growing, we must direct our efforts to keeping the supply line between Oswego and Albany open. This is our prime objective at this time!"

The lieutenant remained optimistic and enthusiastic. "We have been successful in cutting off the French supply lines to Fort Duquesne, and thus have set up its fall, but we have also managed to break the long line of communications between the St. Lawrence and Ohio Rivers."

"We had difficulties in reaching Fort Oswego, however. Once we got there, the incomplete fortifications made it obvious that an offensive against Fort Frontenac was impossible," Captain Bradstreet said.

On the road, Finn, Gus, and Fronto noticed how the French prisoners succumbed to severe dysentery. Usually, when they had fallen, they made an effort to rise. They heard the groans and strangled breathing as the fallen tried to get up, and then lay lifelessly where they collapsed. Finn observed that the British troops paid no attention to the fallen enemy soldiers, and wondered why. The explanation was not long in coming. There was the sharp and regular crackle of pistol and musket fire behind them.

Skulking along, a hundred yards behind their contingent, came a Hessian cleanup squad. As members of the squad stooped over each huddled form, there was an orange flash in the darkness and followed by the sharp crack of rifles echoing through the woods. The Hessians left the bodies where they lay as a warning, so that other stragglers coming later would see them.

The road became more crowded as they marched into a clearing. Finn stopped in his tracks when he saw what was happening ahead of them. There, a mounted Hessian patrol led by Johan Kopf had apprehended the surviving French and Canadian soldiers and observed the troops by the roadside as they marched by. A runt in a raggedy uniform, a toothless imbecile young private hoping to be rewarded, claimed he had information regarding looters.

Johan Kopf admired the surrounding hillsides and sylvan ridges reaching out to the distance, and he thought that perhaps being sent to this new world was, after all, a stroke of luck. He sensed that this place was full of opportunities, ripe for the taking. He stood in the road with his hand on his sword and recalled the days he arrived in America. After his arrival in New York, the British army found accommodations for Johan Kopf in a lodging house run by a merchant in Albany. However, when he arrived in town, the first thing he wanted was a drink. Looking for a tavern, he wandered into a shadowy alley with flickering torches behind the *Stadt Huys*, a three-story building with the lower story built of stone and used as a jail. He chuckled as he remembered meeting a pretty Chinese girl who smiled at him and said, "Hessian numbah one! Two shilling, mistah, and me luv you long time!" She led him to top floor of a Chinese boarding house that had an opium den downstairs. Kopf quickly settled in and thought life could not get any better than that.

On the forested road, the French prisoners stood silently in rows as Johan Kopf in his green uniform watched them with contempt, his hand on his sword hilt. The Hessian troops behind him were nothing like the toothy, bespectacled runts he faced. The Hessian soldiers were cruel, stalwart, and tall in their blue uniforms. Johan Kopf took a canteen, poured the water into a horse's nosebag, and then threw down the canteen. "I could make some of this hinterland into my own domain. I'd say, to each man his own!" He looked about, appraising the rugged forested ridges.

Without a warning, Kopf grabbed one the French soldiers by the shoulder and savagely shoved him down on his knees. Kopf's face twisted in a severe, arrogant smile as he hovered over the poor man on the ground. Then he quipped to the Hessians that he should add a little spice to the entertainment.

Johan Kopf turned back to the kneeling man. "I suspect you are tired, you rabid dog?" he said snarling contemptuously. "Do you want sleep? Just lie down on the road, and you'll get a lovely long sleep!" He pulled his sword out of its scabbard and raised it high over his head, holding it with both hands. The young private near him quickly skipped to one side.

Finn could not understand at first what was happening. Then Johan Kopf's face distorted in utter hatred as he swung his sword. The sun flashed on the sword, Finn heard a swish and a chopping thud, like a cleaver going through beef, and the prisoner's head seemed to jump off its shoulders. It hit the ground in front of troops and rolled over and over between the lines of prisoners. The body fell forward, blood gushing out in long bursts as the heart continued to pump for a few seconds more, during which, at each beat, there was another crimson gush. The gray dust turned into crimson mud. The runt who had pointed out the looters to Kopf scrambled forward and began to gather the headless soldier's possessions.

As they got closer to the execution site, Finn realized that he could not move anywhere without exposing himself. Gus nodded reassuringly to Finn and urged him to loosen the pistol in his belt. Fronto marched on with his head held high and his eyes fixed straight ahead. Finn smeared his face with mud and pulled his hood over his head.

The oxen team driver used a whip. "Duke, giddy up! Doc, giddy up!" The oxen bellowed, and straining the wagon harness, pulled the heavy load on.

Finn was extremely nervous as they came nearer to Johan Kopf and his men. Johan Kopf mounted his horse and moved closer to the road so that he could see inside the wagons. Finn lowered his head and pretending he was pushing the wagon, keeping the wagon in between himself and Johan Kopf. At the same moment Finn was about to pass him, Johan Kopf moved to another position on the same side. They were now only a few feet apart.

The wagon became stuck in a pothole, and the wagoner jumped off, threw his hat on the ground, and swore in a thick Scottish accent. "Bullshit! This is such a load of crap!"

Finn turned his back and contracted his shoulders. He saw glimpses of shadowy figures and a large, shaggy dog like a wolf running in the woods parallel to the convoy. He did not see as Johan Kopf was going to get someone to throw the body away, and not realizing it was Finn, pointed his riding whip at him. "Hey, you, right there!" Kopf shouted to Finn, just as a group of men dressed in green uniforms, buckskin leggings, and moccasins ran out of the forest. They rushed to report to Captain Bradstreet, waving and pointing ahead. Johan Kopf forgot all about the body, and leading his horse, went to investigate what was happening. Finn looked at Gus. He wiped his brow and let out a sigh.

The French and Abenaki warriors led by Colonel Louis launched a well-planned and fierce attack on the convoy. Their ambush initiated perfectly, a salvo of gunfire erupted all at once, and Finn saw how the dark trees around them were lighted with muzzle flashes. A Scottish wagoner and some men riding on the wagons fell off dead. Soldiers marching alongside the road were killed in a fusillade of bullets and arrows, and a militiaman next to Finn was hit with an arrow right through an eye. Finn hopped on the wagon and saw shadowy figures of men running bent double, bounding and descending upon them from the woods.

Colonel Louis leaped on a mound, holding his rifle over his head. From the woods, a deafening uproar and war cries arose. Colonel Louis pointed to the lead wagon and shouted, "Cut off the lead wagon and the last one in line! The rest of them will be trapped in between!"

The French soldiers and warriors fired on the run at the British and colonial militia, inflicting horrendous casualties on them. The British scurried to take cover behind the wagons and the road was soon littered with bodies in puddles of blood. In the heavy smoke, Finn, Gus, and Fronto leaped under the wagon for protection. Bullets hit the wagon, and they were showered with wood splinters. A soldier was hit in the head and he fell at Finn's feet, with the top of his head gone and brains pouring out.

"This is not what I bargained for!" Gus yelled just as two arrows slammed into the wagon next to them.

"We did it again, looks like we jumped from a frying pan straight into the fire!" Fronto yelled.

A bullet hit a bull in the neck and it bellowed in pain, froth flying out of its nostrils. More bullets hit the wagons around them, and next to them, an arrow hit a soldier through his throat.

"We'll have a better chance in the woods!" Finn barked. "I don't think we are going be missed if we get the hell out of here!" Crawling, crouching, and dodging in a shower of arrows and bullets hitting the ground around them, Finn, Gus, and Fronto escaped from the kill zone into the woods.

There was a whopping commotion in the bush behind them, and few shots echoed sharply in the woods. Then a spooky dreadful silence fell over the forest, leaving only an unpleasant taste of burned black powder in the air. Finn could hear his heart beating and felt a drop of sweat run down his neck tickling his back. Suddenly, a horse rushed through the bushes and almost trampled them. Frantic Captain Bradstreet led a motley collection of panicked soldiers in bloody and torn uniforms out from the ambuscade.

"The wagon train is lost! Form small groups and head for Albany!" Captain Bradstreet shouted hysterically and galloped off into the woods. Finn, Gus, and Fronto followed, running through the forest as fast as they could, without looking back.

§     §     §

They avoided contact with other stragglers and groups of retreating soldiers, and stopped only for a brief sleep at night without making a fire. They slept sitting up, back to back, with all their gear on and taking turns on guard. They continued before daybreak following a trail they discovered that left the creek where flat, dark lumps of granite stood out in the cobbles of the creek bed, carried down from the slopes above.

Traversing the western side of a steep valley, they followed a path along the edge of the creek where it gave way to birch forest on the higher hillside. The path climbed gently onto the valley slope and wound upstream around the hillside, dipping in and out of small gullies high above a river. After it crossed a saddle the track ascended onto a broad plateau. Standing on the very brink of the plateau summit, Finn stood in awe as he looked across the amphitheater of the Hudson River, with the varied textures and colors of the immense forests spread out below.

Gus and Fronto stopped to take a breath when they climbed up to the plateau. "So, how long have you known Finn, if I may ask?" Fronto asked Gus.

"On the ship on the way here he tried to fight me first and then bought me free, and he used last of his money for doing that. I can't explain that, but I owe him!" Gus said.

"The boy is more than the sum of all things he is. He has his hands full, learning to live with himself!" Fronto said, and slapped his neck and looked at his bloody fingers. "These damned mosquitos are so big that they stand flat-footed and I'll warrant that they could breed a turkey!"

Standing on the high cliff, Finn saw gleaming lakes to the north and appreciated the vast American wilderness. It was the frontier, and the void between two invading European monarchies. In the distance to the north of the lake, he saw smoke rising to the sky, apparently from a French fortress, designed to defend the area north from any British advance into Canada. Between the two belligerents laid the twenty-six-mile-long lake and to the southeast of the lake he saw other smoke rising from Fort Edward on the Hudson River.

Finn admired the breathtaking scenery and inhaled sharply in approval, as he thought that it was the most beautiful country he had ever seen. The river reminded him of an enormous dark blue snake, its slithering and wet body crawling through sinking soft green, tall grass. The ranges of the mountain wilderness ran south from the plateau like the fingers of an outstretched hand. He stood there, silently marveling at the spectacular river valley below, and his thoughts were flooded with memories. He remembered his friends Machel, Canut and Evert from the home village, and he looked around surprised, as he was sure he heard their voices calling to him, *Earn it.*

Gus slapped Finn on the shoulder, and they followed Fronto down the track along a steep forest ridge, then over a rocky spur and across a small saddle and down to the Hudson River. Following the embankment, they searched a way to get across, and much to their satisfaction, discovered a ferry landing. They saw the ferry on the other side of the river on its way back towards them.

Finn's feet were sore as he sat down to wait for the ferry. He glanced unhappily at Fronto. "Two score leagues, you said. Kiss my ass, old man!" He took his boots off and rubbed his feet. "Anyway, how old are you, old man?"

"Age is merely an opinion. I am content with what I am," Fronto replied.

A young black ferryman slave arrived, dressed in a long tailcoat and tall black chimney-pot hat made of leather and a yellowish vest with dirty white shirt. Gus tossed him a coin, and he promised to take them across the river on his flat-bottomed punt.

"They call me Billy Blue!" the ferryman told them, all

smiles. "I am the master of this ferry, just like my father was before me, and my son will take over after me! I don't know much about anything else, but I know people will always want to go to the other side! Around here, the Rangers are lords in this land of fantastic danger into which you are crossing."

On the ferry, Finn spied boxes of whiskey hidden under coils of ropes and tarpaulin. Billy Blue saw Finn take notice and rushed to conceal the boxes better. He smiled over-eagerly and said, "There's nothing there to see, young sir! Not a thing at all, just a few items for some loyal customers."

They got to the other side, and as they approached Fort Edward, Finn saw a man standing in the edge of the woods wearing buckskin leggings, moccasins, green uniform tunic, and a Caubeen on his head. He had a rope slung around his shoulders and a musket in his hands. A green flash from the setting sun blinded Finn for a second and he shaded his eyes to see better, but in that instant the man had disappeared.

§    §    §

The old man in the Catskill Mountain House rubbed his temple. "I still remember that day just like it was yesterday, Henry," he said. "Tangier Tavern, what a slimy, foul smelling dugout that place was! It was built of rotten wood full of grub, and I could taste the mold spores in the air. Anyways, I kind of liked Marcus Fronto from the moment I met him. He was older than me but his eyes were clear with a sparkle and did not leave anything in the room unnoticed, and his hands were rock steady. He was overweight, but he moved with strength and agility like an athlete. His face seemed to have almost a constant expression carved on it like he was curious and amused by you, and just waiting to see what would happen next. Fronto turned out to be witty and little vainglorious with questionable morals – well, who am I to judge anyone - and he surely liked to party.

"Fronto was too smart for the period, and that made him a disestablished outcast in the society, because he recognized causes and effects other people didn't realize. He seemed to be more aware of the world than other people, which Fronto considered his greatest weakness, because it made him somewhat vain, but also lonely at the same time. Fronto still cared about people and society at large, and he considered it his duty to participate in public debates. But he knew there was little he could do to change things, which made him feel totally helpless. The only thing left for him do was try to remain optimistic about life by practicing his philosophy, which I was lucky enough to learn from him as the years went by.

"Fronto was always getting into trouble with the law, because he didn't give a damn as regular folks did who were white-lipped of the authorities, and particularly aristocrats. He always liked to tell of the time when he was young and rich and elegant - when we met he joked how he was just strikingly good looking by then. He had met a beautiful blue-eyed blonde girl named Drophina, the daughter of some wealthy merchant. He was much taken with Drophina, and she knew of his reputation of wealth and fame from her father Boethius, who was hoping for the match and had seen to that. Anyways, when she laid her eyes on his rough looks, she burst into tears! Fronto adored Drophina, but seeing her plight couldn't bring him to cause her any grief, so he decided not to marry her. Instead, with prudence and sagacity, Fronto succeeded in arranging her marriage to another successful and handsome young man from a good family. But alas! Drophina's new groom was jealous of Fronto's influence with her, and he accused the faithful pilgrim of having managed his master's finances badly. He then incited her father Boethius to request accounts for the expenses, which Fronto did in acutely certain terms.

"I can imagine clearly how Fronto, being umbrageous at such pretension, replied to Boethius saying 'Sir, I have served you a long time, and brought you from low to high estate, and for this, through false counsel of this man, you are ungrateful. I came to your court a poor pilgrim, and since lived modestly on your bounty. Therefore, I shall relinquish all my services, and return to you all I've earned here. Just give back my mule, my staff, and knapsack as when I came.' Boethius, now regretting his own harsh and too loosely predicated claims, would not have him go, but Fronto would not stay, and he departed as he came, and no one knew where he went, until that day we met in the Tangier Tavern."

The old man fell silent for a moment, and seemed to trouble himself to recall events and people long gone. "That's when we arrived at Fort Edward on the River Hudson for the first time. The first thing I saw was the timber palisade and sharpened stakes, and rowing guards' bayonets sticking out on top. There were some log houses outside the fence and a small army encampment with sentries. Facing the fort, there was an island upstream where we had crossed it in the middle of the river with a group of log buildings, and a wooden bridge led from the fort to the island. We entered the fort through the main gate. The guards looked at us without saying anything. We walked along the main street and saw a frontier military fort and settlement in a paradise gone sour. At Fort Edward, to get rid of garbage, people fed it to livestock, threw it about the yard, or tossed it into a nearby pit. Said pits contained anything from broken pottery to rotting vegetables to human waste, making the whole fort look and smell like a giant shithole.

"Fort Edward started out as a stockade and a supply depot at a strategically vital crossing point to make a portage to Lake George. As the war continued on, a chain of forts was built along the frontier. When the French threat against Albany grew, it was decided to expand an encampment on the site to a more effective defensive position, so that was named Fort Edward.

"There was a fortified island on the Hudson River next to the fort, in order to protect it from invasion along the riverside. It was called the Rogers Island, which I... Well, I'll tell you more about that later. On the opposite shore of the Hudson, a smaller fort was also built to prevent enemy landings there. That way the river was effectively blocked and settlements downstream, including Albany, were protected from hostile incursions.

"Where soldiers went camping, followers came along with them. First arrived gunsmiths, and then came whores, thieves, black marketers, drifters, and a bunch of nobodies such as us. The fort grew steadily, and soon there were houses and farms in the vicinity. We were going to learn frightfully quickly that it was no heaven, that life at Fort Edward was exceedingly tough. Those who were crippled or feeble, ill, weak, or lazy had a hard time. There was little kindness or sympathy available, and people in need were often humiliated. I learned quickly that, in the dictionary, you find sympathy between shit and syphilis. Anyone receiving charity had to wear a ribbon around their arm at all times.

"Schools were considered a luxury and of course they were there only for learning to read and write, and that's it. There was no childhood as we know it now! The kids were just little people, like a colt is a small horse not yet fit for a full day's work, and children also were kept busy from dawn until late at night.

"Six-year-olds, if they were lucky enough, could become apprentices for a trade. Apprentices were like slaves or indentured servants, or worse. They lived in the master's house and worked long hours in exchange for learning skills. The master had complete control over the child, and often youngsters were beaten for breaking the master's rules, or just for fun. You can imagine what happened to many girls.

"The locals were suspicious of strangers like us when we arrived, because con men known as strollers traveled from town to town, cheating residents out of money and possessions. Some pretended to be learned gentlemen and then swindled money from people. Others faked disabilities or hardship to get charity. If you showed up in town with no introduction, the sheriff certainly gave you a hint: if you caused any problems he would drive you out of town! Harboring a stranger could anger people, so anyone who invited you to visit would also inform the sheriff. That way, everybody knew you were an invited guest.

"That was what our soon-to-be new home was, Fort Fucking Edward, as I started calling it later, in those days."

The old man fell silent again, lost in thought and memories. He stared straight ahead, and Henry Raymond filled his glass and continued to take notes. After a long silence, Raymond cleared his throat and said, "Go on, sir, please. Tell me more about Fort Edward."

The old man snapped out of his reverie, took a sip, and continued. "The day we arrived, there was a court in progress, and the defendant was none other than the man we were supposed to enlist with, Captain Robert Rogers. We followed the crowd into the town house. Mayor Trevor Glock and Judge Salomon Lynch sat at the table in front of the room and the defendants sat facing them on the long, uncomfortable benches.

"Mayor Glock had bought the first new printing press in the area a few months earlier and started publishing the *Colonial Statesman*, engaging in scandalous attacks on leading Loyalist politicians. Glock was also an avid gambling man, so he was closely connected among the affluent businessmen and political leaders, but he also continued to accumulate debt."

Henry Raymond raised his pen and looked like he had just thought of something. "I remember reading about Judge Lynch. Was he there when you were in Fort Edward?" he asked.

The old man smirked, then laughed softly, and shook his head, and replied, "Oh yes, Judge Lynch was there alright.

That son-of-a-bitch was a self-appointed judge who headed the irregular court in Fort Edward. He was a strong supporter of the Patriotic cause known to equip and organize groups of nationalist zealots, who systematically visited the homesteads of suspected Loyalists, and eagerly punished Loyalist supporters. The nearest proper courthouse was far away, so John Lynch decided to take matters into his own hands. He established a court and simply declared himself the Justice of the Peace, but it amounted to no more than a travesty of justice. In his court, the justice was straightforward. In his self-appointed new role, he eagerly dealt with horse thieves and other criminals and handed out just punishments. His favorite sentence to the accused usually was either thirty-nine lashes, to be strung up by the thumbs, or hung. People soon coined his form justice as being under the threat of lynching. The judge simply considered the wealthy suspects to be Loyalists, and fined thousands of pounds for a misdemeanor, but after receiving the monies only sent them to be hanged anyway.

"As I recall, his mother had died of tuberculosis when he was a young child down in Virginia. Lynch Senior was a devoted husband and loved her much, never remarried and focused on running the family plantation, growing cotton and tobacco.

"The death rate among the slaves was high despite pretty decent living conditions on the plantation, and Mr. Lynch senior treated them pretty well, all things considered. Young Salomon's capable father encouraged his slaves to have children in order to replace his losses, and he even promised the women slaves their freedom after they produced fifteen children. He knew that even after getting their freedom, the women could not leave their children and they would stay on the plantation.

"His childbearing program, as he called it, started when the girls turned thirteen, and by twenty years of age he expected the women slaves to have four or five children at least. Rumor was that being a widower he was intensely involved in making sure the program worked and got many of the slave girls pregnant himself. When Salomon grew up he eagerly followed in his father's footsteps, and lo and behold all girl slaves were expecting all the time! All was well, and the future looked positive, for a while at least.

"One year after the crops had failed again, his father got into temporary cash flow problems, but the British would not grant him any reprieve in paying his taxes. Infuriated when he heard of the new tax hikes, he got involved in a riot against the British, who quelled the riot ruthlessly, and his foreman was killed. Many of his slaves escaped from the fields into the woods, fearing for their lives. Loyalists who coveted the land saw their opportunity and bribed the British to foreclose on the plantation. In desperation, the father hanged himself and Loyalists quickly drove young Salomon out of his home.

"Salomon Lynch swore revenge on his father's body which was still warm hanging from the tree, ravens picking out its eyes, against the British and their loyalist supporters. He had heard of a secret nationalist movement up north, so he decided to steal his own horse, opened the entire remaining slave buildings to release his holdings, and headed north," the old man said. He emptied his tumbler again. Henry Raymond continued to write notes feverishly.

§   §   §

Walking through the gate, Finn, Gus and Fronto passed
the jailhouse. The fort was larger than they expected,
having a main street and several smaller alleys between the
buildings. Deputies guarded some drunkards and paupers
who owed money waiting to be questioned by the sheriff.
They noticed a whipping post on the side where criminals
waited, men and women, to be whipped on bare backs.
The cat-o'-nine tails had a number of leather tails, each
knotted at the end. At each stroke of the whip, the tails
bit into bare flesh. From twenty lashes to more than one
hundred lashes were given, and any more than forty lashes
could be fatal. The flesh on the back eventually ripped
off, causing extensive bleeding and sometimes exposing
internal organs.

Inside the menacing log building that served as the
sheriff's office and town hall, Mayor Glock sat down
behind a large desk next to the judge. Keeping his eyes on
the men in front of him, he muttered from the corner of his
mouth, "Sorry for the delay. I was out of town on business.
What happened to your earlier case, Judge Lynch?"

"He died at the hands of persons unknown. But it was
a clear act of criminalistics in social control anyway," the
judge replied expressionlessly.

At the door, Finn, Gus, and Fronto pushed through a
large crowd of rough men. Hunters, woodsmen, Mohawk
warriors, trappers, misfits, gamblers, soldiers, loggers,
and farmers had all come to see the trial. Women were
not allowed. Inside, armed men stood along the walls surrounding the few rows of long wooden benches that were

filled with even more heavily armed men glaring angrily at the judge's bench at the front. Stern men with severe expressions on the bench wore green coats and buckskin leggings and moccasins.

"I would hate to be the judge," Finn whispered to Fronto.

Fronto glanced at the heavily armed men on the benches. "I can see that the defense could argue their case very well indeed," he whispered back.

In the third row sat Archibald Senior and his son Archibald Junior, both austere-looking hunters who kept a firm grip on their muskets.

In the second row, John Stark sat with his brother William and a large furry mean wolf-dog at his feet.

In the front row sat Captain Robert Rogers with his brothers Richard, James, and John.

James Rogers was the second oldest of the four brothers, the middle child and the family mediator. He was close with his brother Richard.

Richard Rogers was also a middle child, quite often ignored by his parents. He learned early on his place in the family, and he resented his treatment but kept quiet about it. He thought that emotionally James was his only "real" brother.

John, the youngest of the brothers, was nicknamed "Tiny" by his brothers because he was the biggest of them all. He was the youngest of the family and was treated accordingly. The family jester, he was also most influenced by Robert's strong personality. He learned how to manipulate his older brothers to get his way, and sometimes even just for fun.

Then there was Robert Rogers, the oldest brother. At twenty-four years of age, he was an athletic man, charismatic, and of vigorous constitution. His face bore scars, with its weather-beaten and slightly pock-marked skin. He had a serene, full-lipped mouth, aquiline nose, and eyes like two black charcoals ablaze. Finn could sense the sheer unyielding fortitude clustered within.

Being the oldest of four brothers, Robert was their leader and accustomed to getting his way, and he was comfortable bossing them about and being domineering. He loved all of his brothers dearly, but also joked about them, saying that the only skills that were required to bring up three younger brothers were threats, extortion, and bribery. Robert Rogers was sympathetic to the Colonial cause, but because he was an outspoken and controversial figure in the community, Judge Lynch suspected he remained a Loyalist, and found a way to lay on him a counterfeiting charge.

"Will the accused stand up front and center!" Judge Lynch ordered. Robert Rogers stood up and stepped forward. He glared back at the two men.

"The court has no standing in this case," he replied.

"You are out of order, Captain!" Judge Lynch shouted.

"No sir, this whole court is out of order!" Robert Rogers replied.

Judge Lynch pointed his gavel at Robert Rogers. "Captain Rogers, you have been charged with counterfeiting. How plead you?" he demanded.

"I am not guilty!" Robert Rogers shouted, and his three brothers as well as John and William Stark and the Rangers all stood up, vehemently knocking down the bench, and applauded behind him.

"Hear, hear!" John Stark cried, in support of his close friend.

Finn did not really understand what was taking place and as he felt his stomach grumble he became more interested in how to fill his belly, and he motioned Gus and Fronto to follow him outside. He waved his hand towards the saloon across the street. A group of tough-looking rough Rangers and Mohawk warriors sat outside Silver Star Tavern smoking and drinking. Finn stopped a man to ask for directions. He was town crier John Sergeant, son of one of the first missionaries at Fort Edward. Finn pointed at the men hanging around by the tavern.

"Who are they and where have these men come from? Why have they befriended natives? I thought they were enemies?" Finn asked.

John Sergeant spat on the ground. He said, "Beware young man, those ruthless looking bastards are just that: they are brigands, misfits, and dangerous killers."

"That could be," Fronto said, "but there are times when people sleep peaceably in their beds at night only because rough men stand ready to do violence on their behalf!"

Sergeant replied, "Their leader, Captain Rogers, has been involved with a gang of counterfeiters and he stands trial as we speak. Knowing how things work around here, my bet is that the judge will throw the case out of court because of the war. They need killers to do the fighting for them."

Fronto pointed up at the tavern sign hanging above them. "I'm dying. Let's fall in and get a drink," he said, and leaped to the swinging doors to look inside. He rubbed his hands together and continued, "Silver Star Inn, where it seems people do drink well, and the beef are roasted to a turn!"

The Silver Star had a long bar to the right of the entrance with a large painted mirror on the wall depicting half-naked women in red corsets dancing on a stage. Several round tables filled the large room, and a railing divided a few tables for the gambling area. In the back, a scrawny old man in a worn-out wig pounded an old harpsichord with gusto. Wooden stairs led to the balcony and rooms for rent by the hour. The saloon was crowded with roughnecks, farmers, trappers, hunters, Rangers, soldiers and whores.

Finn smelled the roasted beef, and when he saw titanic slabs of copper brown meat being carried across the room on a serving plate, he felt his stomach grumble. He realized as he walked into the tavern that it had been a long time since he had seen that much food.

At the end of the bar, a rowdy group of Rangers in green uniforms were drinking and singing a bawdy song. "Columbo walked the dirty streets of Spain and shat in every alley! What he wanted most was to fuck the Queen in the prone position!"

Finn and Gus followed Fronto who pushed and shoved through the crowd to find an empty place at the bar. Fronto enjoyed the singing, and after getting drinks, he found a table near the Rangers. He motioned the waitress to bring food and more drink.

Fronto shouted to Finn over the noise. "Finn, listen up! They are singing about your beloved Columbia! I think we may have found our new home after all!"

The Rangers got loud and boisterous. Hopping on a

table, one of them started to lead the singing. "The queen, she waved the royal flag, Columbo waved his pecker!"

Finn looked around flabbergasted, and did not know what to think. He was shocked by the vulgar and callous demeanor of men, but at the same time, they were somehow familiar and he felt drawn to them. Then the thought occurred to him that in their green coats, they reminded Finn of Captain Lofving. One of the Rangers grabbed the waitress's ass, and she screamed, laughing. There was much other jostling and laughing, and Rangers spilled their tankards, singing, "Columbo took his whang into his hand and sang, 'Ain't that a beauty!'"

Gus shook his head in amazement. He turned to John Sergeant and cupped his ear to hear him better. "Could you tell me more about the warriors over there?" Gus asked.

John Sergeant leaned closer and shouted over the noise, "The Mohegan nation transferred its Council Fire from the Hudson to the area not far from here. Other families and groups relocated here during the turbulent years, notably, the Wappinger tribe of the Dutchess County area led by Daniel and Aaron Nimham," he said.

"I find intriguing that they are loyal to the colony. Let's get some of that beef!" Fronto shouted, and beckoned the waitress.

Finn grabbed his arm and said, "We don't have any money. How are you going to pay for it?"

Fronto fumbled with his coat. He withdrew a couple of coins from the seams and winked at Finn.

John Sergeant continued, "Far from desiring to remain neutral in the dispute between Great Britain and France, they have taken an active part on our side, enlisting their young men in our Army, while their sachems have sent belts of wampum to the Six Nations, to their brethren in New France, and to the Shawnees, on the Ohio, asking them to defend the Colonies!"

Two Rangers started a fight, but others quickly forced them to sit down and shake hands. Skimpily clad barmaids served more beer and whiskey and the Rangers started singing, bellowing at the top of their lungs again. "That dirty lecher, asshole stretcher son-of-a-bitch, Columbo!"

Fronto laughed and waved his tankard towards the singing. He took large bites of beef and grinned at Finn. "This, my young friend, is home!"

Outside, the townspeople hurried home as it got dark, and in the tavern barmaids lighted candles and oil lamps, and started a fire in the fireplace. The rowdy party went on well into the night.

§    §    §

At the break of dawn, a giant rooster crowed right above Finn's head. Jerked from his slumber, he grabbed the first thing he found and threw it at the bird — it was a bit of manure. Holding his head, he found himself on a pile of straw in a pig stall. A group of Rangers passed by and talked about making it on time for morning formation. Close by, Fronto and Gus were still snoring. Finn shook them, and Gus waved his hands to push him away. Finn found a pail of water and washed his face, then emptied it on Fronto, who woke up coughing and cursing.

Dirty-faced little children in tattered rags crawled among the livestock, looking for anything to eat. Older

children were already busy at work. Three-year-olds
gathered firewood, shucked corn, and did other simple
chores. The older children had more farm duties before
and after basic schooling, and the boys joined their fathers
to feed animals, gather vegetables, cut fire wood, make
brooms, and perform other labor just like grown-up men.
Parents did not allow girls go anywhere, and they stayed
home to help their mothers to prepare food, sew, iron, milk
cows, weed the garden, and make candles and soap.

Finn said, "Let's get the fuck out of here. I'm curious,
let's go and see what is going on at the Rogers Island."

When they crossed the river on a wooden bridge to the
Rogers Island, they saw Rangers standing in formation and
experiencing really bad hangovers. On one side, there was
a contingent of British regulars and colonial militia. Flags
flapped in the gentle breeze blowing across the field. Log
buildings were spread in regular intervals around a large
parade ground. There were troop bays, supply storage,
the commander's office, and a rudimentary mess hall. Finn
noticed that the militia manned the guard towers, and he
saw a training field in the back next to an outdoor firing
range. Sentries were located in key points along the riverbank. The camp was especially neat and orderly.

Finn, Gus, and Fronto loitered around the canteen,
not wanting to draw attention to them. Finn pretended to
examine one of the horses as Sir William Johnson stood
in front of the formation. He was a handsome man with
a strong jaw with a small dimple on his chin and had a
pale face. He wore a quilted canvas coat over his scarlet
uniform and a deer cap, and carried an ornamented rapier
with a swept hilt guard.

"The hardy character of the Rangers, and the experience acquired by their hunting excursions and intercourse with the enemy, enable them to discharge the arduous duties in which they are employed," Sir Johnson said. "Rangers are to scour the woods, and determine the strength and position of the enemy. They are to discover and prevent the effect of his ambuscades and to ambush him in their turn! Rangers will obtain knowledge of enemy movements, by making prisoners of his sentinels, who are often taken and brought away from the gates of Crown Point and Fort Carillon by these daring woodsmen. Rangers shall clear the way for the advance of the regular troops, and lastly, to engage the enemy according to his own style and with his own weapons, whenever circumstances require!"

Officers dismissed the Rangers for a quick breakfast and the men gathered around the canteen and large wooden tables.

William Johnson, an Irishman and First Baronet, was the director of Iroquois affairs for the northern colonies and commander of the Colonial militia. As a young Catholic man growing up in Ireland, William Johnston's opportunities for advancement in the British Empire were limited. Never particularly religious, Johnson had converted to Protestantism when offered an opportunity to work for his uncle in British America. He became hugely successful as a wealthy merchant, building relationships with the Iroquois tribes through trust and goodwill, and when the war broke out, the Mohawks insisted that they would honor their alliance only if Johnson were reinstated as their agent.

General Johnson was an unusually promiscuous

man who had several children with both European and
Iroquois women. Rumors circulated about his one hundred
illegitimate children. He was involved with Catherine
Heisenberg and at the same time with Elizabeth Brant,
a Mohawk woman and her younger sister, Margaret. He
was also intimate with the sisters Susannah and Elizabeth
Wormwood, and an Irish girl named Mary McGrath.
People said that his extramarital accomplishments
explained the paleness of his skin but even so, he seemed
to have no dearth of energy for his soldiering.

Although General Johnson had little military experience, he was a skilled negotiator who had to deal with six
different colonial governments. He received a commission
as Major General, and he worked closely with Captain
Robert Rogers. They both understood the natives on both
sides and realized the need for a new style of fighting in
order to win the war.

Robert Rogers and General Johnson walked by the
mess hall, conversing. Rogers raised his voice so his men
could hear him. "I agree with your excellent talk, sir, but
let me point out that if on our excursions we sometimes
differ from the usages of civilized warfare, inflicting use of
the scalping knife, the barbarity of the enemy, the terror of
retaliation, and the plight of the times must be our excuse.
We are compelled to fight upon our own terms!"

Finn and his friends were standing by the horses listening. Finn saw Bill Stark standing nearby with a large
wolf dog by his side. "These Rangers remind me of certain
very courageous men back home," Finn said. "Redcoats
being dressed too fancy and too strictly disciplined for my
taste, and all other things taken into consideration, I have

decided we want to join the Rangers! I mean, I think we should join them."

Fronto looked at him and then appraised the camp around them. "The camp looks quite professional," he said, "It seems to me that the men who played hard last night, as we witnessed, also work hard. Who was the man speaking?"

"I think he is Sir William Johnson, the superintendent of the northern colonies and commander of the Colonial militia," Gus replied.

In front of the commander's office, Captain Rogers was sitting behind his desk talking with Bill Stark and other Ranger officers. "We must destroy the French fur trade and rob it of mast timber for its navy!"

As Finn, Gus, and Fronto approached, the wolf dog growled a warning, and Bill Stark petted it.

"We came here to enlist, sir," Finn declared. "I fought with Captain Lofving against the Russians and then with Captain Campbell of the Black Watch. I know how to handle a rifle, and I know my way in the woods. My friends here have proven themselves in battle, as well. We are vigorous men for you, sir," he said.

Robert Rogers took a long inspecting look at them. He got up and stopped to face Fronto. "We do not enlist any brigands or vagabonds!"

Fronto made little clicks of disgust with his tongue. "We see that, sir, a fine group of individuals you have here," he replied, staring back at Robert Rogers without flinching. "They are a bunch of misfits who happen to fit together! I can assure you, sir, that on the other hand we are merely gentlemen of the road."

Rogers measured them closely one by one and said, "Perhaps I could use the slave, and the boy, but I'm not so sure about this chubby bastard. He has a big mouth!"

Richard Rogers looked at Finn. "I see him as a suitable prospective member of the Rangers. He's young, dumb, and full of cum! Where are you from?" he asked.

Finn straightened his back and raised his chin when he answered, "My people came from where the majestic river Neva and river Ohta meet, and run into a great lake. They had to flee when the Russians burned everything, and now have built a sizeable city there. They named it Slottburg first, and then later Petersburg."

"What's your name?"

"Finn."

"Your family name?"

"I.... I don't have one," Finn replied with a stiff upper lip.

"What shall we call him, Captain?" William Stark said.

"Shall we call him Alphabet?" Richard Rogers quipped.

"We shall call him just Finn. That is where he comes from, and that shall be his name," Robert Rogers decided.

"Thank you, sir. I will serve you well. But I encourage you to hire my friend Mr. Fronto here, as well. He may look like a brigand, but I swear he is a skilled fighter!"

Robert Rogers waved his hand in approval and returned to his papers.

§    §    §

That afternoon, John Stark led Finn, Gus, and Fronto to the supply room where they received uniforms, weapons, packs, and other equipment. The Ranger sergeant showed them to their quarters in one of the log buildings. It was a barren room furnished only with six cots and lockers, and a stove. A single window allowed some light in.

Fronto sit down on a cot, looked around the room, and said, "So this is our new castle!"

Finn changed into his new green uniform jacket and moccasins. He started inspecting the new musket he was issued. Soon a bugler sounded a call summoning everybody outside to formation so that the Ranger officers could lecture all the new arrivals.

John Stark addressed the men first. "There were great men before us, who were great fighters and taught us the way of the woods," he said. "They carried the fight to the enemy through the wilderness and earned the distinction 'Rangers.' John Endicott and John Mason crushed the Pequot tribe near Jamestown over a hundred years ago! Benjamin Church fought and destroyed Metacom and the Wampanoags during King Philip's War! These magnificent soldiers mastered the raid and ambush like no men before them. Later, John Gorham launched amphibious attacks against the Injuns and even enlisted Injuns as Rangers. His son then commanded His Majesty's First Independent Company of American Rangers."

John Rogers stepped forward and said, "Ranger John Gorman was a convincing man and being a decent gentleman he offered the Injuns a reasonable choice of death, slavery, or enlistment! Many joined him, but then later he sold hundreds who fought with Metacom into slavery abroad. A Wampanoag warrior fighting with Captain Church killed Metacom, ending the war. Life is not unequivocal and black and white. It has many shades of gray, remember that!"

"How does it feel to kill, Captain?" The question was asked by a seemingly meek, naive round-faced recruit named Fat Murray, with kinky, coarse red hair and large protruding ears. Just then, Robert Rogers arrived.

"I can tell you it feels a whole lot better than being killed!" Robert Rogers shouted. "I lived in fear and was afraid of dying, until I killed for the first time. Since then, I have slept like a baby! Now, get ready for training! As if born for the sole purpose of wielding arms, we never take a break from training, and never rest on our lazy asses just waiting for a situation requiring firearms. We practice like we fight! Each and every Ranger trains every day with all his might, as if in battle!"

On the Rogers Island, the Rangers wasted no time. Training started immediately. To begin, Robert Rogers led them on a hike. The men double-timed six miles on a fourteen-mile march and completed it in two hours and forty minutes. Finn and Gus helped Fronto, who leaned on them on the way back. He was badly out of shape and upon returning to Fort Edward he was completely exhausted.

After a short break the men practiced dressing wounds, and how to move a wounded Ranger using a fireman's carry. Everywhere they went they had to run. Mornings began with conditioning exercises that included six-mile runs before dawn. The men carried stretchers and took turns acting as the wounded while others carried their packs and weapons. The exhausted men returned to the barracks dirty, stinking, and sweaty. The Rangers started training again after a short break for a quick shit, shower and a shave, and an even quicker breakfast. Long hours turned into days, and the days blurred together so that soon Finn was not sure anymore which day of the week it was. During a fast and arduous road march, he was surprised to find new energy inside that said *keep going*. He started thinking how could he make himself even stronger.

The Rangers strung up a heavy cargo net between twenty-five-foot-tall poles and the men practiced techniques for climbing up and down the net. They climbed and scaled walls six and ten feet tall, which Robert Rogers told them was necessary training for raiding and sabotage.

The Rangers practiced tactical maneuvering, both offensive and defensive bounding over watch. It was a technique used when contact with the enemy was expected. One fire team advanced while the other team was in good position ready to fire. The key to this movement technique was the proper use of terrain. All men had to exploit all cover and concealment. They practiced moving in a single file five yards between each man, how to deploy in a hasty ambush, and how to retreat under fire. Burly Ranger sergeants held the hand-to-hand combat training in a circular pit and ended with the king of the pit competition.

The supply sergeant issued more equipment, followed by weapons maintenance and several inspections. There were bayonet drills with straw dummies as targets, knife fighting techniques, and tomahawk throwing practice. In the evenings, Finn, Gus, and Fronto returned to their squad bay dead tired, and slumped down on the bunks to sleep.

Exhausted, Gus complained to Finn. "What did you get us into? Have you been sent to torment me?"

The next day during marksmanship training, a Ranger lay in the prone position aiming his musket. The instructor placed a coin on top of the barrel and the Rangers had to learn to pull the trigger without dropping the coin. They moved on to live fire exercises led by William Stark who barked instructions, "Talk through, walk through, dry fire, blank fire, and live fire! That is the way we do it around here, because practice makes champions!"

Two British officers condescendingly watched Rangers in training. "What a waste of ammunition!" one of them sneered.

"Their practice is not very becoming for gentlemen," the other one replied. "The mighty British Army will certainly never adopt such crude tactics!" he said contemptuously.

There was a reloading demonstration. A Ranger sergeant fired his musket and reloaded in rapid succession. He fired the musket three times in less than a minute.

"That is real firepower, men! Three well-aimed shots in forty-six seconds! Well-aimed shots, remember that, and understand it! Then you must learn to do that while running through the woods! Learn that and you might even live to fight in the next encounter!" Bill Stark shouted at them. Finn, Gus, and Fronto looked at each other, impressed with the demonstration.

On their way to the firing range, Finn noticed several Mohawk scouts hurrying in and out of Robert Rogers' office, followed by some dodgy-looking individuals.

At the firing range, Lieutenant Donald MacCurdy demonstrated the three-barreled rapid-fire percussion pole cannon. "This is our secret weapon! We call it the Hog! It is a crew served rapid-fire seventy-six caliber three-barreled pole cannon! It fires either a single shot musket ball, or buckshot!" He showed the massive round projectile he was holding in his hand.

Donald MacCurdy and his assistant gunner fired the cannon three times in rapid succession, with devastating effects on the target.

"Men, we are the most effective fighting force in the world today!" MacCurdy shouted. He was so excited that his hands shook. The Rangers cheered and yelled.

Robert Rogers stormed in with the other Ranger officers. He started kicking and punching and throwing men out to the field towards their gear and packs. "Fall in for forced road march! I pity you, so I will start you off easy! Get ready for a twelve-mile road march with a basic fighting load to be completed in three hours!"

A long line of Rangers disappeared around the bend in the road and into the dark forest, and Robert Rogers' shout echoed in the woods: "March or die!"

§    §    §

Early one morning Finn was fetching a flour sack from the fort and he saw some kids as young as eight years old being sent out hunting with guns, without any grown-ups, who were too busy running the houses and farms to watch carefully over each child.

He carried the sack to the Rogers Island just as Robert Rogers was taking inventory of the supply room. He noticed that the meat lockers were getting low and ordered Finn to go hunting for the Rangers.

As Finn moved through the woods quietly looking for

animal tracks, he saw a war party and immediately took refuge in the bushes. He did not recognize the warriors or which tribe they came from, and he stayed hidden, holding his breath. When the warriors disappeared from sight, Finn started running back to Fort Edward to report what he had seen.

Running through the woods, as he got closer to the fort he saw smoke rising from a chimney in the distance. Suddenly he heard a woman's voice, and knelt down on one knee holding his musket at the ready, alerted. He heard the woman again, and this time she was sobbing. Cautiously, Finn moved forward to investigate, and emerged from the bushes onto a clearing. He encountered a young woman in a green coat trimmed with white fur and a black scarf sitting on the ground. She was crying and holding a dead young man on her arms.

"My dear lady, are you alright? What has happened here?" Finn asked politely.

"What, don't you see what has happened?" the woman replied and seemed to be angry. He took a step back, and felt how his stomach twitched a little.

"Forgive me, my mother taught me to greet all people I meet, regardless if they are happy or in mourning," Finn said and took off his cap, "My lady, I meet you with such an awful, sad sight! May I ask what your name is? I see you are mourning your husband, who seems dead to me, my lady. Who did this terrible deed? Was it done by a rifle, or perhaps with a bow and arrow? Please tell me who is behind this, and I shall avenge your husband, I can certainly still catch up with them!" Finn brandished his musket and tomahawk. He knelt beside the woman and looked at her with concern. He examined the body in her arms. The man was young, in his early twenties. He had suffered numerous wounds to his upper body, and his scalped head was a bloody mess.

She wept as she gently held the young man's body on her lap. "My name is Catherina Brett, and this is my dear brother Joseph," she said, "It's no use, he is dead, and I am in agony, but I thank you for your kind words, sir. He was my only brother, and now that he's gone there is no other family for me! The Abenaki raiding party killed him while he was hunting. Your bravery and respect for my dear brother are highly valued," Catherina almost whispered sorrowfully.

When Finn stepped closer, through her grief, Catherina could not help but notice his handsome looks. She felt curiously as though she had gained some strength from the stranger who appeared out of thin air in the middle of nowhere. She stole a look at his blond hair and blue eyes. She saw his muscular body and suddenly felt an intense attraction to him. Her thoughts made her blush and she turned back to her brother.

"What is your name, if I may ask, young sir?" she asked softly.

"My mother, may she rest in peace, called me by many names," Finn replied, "She called me good boy, dear son, and beautiful son. She raised me alone, but she is gone now, killed by a ruthless enemy. To my friends I am Finn."

When she looked the other way, Finn secretly admired her. He saw a throbbing vein in her throat, and a faint perspiration on her temple. He leaned slightly closer to smell the scent of her hair. He felt time stand still as he stared at her profile, a few curly locks of golden hair under a black lace scarf, long eyelashes, and a dimple in her cheek. Finn was startled when Catherina spoke to him again. He jumped back a little.

"I am so sorry to hear that," she said. "She must have loved you surely much. My brother was a skillful hunter, and he kept our food locker stocked. Now he is gone too, killed by hostile warriors who have raided these parts for years. Maybe he got careless, maybe there were too many of them. I know he did not go without putting up a fight. Now all I have of him is his dead body. He left me with tremendous sorrow, and I miss him so much already!"

Seeing her broken-heartedness, Finn felt a sudden surging need to protect her. He looked firm and hit his chest with his fist. "Dear lady, I know how you must feel!" he said. "I have lost my family to sudden, violent acts too! Like lightning from the clear blue sky, a heartless enemy ruthlessly took them from me. Your sorrow and my shame demands I seek redress for this hideous crime! Show me which way those savages went so I can avenge your brother's death!"

Catherina was first impressed with Finn's excitement, but then she became concerned. "But you might be hurt or killed if you rush after the warriors all by yourself! It's no wonder, I do not want to put you in danger or lead you to harm's way. Surely you could use some reinforcements from the fort, don't you think?" she said.

"No worries, lady! I serve with Captain Rogers' Rangers now, and before that, I fought with Captain Campbell and even before that with Captain Lofving. I am a Ranger, and I am going to become an officer and a master of my own life! I can take care of myself!" Finn exclaimed.

The grieving Catherina held her dead brother, and a tear ran down her cheek as she pulled his clothes closer about him in a useless effort to keep him from cold. She wanted to smooth his cheek, but could not bear to touch his bloody flesh. She looked up and started to point the way, but after seeing Finn's eagerly angry face, she hesitated for a second. She suddenly pointed in the opposite direction. "They went that way," she said, and turned her head away not to look at him.

Finn collected his weapons, and without further ado rushed into the woods. Quite bewildered, with her dead brother still in her arms she watched him leave. Finn chased the war party through the woods searching for tracks, but when he could not find any tracks, he realized that she had led him astray. He became angry at her first, but then her action only puzzled him.

§    §    §

Finn returned to the fort, dodging the hogs running wild out of the gate, leaving piles of shit behind to add to the horseshit that continued to pile up. There were the sounds of clanking hammers, squealing animals, clattering carts and wagons, screaming children, and staggering drunks shouting obscenities.

Finn rushed through the fort towards the Rogers Island when he saw officers in front of the commander's office. He immediately reported to Robert Rogers that he had seen an enemy patrol in the vicinity and that they had a killed a farmer. The officers listened attentively. General

Johnson nodded to Robert Rogers, who immediately rushed towards the island, excited.

"Initiate lock-down immediately!" Robert Rogers barked as he rushed across the bridge. "No one will get on or off the island!"

John Stark ordered more armed guards on the palisades, and the gates were summarily shut down. Finn followed Robert Rogers, a little surprised that his account of sighting an enemy patrol caused such a strong response. He thought he might have missed some essential element.

Robert Rogers summoned the Ranger officers. "I have received instructions from the headquarters to send an expedition against the French fort at Crown Point. We need better intelligence. Get the men ready to move out," he said, and he laid out the maps on the table to study them closely. Lieutenant Stark arrived, and Robert Rogers ordered him to summon the Rangers.

Finn was excited as he got back to the squad bay and met with Gus and Fronto. "Have you heard about what I saw?" he asked. "This might be it! I brought a valuable observation back!"

The bugler sounded a call for the formation and Robert Rogers and his officers inspected the men and their equipment. John Stark told the men to put on their gear and jump up and down to ensure that they did not make any noise. Robert Rogers issued a patrol order, and gave the men some time to make adjustments and corrections, and get their rations. A flurry of activity filled the Island as the Rangers got ready for their first mission.

It was getting dark when the Rangers moved out of the gate toward the guarded docks on the lake. As they passed through the gate, each Ranger threw a coin into a bucket, where they made a muffled clanging sound as the bucket was half-full.

"Why they do that, sir?" Finn asked John Stark.

"They are paying a ransom on their souls," John Stark replied.

Finn dug a coin from his pocket and threw it in the bucket. Gus did the same but Fronto just shrugged his shoulders, and did not say a word as he followed them out of the gate.

Robert Rogers led the men in a single file toward Lake George. Although they were still in what was considered friendly territory, he sent out scouts in three directions, twenty yards in front of the main body and twenty yards to the left and right. The men marched in silence through the darkness. When they arrived at the lake, the Rangers embarked in canoes. They stayed close to the shoreline, and their canoes glided silently across the dark lake. The men moved their paddles forward and each man rotated the grip of his paddle in the palm of his upper hand. Then, carefully and effortlessly as a result of long experience, the men were ready for the next power stroke without taking the blade out of the water. There was no sound from their paddles. The air on the lake was chilly, and it took them hours to reach the planned landing site. Robert Rogers motioned the canoes to stop and then sent one of the Rangers ahead to recon the landing site. When they saw a faint sparks from flints being struck against steel as a signal that the site was clear, the Rangers debarked on the west shore.

Security guards were sent out. Robert Rogers told the

men to get close, and he whispered his orders. "Alright men, I know this is your first mission so we will play it safe," he said, "We will recon the French forts and will not seek contact with the enemy, but there is more to this mission. This is, in fact, a prisoner snatch mission! Our scouts have reported that there is a French communications officer traveling between the two forts regularly. We are convinced he is carrying valuable intelligence. On our way back, we will intercept this officer and take him back with us. Keep your eyes and ears open, is that clear? Take only the basic load with you when we move out!"

John Stark ordered two privates to stay behind and guard the boats and gear, and they grasped their rifles nervously and exchanged scared looks.

The Rangers marched in a single file through the night to a small knoll overlooking the enemy fort, where they got a fair view of Fort Carillon. The men lay in the tall grass and brush, camouflaged with vegetation. At dawn, they saw a large group of Abenaki warriors shooting at something.

"What do you think they are shooting at, sir?" Finn asked, whispering.

"The irregular firing tells they are shooting at marks, a pastime which they are very fond of," Robert Rogers replied, without taking his eyes off the enemy.

They stayed in place all day, without moving or eating. At night, the Rangers moved out again and crept past the French guards, so close they could almost touch them. One guard turned around to take a piss and almost stepped on Fronto's hand. His stream narrowly missed the Rangers lying frozen just below him in a gully. The guard returned to his comrades, and like shadows, the Rangers passed through the village south of the fort, to an eminence on the southwest.

From the new vantage point, the Rangers saw that the French were erecting a battery and had already thrown up an entrenchment on that side of the fort. The Rangers moved, creeping and crawling, to another rise a short distance from the former.

Finn held a bunch of small branches in front of his face as he slowly raised his head to see better, and realized the patrol was in the middle of the enemy formations. They were smack dab in the center of a fortified enemy encampment. From the new location, they discovered that the encampment extended from the fort southeast to a windmill at thirty yards distance. The Rangers used only hand signals to communicate what they saw. Gus put his head right next to Robert Rogers's ear to whisper his report.

"I count that the troops occupying it amount to about five hundred men," he said, so quietly that Finn next to him just barely heard him.

"I don't see an opportunity for procuring a prisoner here. Our small group might be discovered, so we will start heading back to the boats," Robert Rogers ordered, and one by one, the Rangers crawled backwards away from the enemy camp. Once a safe distance away, they ran crouching down another few hundred feet before stopping to regroup.

The Rangers passed within two miles of Fort Carillon on their route homeward, and Robert Rogers observed it from a hilltop with his telescope. Finn tried to see the enemy fort. "There is a lot of activity. How can we get a single man out of there without being noticed?" They could see smoke rising from fires to the sky and heard the French firearms echoing in the woods.

Robert Rogers decided to move closer to get a better view. "I will move closer to count the number of the French and the Abenaki." He was ready to go out when Lieutenant MacCurdy came to report.

"Sir, our provisions are almost expended, at a level so that we cannot carry out a new mission to ascertain the enemy's force," Donald MacCurdy said.

Robert Rogers looked back at him, furious. "Damn it! Well, we better head back and regroup," he said.

The Rangers moved swiftly and reached the place where they had left the boat in charge of two privates. To their utter surprise, the two men had deserted, leaving them no provisions whatsoever. Robert Rogers was enraged. "I will find those fucking yellow-bellied, lily-livered sons of bitches!"

Gus and Fronto asked Finn what had happened. Finn shook his head and told them, "Looks like that fat bastard and his butt buddy high-tailed it out of here taking all the rations with them!"

The Rangers were fatigued and upset with hunger and cold. No fires were allowed, and the men ate the cold rations they had been carrying on their persons.

Robert Rogers decided it was time to take the prisoner. "We are going back to Fort Carillon," he said. "We will land on the west side, twenty-five miles from here, and march the remainder of the way to the fort." He took out a pistol. "This," he said, "is an especially loaded pistol! It has only one third of the powder as usual. Therefore, it is remarkably quiet and only intended to incapacitate the target so he won't be able to run away. To be effective, I must first get really close to the target. I will shoot him in the leg, you will put a burlap bag over his head, and we will carry him off on a stretcher. Are there any questions?"

Finn shook his head as he realized that all those stretcher runs during training had prepared them for this mission. The Rangers moved silently through the night in single file again. At dawn, they were within three hundred yards of Fort Carillon and lay down, concealed in a clump of willows. It was dark, and the men got their weapons and gear ready quietly. Finn adjusted his gear and fumbled to get a pistol in the darkness. Before sunrise, Robert Rogers crept closer to the enemy fort by himself and lay concealed behind a large pine log, camouflaging himself further by holding bushes in his hand. The rest of the patrol stayed behind in an overwatch position on a hill where they could provide supporting fire if required.

Donald MacCurdy set up defensive positions and assigned men fields of fire. "Keep your eyes and ears open!" he whispered.

Shortly after sunrise, a large formation of French soldiers spread out in such numbers that the Rangers could not leave their secure positions without discovery. The men became acutely tense, and Robert Rogers stayed quietly in his hideout. The French soldiers approached their positions, and then passed them close without incident. Donald MacCurdy glanced at his watch at ten o'clock, when a French officer came out alone and advanced directly toward the Rangers on the trail. The men watched the man approaching over the barrels of their muskets. Robert Rogers sprang over the trunk and offered him mercy.

"Halt! Surrender or be killed!" he shouted, and pointed his musket at the man.

"Fuck off, you crazy wank!" the Frenchman shouted and lunged with his dirk at Robert Rogers.

Finn pulled out his firearm, and was dismayed to see that he had the wrong pistol. In the darkness he had grabbed the wrong weapon. He was holding the suppressed musket in his hand, and Robert Rogers had Finn's standard pistol. He almost panicked and started to get up and run to the trail, but Donald MacCurdy, his eyes not leaving Captain Rogers, placed his hand firmly on Finn's shoulder and pulled him back down. On the trail, Robert Rogers parried the Frenchman's dirk and aimed his pistol at the man's legs.

"I said surrender, mother fucker!" Rogers demanded and cocked the musket. The Frenchman still pressed ahead with determination. He crouched down low ready to leap just as Robert Rogers pulled the trigger. A thunderous shot echoed in the morning air, alarming the enemy in the fort. The bullet hit the man in the face, and he slumped dead at Rogers's feet. He stared slack in amazement, looking at the pistol in his hand, and his mouth formed the words "What the fuck..."

Enemy troops assembled, shouting, inside the fort, and the party in the woods that had left earlier turned back towards the Rangers. Donald MacCurdy barked commands: "Cover Captain Rogers' retreat and get ready to move out!"

Without a second thought, Fronto was up and running

through a hail of fire, breaking cover and drawing fire away from Robert Rogers. He fired on the run, stopping to quickly reload behind trees and rocks. The Rangers fired a volley at the approaching enemy who dove for cover, and the Rangers peeled off in turns, breaking contact.

Robert Rogers was able to get away and he ran back to the Rangers, and they retreated to the mountains. "Who in hell changed my pistol? What a fucked up mission!" Captain Rogers demanded. Finn hid the pistol under his jacket, and whistling quietly looked the other way.

The Rangers moved out at a brisk pace through the woods. When they stopped for a short rest, Finn asked, "Captain Rogers, may I ask, weren't you afraid when you attacked that Frenchman?"

Rogers spat on the ground and grinned as he replied, "When I was born my mother gave birth to twins: myself and fear. So it must remain until the moment when I utter my last words and take a grand leap in the dark. Fear motivates me to keep going."

Early the next morning, the Rangers returned to Fort Edward, appearing like ghosts from the dark forest and the fog rising from the river. Donald MacCurdy took the position by the gate with a pistol in hand and identified each man before letting him pass. The men marched in quietly and removed their equipment and started immediately cleaning their weapons and checking their gear.

Robert Rogers was still furious. He went looking for the two privates who had left their post. In mad frustration he threw gear and furniture out from one of the squad bays as he searched for the deserters.

The whole island heard Captain Rogers shouting.

"Where are those two maggots? I will tear their lungs out and feed them to the pigs! Where are they? I want their heads on a platter! And if I ever find out who changed my suppressed pistol I will tear his head off and shit down his neck!"

John Stark returned from the fort. "Sir, it appears that they might have never returned here. They must be hiding somewhere, or more likely, they are still running, probably all the way to Pennsylvania by now. They know better than to show their faces here ever again!"

The men cleaned their weapons and equipment. Everything was unpacked, cleaned, fixed, and repacked, ready to go again.

"Supply sergeant! Make sure each man has a new load of sixty rounds of ball and powder, and three days rations! Men, always be ready to march on a moment's notice, and be ready to stay out there for five days!" Robert Rogers barked.

"Did you see Captain Rogers when he shot that Frenchman dead on his feet?" Finn asked Fronto.

Fronto laughed as he replied, "One of the guards almost stepped on my hand in the village! He was so close I could smell his fear!"

Donald MacCurdy arrived to talk to the men. He stepped his other foot on a chair and leaned on his knee. "Listen up, Rangers," he started. He farted and continued, "You did well out there. We gained valuable intelligence. Debriefing is tomorrow. If your musket is clean as a whistle again and your gear is squared away, you are free to go. I'd suggest you get some rest. But if you go to town, for the ladies' sake, wash yourself first! You people stink to high heaven!"

The Rangers laughed and hollered, pushing and jostling each other. Finn joined some Rangers at the horses' feeding trough to wash. The Rangers grabbed one of the privates and threw the man into the trough. "You stink!" A wild water-fight erupted.

In small groups, some of the Rangers left for Fort Edward. Others went back to their bays. A group of Rangers who were heading to the fort called jokingly when they walked past Finn, "Hey, Alphabet, want to join us?"

Finn waved a hand at them, and he walked to the squad bay where Gus and Fronto were working on their gear.

"Now I'm surprised. What's the matter with you two? You are not going to the tavern?" Finn asked.

Gus glanced at Fronto and winked. Fronto smirked and dug out a small purse, "Yeah, we might have to fix that. Are you going to come along or what? Come on, you black brute, let's go!"

Finn, Gus, and Fronto walked over the bridge to the Silver Star. There were stars in the sky and a full moon lighted their way.

Gus watched the night sky. "This place may not be much, but it feels good to be back," he said, lost in thought.

Finn jumped playfully on his shoulders. "Sure does! Hey, did I tell you about the woman in the woods?"

They arrived at the tavern, and Fronto was a happy man again, and in his element. "No, you didn't tell us, and luckily here we are, at the fine Silver Star establishment, where you can live today for your own funeral tomorrow!"

"You shouldn't be so morbid, old man," Finn replied. "You heard Lieutenant MacCurdy, and we did well out there! Live it up!"

Fronto laughed and grabbed a waitress by the waist and squeezed her breast. "That's what I was saying! Shall we dance, my fair Delilah?" She giggled and playfully knocked him on top of his head with an empty tankard.

Finn turned to Gus. "Anyways, that woman I was telling you about? She was the most beautiful woman I have ever seen, but she was slightly scary too, you know what I mean? I don't know, but it's like she saw right through me!"

Gus took a long drink. "Yes, I know what you mean, some ladies do that. What do you think of Fronto?"

"I have this strange feeling that I have met him before, but I have no idea where or when," Finn replied.

"I think so too. Fronto reminds me of someone I read about in a book or something. He's familiar, yet a little strange."

Finn took a place at the bar and started bragging. "Now if that is all there is to it, waging warfare in Ranger style, well then, I will win the whole damned war all by myself!"

Finn stood a little separate from the others in the bar. Images of battles and men dying were running through his mind, and he quieted the noises of brutal combat in his head by emptying his tankard and ordering more. More Rangers arrived in the tavern, and the noise became louder. Outside in the darkness, lights shone from tavern windows. Thievery was not that common in Fort Edward, but there were roaming night guards checking to be sure that the lanterns were lighted, watching for fires and thieves, and during days calling out the time and the weather. The guards were often scared stiff, firing first and asking questions later, rattling a bell as they patrolled to keep the pilferers at bay.

Nestled in the vast wilderness, Fort Edward winked as a few spots of light in a vast sea of darkness. The moonlight shone on the Hudson River, and in the distance, Lake George and Lake Champlain glistened between the dark mountain ridges.

# Chapter 5

LATE FALL WEATHER ARRIVED, sunny and cold with brisk north winds. Out of the chilly mist rising from Hudson River, two swans appeared, swimming among small floes of ice. On the shore, a thin layer of ice formed on puddles, and patches of snow dotted meadows. Freezing air preserved red rose hips pristine under frost, and yellow and red leaves clung frozen to birches and maples. Busy squirrels gathered nuts and pine cones for the oncoming winter.

After an unusually wet mud season, the falling temperature was received with relief by townspeople. Dirt roads and paths became passable again across the hard frozen ground, and John Morton traveled to Cambridge in the Province of Massachusetts Bay to meet with Governor William Shirley. Morton was troubled by certain plans he had heard rumors of, and wanted to get firsthand information. When he arrived, he encountered several armed guards around the governor's house, hardnosed looking brutes in uniforms, who stopped all visitors. He remembered hearing about occasions when the Governor had not hesitated to order his guards to shoot at protestors, and that he used them as debt collectors. There was a persistent rumor that Governor Shirley also provided what he called "protective services" to local merchants.

John Morton met Governor Shirley in his library. They exchanged cordial greetings, but the governor did not seem pleased to receive his guest from Pennsylvania. John Morton noticed that no refreshment was offered or served to him, which was highly unusual. The aristocratic Governor seemed condescending and self-absorbed.

"Sir, without further ado, I am here because several people have expressed concerns about the planned deportations of the Acadians," John Morton said, getting straight to the point. "Perhaps we should talk to Governor Lawrence about adjusting his tribal purging operation."

Governor Shirley was one of the planners of the operation, and he barely had any sympathy for the Acadian people. He was devoted to the Crown first and foremost, and had plans to return to England as a rich man after his obedient tour of duty in the colonies. He despised the Colonials and considered them fools useful for exploitation.

Governor Shirley sneered. "No need for your concern, Mr. Morton. This impressive campaign was launched earlier by General Braddock, before he died in humiliating and most unfortunate circumstances. The Acadians have pretty much ignored the changes taking place in America for the past forty years. The French certainly don't care about them, never having lent a great deal of help or support to them. So we are usually in control of the situation and will act as we see fit."

Governor Shirley played with a small knife and looked slyly at Morton. "For your information, even the French colonial government in Paris considered exporting the Acadians from their homeland!" he said, looking bored.

John Morton did not agree. "Many Acadians have taken oaths of allegiance to the British throne, which gives them a verbal promise of neutrality in case of a war between the British and the French. In order to maintain law and order, we must respect their assurances!"

Governor Shirley let out a dry, insincere laugh. "Ha! By and large they have refused to sign an unconditional oath of allegiance to Britain!" He slapped his hand on the table hard and continued, "There is no such thing as Neutral French, as Acadians are called! It is a matter of record that France sacrificed Acadia and its people when the Treaty of Utrecht was signed."

He threw a rolled-up map on the table. Unrolling it, he pointed to the area with his finger. "What is imperative, Mr. Morton is the fact that the Acadian settlement is the only direct link to Quebec by sea, and it is also the link to get our ships from here to Fort Louisburg. The time has come for the so-called neutrals to choose sides! They are either with us or against us!"

Morton remained firm. "I see the military aspect, sir. We must neutralize any military threat the Acadians present, and interrupt the vital supply lines Acadians provide to Louisburg. But we must also make distinctions between the Acadians who have been peaceful and those who have rebelled against the British!"

Governor Shirley looked disgusted. "Be assured that the ingenuity of our superb military will vigorously take care of that dilemma, once and for all! I'd say deport them all and let God sort them out later!"

"Sir, there are more than fourteen thousand of them! Surely there will be problems," John Morton said. The rude aristocrat disgusted him, but he maintained his decorum.

"Mr. Morton, the absorption of Nova Scotia with its Acadian people into the British empire poses, at first sight, no substantial or unusual problems." Governor Shirley stared back at him condescendingly. "The high court in London has already coped with raggedy people living at the end of long lines of communications and who are inclined to riot for their petty vision of political liberty, namely, the British fiefdom in North America!"

John Morton realized there was nothing he could do, but he wanted more information. "I heard that some of Captain Rogers' Rangers from Fort Edward might be ordered to take part in this operation. Is that correct?"

The governor paused for a moment. He stared coldly at John Morton, briefly contemplating before replying, "That could easily be. This is, after all, a special operation, but that is classified information! In the grand scheme of our strategy, the ultimate solution to the Acadian question does require flexibility of mind and imagination from us! But don't worry, Mr. Morton, about the approved plan. It is not to kill all Acadians as I suggested, but instead settling them in small groups throughout the thirteen colonies, so that they will simply disappear as a people. And now, sir, if you don't mind, we are done here. Have a lovely day," Governor Shirley said, and turned his back to John Morton.

At the same time up north, unpredictable events were unfolding. Fort Beausejour was under the leadership of Governor Charles Lawrence, who was not only politically motivated, but also greedy, and the lands held by the Acadians were high on the list of things he wanted. Unfortunately for the Acadians, they were not British and their lands were the lushest around. That was all Governor Lawrence needed for an excuse. He decided to get rid of the Acadians.

To expedite his ambition, Governor Lawrence set up a bounty of thirty pounds sterling for the scalp of each Acadian male over sixteen, and twenty-five for younger males, or any females.

Although the bounty was supposedly limited to the natives, in practice, the British paid the bounties without inquiring about the race of the original owners of the scalps.

"The enemy will soon find a way to wrest Acadia from us if we do not remove the most dangerous French inhabitants and replace them with British families," Governor Lawrence told his officers. "The Province of Nova Scotia will never be out of danger so long as the French inhabitants are tolerated under the present mode of submission."

Colonel Monkton, the Governor's military adviser, reported his intention. "We will bring six thousand new, loyal families to Nova Scotia. Two thousand of them will come from the British Isles and two thousand will come from New England. The remaining two thousand will be soldiers sent to North America who would be given land if they would retire there."

As soon as the British forces arrived, the fort was taken easily, and nearly two hundred Acadians warriors were found within the walls of the fort when it surrendered. All men and boys over the age of ten were taken prisoners and forced into the church at Chipoudy, and women were left outside to watch. The families were torn apart, and all their possessions were taken from them. When all of the men were inside the church, the doors were closed and locked. The British told them that they no longer owned their land and property and that both they and their families were going to be put onto ships and sent away.

The Acadians protested, arguing that the question had been settled with the oath of neutrality that they had taken to the British monarch twenty years earlier. Their leader, Joseph Broussard, declared that the Acadians had signed oaths on the condition that they would not be forced to fight against France, insisting that they had been forced to bear arms against their will.

Joseph Broussard addressed his people. "The majority of our people are ready for demarche, not to take yet another oath that the King requires of us! We want to be farmers untouched by war! This is not our debut as fighters involved in the ongoing guerrilla battles over which European government would control North America!"

Waiting for the crowd to quiet down Broussard continued, "We are still proud Acadians, a people who possess little loyalty to any foreign nation, who have received little from either Britain or France, and who feel no strong loyalty to either. We are sometimes French subjects, but Acadians first and foremost!"

For some British officers, the mere Acadian presence was evidence of treachery. Having received his orders, Colonel Monkton's intention was to deport them all. He declared, "The Acadians are stubborn, insisting upon the condition of not carrying weapons against France. Leaving the country to them is unacceptable, because it strengthens the enemy."

Governor Lawrence considered the Acadians to be arrogant and cunning. He had fifteen warriors taken from the church and under pain of torture tried to force them to join the British ranks. The oldest warrior of the group replied by holding one hand curved and waved it back and forth as if masturbating. The angered British pushed and shoved the group behind the barn and shot them against the wall. Lawrence then issued an ultimatum to the Acadians in the church: fight against France with the British or face the consequences. Refusal would mean slow death, or in the best case, expulsion from the colony.

The Acadians were offered one last chance to join the British, but they refused. Governor Lawrence was infuriated but at the last moment he balked at shooting so many civilians and ordered the deportations to begin. The Acadians were told that their lands, goods, and chattel were forfeited to the crown. Moreover, they were to be held as prisoners until the ships arrived for their deportation.

"In the meantime, it will be necessary to keep this measure as secret as possible to prevent any attempts to escape," Governor Lawrence continued.

The deportation was heartbreaking and it lasted several hours as people were gathered together at bayonet point. The distressed Acadians prayed, cried, and wailed. The two hundred warriors from the church were brought outside to be taken to the harbor, and sadly and with consummate sorrow they watched as their homes were torched. The women, in great grief, carried their newborns or their youngest children in their arms. Others pulled carts loaded with their household goods and perhaps crippled parents. It was a scene of utter confusion, despair, and desolation. After the long column of people was gone, the British looted the Acadian houses and then burned down everything, including the church at Chipoudy.

The British were overconfident and did not guard the prisoners well enough. On the way to the harbor, leading one hundred twenty-five Acadian warriors, Joseph Broussard attacked and killed few British guards and escaped into the nearby hills. They recovered caches of arms and ammunition they had hidden earlier. Organizing a resistance movement, they soon saw an opportunity, and overtook a company of British regulars sent after them at the Pelkoudiak River. The Acadians attacked and fought the British for three hours, and inflicting heavy casualties, drove them vigorously back to their ships. Regardless of their initial success, Joseph Broussard remained bitter. He was keenly aware that one victorious battle does not win the war.

§       §       §

White wood smoke rose from chimneys in the river valley, and in Fort Edward, first snow covered shingled roofs. Hoar frost formed delicate swirling patterns on windows and a door to one of the log houses was frozen shut. Finn forced it open and pulled a cloak over his head as he walked to the command post. Frozen grass made a crisp, crackling noise under his feet as he traversed the open training ground. At the command post he met Lieutenant Richard Rogers outside.

"Sir, you summoned me." Finn pulled his jacket tighter against his body in the shiver-inducing weather.

"Right, the temperature is plummeting, and we still need more provisions to last the winter. Take a few men and facilitate a hunting party, and pick up supplies from the fort on your way out." Rogers pointed out the directions. "Scour the woods south by southeast. There should not be hostile warriors in the area, but stay alert just in case."

"Yes sir! You picked the right man for this job! I am an experienced hunter!" Finn saluted crisply and speedily returned to the squad bay. Gus and Fronto were excited as he told them to get ready for a hunting trip.

"Yes! I was getting bored." Fronto rubbed his hands together. "Taming or killing wild beasts for pleasure is an attempt to control nature, but man is incapable under her rule! We must nourish ourselves. There's nothing like a good hunt to stimulate an old man!" Fronto started getting his gear ready.

Finn, Gus, and Fronto, dressed in fur coats and winter leggings, stopped at the supply sergeant who handed out hunting rifles, ammunition and some beef jerky to last for a day, and told them to get a sled from the shack by the gate. As they were going through Fort Edward, they observed townspeople involved in an animated argument.

Rumors were running rampant in the area. The people gathered to exchange the latest news they had heard around the whipping post. A man in a long hooded coat had arrived from Albany. "The horse traders always hear the latest news," the man claimed, "and from reliable sources, they heard that the French have a secret weapon to be launched against anybody who challenges them!

Beware of their terrible wrath!" The man's proclamation had made the people around him seriously concerned.

Catherina, the beautiful woman whom Finn had met in the forest, was standing among a group of women. Finn was smitten by this determined woman who had braided blonde hair under a scarf and strikingly blue eyes. He admired her firm mind and slender body, and wished to know her better.

"That's her," Finn said.

"And who is that?" Gus asked.

"She's the woman I told you about, whom I met by chance in the woods. Her brother was killed by Abenaki warriors. There's something about her..." Finn replied, watching her as they headed to the gate. While he was fetching the sled, he took the opportunity to gather information or opinions from some of the townspeople about her.

An old woman narrowed her eyes and looked at Finn. "Any decent man would regret a relationship with her later and feel shame. She is stubborn and will not tolerate any ordinary men - she calls them all cowards," the old woman said.

"In that case, Finn, you might have a chance! You're no picnic either!" Fronto teased him.

"Oh yeah, and you're the mule who gets to pull the sled!" Finn replied, slapping the harness in Fronto's hands.

Fronto picked up the harness and slung it around his shoulders. "There is hardly any snow, and I don't feel like a reindeer," he said.

"We'll fit antlers on your cap and a hairy tubby tail on your ass, and you sure would look like one!" Gus laughed.

"How would you know? Are there any reindeer in Africa?" Fronto quipped back.

"Listen old man, Gus is the smartest guy I have ever met, and a straight shooter to boot. That's why I want him on my side!" Finn said.

"You're right, not only can he read, but he also understands what he reads!"

They moved out, Finn leading the way, followed by Fronto pulling the sled with Gus bringing up the rear. They pulled the sled by turns and continued along the trails following the ridgelines, which gave them some protection against the harsh wind. When they had progressed far enough, they looked a place to set up a camp. Gus pointed to a group of trees, "This place looks as fine as any other. Should we split and start tracking alone?" He looked at the others.

Finn pointed further towards a ridge across a plateau some distance away. "No, I think we ought to move in that direction," he said, "I saw some meadows and good feeding grounds for deer along that small ridge."

They crossed a ravine with a frozen stream and continued to move cautiously through the trees and around thickets. The forest was silent, and Finn started daydreaming about the woman he had seen again. He imagined her in the winter forest naked except for furs, and she was holding a colorful orchid in her hand. He fantasized her fur coat opening slightly, revealing the hypnotic seduction of large, voluptuous breasts.

Fronto noticed Finn beginning to drift off, and slapped him angrily in the back of the head. He noticed a pile of moose droppings and knelt down to pick some up. He broke a piece in two, still steaming a little inside. He raised a finger in front of his mouth and whispered, "Not completely frozen yet, so it is pretty close."

They spread out as the morning turned into afternoon. Going through heavy brush, Finn heard an animal snort. He moved the branches slowly out of the way. There, across a clearing, he saw a giant bull moose with massive, broad and flat antlers, covered with soft furry skin. The animal that stretched seven feet across was staring straight at him. Finn held his breath and raised his musket slowly and stared back at the animal over the rifle barrel. *That son of a bitch must weigh fifteen hundred pounds at least!* he thought.

Behind Finn, Gus and Fronto looked in the direction he pointed his rifle. They moved quietly to get a side shot. The moose's heavy exhalations in the cold air shot a cloud of smoke from its nostrils. It lowered its enormous rack, scraped the earth with its hoof, and its loud bellow echoed in the forest.

Without any warning, the moose charged Finn, its hooves sounding like drums beating against the frozen ground as it trampled the field toward him. Finn aimed calmly at its chest and the heart, but a split second before he fired, the beast jolted and the mist from its breath clouded his aim. The shot hit the moose in the thick-boned midline of its skull and ricocheted off harmlessly.

Holding his breath, Finn started to reload hastily. The huge, red-eyed wild beast was almost on top of him now, rushing right at him like a Minotaur straight from hell. Two shots rang out when Gus and Fronto fired almost at the same time. Their bullets hit the moose twice directly behind its shoulders, blowing right through the animal, spraying the ground with blood and pieces of flesh, and its front legs gave out from under it as it plowed into the ground.

Finn let out a sigh and wiped his brow. "Whew! Thanks but I was going to get him, you know!"

They approached the moose which lay motionless on the ground, its carcass steaming in the cold air. Finn stepped closer and drew his knife. Suddenly, the moose bellowed again and jumped up on its feet, rearing up on its hind legs. Finn fell backwards, landing hard on his back.

"Holy shit, it's alive! It's alive!" he exclaimed, taken totally by surprise. The moose tried to kick him with its front legs, and Finn rolled sideways as the hooves, like giant sledge hammers, pounded the ground around his head. Gus and Fronto fired again, and the moose fell on Finn's legs, pinning him down. Finn frantically hit at the animal with his knife, and Gus and Fronto ran up to help him. Fronto reloaded on the run and shot the moose in the head one more time. Finn lay in the snow on his back, his legs pinned under the dead moose. He moved his arms making patterns in the snow and laughed, relieved. He left an impression in the snow, a human form with wings. Gus and Fronto finally managed to move the carcass off his legs and pull him back up.

"Finn, you are one lucky bastard! You sure did have a guardian angel with you today!" Gus shouted.

"The hunter almost became the hunted!" Fronto said as he slapped Finn on the shoulder.

"There's nothing to it, nothing at all!" Finn said, breathing heavily, "I tell you, one time we had to fight off a pack of wolves to claim our prey," he said grinning, and brushed some leaves and dirt off his jacket.

Across the clearing behind a bush, two Abenaki warriors watched them. One of the warriors aimed his musket at them when the other warrior stopped him, pointing at Finn, and the moose head necklace around his neck. The warrior lowered his rifle, and the two warriors disappeared into the woods without a sound.

Finn, Gus, and Fronto started to field-dress and quarter the moose. Finn inserted a sharp knife at the base of its throat and sliced across the main blood vessels with a broad and deep crosswise cut. Gus and Fronto worked together to break the breastbone using one axe for cutting, the second as a hammer. Finn severed the windpipe and gullet close to the head, pulling it clear of the carcass. He then carefully cut through the abdominal muscles, exposing the stomach and intestines. Gus and Fronto spread the body wide open, and rolled the carcass lying on its back on logs to provide free air circulation between the ground and the carcass.

They allowed the carcass cool down for a couple of hours, and then loaded the quarters into the sled and tied the large antlers on top.

§        §        §

The return trip back to Fort Edward with the heavy load lasted the rest of the day, and they were sweaty and exhausted as they walked through the gate in the early evening. Finn saw a group of townspeople and thought they looked so poor that they probably never threw anything away other than their hopes and dreams. When those people slaughtered a pig, Finn thought, they would make sure everything was used except the squeal. A woman sold utensils, spoons made out of clamshells, cups made of gourds and a turkey wing to be used as a brush. The townspeople wore every garment until it was falling apart and then made quilts from the scraps.

As they pushed and pulled the sled through the fort, they heard clamoring and saw a group of agitated townspeople in an animated argument. "What? They are still fighting?" Gus wondered aloud.

Finn walked closer to see what was happening and found out that Catherina had defended a chief against the townspeople who were gathered around them. The chief was Daniel Nimham, a fearsome young Wappinger warrior. Wearing a red shirt and black overcoat, he also sported large golden earrings and a thin blue headband with green and white feathers. His plucked-out head had only a square of hair forming a ponytail on the back. Around his neck he wore a beautifully etched military model copper-gilt plate, engraved with a crown above the Royal cypher within a wreath. Finn noticed a heavily decorated war club under his belt.

Catherina glared angrily at the townspeople with her hands on her hips. "I wonder, what is the meaning of this? It is unfair to blame Chief Nimham! He has done nothing wrong! He is well-known for trading on quality horses for a living!" She said.

The leader of the agitated crowd was Harold Ferrara, a sturdy Scot wearing a blacksmith's apron. He ignored her and pointed his rough, blackened finger at Daniel

Nimham. "Injun horse traders can't be trusted! He sold me an overpriced horse, which turned out to be lame, as well! I barely made it back from my trip to Boston!" As he shouted, spit flew from his foul mouth. Harold Ferrara's skinny neighbor stood behind his broad back supporting him and waving a clenched fist at Daniel Nimham. He turned, and Finn saw his face better. The chief's facial tattoos were scalp and war wound tallies crossing his face, and a sunburst streaking off the face adjoining his mouth on the lower jaw.

Chief Daniel Nimham stood his ground proudly, defying the two men and the crowd. He stared Harold Ferrara directly in the eyes, and ran his tongue ring against his top teeth. "The best chief is not the one who cheats his customers! The horse I sold to you was in fair condition! The white people should pay attention, the price was reasonable, an average going price in the market, not a shilling more!"

Harold Ferrara was infuriated. "I have never seen such insolence! We don't even know whose side you are on anyway!"

Daniel was insulted by the accusation because his loyalties were questioned. Ferrara took a swing at him. Daniel ducked the blow, but Ferrara's neighbor seized him by the arms and held him down. Ferrara got ready to hit him again. Catherina, jumping between the men, tried to stop them from fighting. Ferrara slammed her aside harshly against the wall. Finn had seen enough, and he jumped over the sled to grab Harold Ferrara by the arm.

"Back off, mister!" Finn shouted, "No pushing ladies

around here, I will see to it! Besides, there are two of you against one of him, which hardly is a fair match, so you can count me in on the chief's side!"

The two men looked at him in aversion, and Harold Ferrara gripped his sword handle. Gus and Fronto lowered their muskets, ready to join the fight.

Harold Ferrara spat out and glanced at them, his face twisted in fear and loathing. "You Rangers... You think you're something remarkable! But this ain't over yet! Remember this, we know who you are!" he said, hissing between his teeth and wiping the corner of his mouth on his sleeve. The two men stepped back, picked up their hats, and pushed through the crowd.

Catherina hopped in front of Finn, all fired up and her long blonde hair blowing in the wind. "Let's go after them! You know they will be back!" she said, waving her arms.

Daniel placed his hand on her shoulder to calm her down and looked at Finn. "You are a newcomer, yet you intervened. That's not the way people do things around here. Why did you help me?"

Finn did not answer, and just shrugged his shoulders. He turned to Gus and Fronto. "Nothing more we can do now. Come on, we must report back." He helped Gus and Fronto pull the sled loaded with game meat towards the mess hall.

Gus helped Finn with a large chunk of the moose meat. "I can see now what you meant. Her character is stout and proud, but a woman like her needs a counter-balance. Otherwise, she won't be happy!"

"The young woman strikes an imposing figure, yet I bet she can be disarmingly charming if she wants to!"

Fronto replied. He absent-mindedly pinched and pulled the tiny little hairs from his earlobes.

Back in the fort Catherina was still upset. She did not want to talk to the townspeople and Daniel kept calming her down. Glancing over his shoulder, he watched the three men pull the sled towards the Rogers Island. "Catherina, I appreciate your help. Manitou says that the one who is most adaptable to change survives!" he said, and with that sudden realization, he made up his mind about his fate and ran after them, leaving the very upset Catherina to watch him go.

Daniel caught up with them and said that he had decided to see if the Rangers would take him as a scout. Finn told him to accompany them to the Rogers Island to meet with Captain Rogers.

Gus and Fronto took the sled to the supply sergeant, and Finn showed Daniel to Robert Rogers' office. He was immediately willing to enlist Daniel because he was anticipating a vital mission and needed more warriors for scouting. Robert Rogers was reloading his musket and had several packets of black powder and ball ammunition on the table in front of him. As they were talking about possible new missions, all of a sudden, the door slammed open and Catherina burst in, her long blonde hair waving free and a musket in her hands. "Captain, I want to enlist, too!" she exclaimed, and stood in the middle of the room facing the startled men.

The Rangers were all taken totally by surprise. Finn was dumbfounded and could only ogle at the most stunning woman he had ever seen. He noticed a coiled shaped brooch in silver with clear, black stones, representing a two headed snake. Robert Rogers was almost speechless, and glanced at the men around the room looking for support as he turned back to her. "I-I'm sorry ma'am, but... but you're a woman," he stuttered. "Only the most able-bodied freemen and Iroquois may enlist!"

Richard Rogers stepped forward and looked sternly at Catherina. "Ma'am, cover your head for the common decency!" he said.

Catherina ignored him and threw a sachet of ball ammunition and black powder on the table. One packet opened, and a musket ball rolled out next to Robert Rogers' ammunition. "My aim is just as sure as any man's, and my balls are just as big!" She raised her musket and took a shooting stance, then lowered the rifle slowly, and glared back at the men around her.

Robert Rogers again glanced around the room for support, but the other men looked away quietly. He started to respond, "Well, ma'am, I am sure of that, but..."

Catherina cut him off. "I can carry my own weight, Captain!"

Robert Rogers tried to remain calm. "Well, maybe so, but you see, we recruit only hunters and trappers and farmers hardened by hardships in the frontier. Sure, women may follow and do some tasks in the camp and..."

"I am no camp follower!" she shouted angrily. "I want to fight! Abenaki warriors killed my brother! Have you ever paused to wonder that I have the right to fight! Listen Captain, women are driven into battle by their commitment to kinship ties, and they will abide by their families through strife and bloodshed!"

Robert Rogers ran out of patience with this impudent

woman, and his expression became grim. "I am sorry about your brother, but maybe you can find some tasks with the artillery battery," he said between clenched teeth. "Our forays deep into the enemy territory are far too demanding for any woman!"

"So, you are saying women are only good to bear your children and then bury them for you when they are killed in one of your wars?" She stormed out, slamming the dusty door hard shut behind her. The men in the room stared at the door in stunned silence.

§    §    §

In the Catskill Mountain House, Henry Raymond looked up from his notes at the old man. "I remember reading that some of the winters were bad in those days," he said.

The old man smirked. "Winters weren't that dreadful really. People actually preferred them in many ways, because frozen shit and filth didn't stink so badly!"

The old man smiled as he remembered. "That particular day was one balmy day after all. Catherina was a beautiful farmer, charming and sweet, but stormy and forthright when she got angry. She was raised on a frontier farm, and the people were constantly being tested by deep passions. They were farmers who toiled the land and their reactions to life were rudimentary, and violence was their native language. But Catherina was unusually persistent and she refused to settle in the traditional role townspeople had reserved for her sex. She was determined to be her own woman. She grew up brave, uneducated but smart, pigheaded and independent.

"She felt she had a big problem because she could not read, and she wanted something she was not expected to need because she was a woman. She wanted to own and operate a farm all by herself. Being alone, she was in danger of losing her independence as well, because people would try to fit her into a marriage since, supposedly, a woman could not take care of herself. She was young and innocent, full of grand passion and sense. She was also a rebel who acted impulsively and consumed by her irrational feelings. She became agitated when she was hungry.

"She did not tolerate being underestimated, as she had been when she stormed into Captain Rogers's office. Being treated as a member of the 'weaker sex' and not being allowed to participate in any missions infuriated her. She lambasted the townspeople for their permanent closed-mindedness at a time when righteousness was considered a hallmark. Catherina also hated clergymen, because their power came from somewhere outside, and they could hide behind their omnipotent power, and she was not able to fight against it. She feared being the helpless target of someone's omnipotence."

The old man glanced around his shoulder and whispered. "She had a secret: as a child she had stolen a brooch. She had seen it during a church sermon, and because it reminded her of her mother, she coveted it so much that she took it. She knew to whom it belonged, but pretended not to know. She was afraid that, if found out, the clergymen would take it away from her."

He resumed his normal voice. "She learned early on to overcome hardships and hoped one day to learn the qualities she needed to make her world a better place. She had to work her way through a childhood of abandonment, and then there came the tragic day that her brother was gone, too. For reasons that left her baffled and unsure about herself, at first she became angry at her dead brother for leaving her alone, as if it was his fault."

Henry Raymond pressed on about a related question that he was interested in. "The Iroquois nation was troubled in those days, and they found it difficult to choose sides. The Iroquois nation was divided. Who was the chief?"

The old man replied, "He was proud Chief Daniel Nimham of the Wappinger, and he was a sight to see. I can tell you that Daniel was bright and proud. He was a religious man with multicultural skills and a firm believer in justice, and a strong advocate of the Iroquois cause. He was optimistic about the future too. He was committed and hardworking, natural and social, and a skilled negotiator! He dreamed of starting his own horse breeding business one day. He was worried a little, because he also knew that other Iroquois business owners had unfortunate experiences in the past, particularly those who dealt also with Colonials and British, not just other tribes. They had experienced prejudice and discrimination in their interactions with investors, suppliers, customers, and competitors.

"Daniel had realized early on that the Iroquois entrepreneur who had both local and colonial customers, and whose business activities did not have anything to do with horses, experienced more inequality and discrimination. When they were able to sustain business activities for some time, the prejudice and discrimination slightly decreased, but even so the majority did not treat Iroquois entrepreneurs equally. Daniel saw the answer to the problem was in building trust between different people because familiarity with each other lowered barriers and built rapport. He had visited Boston and Albany where he had seen the white man's ships, technology, and weapons. He realized that if they were to succeed in the future, both sides would have to participate in building trust.

"Daniel was self-reliant and confident that all people, Iroquois, the Colonials, the British, and even the French, could live together in peace. But he was also a realist and accepted the fact that war was inevitable. It was something he could not control, but he had to deal with it. In private, he had thought about proving his loyalty by joining Captain Rogers' Rangers, whom he had seen in action against the hostile tribes and Canadians. Being young and a little naive, he thought military service would lessen the bigotry against him and improve his standing in the white man's society."

Henry Raymond asked about the man who had caused the problems. "The Colonials came in all shapes and sizes, and from different backgrounds. Who was the man who confronted Chief Nimham that day?"

The old man replied, "It was a bitter Scotsman who rode on a limping horse back to Fort Edward that same day with a pack mule carrying the tools of his trade and more supplies from Boston and Albany to his blacksmith's workshop. Harold Ferrara was originally from Doune in Scotland, which had been the center of rebel fervor. His father worked at the local distillery, but because the family was poor, young Harold spent most of his time with his uncle who was a gunsmith. His Jacobite father and older brother had gone out poaching one night. Upon hearing his opponent was out of town, a competing chieftain decided it was an opportune time to make a move on his mother who was known for her beauty. Young Harold intervened, and after a brawl, the chieftain ran away, Harold hot on his heels in drunken chase over rough terrain in a thunderstorm. It was midnight and the chieftain's horse lost its footing, and he broke his neck. Young Harold realized that he stood no chance for a fair hearing so he left for the New World, and a new place to live.

"In America, Harold assumed a new name and started out as a fur trader. Unfortunately, on his first trip he was captured by Abenaki warriors. He spent one winter in Mount Royal, Canada with the tribe who adopted him as a brother. As was the way, he took a country woman to keep him warm, a native, by whom he fathered a child. In the spring, he managed to escape, and with the help from some trappers and hunters, found his way through the wilderness to Fort Edward.

"As soon as Harold Ferrara made it to Fort Edward, he swore he would never set foot outside the civilized world again. He spent all the money he had to build a gun shop, and set up a workshop in the back. It was a stately building with a high facade and a door and window in the front. He painted his own signage with stylish lettering to say "Gunsmith." He took out a loan to buy benches for boring and rifling, and a range of blacksmithing tools and woodworking tools, a forge to make the brass and steel parts, bellows, anvils, hammers, reamers and files in addition to planes, saws, and rasps. He also made gunpowder from potassium nitrate, charcoal, and sulfur. He experimented so as to make sure he would have those in the correct proportions and then simply ground it up. He cast cannon barrels and balls, and made rifle barrels by forging or hammering a heated iron bar around a cold iron bar. Hunters and trappers favored his .74 caliber smooth bore musket stocked in walnut with checkered wrist, and musket balls of course were always in high demand because there was so much killing to be done!

"Harold Ferrara was especially skillful, and his reputation spread quickly. His swords, made from Damascus steel, gained an excellent reputation for being unbreakable. Once, the French even sent a war party in an attempt to kidnap him. Unarmed, he fought the Abenaki with his bare hands and managed to escape. He started always carry a basket-hilted broadsword wrapped up in his bonnet and a Scottish all-steel double-barreled pistol in his belt after that incident."

The old man fell silent, and Henry Raymond shuffled through his notes.

§　　§　　§

Late one night, Finn walked over to the Silver Star tavern. Fronto was devouring fun, drinking and singing to one of the tavern wenches in a scanty German barmaid dress. He saw Finn entering and shouted, "Finn, take a look at these breasts that are just begging for a caress, and curves that'd change your blood flow!"

Finn joined Daniel at the bar. "Chief Daniel, how well do you know Catherina?"

"The young chief should pay attention, her dedication must be earned! She demands a lot, but she'll do everything, to the right man!" Daniel replied.

Outside the tavern, unrest was breaking out. Judge Lynch, Mayor Glock, John Sergeant and Harold Ferrara tried to calm down the crowd but the agitated people pushed past them through the door shouting and yelling, filling the room with the stench of sweat and dirt. Fronto saw the restless crowd, and he patted the waitress on the butt and sent her away. "Girl, gather your roses," he said.

The townspeople passed around a bottle of whiskey. They argued noisily about some tools and camping equipment that had disappeared, and foodstuff that had been stolen from storage, as they gathered to find out what had happened. A young woman in a raggedy dress and a scarf pushed through the crowd shaking her fist and cried, "This morning I went to fetch some meat from the meat locker, and I saw that a whole deer flank was gone!"

Someone had seen a shadowy stranger in town. Another villager had seen a mysterious figure near his farm, too. But no one seemed to know what they had seen, exactly.

"I noticed a stranger in the alley, but when I approached he ran away!" said a skinny man with long, greasy hair.

A second, older woman, in a black dress with ashen skin and her hair in a tight bun had seen someone too. "I was carrying water when I saw a dark man standing in the wood line. When I asked who it was, he disappeared into the woods!" More wild rumors began to spread, and the people pointed their fingers at each other.

Fronto tried to get some clear answers to figure out what was going on. "Was it a man or a woman? Can you tell if it was a local or was it an Iroquois? Was it a soldier or a civilian?" He asked, but the people could not answer anything specific. The townspeople kept glancing at each other and shrugged their shoulders.

"Last time we caught us a thief we gave him a terrible whipping, yet he survived," a third man said, looked around and made some heavy knots to a rope, and continued, "This time we will finish the job!"

Finn was almost beside himself that the townspeople acted so distressed over what was to him a minor issue. "Calm down everyone! All this fuss and noise sounds like Major Oak is on the loose again!" He said, and winked at Gus and Fronto as if he were telling a hilarious joke. The villagers were stunned and terrified upon hearing his words. They looked over their shoulders, eyes wide, and huddled closer to each other. "Major Oak! Now that is a name we do not want to hear in these parts!"

A woman in the back gasped loudly, "Major Oak is robbing us!"

Finn realized the townspeople took him seriously. He cleared his throat and raised his finger, as Catherina walked in. He said, "It might not be a thief after all, but maybe there is a spy in the town? And who is Major Oak actually? Isn't he only a legend?"

"I don't think so." A woman held her hand in front of her mouth as she whispered, "Why would a spy risk being caught by stealing items? Major Oak is also known as James Robbie, a notorious cattle thief and a robber who claims to have mended his ways. Supposedly, he lives a quiet, secluded life." She looked around, worried.

The terrified villagers were not so easily convinced. "Maybe it is the Mohegan again! It is difficult to say which one of them behaves well and which does not!"

All of a sudden the tavern doors slammed open against the wall and Johan Kopf, wearing leather gaiters and hunter green field uniform coat and his trademark cap with a skull and bones emblazoned in front, marched in. Right behind him came in Sheriff Jimmie Dick, a man of short stature, bulky frame, and shaggy dirty hair framing his grimy face. Three more men barged in, all of them hard-looking gunslingers of shadowy appearance, and eyes glinting with greed. Johan Kopf took off his buff goatskin gloves and triumphantly pointed his finger at Finn. "There is your perpetrator!" His face twisted in hatred as he shouted his accusation. "I happen to know that back in the old continent, he is a wanted man! He is your villain!"

Kopf took a step closer and pointed his finger at Finn. "You fucking nitwit! You managed to escape from me too many times! You figured you could hide here in the colonies, didn't you? Hah! I inspect ship records regularly, you asshole!"

Finn felt everything go quiet, as if he were hearing Johan Kopf's voice filtered through a pipe. The sound was drained out of the rest of the world. He heard everything muted, surreal and ghostly as he gazed up. "Is that you, Totenkopf?"

"He is behind all this! Seize him and bring him to me! I will take care of him once and for all!" Kopf shouted. The townspeople were stunned. Sheriff Jimmie Dick and his men pulled out their guns and stepped forward to seize Finn, who stepped back away from them.

The Rangers around the saloon pulled out their guns. Johan Kopf and Jimmie Dick faced dozens of musket barrels. The three men who came in with them raised their hands and stepped back, leaving Johan Kopf and Jimmie Dick to face the Rangers. Finn stayed back behind the Rogers and Stark brothers. He looked around for a way to get out from the back.

"Don't believe him! That... that Hessian monster killed my family!" Finn yelled.

Robert Rogers stood up and pointed his finger at Johan Kopf. "I am not going to let anybody blame any of my Rangers without any evidence, or based only on rumors! And particularly I don't listen to any Hessian mercenaries!"

The Rogers' brothers and Stark brothers cocked their pistols, and the Rangers pulled out their cutlasses, and stepped closer surrounding Finn, ready to defend him.

"There is no honor in fighting against vermin," Kopf snarled, and bared a golden tooth.

"A murderer like you has no honor!" Finn barked at him.

Kopf's right eye twitched and he pulled his earlobe to stop it as he glared victoriously at Finn. "Like I say, to each man his own! Remember when you met us on the road? You ran away, remember! I followed you! You led me to your village!" he said, sporadically sucking air through his teeth.

Johan Kopf's words struck Finn like a blow to his face. His heart sank, and he felt his blood curdling. His face distorted in pain, and tears swelling in his eyes, he let out a hellish yell. "No! Jesus fucking Christ! No! Holy shit! No!" he shouted. Seeing the effects of his words on Finn, Kopf gulped and took a step back.

Bill Stark stepped forward. "I once had a dog who fed off a scum-bucket like you, Hessian. He fell ill and puked it out. I still had to shoot to let him out of his misery," he said in a low voice, and poked Johan Kopf in the chest with his finger.

"Make your move, Hessian," John Rogers said in a hoarse voice, and raised his hunting knife. Johan Kopf looked at the row upon row of musket muzzles pointed at him and realized he was totally outnumbered and was forced to withdraw. He shook his fist at Finn and turned towards the door. "You're a sorry-ass lucky son of a bitch! I will get you one of these days!"

"Fuck you, Totenkopf, and the bitch's womb you crawled out of!" Finn shouted back. "You are nothing but a murdering thief and a coward! I swear I will kill you!"

Johan Kopf spun around, ready to fight Finn, but the wall of musket muzzles and razor sharp cutlasses stopped him. He snarled, the light catching his gold tooth, and walked slowly backwards out of the door. Outside Sheriff Jimmie Dick rose up from cowering behind a water barrel and followed him.

Inside the tavern, everyone was still breathing hard as Johan Kopf's voice echoed outside. "Fuck you, and your pathetic friends! None of you belongs! I belong!"

Robert Rogers looked sternly at Finn. "Not now, not here! Do I make myself clear? We have a war to fight and I need every swinging dick ready for battle! Besides, he is, after all, an officer in His Majesty's service! You will get your day, some day! Do you understand?"

"Roger that," Finn replied.

Fronto looked at Finn. "What did you ever do to him? Did you piss in his ale tankard or something?"

"That man killed my family! His soul is dark like the

deep waters, and he's gazing at his own reflection! I want his ugly head on a platter!" Finn was trembling.

"Justice, whippersnapper," Fronto said to him. "Don't be swayed by those whose ruling principles are guided by animal drives or unregulated emotion, even though they may appear to have our interests at heart. There is no reason to fear men like that because they hold no power over those who are ruled by reason. People like him are concerned only with their self-preservation. Men like that take part in the sport exclusively for themselves, and have an interest in us only insofar as we may advance their predatory and reptilian agendas. The moment when we are no longer able to meet their needs, we become expendable. We do have a duty to excise the reptiles and predators who roam amongst us," Fronto said and patted Finn on the shoulder.

Gus tucked his pistol in his belt and said, "Finn, the old man here got me thinking that maybe it truly is us who controls our own will at all times. Maybe it is we who decide how we should respond to events in our life. Maybe that is in our control. Rest assured, you will have your chance, and in the end justice will prevail," Gus said, talking with his hands.

Robert Rogers patted Finn on the shoulder. "Relax, Ranger. There are no virgins with zero defects around here. We are all damaged goods from the get-go."

Catherina pulled Finn and Fronto aside. She looked worried, and Finn wanted to calm her down. He said, "Catherina, I must be true. My innocence may not be so straightforward, but his quilt is easy enough to see."

"Finn, I'm so sorry to hear about that horrible Hessian," Catherina replied. "Skunks live by night, and so does he! You must listen to Captain Rogers, and do not try anything stupid. And I think Fronto is right, but people are getting restless and anxious about all this. I'm afraid that if this thievery is not solved, then there is going to be trouble against the friendly natives. We must find the perpetrator!"

Finn realized he had caused much trouble by his careless joke. "I might have sent these people after an innocent man! We must catch this Major Oak or Robbie, or whomever it may be and bring him in for a fair trial before he is hanged by the mob! Let's go and get Daniel," he said.

The townspeople continued to become increasingly agitated. "We must get the sheriff to arrest this Major Oak! This time we will fix a rope around his neck!" The crowd started to disperse shouting, and shook their clenched fists calling for the sheriff. Finn looked into his empty cup and placed it on the table upside down. Images of combat and soldiers dying ran through his mind.

Finn looked worried and tense as he gazed Fronto in the eyes. "Anyways, why did I live when all those others died? I thought I wanted to be a soldier and an officer. Now I'm not so sure anymore. There is no honor in horror," he said and fumbled with his moose head necklace.

Fronto took a long drink from his tankard. "Stay focused, my friend. We all wrestle with our own demons. Some will win, some will lose. Look, I'm just a knight without a lord who is condemned to wander aimlessly until I find a purpose again," he said.

"Old man, everything has been taken from me, but you keep saying that I still have my only freedom – to choose my attitude no matter what happens, to choose my own way. What the hell do you mean?" Finn asked.

"It is up to you, my dear whippersnapper, to be totally independent! Who said it would be easy? You may be sick and yet happy, in peril and yet happy, maybe you're dying and yet happy, you might get exiled and still be happy, you may find yourself in disgrace and yet happy," Fronto said. Finn shook his head and looked back at him, confused.

§     §     §

One afternoon Finn was riding about on errands, and on his way back to the fort, he met Robert Rogers on the road heading out to a meeting. He saluted, but Rogers hurried past him and barked, "You better get back to the fort, double-time, Ranger!"

Finn watched him go and then turned back towards the fort. He passed some small farms and saw women wearily doing their chores. Stalwart countrywomen ran large households in Fort Edward. They tilled and toiled gardens, milked cows, churned butter, raised and butchered animals, prepared and preserved meat, spun yarn, and sewed. When times were unusually tough, women labored in the fields alongside their husbands and children. But above everything else, the women were expected to satisfy men's needs and bear children. Children were needed to help keep the house and farm and join the militia to fight the hostile incursions every so often. But because so many children died as babies, women spent most of their childbearing years either pregnant or nursing infants.

Finn came to a junction in the road, and remembered the orders to report back to the base. Instead he looked around to make sure Robert Rogers was gone, and he decided to visit Catherina's farm. It was slightly out of the way, but not too far from the fort. The rocky lane followed an old moss-covered fence and led across small fields of crops and old stone walls to the house, which was nested under large oak trees and hemlocks. The house had a wraparound porch and was built partly on top of a small stream, providing quick access to running water from the back. A cattle path led from the house, passed a stable and cow shed, down to an even lower level that adjoined the stream. Finn did not see anybody and rode slowly closer.

"Hello! Is anybody home?" Finn called out, shifting his worn-out leather messenger bag.

"Yes, just a minute!" Catherina answered from inside the house. Finn dismounted and tied his horse to a tree. He took off his musket and hung it on the saddle knob. He stepped towards the house.

"Hello? Is anybody home? I would like to get some water, if possible?"

Catherina hastily arranged her clothes, and making sure Finn did not see her, did a little butt wiggle. Outside Finn saw her head in a mobcap appear in the open window, and she was holding a book in her hand. She looked at Finn for a moment and then motioned towards a bench. "There is a bench on the porch by the window. Please have a seat," she said.

"Will you join me?" Finn asked.

She thought for a moment. "I was in the middle of something, but it's okay, we can talk." Catherina said. Finn sat down on the edge of the bench.

"What is it that you do?" Finn asked, suddenly feeling slightly anxious and shy. "That is, if I may ask, why do you live in a place like this? I mean it is a little remote, and you are by yourself now," he said.

Catherina walked out on the porch her long, curly blonde hair flowing freely. She tossed her mobcap on the chair and looked at him, her chin held high. She was wearing a light mint green dress with lace and ribbons, small diamonds and stripes. The sleeves hit just above the elbow, but with the ruffle, it hit in the middle of her arm.

She toyed with her hair and tapping her toes replied, "This is my farm where I was born. Some people wonder, but where else would I live? I am learning to read, if you must know. The thing is not to stop questioning! My brother was an expert hunter and fisherman, so I had no worries about food, and I still have some livestock. Other than that, I am not so sure anymore." She stopped talking, realizing suddenly that she had said too much.

"You made quite an impression at Captain Rogers' office the other day," Finn said.

"They dared to call me insolent! Telling the truth cannot be insolent! I'm just saying the way it is!" Catherina replied, raising her chin.

Finn felt a surge of shyness all of a sudden, and stood up to make a slight bow. He was taken with her gorgeous looks and gazed at her admiringly. He said, "Your name must be Deborah. I look at you and see the definitive trap of love. Where is the man who gets your attention?"

Catherina frowned, and taking a deep breath, folded her arms in front of her. "Excuse me?" Seeing the sincere look on his face she paused for a moment. "I find your tasteless remarks demeaning, but maybe you don't know what you are implying, mister. You helped Chief Daniel

Nimham so I think you are a friend, and you may call me Catherina, if you wish." She turned to look away because she liked him, but did not want him to see.

Finn nodded in agreement and replied, "I am sorry, I did not want to offend you. Catherina is a beautiful name. I am called Finn, but you already know that because that's where I'm from, the old country. I have been riding on errands all day, and now I am thirsty. What can I do to get some fresh water to drink?"

Catherina relaxed and smiled, and making a humorous curtsy disappeared inside to fetch some water. Finn heard a crashing sound, and a bucket dropped, clanging. "Ouch! Damn it!" she yelled. Finn jumped up and bounced in through the door. He saw Catherina holding her hand, looking at a splinter in her finger.

"What happened? Are you alright?"

"The water bucket needs a new handle, that's all," she said, and removed the fragment with her teeth.

Finn looked around the room and noticed a heavy chessboard and chess pieces on the table. He heard the running water from the stream under the cabin. Catherina took another wooden bucket and opened a small door on the floor, lowering it into the stream by a rope. She pulled the bucket back up and filled a wooden cup with water and handed it to Finn. He took a long drink while watching her over the rim of the mug. As he handed the mug back to her, their fingers slightly touched. She gasped, a little surprised, and withdrew her hand quickly.

She felt a little awkward and hesitated for a moment, but she wanted to be courteous. "Back in the forest, you said such beautiful things about your mother who called you many beautiful names. You must miss your family a lot?" She smiled at him bashfully.

Finn turned solemn, and he looked bewildered. There was an awkward moment of silence. Finn wiped his mouth to his sleeve and pointed outside with his thumb. "I noticed there is a pile of firewood that needs to be chopped. I can help, if you want?"

Catherina noticed how uncomfortable he had become, and thought she had said something wrong. "That would be nice, thank you," she replied softly, pleased at his asking to help her. Finn stepped back out and walked briskly to a pile of wood and rolling up his sleeves, picking up an axe on the way.

Finn waved his arm and boasted. "I'd say that a long, straight row of firewood standing in the yard in the spring is like silver in the bank indeed. As it dries in the summer sunshine, you're collecting interest! And it keeps you warm in the winter!" He swung the axe, purposefully flexing his muscles.

Standing on the porch, Catherina pretended not to notice and appeared to check the seams on her dress. "Uh-huh..." She mumbled, but she felt strangely curious about this man. It was a feeling she had never felt before.

Finn continued chopping the wood, and wanting to impress her even more he said, "I know how to stop the slugs from eating your garden, and I could feed your cow, too!" He gave her a bright smile.

"Men love to wonder, like I needed your help..." Her voice trailed off as she looked the other way, but she glanced at him around a porch column as soon as he went back to his work.

Finn hit a stout log hard with the axe, and it became stuck. No matter how hard he pried he could not get the axe free and he moved so that she could not see it. He noticed a goose by the barn, and to deflect her attention away from himself struggling with the axe, he exclaimed, "That's an excellent bird you have there, and such splendid feathers too! He shines a long way off. If one had such lofty feathers, one needn't be chopping firewood!"

"That's my brother's axe," she replied and looked away to hide her smile. "It's unusually heavy and hard to get off when it gets stuck like that. Do you always talk so much? Anyway, you seem to like birds, and so let me introduce you to Marlyon." She spun around on her heels and disappeared inside.

"Who is Marlyon? Perhaps you have a nightingale in a cage or something?" Finn asked, and stopped struggling with the axe. "I have heard that fine ladies like to keep little birds as pets."

Catherina reappeared after a moment wearing a thick leather glove and carrying a hooded falcon on her arm. The falcon was feeding on a small rodent in her hand. "Marlyon is my hunting partner," she said proudly as she admired the bird. "She also keeps me company on long dark winter nights and takes care of the mice, too."

Finn was hugely impressed and looked at her, astonished. "A mighty hunting bird you have there, my lady! She is such a superb specimen! I think it truly exhilarating that you have such an esteemed and noble skill as falconry!"

She turned her back to him to hide her smile.

§    §    §

The weather changed. All the plans and activities on both sides of the frontier had to be postponed. A fluke nor'easter storm started as a drizzle, which developed into freezing rain. As the temperature kept plummeting, it turned into an ice storm and heavy snowfall and finally transformed into a terrifying blizzard.

Finn brought more firewood in the squad bay, and dumped the wood in the pile and brushed the snow from his clothes, "That should keep us warm for a couple of days at least," he said.

The townspeople and farmers around the fort hastily prepared for the storm by boarding their houses as heavy gales blew through the town. The farmers fought strong winds to collect their cattle from rolling pastures and herded them into shelters.

A spooked horse galloped away, and a young farmer chased after it. Both disappeared into the storm, never to be seen again.

Big old oak trees became weighed down with snow and ice, and the tops broke off. One of the tops crashed on a farmhouse, breaking the roof, and injured the people inside. They sought refuge in the town hall from the storm, which became worse by the hour. The storm and bitter cold temperatures lasted three days, burying the houses in ten feet of snow. The firewood started to run out, and soon the food and drinking water became scarce, as well.

As the weather intensified, the Rangers were ordered to evacuate the farmers to the fort. Finn, Gus, Fronto, and Daniel donned heavy caped sheepskin coats, fox fur hats and winter moccasins with wool leggings. They waded through the heavy snow to Catherina's farm. Frozen trees and branches broke under heavy snow around them. Finn heard loud cracking noises like muskets firing from the forest and dove head first into a snow bank.

Daniel laughed at him, "It's just trees breaking under the heavy snow!"

"Right, I knew that!" Finn looked embarrassed as he crawled out of the deep snow.

Catherina stubbornly resisted the evacuation order, and refused to leave her farm voluntarily. Finn and Daniel pleaded with her while Gus and Fronto gathered some of her belongings. She glared back at them adamantly, "I will not leave my livestock! My life depends on it! I must stay here to see to it nothing happens to them!"

Finn was frustrated with her. "Don't be so pigheaded! Your life depends on getting to safety in the fort!"

"You heard him, now come on, let's go!" Daniel told her.

Suddenly the window came crashing in startling everyone, and that allowed the storm's fury to enter the room. Finn and Gus fought the wind to board the opening. Watching their efforts, Catherina finally accepted that she was forced to leave her livestock on the farm. She propped the door so it would remain closed and could only hope the animals would survive the storm in the shed.

On their way back to the fort, they got lost in the white blizzard, and the situation quickly became precarious. They simply could not go on any further and were forced to seek protection from the storm. Looking for shelter under a hefty snowbound fir tree that looked like giant white ghost, they tried to start a fire in vain.

"Right about now, I'd rather be back in Tuscany!" Fronto shouted over the howling wind, rubbing his hands together. Suddenly, Finn caught a glimpse of a shadowy figure running in the blizzard, which to him looked like a wolf. Alarmed, he cocked his musket, but to his utter surprise it was Sergeant Beaubien who appeared from the blizzard wagging his bushy tail. The husky dog licked Finn's face and guided them to safety.

Finn, Fronto, Gus, and Daniel arrived back on the island with Catherina and hurried inside. Robert Rogers, who had gone out to relieve himself, seeing them go in came inside after them. He was sitting down on a bed and turning to Fronto said, "Ranger Fronto, I might have misjudged you at first when you wanted to enlist. I was against it. Now, I am glad your Finnish friend stood up for you. You have proven yourself out there, and that's all that matters to me. I am man enough to admit my own error. Ranger Finn here was right, and you are one hell of a fighter!"

"Well, thank you, sir, for your kind words," Fronto replied, obviously not accustomed to hearing such praise. "You are indeed a man of strong character, and I see no one else more fit than you command the Rangers. I do what must be done simply because I have a mission."

Finn tossed the last of the firewood in the fireplace. "This is lousy weather! I hate snow! Weather like this, we don't need any enemies! Now it's someone else's turn to go get more firewood!" he shouted over the howling wind.

Fronto filled up his pipe. "Temperance, whipper-snapper! You should have learned by now that there are always night and day, winter and summer, perfect and foul weather, which are constantly taking turns. Night will be positively changed by day, winter by summer, and severe weather by loving," he said.

Finn glared at him, "You think you are so funny, don't you? Anyways, you go get more firewood this time!"

"And in like manner, your dark mood will be replaced by a brighter one," Fronto said.

Finn noticed Catherina's blinking blue eyes and the tip of her reddish nose from under a thick pile of blankets and fur on one of the cots.

Without saying a word, Gus picked up his coat and walked out into the wailing wind to get more wood.

A moderate breeze and a thick fog from the southwest finally replaced the nor'easter, and the townspeople ventured outside to assess damages from the storm. People noticed no one came out from one of the poorest houses in the area, and went looking for survivors. It was a shack made with rough planks and wide cracks in the walls. They discovered inside that firewood had run out, and the entire family of five was found huddling together under a blanket, clutching a single candle without any means to light it. The parents had placed their three small children in between them in an effort to keep them warm with their body heat. The whole family was frozen solid.

Back in the squad bay Finn took a needle and some yarn to patch his torn coat. He kept poking his fingers with the needle. "Anyways, I'm glad this shit will be over soon! I mean, we have suffered enough! I believe you, old man. If you say so, it can only get better from here on!"

§   §   §

The French headquarters were located in Chateau St. Louis on top of the Cap Diamant. Canadian militiamen guarded the gates as supply wagons rolled in along the road toward the fort. The French troops marched in formation in the courtyard.

Colonel Louis arrived with his band of Abenaki warriors to collect reward money for the Ranger prisoners who were beaten and bruised and bleeding. Behind them, Captain Langdale rode in to report to Governor Vaudreuil, who was in discussion with Captain Villiers.

"Milord, the British *coup de main* on Fort Carillon was repelled." Captain Langdale, who resembled a weasel, was still in his torn and muddy field uniform, and reported his news. "They have been sending out fighting patrols led by Captain Rogers. I discovered their rendezvous and inflicted heavy casualties upon them!"

Captain Villiers sat by the window, smoking a long pipe. Governor Vaudreuil drummed the table with his fingers as he contemplated the story.

Canadian-born Marquis de Vaudreuil-Cavagnal had been recently promoted to governor of New France. He had risen quickly through the New France military and civil service, in part owing to his father's patronage, but also due to his own innate ability. At the age of six, he was commissioned an ensign in the French Marines, at age thirteen a lieutenant, and at fifteen, he was promoted to captain.

Now at age fifty he was already looking forward to retirement and was not at all excited about yet another war. Adding to his troubles, Governor Vaudreuil had also failed to grasp the schemes of his intendant Francois Bigot. The Governor did not know that General Montcalm had secretly bribed Bigot to systematically loot the province behind the Governor's back and defraud the Crown of millions of *livres* so that the general could then blame the Governor for it.

Governor Vaudreuil had a real problem in that while he was responsible for the conduct of war, General Montcalm commanded the troops in the field. The general was also more than eager to examine Governor Vaudreuil's leadership, and other high-ranking officials of the regular French army, who judged him to be "too Canadian," and ignored his orders selectively.

Governor Vaudreuil and General Montcalm grew to loathe one another, much to the detriment of the French war effort. Governor Vaudreuil had excellent relations with the Canadian militia, and with the tribes allied with France. General Montcalm looked down on both, and preferred to rely upon French regular troops and made limited use of irregular Canadians and the Abenaki. Governor Vaudreuil constantly sought to discredit General Montcalm at the court and intervened in his military affairs. He launched his plan, because General Montcalm was away traveling to defend himself in Europe and looking for support from the King, and the Governor intended to carry on the war effort as he saw fit.

First, Governor Vaudreuil planned to use his irregular forces and allied warrior to harass the frontiers of the British colonies, forcing the enemy to remain on the defensive. Despite General Montcalm's objections and inveterate defeatism, Vaudreuil was convinced that his strategy would be victorious.

"Sommelier, more wine!" the governor ordered.

Captain Villiers commented, "My scouts have reported weaknesses along the British supply lines. I moved out my forces en masse and easily destroyed one of their wagon trains in the vicinity of Fort Oswego, and even their Hessian cohorts could not help them!"

Governor Vaudreuil paced around his desk, contemplating.

Captain Langdale stepped forward, "If I may suggest, sir, now might be a good time to launch a reprise attack!"

Captain Villiers nodded in agreement. "The British rely heavily on their regular regiments and tactics more suitable for the European battlefields. They have difficulties in heavily forested areas. I think we, on the other hand, should face them with the help of our Abenaki allies."

Governor Vaudreuil looked at the two officers. He motioned to an aide. "Fetch Captain Lignery!" The aide left the room, and Governor Vaudreuil paced tensely around his desk.

Captain Lignery arrived quickly. "Sir, you summoned me," he said and stood at attention.

Governor Vaudreuil turned to him. "Captain, have you read the reports and heard the latest news. What is your opinion of our strengths in this situation?"

Captain Lignery glanced and nodded at the two other captains. He cleared his throat and replied, "The reports keep coming in from all directions, milord. It is like a marquee on the wall. They all indicate that the British are weak, and to capitalize on that weakness we have sent out agents to spread false information among the British."

"Those scabby beasts they call Rangers," Captain Langdale spat in the fireplace, "they have been running loose too close for comfort to Fort Carillon. Obviously, they are planning something vile! With your permission, sir, I will take my épée and cut off their heads!" he said, his voice rising to a high pitch.

Captain Villiers supported him. "Our military have proven themselves to be effective in combat!"

Captain Lignery addressed Governor Vaudreuil. "I agree that we should make a decisive move against them. We could finish this war in our favor with one offensive campaign! We control the dice, sir!"

The headwaiter entered the room and stood quietly waiting in the doorway. Governor Vaudreuil stopped and motioned the servants to bring them drinks. The headwaiter motioned with his hand, and servants brought in crystal goblets on trays. Governor Vaudreuil picked up a goblet and gazed anxiously at the three officers. He made his decision and snapped to attention. He raised the goblet, and the officers followed the example.

"*Vive la France! Vive le Canada!*" Governor Vaudreuil shouted.

"*Vive la France! Vive le Canada!*" Captain Lignery, Captain Villiers and Captain Langdale replied in unison as they raised their glasses.

Governor Vaudreuil threw his empty goblet into the large fireplace, smashing it to pieces. The officers followed suit.

"You are right, the time is right!" the Governor

exclaimed, "This could easily be the *coup de grace* against the British in America! We will call all friendly nations to join us in an action to repel the British vermin! We shall tell them that the British dogs have come to drive them out of their land. We shall pay them considerable rewards for the pitiful British, every man, woman and child, dead or alive! Start preparing the marching orders! We shall strike against the British forts when the snow melts in the spring!"

§     §     §

The British high command decided to change some of their senior officers, and General Daniel Webb was ordered to take command. General Webb was nervous in this high-visibility command post, and he had also never been so close to the enemy. He arrived at Fort Edward and immediately sent the Rangers patrolling the woods around the fort constantly.

"Lord Howe and Lord Loudoun are going to be here soon," he said. "Captain Rogers, I want you to send patrols out between here and Carillon. Double the guards on the island and Fort Edward, as well!"

The commander's nervousness was contagious, and all the British officers soon became anxious and edgy about the arrival of two Lords. Officers in the fort were nervous and barked orders, inspected uniforms, and made troops perform additional parade drills. The Rangers were exempt from guard duty and other tasks, because they had to be ready to march at any time. They disappeared from sight, each pretending to remember some very important task they had to do away from the fort.

Robert Rogers met with his brothers and John Stark who were hanging up a log to a tree branch to be used as a training aid in tomahawk fighting. Bill Stark joined them and waved his arms at the parade drills. He said, "Captain, aren't we glad to see that we are supported by the people in highest places. Aristocrats are the scum of the earth!"

Robert Rogers nodded and shrugged his shoulders. "Watch your words, Stark! Two lords are arriving for the change of command ceremony, and our new general is getting the jitters," he replied, and turned to his brother and Lieutenant Stark. "Tiny, have your men ready for patrol. Lieutenant Stark, you send patrols out as well to make sure nobody surprises us while the lords are here. In any case, that'll take you away from this madhouse!"

Lord Howe and Lord Loudoun arrived at the fort for the change of command ceremonies, and the band started playing marching music. The Rangers paid no attention to them and nonchalantly continued getting ready to go out. Seeing them prepare for a mission, Lord Howe wanted to join the Rangers in one of their patrols, being desirous to learn their method of fighting.

John Stark spoke to his brother, and whispered, "Bill, you have covered my ass in combat more than once, so now I will return the favor and let you take it easy. Take Lord Howe with you on patrol and walk around the woods for a while, in the opposite direction, to keep him out of harm's way."

Bill Stark winked to his brother. "Roger that!"

Ranger Moses Hazen, a rough looking man with a

scarred face, noticed that Lord Howe was going to join them on patrol, and he turned to Bill Stark. "Who's the package? I gather this is not a typical patrol?"

Bill Stark was petting Sergeant Beaubien. "No, we are just going to take him for a walk in the woods to keep him busy, that's all," he replied and winked.

Moses Hazen grinned and replied, "Nice, what a lovely day in my neck of woods."

The patrol walked around the woods all day, taking a long detour to the south. The general stopped them once for a field lunch, which was more like a picnic on a meadow and then they continued marching in a wide circle southwest before returning to the fort. Lord Howe expressed his favorable opinion of the Rangers to Lord Loudoun.

"Lord Loudoun, I participated in one of the Rangers excursions, which are, as you know, very dangerous, and I can tell you firsthand what spiffing woodsmen these Rangers are! We moved like ghosts through the woods! We need more men such as those!" Lord Howe said.

"I take your word for it, Lord Howe," Lord Loudoun replied. "We will add a number of volunteers from the regulars to the Rangers, to be employed hereafter as light infantry under Captain Rogers's command."

Troops from the 42nd Regiment of Highlanders marched into the fort, and their kilts drew attention from the colonials who smirked and pointed their fingers at them. The new arrivals were quartered in huts on Rogers Island, and Finn recognized the Black Watch tartan.

The Rangers were ordered out to the parade ground in formation. Lord Howe and Lord Loudoun were sitting on comfortable chairs brought out just for them. General Webb kept glancing at them fretfully when he walked out in front of the formation to address the Rangers.

"Rangers, on receiving accounts of your operations against a tough and determined enemy, we sent an express to Boston. You cannot imagine how all ranks of people are pleased with your performance under fire," General Webb said in a loud voice. "I am sorry for the loss of so many Rangers you sacrificed in action, but that was their fate as soldiers and Rangers in this struggle. We shall seek revenge for the losses in due course! I wanted to be out there fighting beside you, because I know that as Rangers, you accept the fact that you might be killed in action. The principle of King George II of Great Britain is the best for the Rangers, that every bullet must have its target! It is in the King's hands how every man shall die, and it is better to die with the reputation of a brave man! Rangers set the example for others to follow, to fight and die for the King, in a good cause! It is far better than preserving one's life by shamefully running away! The worst any man of honor could do is lingering to an old age, and die in his bed without having done his country and the King any service!" The general saluted the Rangers who stared back at him without returning a salute, and walked off to meet with the two Lords who stood and followed him to his command post.

Robert Rogers stepped out front and center and saluted, and his men returned his salute. He stared at the formation for a while, and then said, "I must also say that Lieutenant Stark's courage and prudence saved the party and that to the bravery and skill of Rangers William and

John Stark, the Rangers are indebted for much of our success."

The officers released the Rangers and the men walked back to their barracks. On the way to the squad shack, Finn saw some Scots and stopped to talk with them. "I remember the Black Watch regiment well, but I think I might have seen some of you fighting for Bonny Prince Charlie and other clans, but yet here you are also fighting now under the Union flag. Why is that?" Finn asked.

"We do this to punish the French for their treacherous promises in the Forty-Five," one of the Highlanders replied.

Inside the squad bay, Finn, Gus, Daniel, and Fronto started to clean their weapons. Finn remembered he had some leftover boiled eggs and taking one of them, cracked the shell against the table and started peeling it. As he was ready to eat it, Daniel looked utterly repulsed as he watched what Finn was doing. "White people work in mysterious ways. Young chief doesn't know where those come from?"

John Rogers peeked in. "Finn, there is someone to see you," he said. Finn looked at the others and shrugged his shoulders. He walked outside, and to his pleasant surprise, he met Dugald Campbell, now a Captain, who stood proudly in his uniform with his hand casually on the hilt of his sword. They rejoiced at meeting again.

"Captain Campbell! It has been such a long time! Gus, Fronto, Daniel! Come meet an old friend! Err -- I hope I can call you a friend, Captain Campbell?"

Dugald Campbell laughed. "Hey! Finn, glad to see you are alive and well! We fought that day together on the moors and took a valuable prisoner, I must tell you about her! And of course, you can call me your friend!"

Gus, Fronto, and Daniel shook hands with Dugald Campbell. Finn invited him in to their bay and dug out a bottle and a dusty tin cup from a footlocker. Dugald Campbell was sitting down and said he wanted to tell Finn what happened to Lady Ogilvy after the battle.

Finn turned serious and paused for a moment, as he noticed the solemn tone in Dugald Campbell's voice. "Tell me what happened, please, and do not spare me. Just tell me what happened after I left."

Dugald Campbell took a long swig from his mug, and wiped his mouth on his sleeve. "No problem, but give me a moment, please. I will do my best and not leave anything out," he said

Dugald Campbell scanned the faces around him, and then addressed his words to Finn to tell his story of what happened after the battle in which Finn captured Lady Ogilvy.

"After you captured her, Lady Ogilvy was charged with treason against King George II. She was thrown in jail in the castle of Edinburgh to wait her pending execution. No date was set, so she had no idea when her day of judgment would come and the executioner would come to take her. But as bold and bright as she was, she immediately started making plans to escape.

"She had been an avid partaker in the Stuart cause, and even imperiled her own destiny and life, and everything, save her honor, in order to ensure the triumph of the Stuart tartan. That's why she had advised and convinced her husband to support the Bonny Prince Charlie and even rode by his side to battle. She did not actually join in the battle fray, and only remained a spectator, but when the massacre came, she held a fresh horse all ready for her husband to mount and escape to France. But you took her prisoner, and she was quickly tried and condemned to death as a traitor." Dugald Campbell paused to get a drink.

"The Duke of Cumberland wanted to hold her up as a lesson and a warning to the rest of the rebels. He planned her execution, beheading with a sword, to take place six weeks after her trial. In vain her friends tried to get her sentence reduced, but the King turned down all appeals for mercy. She was going to die in the very flower of her youth and beauty."

Finn listened attentively. "Go on, please."

"But there is many a slip 'twixt the cup and the lip. Fortunately, she was allowed to have friends to see her in jail, and with a little sly help from her friends, she intended to gain her freedom back."

Fronto, Gus, and Daniel edged closer to hear well.

Campbell continued, "The best agent willing and ready to help her was a poor, ugly, crippled old woman, with an ungainly hitch in her walk, who brought her clean linen once or twice a week. Lady Ogilvy started to study that hobbling gait, and the old crone willingly helped her. She kept practicing the clumsy movements, until she became quite skillful."

The door was open, and Catherina came in following the Rangers who gathered around them, attracted by Dugald Campbell's captivating voice and the story.

"The old crone was more than willing to play her part and exchanged clothes with her." Dugald Campbell waved his arms to complement his story as he spoke, and continued. "Lady Ogilvy guaranteed her that her help would be rewarded. Taking up the basket, she assumed the old washerwoman's limping gait and walked coolly and calmly past the sentinel on guard. She was not challenged and was soon out of sight."

"Lady Ogilvy found friends who most eagerly helped her with a saddled horse. Hurrying over her goodbye, she was soon far away on one of the southern roads. She stayed away from the way to London for fear of being discovered.

"Everywhere the story of her flight was announced, and it was the talk of the common people, yet she managed to make her way to the seacoast. No one knows from what port she escaped Britain, but after her long and perilous journey, she found a place on board a vessel bound for France. Lady Ogilvy built a new life in Bretagne after her gallant escape from the block, and she never returned to the country that she fled." Campbell fell silent and emptied his mug.

Finn lowered his eyes and shook his head in disbelief. He took his necklace out and rubbed it uneasily. "I am saddened beyond belief hearing this story," he said. "Greedy as I was after some thirty coins of silver when I apprehended her, but how much misery I caused to this fine lady! It is no consolation to me that I have been so stupid as not to understand the consequences of my actions."

Catherina leaned against the wall, glanced at Finn and did not say anything. Fronto watched Finn with sad compassion and patted him on the shoulder. "Wisdom, whippersnapper! I am not going tell you to cheer up, but maybe not everything is lost," he said. "Maybe, just maybe, you have started to learn something, and you might understand now that you are entirely independent in the actions you take and in the opinions you hold. This is a matter of choice. But whatever your choices are, you also accept the consequences for your actions."

§     §     §

Robert Rogers was summoned to General Johnson's mansion, a two-story stone house enclosed behind slate, stone walls where he received a warm reception. Although they were from vastly different backgrounds, the two men got along remarkably well and shared a common view on how the war should be conducted. Both had extensive experience in dealing with the Iroquois tribes in the area, and spoke their language.

"Sir, thank you much. We are ready to commence an action at your command," Robert Rogers said, pleased by the attention the general gave him. He actually liked the general, who had shown considerable flexibility and understanding in the past in his dealings with the tribes and chiefs who were often difficult to manage. Robert Rogers had been born and raised in a frontier farm in New Hampshire, and at an early age had learned Iroquois traditions and customs. During his forays into New France, he had even learned some French.

"The headquarters has been very pleased with the results from your earlier mission," General Johnson said. He handed him a drink and continued, "Good news, Captain, you are commissioned to hire an independent company of Rangers! Congratulations!"

Robert Rogers was stunned at first, as if he had heard the general wrong, then turning jubilant almost shouted. "That is excellent news, sir! Excellent indeed! We shall shape our place in history! My Rangers shall be like a magnificent sword whose finely edged blade, though splattered with blood, still catches the light!"

General Johnson smiled at the younger officer's enthusiasm. He handed him the papers and said, "It is ordered that the company shall consist of sixty privates at three shillings, York currency, per day, an ensign at five shillings, a lieutenant at seven shillings, and a captain at ten shillings."

Robert Rogers moved his lips while reading the papers and nodded in agreement, "This is quite reasonable payment, if I may say so, sir. I shall commence recruiting immediately."

General Johnson continued, "Furthermore, each individual is allowed ten Spanish dollars towards providing clothes, arms, and blankets. The company is to be raised immediately."

Robert Rogers contemplated his new orders. "All this is going to cost a considerable amount of money, sir. Luckily, I do have resources to collect more funds for the war effort as required," he said making sure no one overheard them. He lowered his voice and glancing around continued, "I have two questions, sir. May I count on legal aid if there are any needs in that regard, and when can I expect to be reimbursed for my expenses?"

General Johnson looked unconcerned. "Captain, the earlier charges brought against you were dismissed by a direct order from the highest level in London, and you know what that means, don't you? I am confident that the headquarters and the King shall promptly pay for all the costs as they are accrued. You must keep accurate books and submit an itemized invoice in due course, Captain," he said, and nodded in affirmation.

Robert Rogers had no reason to doubt the general, who after all represented the King, and his name was law. Anyone who dared to question him would find himself quickly decapitated. Excited, he hit his chest with his fist and exclaimed, "I will recruit only men who are accustomed to traveling and hunting and in whose courage and reliability the most implicit trust can be placed. We are hunters of men, and it is our intention to dominate the enemy totally, both body and soul!"

General Johnson raised his finger as he reminded Rogers of a key principle. "They are, moreover, to be subject to strict military discipline, and the articles of war."

Robert Rogers frowned. "Discipline absolutely, but the articles of war, what the fuck are those?" he asked, half-jokingly.

"You know what they are, is that clear?" The general was in no mood for jokes.

"Absolutely, sir," Robert Rogers said, straightening his posture.

"Listen carefully, Captain," the general continued, "The Rangers are to use their best endeavors to torment the French and their allies, by sacking, burning, and destroying their houses, barns, barracks, canoes, bateaux, and whatever else they find. You will carry on with killing the enemies' cattle of every kind, and at all times to endeavor to waylay, attack, and destroy enemy convoys of supplies by land and water, in any part of the country, anywhere they can be found! Is that clear enough for you, Captain?"

Robert Rogers hit the palm of his hand with his fist. "Yes sir! I couldn't ask for more! Raid, recon, and ambush! That is what we do best! He who dares shall win!"

"Captain, there is a special operation planned in Newfoundland when the sailing season opens. But first, there have been persistent rumors across the frontier about secret weapons the French have somewhere in the vicinity of Lake George. I want you to go there and find them! Your mission is to bring those weapons to us!"

Robert Rogers saluted the general, rushed out, and hurried back to Fort Edward. Arriving in his command post few hours later, he immediately summoned the Ranger officers, and gave an operations order for a patrol of Rangers to go out on a new mission. The officers leaned over maps on the table, and Captain Rogers pointed out to the route as he talked.

"I have been planning this new mission for some time, and now I have been given the green light! We are going to reconnoiter, by force, and seek the secret French weapon reportedly in the area around Fort Carillon, and monitor for enemy activity and engage targets of opportunity." Rogers paused to look at the officers, and continued, "Men, this is a combat patrol. We will take full combat loads and engage the enemy when we meet him and turn his vile efforts into rubble, is that understood! The Black Watch shall stay here as a strategic reserve for us. We will depart from here early in the morning on the fifteenth. Then we shall commence our incursion north on the frozen Lake George towards our objective. Are there any questions?"

John Stark raised his hand. "Sir, we need some supplies, our men are low on ammo, and quite a few are sick. Another thing: the heavy snow fall last night is bound to make our movement difficult."

"Good points, Lieutenant Stark," Robert Rogers said. Pointing the way on the map, he continued, "You, Ensign Page of Richard Rogers Company, and fifty privates are to proceed immediately to the forward staging camp at Lake George, where we have a stash of supplies, snowshoes, and rations. There you will be joined by Captain Spikeman with Lieutenant Kennedy, Ensign Brewer and fourteen men of his company, together with Ensign Richard Rogers with twenty men of Hobbs' company, Captain Campbell of the Black Watch, and Mr. Baker, a volunteer from the 44th Regiment of the line. That will make our patrol eighty-seven Rangers strong. That is enough to scare the living shit out of tenfold that many French and Abenaki! Is there anything else?" Robert Rogers looked around the room. The men looked back attentively.

When no one said anything, Robert Rogers continued, "We expect to make enemy contact, and by inflicting massive casualties on him, we shall conquer him in the field of battle! Each Ranger will take a triple load of ammunition! We will take the pole cannons with us, too. The hogs will give us victory through superior firepower! If there are no more questions, get your men to be ready! We shall continue down Lake George on the ice at night. We will move out at dusk!"

§    §    §

The Rangers moved cautiously through the snow-covered forest on snowshoes. When they came to marshes that had frozen over, where the ground was low and they were more exposed, they changed their position and marched abreast of each other until they reached the other side, and then resumed their first order. They continued to advance through the night to a high ground, which Robert Rogers judged afforded their sentries the advantage of seeing or hearing the enemy from a considerable distance. As they rested, the Rangers kept one-half of the whole party awake and on watch, alternating in two-hour shifts for sleeping, throughout the night. Before daybreak, the entire patrol was awakened and ready. At first light, they advanced single file towards the lake barely visible two hundred yards in front of them. When the trees became sparser, Robert Rogers gave hand signals to his men to spread out. Finn, Gus, Fronto, and Daniel formed the point squad. When Finn got close to the shoreline, he saw movement on the icy lake and gave a hand signal for the patrol to stop, and ran back to Robert Rogers.

Leaning close, Finn whispered his report. "Sir, there is a sled moving on the lake towards Fort St. Frederic!"

Robert Rogers nodded and motioned to John Stark. "Lieutenant Stark, get your men and intercept that sled. We will gain valuable intelligence from the prisoners!"

"I'm on it, sir!" John Stark replied and pointed at Finn. "Bring your men!" Without waiting for a response, he moved out in front of Finn, Gus, Fronto, and Daniel to catch up with the enemy sleds.

Robert Rogers observed their movement from the high ground, when suddenly he saw another ten enemy sleds appear from behind an island, going down the lake. He signaled to John Stark to stop, but it was too late: they had already moved out in the open.

Seeing the new sleds just as they emerged from the trees on the ice, Stark signaled his men to fall back into the woods, but the enemy had already seen them and turned their sleds back toward Fort Carillon.

Stark made a quick assessment and pointed at the sleds. "Rangers, go after them! Don't let them get away, but don't shoot!" He barked his orders and his men sprang into action. Finn, Daniel, and Gus started running after the sleds, Fronto falling behind and struggling in the deep snow. Running with the snowshoes on slowed them down, and the sleds started gaining distance. Suddenly, one of the enemy sleds overturned, spilling the men and its cargo onto the ice. John Stark, followed closely behind by Finn, Gus and Daniel, rushed the occupants and succeeded in taking seven prisoners at gunpoint. The rest of the French sleds managed to escape, and the Rangers returned with their prisoners to the main patrol camped behind a small knoll, which provided cover and concealment.

The prisoners were separated from each other so they could not talk amongst themselves, and were kept under close guard, muskets pointed at them. Temperatures kept dropping, and since it was daylight Robert Rogers allowed small campfires for warmth. The Rangers carried a bundle of dry twigs and small sticks to start small campfires that would hardly produce any smoke. Robert Rogers decided to interrogate the prisoners who wore uniforms of the French Marines, long, greyish white collarless single-breasted coats with deep cuffs of blue. Sullen prisoners stood silently and stared defiantly back at him, their eyes glaring with rage as he appraised them. "What a bunch of sad assed mother fuckers! Nevertheless, I doubt that they'll tell us anything voluntarily and we do not have a moment to waste!" Robert Rogers nodded to Finn and Daniel continued, "Men, make them talk! We need information on enemy numbers, movements and locations."

Finn did not know what to do and was about to ask for instructions when Daniel pulled out his hunting knife and approached one of the prisoners, a young boy in his late teens. The older prisoners, seeing what was happening, attempted to intervene and protect the lad, but were pushed back harshly with bayonets. Daniel grabbed the boy by the hair, yanking his head back and exposing his throat, and raised his knife, its blade catching the faint sunlight. One look at the Wappinger warrior's painted face and the raised knife was enough. The terrified prisoner started crying and pleading for mercy, his voice shaking. There was a dark spot spreading on the front of his pants.

"Stop, please! Show mercy! I tell you everything! There is a powerful war party that just arrived at Fort Carillon! It is garrisoned by a thousand regulars!" he said.

Robert Rogers heard a faint whistle like a quiet bird song and jumped on top of a knoll. He saw a Mohawk scout some distance out who made hand signals indicating the enemy was on the trot back towards their fort. He turned back to the patrol, signaled to put out the fires, and ordered his men to dry their weapons and prepare for combat.

"Good job, Ranger Nimham, you can spare the boy. I think he was telling the truth. That is a sizeable enemy force, too large for us to handle, so we'll need rein-forcements," Robert Rogers said. He assessed the situation and continued, "We must return at once and inform the general. No doubt the sleds that got away will trigger an alarm. Lieutenant Stark, get our men ready to move out immediately! We will take the same route back."

John Stark looked at him, surprised. "But sir, that is not wise, and it is against all the rules!" he said.

"I realize that, Lieutenant," Robert Rogers replied, "but right now the need for speed is of the essence, and the deep snow is against us. Regarding the enemy, my bet is they will not dare follow us. They know who I am and what I am capable of! I would fuck them up so bad their children's heads would spin! We must take the chance and use our own tracks!"

Daniel moved out to take the point with Finn, Gus and Fronto following close behind in wedge formation to provide flank security. Twenty yards behind them, the Rangers marched out in single file, Richard Rogers and Ensign Page leading the point element. Robert Rogers and Lieutenant Kennedy were in front of the main patrol, and Captain Spikeman in the center with the prisoners. John Stark and Ensign Brewer led the rear element. The last man of the rear guard was Corporal Walker, who walked backwards to make sure they were not taken by surprise from behind.

Robert Rogers talked to John Stark as the men filed past them. "Lieutenant Stark, after a league or so let the men rest awhile before we continue on our way south."

The Rangers moved through the forest cautiously, keeping up a respectable pace, with each man facing out alternately left and right. The forest floor was covered with broken trees and branches, adding to their difficulties as the Rangers probed forward. They followed along the base of a ridgeline leading towards a high ground two thousand yards to the front.

In the meanwhile Captain de Rouilly, the leader of the French supply convoy intercepted by the Rangers, returned to the Fort Carillon with his shaken men. The fort was manned by the French Marines and Ottawa warriors. He alerted Colonel Paul-Louis de Lusignan, the commanding officer.

"Sir, our supply sleds were ambushed by the British a few miles south on the lake! It was that son of a whore Rogers, no doubt! There were less than a hundred of them. Nobody else would dare to challenge us in our own front yard!"

Commander Lusignan studied the map Captain de Rouilly handed him. "They must be returning towards their lair by now like there is a fire under their tails! Captain de Rouilly, your men can rest for now. Captain Langdale, get your men ready!"

§    §    §

The Rangers advanced half a mile over broken ground, and they crossed a steep dale. Daniel, Finn, Gus, and Fronto gained the summit of the hill on the west side, and stopped to wait for the main patrol. The sun was descending from a canopy of clouds.

John Stark heard the sound of muskets being cocked, but he first thought it came from one of the Rangers in the point element. The ambush was a complete surprise, and a barrage of two hundred shots ripped through the Rangers' ranks, killing a dozen Rangers immediately. Lieutenant Kennedy and Ensign Gardner, the volunteer, were killed instantly, both shot in the head at close range. Several Rangers fell down, wounded. One of the Rangers was hit in the shoulder, and went down on one leg. He tried to crawl for cover, but his body was shaken with multiple hits. Finn fell backwards, pulling Fronto and Gus down with him, and shot a French soldier whose musket had misfired, hitting him in the head in a spray of blood and brains. Daniel dived behind a log next to them, killing an Ottawa warrior with a single shot.

The Rangers were fortunate that many of the French muskets misfired due to wet gunpowder. Finn, Gus, Fronto and Daniel scrambled for cover behind some fallen trees and returned fire. Dirt exploded around survivors, and they were showered with splinters from the tree trunks. The Rangers returned fire, aiming at the muzzle flashes in the dark woods. They realized that the French Marines and Ottawa warriors were drawn up in the form of a crescent to surround the Rangers.

A shot plowed across the top of Robert Rogers' head and he slumped down to the ground, unconscious. The fusillade was tremendous from both sides, and thick black smoke filled the forest as the Rangers fired and reloaded as fast as they could.

Finn fired and was reloading when a French Marine, screaming bloody murder, charged at him with a bayonet. Finn realized in a flash that he was not going to make it, and his body tensed to receive the shock. *Oh shit! Oh shit!*

*Oh shit!* he thought, just as he felt a sucking draft across his cheek; a tomahawk flew by his head and hit the Frenchman in the face. Finn glanced over his shoulder and saw Daniel let out a blood-curdling war cry and with a single bound jump over to the body, and then, with one swift motion, scalp the man.

Richard Rogers shouted commands after his brother went down. "Keep firing, men! We must gain fire superiority!" He raced the bullets across the open and dived for cover, bullets screaming over him. Robert Rogers lay still on the ground, and Richard Rogers covered him with his own body.

Robert Rogers regained consciousness, his head spinning from pain. Wiping the blood off his face, the first sight he saw was his brother Richard dressing his head wound to stop the bleeding.

John Stark, who was bringing up the rear, saw what happened at the front of the column and rushed in to take charge. He shouted his orders. "Rangers, form a defensive line along this rise! Lay down a covering fire!" He saw Robert Rogers was getting up and shouted to him, "Captain Rogers, retreat to my position!"

Robert Rogers, with his head wound dressed, tried to get up to shoot. Out of the brush an Ottawa warrior attacked Richard Rogers and engaged him in hand to hand combat. The two men wrestled in a deadly struggle and rolled out of sight into the woods. Two young Ranger privates were separated from others, and six screaming Ottawa warriors attacked them. With no time to reload, the privates threw their tomahawks in terror and missed, and desperately tried to defend themselves with dirks only.

They were no match for the merciless and skillful knife fighters, and the Ottawa warriors swiftly cut the privates down and hacked them to pieces.

Robert Rogers managed to get up, in tremendous pain. In order to shoot he leaned on a tree stump, but a bullet slapped into his arm. He spun and dropped down on one knee again. Clutching his grazed arm Robert Rogers managed to crawl behind the fallen trunk of a giant alder.

Robert Rogers was covered in blood and though clearly in great pain, resumed command. "Captain Spikeman, take charge of the detachment to be left in the contact! It's your job to buy the rest of us enough time to get out of here! Die in place if you have to! Take forty men and cover our retreat. The rest will run for the opposite hill, to Lieutenant Stark's and Mr. Brewer's position!"

Behind the knoll some young, nervous Rangers witnessed what had happened to their two young comrades. They started looking back over their shoulders, looking ways to run for their lives. John Stark cocked his pistol and raised it. "I will shoot the first man who flees! We have a strong position, and we will fight the enemy until dark and then withdraw!" he said.

While John Stark was speaking, a French Marine took a shot at him, and the bullet broke the lock of his gun. An instant later a bullet ripped through the Frenchman's chest, killing him immediately. He had been shot at close range by Bill Stark. John Stark sprang out, seized the dead Frenchman's musket before it hit the ground, returned to his position behind the tree, and giving a thumbs-up to his brother, continued to fight.

The Rangers pulled back under withering enemy fire.

The pole cannon roared and cut down attacking enemies in large numbers, splattering the woods with blood and pieces of flesh. The gun crews hammered away at the attacking French, displacing, taking turns falling back and hammering away again. Ignoring their dead and wounded, the French pressed their attack. They managed to overrun Captain Spikeman's position, bayonetting him and several Rangers dead, and taking the few dazed Ranger survivors prisoner.

Robert Rogers quickly assessed the situation and barked new orders. "Get rid of the prisoners! They are slowing us down!"

Without hesitation, a group of Rangers turned their muskets on the French prisoners. Finn rose on his elbows, still dazed, trying to clear his head. He turned and rolled over to see a young French soldier looking at him pleadingly with his teary eyes. As Finn watched in horror the boy was shot in the back of his head, the brains scattering all over a spruce tree. The rest of the French prisoners were shot at point blank range.

John Stark repulsed an enemy attack by a brisk fire from the hill, killing several and affording Robert Rogers's men an opportunity to get behind the mound and take cover. John Stark calmly directed his men's fire: "Don't waste your ammo! Take well aimed shots!"

The firefight continued while in the background the deep red sunset cast an eerie glow over the smoking battlefield. On the hilltop, John Stark took a position in the center, with John Rogers, Corporal Walker and Sergeant Phillips acting as reserves, to protect their flanks and observe the enemy's movements.

Soon after, the enemy attempted to flank them, but Finn, Gus, Fronto, and Daniel fired a deadly volley that killed four French and Ottawa warriors. They charged the survivors with bayonets and forced others to fall back to the main body.

Finn used his musket like a bat and hit an Ottawa warrior in the head. The stock of Finn's musket splintered, cracking the warrior's skull, and Gus, who was standing close, was showered with spit, blood, and teeth. Finn tossed the broken musket away and picked up a new musket from a dead soldier.

The French officer Langdale shouted to the Rangers, demanding surrender. "Hey British ass bandits, you are surrounded! It is useless to fight any longer! Surrender now and we will spare your miserable lives! Captain Rogers, we know it is you, and I am pleased to tell you that your position is hopeless. Be a professional and save your brave men and yourself!"

Robert Rogers looked around his men. The Rangers looked back and Gus spat a tooth on the ground while cocking his musket. Daniel gripped his tomahawk and said nothing.

Robert Rogers recognized the voice shouting at them, cupped his healthy hand in front of his mouth as he shouted back, "Fuck you, Langdale, you cum-guzzling French faggot! You still can't shoot worth a shit! Your bullets are just as soft as your dick! You hit me twice and couldn't even kill me!" he said.

"Hey Langdale, you girly asswipe, is that you?" John Stark barked. "Bring your toothless mouth over here and make it useful and suck my cock! You still sound like a man who is made smooth between his legs!" He quickly ducked back as bullets chewed the tree trunk to splinters next to his head, and he grinned at Robert Rogers.

"The French are at a disadvantage now, since they don't have snowshoes and they're floundering in snow up to their knees," Robert Rogers said. "We shall hold them here until sunset, and then withdraw!"

The French Marines and Ottawa warriors tried to push forward, getting closer, threatening to overwhelm the Rangers. The Rangers had the advantage of the ground. Sheltered by large trees, the Rangers hit the French with everything they had, hammering them with constant fire from pistols, muskets and the pole cannons.

The Rangers forced the attacking French to retreat back to their main body. The French attempted to flank the Rangers once more, but were repulsed by John Rogers, Johnnie Walker, and Ranger Baker, who was hit several times, his body twisting and shaking from multiple hits. All of a sudden, Richard Rogers appeared like a ghost covered in blood from head to toe, running and ducking from the enemy's side, scalps under his belt. He joined his brothers James and John and they scrambled for cover.

Robert Rogers whispered his new commands to a Ranger next to him, and told him to pass it on. "As soon as it is dark, we will break contact and retire in buddy teams. Make sure everybody is ready," he said.

The Rangers kept up a steady, sure fire, forcing the French to stay behind cover, and the Rangers kept their position until the enemy fire ceased. The sun finally set below the horizon, and darkness fell like a curtain upon the battleground.

At last light, Robert Rogers ordered his men to action. "Men, rally again after six miles in that direction! No Ranger is left behind! Lay down suppressive fire. Now, move out!" The Rangers started retreating and left their position in two's while others took well-aimed shots at the enemy positions. By peeling off in buddy teams into the dark forest, the Rangers were able to slip away.

The Rangers moved through the dark woods quietly and quickly. They reached Lake George, and John Stark rushed to Robert Rogers, who was leaning on a tree for support. "Sir, I will take two men with me to the base and procure sleighs for the wounded!" he said.

John Stark took off running with two able-bodied Rangers. The others formed a defensive circle to wait for him to return with sleds. Hours passed, and everyone tensed as a dark figure approached them on the ice. The man identified himself as Ranger Joshua Martin of Goffstown. He was severely wounded, leaning on his musket. A bullet, which had passed through his body, had shattered his hip joint, and he had been left for dead on the field of battle. He recovered himself and followed his comrade's tracks to the lake. He was so exhausted that he fell down.

It was a cold, long night. Finn, Fronto, Gus, and Daniel took turns huddling under a blanket. Finn could not sleep and was thinking about the young French boy who was killed, but he said nothing. The wounded were in agony, but they kept quiet in order not to disclose the Rangers' position. The Rangers breathed a little easier when at first light they saw sleds approaching them on the ice from the direction of Fort Edward.

John Stark traveled a distance of forty miles through

the wilderness on snowshoes when the snow was four feet deep, and in utter fatigue still managed to reach the fort on the evening of the same day, whereupon the relief party was immediately dispatched to the support of the Rangers.

The wounded were hastily loaded on the sleds and the return trip to Fort Edward took most of the day. In the evening, the sentries on the palisades saw Robert Rogers's Rangers return from the woods with only half of their original number of men. Catherina and the other townswomen rushed out to help them. The Rangers looked frightfully grim, haggard and unshaven. She was relieved to see Finn, Gus and Fronto, who supported the walking wounded, covered in blood as they straggled towards the safety of Fort Edward. John Stark took up a position at the gate holding a pistol in his hand and somberly checked each Ranger closely to identify him.

§    §    §

The old man in the Catskill Mountain House placed his empty tumbler on the table and looked at Henry Raymond sternly. "So there we were, falling head first into the abyss of humanity's worst nightmare, the first war of the world! Initially I thought we had found a paradise, but I quickly realized we lived in a man-made world that was full of suffering, famine, and fighting. The war had only begun. We were already on the run, and it was only going to get worse. Wise men say that strength resides in reason, with its capacity to overcome any impediments to justice, but that day I realized mankind had lost its mind, and the sleep of reason produces monsters. Henry, pain and suffering are extremely unpleasant experiences, but this, too, is a matter of choice – in a peaceful world. I thought that if I chose to regard pain and suffering as the end of the world, then I would feel anger, fear, distress, and unhappiness. Why do that? It achieves nothing. We were just lucky enough not to know what calamities still lay ahead of us. Ignorance of the future turned out to be a blessing, and no prayer was going to save us," he said, and stared at his empty glass. His thoughts were lost in blue, reminiscing.

32686650R00214

Made in the USA
Lexington, KY
29 May 2014